"Murder, kidnapping, secrets, e:_____ abiding in the Lord regardless are all _____ etzer's *Lights of the Veil*. Wow! What a g_____
G_____
AWARD-WIN_____ ____HOR OF
THE DECISION AND SPRING RAIN

"An intricately woven plot, a clash between family honor, cultures, and kingdoms. *Lights of the Veil* is reminiscent of *The King and I*, except at its very core, Jesus Christ and a faith question are firmly imbedded in the movement of the story. Metzer's writing swept me away."
DEBORAH BEDFORD
AUTHOR OF THE NOVELLA *A ROSE BY THE DOOR*

"Patty Metzer aptly illustrates the parable of the rich young ruler who must give up all to follow Christ. A pleasant mix of romance and adventure, *Lights of the Veil* will keep readers entertained to the end."
SYLVIA BAMBOLA
AUTHOR OF *REFINER'S FIRE*

"Patty Metzer combines her gift for storytelling with well-developed characters who are real and unforgettable. Nestled among these pages are nuggets of God's truth. Read slowly—you won't want it to end!"
JANICE L. HALEY
PRESIDENT, FOCUS PUBLISHING, INC.

ALSO BY PATTY METZER:

Keeper of the Light

Patty Metzer

Lights

of the

Veil

Multnomah•Publishers *Sisters, Oregon*

LIGHTS OF THE VEIL
Published by Multnomah Publishers, Inc.

© 2001 by Patty Metzer
International Standard Book Number: 1-57673-627-X

Cover design by Uttley DouPonce DesignWorks
Cover image by Martin Salter/Tony Stone Images
Author photo by Kathleen's

Scripture quotations are from *The Holy Bible,* King James Version

Multnomah is a trademark of Multnomah Publishers, Inc., and is registered in the U.S. Patent and Trademark Office.
The colophon is a trademark of Multnomah Publishers, Inc.

Printed in the United States of America

For information:
MULTNOMAH PUBLISHERS, INC.
P.O. BOX 1720
SISTERS, OREGON 97759

Library of Congress Cataloging-in-Publication Data:
Metzer, Patty.
  Lights of the veil / by Patty Metzer.
      p.cm.
  ISBN 1-57673-627-X
  1. Custody of children—Fiction. 2. Kidnapping—Fiction. 3. Uncles—Fiction
  4. India—Fiction. I. Title.
  PS3563.E74639 L54 2001
  813'.6—dc21   00-011027

01 02 03 04 05 06—10 9 8 7 6 5 4 3 2 1 0

To

Jon and Cheryl Henry.

You are living proof that God still uses

His people to build bridges.

Thanks for raising the standard in my life.

Satyameva jayate

"Truth alone triumphs."

"Having therefore, brethren, boldness to enter into the holiest by the blood of Jesus, by a new and living way, which he hath consecrated for us, through the veil, that is to say, his flesh; and having an high priest over the house of God; let us draw near with a true heart in full assurance of faith, having our hearts sprinkled from an evil conscience, and our bodies washed with pure water. Let us hold fast the profession of our faith without wavering; for he is faithful that promised; and let us consider one another to provoke unto love and to good works."

HEBREWS 10:19–24

❧ ONE ☙

OAK TREES LINED THE STREET, spilling their final sacrifice of leaves. An ocean fog joined in the vague dance, that slow-motion spiral from lofty branches down through ink black night onto an altar of cracked and heaving concrete sidewalk. Having grown bored with the yearly ritual, several street lamps slept through their watch, leaving but a faithful two or three. Even they seemed tired.

Autumn had created the perfect background, the ultimate stage for the cast of emotions that had driven her here. Any moment, she expected some giant hand to draw the final curtain. Then a dismembered voice would announce The End and she could go home.

In truth, she would look back upon this night and know it was not the end.

It was the beginning.

Erica Tanner steered her car toward the curb, disturbing a frenzy of leaves and fog against the windshield. The car skidded into its final resting place, one tire straddling a pothole; the other buried in what remained of a water puddle.

This can't be the place. For a few seconds, Erica stared at the newspaper clipping in her hand, and then her gaze clung to a wobbly signpost. Something didn't feel right. On the other hand, nothing had felt right since she opened the letter.

Shutting off the engine was an automatic reaction. Killing the headlights took sheer determination. The world around her settled into a gloomy scene. No fires, no chanting voices, no insanity. Erica felt little girl memories fight their way to the surface, threatening to capture her spirit away to India.

She fought back. She had to fight back.

Leaves rustled against her door, begging entrance. A dog was barking somewhere down the block. She heard sirens, but they died upon the doorstep of Portland Memorial's trauma unit half a dozen streets away. In her mind, she pictured the doctors and nurses flying into action, unafraid, trained to handle such emergencies.

Part of her wanted to return to work and help. The stronger part, the sister part, forced her onto the street. She still wore her uniform; the standard-issue blue scrubs topped by a white lab coat. Her rubber-soled shoes didn't make a sound as she dispatched the length of sidewalk leading up to an ancient, remodeled factory.

With her, she carried a mental image of the people who inhabited such spaces. They weren't the kind of people she wanted to meet this time of night. Yet someone had robbed her of that choice by mailing the newspaper clipping complete with this address scrawled at the bottom.

No security was required to enter the building, no surprise. She tugged on the heavy door, bracing herself. Just inside was a bank of rusty mailboxes, and then scuffed stairs leading up and up and up. Though her gaze traced the wood treads, she could not possibly see all the way to the fourth floor. That journey demanded another dose of determination. It came simply by looking at the clipping clenched in one hand—Ellyn's obituary.

Thick walls stifled any sound from the apartments she passed. Some doors allowed pools of light to leak beneath them. Others entombed nothing but darkness. She heard her own breathing, less regular once she reached the top floor. Fewer doors here, none of them showing signs of life.

407. The number had been burned into her thoughts over the past few hours.

After finding and opening the letter, her entire shift had become a blur. Funny how acting upon her convictions brought such clarity. She envied how her shadow had managed to drop a few pounds from the real thing, making her look like a leggy supermodel instead of a petite size six. She smelled food, and her long empty stomach curled into a knot. She noticed the central skylight and appreciated the unique grillwork. Absurd to appreciate anything. The floorboards protested when she stepped closer to 407. Brass numbers. Oak door. Weak knock.

Come on, Tanner. Two minutes ago you were ready to declare war. Now she wanted to chicken out. She wanted to walk away.... Ellyn would never have walked away. Ellyn would have taken a deep breath and confronted her tormentor head on.

Erica didn't expect the door to swing open when she turned the knob. She only wanted to scare whoever was on the other side. Instead, she found herself stumbling into a darkened, cavernous space.

"What are you doing?"

She whirled around.

A few floorboards and a yawning stairwell lay between them. Details, clear details, jumped the distance. His dark blond, almost brown hair was liberally streaked with gray. Strong jaw. Brown eyes. Late fifties. He was just tall enough to block the number stamped upon his now open door. Under a limp navy bathrobe, he wore the expected white T-shirt and gray sweatpants. The wool socks adorned with red heel and toes were not expected. Neither was the gun he held on her.

It was an automatic reaction to slam the door, to lock herself inside the room.

"Hey!" the man yelled.

Erica heard him run around the perimeter of the stairwell. The second she remembered how bullets could pierce through wood, she was peeling herself clear of the door. She was halfway across the room, nearing the drop-off into panic, when light flooded the loft.

Bathrobe Man stood silhouetted in the now open doorway. Gun in one hand, key in the other. He was undoubtedly pleased to see her. "I've been waiting for you."

Waiting for her?

Using the hand that held the gun, he silently invited Erica to be his guest in an overstuffed, rather overused leather wingback. On her way, she noted every detail about the room, a huge, open loft with outer walls of brick. Predominately masculine in taste, it contained more sporting equipment than furniture. A scarred wood table and mismatched chairs were season ticket holders near the basketball hoop. The iron bedstead modeled rumpled covers in the same way a treadmill displayed no less than two changes of clothes. Her gaze skidded past a sink full of dishes and finally stopped on a living room complete with *the* chair.

Any moment now, Bathrobe Man would produce a king-size roll of duct tape, securing her fate at the same time he tied her to the chair. Another quick, careless gun gesture on his part and Erica decided she'd better sit down. "What now?" she asked, chin raised, blue eyes flashing. "I suppose you'll demand a ransom? Well, there isn't any money, so there!"

"Surely, there's a rich boyfriend."

"Surely there isn't."

"Life insurance?"

"You think I'd sign over the policy?"

"Preferably before you faint dead away. You look a little peaked."

"And you think that's unusual considering I've just been kidnapped?"

"Interesting."

That's all he said—interesting. Erica laced shaky fingers through her short blond curls and squeezed, hard. "Ohhh, would you stop that! Just tell me what you want." He came close, grabbed one of her hands, and gave her the gun. She almost dropped it.

"The safety, this button, is on. If at any time you want to shoot, there's a proper order to firing."

"I'm not an idiot." She clicked off the safety.

He smiled, straightened to his full height, and dared to walk away, edges of his blue bathrobe flying out like Superman's cape. He was too old to play Superman. "You hungry? I thought I smelled sauerkraut. You aren't German, are you? More Scandinavian, I'd say. Anybody ever tell you that you look like Shirley Temple?"

"Not since I was six." It was awkward trying to keep the gun leveled on a very mobile Bathrobe Man. Erica stood, concentrating on his movements. "Listen, I don't have time for all this cloak-and-dagger stuff. All I want to know is why you sent the clipping." He opened the fridge and was scanning the contents. "Hey, I'd like an answer."

"Me too. Are you hungry or not?"

"This gun isn't loaded, is it?" That got his attention. Erica saw a grin spread across his face. He needed to shave. He scratched his chest where the *S* should have been. *Concentrate, Tanner. Prove to him that you're no wimp.* She aimed at the stack of dirty dishes.

"Actually, if you pull that trigger, you'd be doing him a favor."

"Who?"

"Me."

Erica swung around, all off balance. A younger, taller version of Bathrobe Man stood several steps inside the room. His appearance, or rather his sudden, silent appearing shook Erica's resolve. Inch by inch, heartbeat by heartbeat, she lowered the gun until it hung limply at her side.

"Don't shoot yourself in the foot, kid."

"No, I—I won't." She shook her head in a confused sort of way. "Grant?"

"Finger off the trigger, okay?"

Right. She watched him cross the room. Not only did Grant Stevens reclaim the Bathrobe Man's gun, he supported her through the dizzy-all-over feeling. Erica had to tip her head back to meet his eyes. "This is so…silly. Kidnappers and—he's your father? You're his son. I was so stupid." Her little laugh ended in a strangled breath.

Unlike his father, Grant didn't offer her a chair. He more or less planted her in the wingback, then pulled up the ottoman for himself, each action stretching well-toned muscles beneath his gray sweatshirt and jeans. "You cut your hair, kid."

"It's easier. Grant, about Ellyn."

"I know."

He didn't know. Erica looked down at Ellyn's obituary still scrunched in one hand. A dozen thoughts skated figure eights in her head. Unfortunately, they all started crashing at the same time. "Did you send this?" He frowned back at her, prying the newspaper clipping free in order to see it for himself. "Please, Grant. Just tell me. I need to know where it came from. It's important. Really important."

"Dad, coffee. The hotter the better."

Erica saw the older man wave an okay, but Grant had his nose buried in newsprint. It was still an attractive nose, she decided. *Get a grip, Tanner! He dated your sister. A long time ago. That doesn't mean he's still your teen idol. It doesn't mean he even remembers those rides on the back of his motorcycle or ice-cream cones melting at the zoo.*

Without looking, he gently took her hand. That's when grief wrote itself into his expression. He had loved Ellyn. Obviously, he still cared, very much. Erica couldn't stand it. Five years of conditioning to keep her mouth shut and she wanted to spill it all out just to ease Grant's heartache? She bit down on her lip instead.

"Maybe one of you could fill me in on the details here." Bathrobe Man—Mr. Stevens—perched his still youthful frame on the arm of the sofa, eyeing Erica with renewed interest. "You can call me Bill."

"And you can take this." Grant twirled the gun around, handing it to his father grip first. "If I ever catch you doing that again, you're in big trouble. Got it?"

"What I ain't got is a little r-e-s-p-e-c-t. Respect, son. I knew what I was doing. Now, maybe you could introduce me to our little cat burglar. I'm losing my beauty sleep here." Bill smiled at her in such a way that she couldn't help but smile back. "That's better."

"Knock it off, Dad. She's too young for you. Besides, she's Ellyn Tanner's little sister."

"Oh." Bill nodded, a suave gesture. "Very interesting."

Grant wasn't in such an agreeable mood. "You're lucky she didn't shoot."

"That's right. You taught her how, didn't you? Guess I'd better put it away before she hurts me." He shoved the gun into the pocket of his blue robe, totally unconcerned that such a thing could happen. When Grant introduced her, Bill did a knightly bow over her hand. His next move was to take the obituary from his son. "Back to business. By any chance was this in a plain, brown envelope, no postmark?"

Erica withdrew said envelope from the pocket of her lab coat. This was getting too complicated. "It showed up while I was at work. Someone slipped it among the charts."

Bill watched his son take the envelope from Erica. "Ours was slipped into a mailbox downstairs, with a note attached urging us to wait for *the woman* to show up."

"What woman?" Grant asked. "Erica?"

She would have been offended that his tone made it sound like a huge surprise someone considered her a woman, but Bill was already asking, "When did your letter show up, honey?"

"A few hours ago." Though barely whispered past the constriction in her throat, her answer seemed to thrust Bill into motion—faster than a speeding bullet.

"Dad."

"Keep your shirt on," Bill said, just before he disappeared.

It was quiet afterward, so quiet Erica found it awkward holding Grant's steady gaze after he removed a pair of disturbing photographs from the envelope. She chose to leave the chair and pace about the loft. "You live here? I didn't know where you ended up after you dumped Ellyn. What's through there?" She pointed to the door Bill had used.

"An office. Dad and I share the space. He's a lawyer."

Right. She remembered now.

"Are you in trouble, Erica?"

She took her time facing Grant, but it still wasn't long enough to make her half-truth sound like nothing but the truth—*so help me God. Please, help me, God.* "No, I'm not *in trouble.*"

"Just checking."

His teasing disarmed her. Ellyn used to say he had a knack for it, making friends from foes and good things out of bad. She pretended interest in his treadmill before he could see the tears well up in her eyes. If Bathrobe Man didn't come rescue her soon, she'd make a fool of herself and cry all over the place. Erica wrapped both arms around her middle to keep the doubts inside. Sometimes it worked.

"You okay, kid?"

"I'm not a *kid* anymore, Grant. And you aren't old enough to be my father. Besides, I've done a lot of growing up since you decided your career was more important than marrying my sister."

A hint of red flushed his handsome face, defining everything that made him hero material, whether he liked it or not. Erica happened to know he didn't like it. Beneath the charming, all-American exterior was a man so grounded it took a bulldozer to sway him. Or a pint-sized ex-fan. "What happened? Didn't you like playing cops and robbers in the Big Apple?"

"It's more complicated than that. Life in general is more complicated."

"Meaning it was a mutual decision that you and Ellyn split up?"

"Meaning neither your sister nor I felt ready to be married. Meaning you could have trusted us to make the right choice even if it wasn't your choice."

She looked away and he knew exactly why.

"No comment? I guess you haven't changed all that much then. The kid I knew didn't like confrontation either."

"She didn't like being lied to, Grant."

"Eight years is a long time to carry a grudge."

It was her turn to blush. What she was doing to him now was worse than his breaking up with Ellyn. Erica felt the heat begin to melt her defenses, especially when Grant came closer. *Think quickly, Tanner. Don't give in.* "So, you and your dad, you're a team? He's the lawyer and you're the cop."

"Not anymore. I do investigative work now. Private cases."

"Oh."

"Oh, nothing," he said around a half smile; the smile Erica had once labeled as fake because it masked irritation. "I know you too well, kid. In fact, I've kept an eye on you since the funeral. Do you mind telling me if you're over Dr. Wilkes yet?"

He knows about that? Erica squirmed a little. "It turns out I was never in love with Jon."

"He was never in love with you either. But that's not what I asked."

"Well, why don't you tell me what the answer should be? You know everything else about me from orphan to foster care to Ellyn rescuing me and my job at Portland Memorial."

"Wait, you forgot the scholarships and the part about graduating from nursing school in record time, top of your class. Then it's the instant job, where, by the way, you have received accolades from every doctor who's ever had the privilege of working with you. Go on, what comes next."

"I could punch you now."

Grant was grinning again. "Nope. You'd end up hurting yourself. You're still just a half-pint, Tanner."

"And you're still an overgrown quarterback."

"Running back. You never could keep it straight. Just like Ellyn."

No. She shook her head, looked down at her clasped hands. She'd never be like Ellyn. The pain throbbing in her temples was not eased by the way she kneaded the area with her fingers.

"Hey." Grant chucked her under the chin with the same gentleness he would have shown a baby. "It doesn't matter anyway. Haven't played football in a long time. In fact—" he rubbed his shoulder— "I'm starting to feel my age a little."

"Too bad you don't act your age a little."

"Amen," Bill added, announcing his return from the office. He was carrying a second envelope, which he immediately handed over to Grant. "I was planning on showing this to you in the morning until Half-pint came charging in." Erica noticed his grin carried the same fatal charm as Grant's. "Anyway, do either of you recognize the handwriting?"

Grant shook his head. So did Erica, after she gave up trying to see around his broad shoulders and stepped right in front of him, extricating the envelope from his hand. She was the one who dumped it over until the key fell out. It was cool silver against her palm. "Why, Grant, you finally bought me that Harley I always wanted."

"No way." He took the key in the same way she had stolen the envelope. "You'd be trying some Evil Knieval stunt."

Bill used his superpowers to snatch the key and pocket it all in one motion. "Enough with the comedy act. This—" he produced a newspaper clipping—"was in the envelope, too."

Grant reached for it.

Erica only read the caption: Five-Year Mystery Solved. She couldn't breathe, couldn't think beyond reaching for the photographs Bill was holding. Grant beat her to it. They were the same photographs as the ones from her envelope: a burned-out car, coroners removing the unrecognizable body.

A brief glimpse was enough to make Erica back away. The room seemed to get too small, too fast. One of the huge brick supports finally stopped her. When Grant looked at her, she knew the truth was unraveling. But it couldn't be. "Nobody is supposed to know. I don't understand." She tried to rub at the pain behind her forehead, until Grant drew closer and captured her hand into the strength of his.

"Nobody is supposed to know what?"

"About Ellyn," she whispered, feeling disbelief rush through her body. "It's too dangerous. People will start getting—curious, and the Sikh will want revenge, and it's too dangerous."

Grant held her firmly by both shoulders. "Listen to me, kid. You aren't making any sense here. Tell me what's going on."

"She wasn't in the car, Grant."

He dropped his hands, looking as shocked as she felt.

"Ellyn isn't dead."

"Breathe, kid."

Right. Breathe. The rush of oxygen to her brain made her feel a little dizzy, or maybe that was caused by the speed with which Grant ushered her across the room and sat her down at the table.

"You aren't moving until I know everything." He pulled his chair to the guard position, straddling it with his arms layered across the top. Then he waited.

"I can't tell you everything."

"Why not?"

"Ease up a little, son." Bill paused at the table long enough to collect the article. "I've got some research to do."

"If you can't raise the journalist, try going on the Internet."

"Yeah, I know. The newspaper's Web site—it's listed here. Just keep your shirt on."

When it was the two of them again, Erica felt a second wave of guilt wash over her. Not that Grant had accused her of lying, but he seemed to be a little...tense. "I can't tell you what I know because that puts you in danger, too."

"Danger?"

Bad choice of words. She worried her bottom lip a moment, struggling with the need to pour out five years' worth of suppressed frustration. "Ellyn is still in India."

"And?"

"And she's still doing missionary work."

Grant didn't move a muscle, especially not to smile.

That made Erica feel more nervous. She countered like a true trauma nurse—distract the patient long enough to deliver the shot. "You are so stubborn, Grant Stevens. No wonder Ellyn married somebody else." No reaction. Maybe she should take his pulse. She reached forward to do it, but he avoided the effort and scowled.

"How long have you known Ellyn is alive?"

"Since a week after the funeral."

"The government contacted you?"

"No, Ellyn contacted me. It was a five-minute phone call." Erica traced a scratch in the tabletop with her finger. The abrupt question-answer thing they had going wasn't right. Hearing Ellyn's voice on the other end of that phone had created in her some of the same emotions Grant must be feeling now.

There wasn't another person within a million miles who could share that. Once she told him, there would be no going back...but maybe there could be some going forward, some resolution. Maybe Grant could figure out a way to help Ellyn. Really, it all came down to a matter of trust.

She looked at Grant and knew in that instant she had to trust him. It's what God wanted her to do. "I was stunned. It hurt at first that Ellyn let me think she was dead. Then my heart started opening up and it was—overwhelming. It felt like Jesus had just given me a New Testament miracle, you know?"

"Yeah, I think so."

"The first couple of days—" Erica shifted forward on her chair—"I never thought about all the stuff she didn't say. I was just thrilled that she was alive, that I wasn't alone in the world. I didn't question why she would tell me to keep quiet. Almost a month passed before I heard from her again."

"Another call?"

"A letter. I've only spoken to her that one time. All of our contact has happened through letters. Hers are mailed from small towns, never the same one twice. Mine go to a woman named Pali. Ellyn depends on her for a lot of things. Mostly to be discreet."

"So, we're back to the danger part."

Right. The confusing, frustrating, pivotal part. "The car accident five years ago wasn't an accident. It was supposed to be Ellyn in the car, but at the last minute a woman from Seattle decided to go to Cawnpore."

"Are you saying someone targeted Ellyn? They wanted to hurt her?"

A quick nod would never tell him enough. "That's the first Ellyn knew about their intentions."

"But why? She was doing humanitarian work. That's hardly the kind of thing that gets a person hurt."

Erica studied the intensity written on his face. "You kept track of Ellyn too, didn't you? You knew when she went to India."

"She always wanted to go back, kid. It's in your blood."

"God called her there, Grant. To take up where Dad and Mom left off."

"I know. I was praying with her when it happened. That's one of the reasons why we didn't get married. And if she married someone over there, that's the other reason. God had it all planned out."

"Except the danger part." Erica took a deep breath to calm what had become a familiar surge of emotions. Every time she thought about Ellyn, the danger part came with it. "It was never proven, of course, but Ellyn said a group of Sikh extremists set up the accident."

"Sikh—that's a religious sect, isn't it?"

"From Punjab. They blend Hinduism and Islam. It's complicated. Ellyn only mentioned them in the phone call. I had to look up the other stuff, like the fact that this group of extremists makes it their business to oppose Christians." She watched Grant stand. Despite what she was telling him, he seemed in perfect control of himself as he went to the kitchen and finished making the coffee his father had started. "The disapproval of missionaries is worse now than when we were there as kids."

"There's more at stake." Grant dumped coffee beans into a grinder. "A lot has happened in twenty years. More Hindu people are being saved. That makes the powers that be restless. Has Ellyn ever said why she was targeted?"

"Because of Sam." Erica moved to join him in the kitchen. "Sam is her husband, but that's not his real name. Ellyn wrote it was best if I didn't know real names. Got any doughnuts?" He pulled a box from the cupboard and handed it to her. "You ate all the chocolate-covered ones."

"You'll survive." When she picked out the fattest powdered sugar doughnut, he stole it from her. "Could you back up to the first phone call. I'm not getting a good sequence here."

That would help. Erica boosted herself onto the counter. "Okay, so it's a week after the funeral. I get a phone call. Ellyn said she couldn't talk long. The Sikh were angry because they had killed the wrong person. She had to lay low."

"So they were the ones who covered up that the body in the car was that girl from Washington?"

Suddenly, the doughnut tasted like sawdust. "Yes. I can't imagine what her parents have gone through all this time. I feel awful about that. But Ellyn said if the press found out, the Sikh would use it as a springboard to try something else while they still had the world's attention. She couldn't take the risk of provoking them. Ellyn was pregnant. The baby, Joey, was born soon afterward, premature but otherwise healthy."

Grant paused in getting a pair of mugs. "That was your dad's name."

"But it's like Sam, a made-up name. She wrote that she could never risk mentioning the boy's given name. That's how much she loves them, Grant. And somehow, despite it all, she's happy."

"Except for being threatened by the Sikh."

"It's not as frantic as it used to be. As long as Ellyn and Sam don't confront the extremists, they'll turn their focus to other things." Mostly. Erica remembered the underlying thread to her sister's letters, the unwritten risk—Joey. While Ellyn seemed to mention Sam and their work quite often, there had been few references to Joey. There had never been a photograph, never a description of his first steps or his first haircut.

She was startled when Grant took her half-eaten doughnut and threw it into the sink. He frowned at her. "What's the rest, kid? You're worried about something."

"I don't know. Ellyn wrote about God a lot, how He was using her and Sam to reach the Hindu people. Some awesome things have happened for them, Grant. It's made my faith stronger to read how she puts everything on the line just to go where they feel led."

"But?"

"But I can't help thinking about Joey." Neither could Erica keep the tears from stinging her eyes. "My heart just breaks for him sometimes, and I don't know why. I find myself wondering if he's happy, if he has friends to play with, if he misses Ellyn and Sam when they're gone so much."

"He doesn't go with them?"

Erica heard disapproval in Grant's question. "The Sikh weren't after Ellyn as much as they were after her unborn child. Ellyn told me over the phone that they wanted to hurt Sam's family. If they got to Joey now—" She shook her head, not wanting to even imagine it. "The only way I've survived five years of not seeing Ellyn, not really being part of her life, is to remind myself that Jesus did what He had to do, even when it was hard."

"Even when it was the cross." Grant touched the tip of her nose and made her smile. "I told you it was in your blood, kid, loving people the hard way, the servant way."

"Does that earn me another doughnut?"

"Help yourself, but hands off the one with sprinkles."

While his back was turned to pour the coffee, she chose the one with sprinkles. "Your dad is taking a long time."

"He's not very good with computers yet. What do you think about the letters? Who do you think sent them?"

Sawdust again. Erica swallowed, feeling no satisfaction in the big bite she had taken out of Grant's doughnut. "The journalist?"

"Too underhanded. He wouldn't have a reason to scare you like this." Grant gave her one of the mugs. "It wouldn't have been easy, but given that the article is a week old, Ellyn could have gotten her hands on it. She could have sent it to let you know that the story broke."

"But I got the obit; you got the article. She would have been letting *you* know the story broke."

"Trusting I would get the hint and step in to protect you in case things went south." Because she squirmed a little atop the counter, a frown quickly formed on Grant's brow. "What, you don't like that conclusion?"

It was the one she wanted to grasp, the one she wanted to be true instead of the conclusion that tied her stomach into a knot. Erica stared at the sprinkled doughnut a moment before handing it to Grant.

"Gee, thanks. Tell me what you're thinking?"

"I'm thinking Ellyn should come home and buy a nice house with a white picket fence and two cats. I don't like this, Grant."

"Erica, look at me."

If she did, he would be able to tell she was scared. Better to be thoughtful. She tried that, and failed miserably. As soon as Grant took the cup from her, she was praying for strength. He plucked her off the counter and stood her in front of him. Erica was grateful that he didn't let go. "Grant, if it's the Sikh, if they know about me—and you—it's gonna get ugly."

"I can deal with ugly."

❦ Two ❧

A BRILLIANT STREAM OF SUNSHINE awakened Erica from her restless sleep. Upon opening her eyes, she found her face inches from the aggressive tread of a bicycle tire and directly beneath a punching bag. It was enough to pull her ramrod straight on the rollaway bed Grant had produced during the wee hours of the morning.

His deep male chuckle swiveled her gaze toward the kitchen area where he sat on one of the high stools. "You snore like a fish, Tanner."

"I do not!" Her legs and bare feet got all tangled in the blanket when she tried to stand. Of course, Grant laughed again. "For your information, fish don't snore. And I'm very cranky in the morning until I have at least two cups of coffee. Sugar, no cream, thank you." His gesture indicated she could gladly help herself. "Never the gentleman, I see."

"You got me all wrong, Tanner. I'm always a gentleman, even when the lady doesn't always act like a lady."

"Okay, so it was all a lie. I'm cranky because *you're* here." As soon as his mouth hinted at a smile, she was standing in front of the sink, attacking his dirty dishes like she had wanted to do the night before. Well, almost like she had wanted. Today, she wasn't packing a pistol. "I should have put the dishes out of their misery when I had the chance."

"You couldn't hit the broadside of a barn."

"Maybe I've been practicing."

"Now, that I would have heard about." He leaned into the counter next to where she was working. Sometime, Erica didn't know when, he had changed into a plain white T-shirt and jeans. His hair was still damp. "Why don't you try acting twenty-six instead of six and I might believe you."

Erica attacked a spot of dried egg yolk. "Why don't you try acting thirty-three? What does that feel like anyway? Are your teeth falling out yet?"

"Very funny, kid."

There it was again, that word *kid*. She didn't really mind. In a way, it made her world seem steadier than last night's events would allow.

"You used to wake up singing. At least that's what your sister said."

"Yeah, I sang so good, Ellyn left the country. We shared the apartment for a whole six months. Then she skipped town."

"I wouldn't take it personally. Your voice is okay—for a girl."

The girl wanted to stick out her tongue at him, but it was a little early for picking on old people.

"If I had a piano, you'd sing for me, wouldn't you, Skylark? I could play spoons or something."

"Enough with the singing. When will you hear from your friend in Washington?"

"Later. I guess you're gonna be too busy to sing anyway. Before Dad left to go jogging, he made some comment about the smell of bacon luring him home. How about pancakes, too? Ellyn used to make great pancakes."

Ellyn made great everything—pancakes, jokes, flower arrangements. She had inherited that from their mother. All Erica seemed to have inherited was an overactive imagination. She coiled a dishtowel around her wet hands. Why the key? And the photographs—

why send them to Grant? That didn't seem right at all.

Wouldn't Ellyn have called if the Sikh were stirring up trouble? Unless she didn't know they knew about her little sister. Which, now that Erica thought about it, would put the Sikh at an advantage. They could do all sorts of mind games with Ellyn using her sister as the pawn.

"Did you hear me?" The sound of Grant's voice dragged her back. He was holding out a thick, navy blue sweater. "You're cold. Put it on."

"I'll get my lab coat." Too late. He was already pulling the sweater over her head. Its warmth was welcome. His scent clung to the wool fibers. "Thanks."

"You know—" he held a sleeve as she poked her arm through— "there's something I didn't tell you last night." His older, wiser brother tone released a flurry of butterflies in Erica's stomach. "I'm glad you didn't marry Wilkes."

"I wasn't his type anyway. Too dull."

Grant's eyes lit up with amusement. "Hardly." They shared a smile. An easy, best friend kind of smile. It was as if God had brought them full circle again. Grant had been there for her first crush. It seemed fitting somehow that he was ready to offer advice on a botched engagement. "I checked him out, you know. Wilkes had some bad habits."

"Everybody has bad habits, Grant. Even you."

"Especially me," he agreed, still serious. "You don't mind, do you? That I kept an eye on you and Ellyn."

She shrugged and turned a little until she was looking at the ocean. Seeing part of it through the windows made her want to see all of it. Once she was standing in front of the brick sill, she lifted a hand to where the sun was warm upon the huge panes of glass. "I guess it makes me feel like your little sister. Which is weird after being on my own for so long." Without looking, she knew he was standing nearby. It was a nice feeling, a secure feeling. "Are there any empty apartments here? It would be nice to wake up to this view every morning."

He leaned into the windowsill too, arms crossed, eyes scanning the horizon. "There are tons of empty apartments. So far, Dad and I are the only ones who live here. We started at the top. I guess it's taking a while to remodel our way down. Maybe if we had *tons* of extra money." He lifted one shoulder in a casual shrug.

"I saw lights in the other rooms when I came last night."

"They're on timers. If it looks like somebody lives here, it discourages teens from using the place as a hangout. Dad's idea."

"He seems kind of quirky. You know, the lawyer-comedian-super-hero thing he has going. I'm surprised he's not starting an inner city church with all this extra space." She looked up in time to see Grant's totally amused expression. "Don't smile; I bet he'd do it in a heartbeat."

"He's praying about it," Grant admitted.

"Maybe that's what is taking him so long this morning. He's praying and jogging at the same time. Shouldn't he be back by now?" There was something about the way Grant turned toward her, the way he sank both hands into the front pockets of his jeans that alerted Erica to a change in mood from pleasant to strained. She unconsciously braced herself. "What?"

"I asked Dad to give us some time alone."

"Why?"

"So you would relax and tell me whatever it is you left out of last night's conversation." He rushed on before she could stop him. "Why did you come here, Erica? You took a big risk, not knowing who had sent the letter."

She dipped her head, rubbing her cheek against the warm sweater. "It was instinct, I guess."

"Nope. I'm not buying it, especially since you never suggested I try to find Ellyn in India."

Erica's eyes met his with a measure of caution.

"Based on what you told me, that would've been my first choice. What was in the letters that would keep you from trying to find your sister?"

"Ezekiel."

"What?"

"Verses from Ezekiel, chapter 6. Ellyn writes them at the end of every letter. *Every* letter, Grant." Her gaze followed him when he crossed the room to retrieve a Bible. Erica didn't need to see the words anymore. She knew them by heart. "'And I will lay the dead carcasses of the children of Israel before their idols; and I will scatter your bones round about your altars.'"

Grant was looking bewildered now.

She knew what that felt like. "It was like she constantly tried to warn me that our lives were hanging in the balance."

"So why wasn't the same warning on yesterday's letter?" He answered his own question. "Because it's not just a warning anymore. It's real."

Erica was grateful that Grant came back to take her hands in his. "I'm really scared."

"Scared like when I taught you how to drive?"

"No. Like when I got pulled into the riptide." His silence told her the memory wasn't very far away from his thoughts either. He had saved her life that summer day. "The harder I try to make sense out of it, the more confused I get. Part of me feels so empty, and I don't know why. I've prayed and prayed about it. I pour in as much living as I can, but that part, that place deep down inside never gets filled up."

"Would a stack of pancakes help?"

"I'm serious, Grant." The thickness of tears in her voice erased his smile. The fact that the telephone rang didn't help either. She watched him stride to the kitchen area and pick up the portable handset.

"Stevens...yeah."

She knew at once that it was his friend from Washington. Just the way Grant became so focused told her it was the call he had been waiting for. She moved closer to him, listening to one side of what seemed like an intense conversation.

At one point, Grant steered her to a bar stool. He even made her sit down, cornering her there with the width of his shoulders. "I need to know when the journalist disappeared and what story he was working on. If you can get into his computer, e-mail me a copy of whatever files look suspicious. Any mention of the Sikh and I need to know it."

Dear Lord. Erica felt her heart pound out of control. They knew. The Sikh knew.

"Right," Grant spoke into the phone, but his free hand was holding onto Erica's so tightly it hurt. "Yeah, I'm still here.... No, don't go to the girl's family yet. Put drive-by surveillance on them. Are you sure about the journalist being expected in London? Okay. Thanks for your help." Erica slipped off her stool. She was at the door when Grant ended his phone call. "Hey, where are you going?"

"My apartment."

"Erica, wait a minute." He was across the room, gripping her elbow in a firm hand before she could get her purse off the coatrack. She felt more anxious when his gaze swept over her face. "Breathe, kid."

"Grant."

"Humor me. I don't need you fainting all over the place."

"I've outgrown that particular reflex." When his expression said he highly doubted it, Erica freed herself. "Ellyn's letters are at my apartment. I'm going to get them for you to read. Maybe there's something in them you can use."

"I thought you were panicking."

She became perfectly still. "I'm past panicking. Will you come with me?" He didn't answer. "Grant, I asked if—"

Without warning, he jerked her sideways, half hiding her behind him. In the next heartbeat, he flung open the door.

Grant felt Erica clutch his arm with white-knuckle intensity. A reaction that only worsened when they saw his father gain the top of the final set of stairs, carrying a little boy. "I wasn't...sure...I'd make it. Must be gettin' old."

Even to Grant's ears the hushed words sounded too stressed, a result of carrying the sleeping child up three long flights of stairs. Or perhaps a result of something the woman with him had said. She was just two steps behind his father—small, older, and exhausted. Anyone could see that. Dark circles rimmed her eyes.

Bill moved into the apartment so he could place the boy in Grant's big iron bed. When laid upon lumpy covers, the boy only curled himself into the softness. Erica would have gone to him except the old woman set herself in the way. "Please," she spoke quietly. "Do not awaken him. He is very tired. We have traveled far."

Yes, but how far? Grant wanted to know. *How far and how fast and why?* The questions clicked rapidly in his mind, becoming tangled with a handful of other impressions: the woman's heavy accent, her dusky skin, her clothes. And a little boy not quite five years old. When Grant looked down at Erica he knew she was thinking the same thing.

The boy was Ellyn's son.

Grant set his arm around Erica. "Let's sit down, kid."

She twisted free and stared at the Indian woman, waiting.

Aging brown hands were pressed palms together beneath the woman's chin, followed by a servant's bow. *"Namastey,* Erica. I am Pali."

"Where is she?" Erica's whisper pierced the room more completely than any shout could have. "Where is my sister? Is she here? Is she downstairs?"

Bill answered, or rather, didn't answer. "There isn't time to explain everything. I'm going to stay with you while Grant and Pali go to the airport."

"The airport?"

Grant noted how his father's shoulders were already squared against whatever Erica would say. There was purpose in how Bill Stevens retraced his steps, how he stopped by the coatrack long enough to remove Grant's leather bomber jacket. "Do you have your keys, son?"

Grant nodded. "If Ellyn is at the airport—"

"You're going to a security locker." Bill threw the jacket at him. Grant caught it. He also caught the way his father motioned for Pali to precede him through the door. She did so without looking at Erica again. Nothing about this felt right. Too much tension. Too many careful responses and no real answers.

"Bill." Erica practically threw herself onto the landing. "Just tell me what's going on. Please. I don't understand. A security locker?"

Grant felt an invisible fist punch him in the gut, especially when his father took so long turning around.

"Erica, the security locker contains money and a will."

She took an involuntary step backward, colliding with Grant. He would have steadied her, but she shrank into herself. Her gaze was still locked on his father.

"Honey, I'm sorry. Ellyn died over a week ago in an airplane crash. Her husband is dead, too. Pali brought Joey to you because that's what Ellyn wanted. I found them downstairs, huddled in a corner. She was too exhausted to carry him upstairs."

Erica reached behind herself for the wall, then sagged into it. Her tear-filled eyes were fastened on Pali now. The explanations would be painful because they shared the same grief. Grant knew how they felt. He was ready for the moment Pali's wise, brown eyes shifted from Erica's face to his. Behind the physical signs of exhaustion lay a deep inner resignation.

She nodded.

Grant nodded. Time to go. He didn't want to leave Erica right now, but there was no choice.

"It's taking too long," Erica repeated. She had paced across the room, around the room, even from one room to the next. Nothing helped. Each journey ended in the same place, at the foot of Grant's iron bed, watching the boy sleep. She didn't even know his real name. Sunlight caressed his dark hair, warmed the light brown of his cheeks. He wore black pants and a white shirt, like a little man. Erica wrapped both arms around herself to keep from wrapping them around the boy. *He belonged to Ellyn. He is a part of Ellyn. He's so little....* The pain that came with biting down on her lip was nothing compared to the pain tearing through her heart. Ellyn was dead. When she sensed Bill behind her, she turned toward him. "This can't be happening."

"I wish it wasn't."

The compassion she heard in his words brought fresh tears rushing to her eyes. He must be thinking of Grant, how news of Ellyn's death would tear a huge hole in his life too. Only by concentrating very hard did she keep from crying. "I don't know what I am going to do."

"Well, when Grant gets back, we'll sit down and talk it through. He's a good man to go to in clutch situations. Until then, we pray a lot."

Her nod was feeble at best.

"Look, I think Joey is waking up."

Though Erica would have whirled around, Bill's hand on her arm cautioned her not to frighten the boy. She was grateful to have him stick close when she sat on the bed.

In a moment, the little boy rolled onto his back, opening sleepy eyes. Incredibly, he smiled. "You are Aunt Ricky. We saw you at the hospital yesterday." He frowned. "Where is Pali?"

Bill knelt next to the bed. "She will be back soon. Did you and Pali deliver the letter for Ricky?"

"Mmm." He was looking around. "The secret letter. We brought one here, too. Do you live here? Am I sleeping in your bed?" One of his tiny hands glided over the warm blankets. "I like your bed. I do not have a bed like this." The way he so quickly bounced onto his knees caught Erica by surprise. He had dimples in both cheeks. Sweet, kissable dimples. "I do not have a bicycle or...that thing." He pointed to Grant's weight bench. "Or that." The stereo system.

His bright eyes sobered instantly when he saw the tear that slipped down Erica's cheek. She braved a smile but couldn't talk so Bill took over. It touched something in her to see him stick out his hand for Joey to shake. "Hi, champ, I'm Bill."

"Where is Grant? Pali told me Grant would be here."

"I'm sure he's on his way. How about if we make a couple of man-sized sandwiches?"

"I'd rather have American pizza or macaroni and cheese. Or peanut butter and jelly." He giggled when Bill tickled his tummy. The sound of paper rustling reminded Joey of what he had in the pocket of his white shirt. He pulled it out. "I forgot. Here, Aunt Ricky."

Erica accepted it with a feeling of trepidation.

"It's another secret paper. Pali said I should keep it safe and give it only to Aunt Ricky. What does it say?" He was on his knees now, leaning against Erica, so content she knew Ellyn must have told him all about her. She was not a stranger to him. She *was* his Aunt Ricky. "Read it to me, please. I like secrets."

Thankfully, Bill distracted him with a piggyback ride to the kitchen for food. Erica could not have found the strength to read it out loud.

Dearest Ricky,

    If you are reading this letter I know it will mean that I'm dead and—unimaginably—that Sambhal has died also. We send Joey to you in faith that God will allow our son a rich and long life, a life made more complete as you impart to him our heritage of Christian faith. There is enough money to raise him well into adulthood. We leave him in your hands. He is your son now, Ricky. Love him as we have loved him. Now, I must write the difficult words, words that grieve me and stain my contentment with its only shadow of regret. Life with Sam has meant taking a certain amount of risk. You know about the Sikh, but I have never told you that a seed of contention has driven bitterness into the very heart of Sam's family. There is not time or space to record here every concern, but you must let Grant help you find a safe place to raise Joey. Pali has been instructed to give Grant a letter describing the precautions that must be taken. Sam's family will seek revenge.

There was more, but Erica had read enough to feel fear freeze in her veins. She stumbled to her feet. Bill and Joey were safe in the kitchen, laughing over peanut butter and jelly sandwiches. But Grant and Pali were in danger.

Bill just happened to look up and catch the look of terror that contorted Erica's expression. Within seconds, he was taking the letter from her, reading Ellyn's sobering words. No wonder Erica was shaking.

    "You have to—do something," she whispered. "Please, Bill. You can't let Grant do this."

"I sure can." Bill led her several steps away from Joey's hearing. "Grant is the best person I know to take care of this mess. He'll protect you and Joey and Pali."

"But the Sikh—"

"Are about to meet their match. Listen, honey." He held both of her hands, the letter crumpled between them. "Grant has his gun. I felt the weight of it in his jacket. He also has eyes in the back of his head. The first sign of trouble and he'll be calling Tom Chainey."

Tears came to flood her eyes. When he wiped them away, more came. "Hey, now. That little boy is going to think you're a leaky faucet." She glanced over Bill's shoulder in Joey's direction. That stopped her tears. "Better. Add a smile for him and pancakes for me."

Erica's giggle was shaky. "Pancakes?"

"Yup, pancakes. I'm too old for peanut butter and jelly. Is it a deal?"

She might have answered yes, but the word was torn away by the sound of angry voices erupting upward from the lower floors. Bill ran for the door, ordering Erica to stay with Joey.

The first flight of stairs passed by in a blur, then he moved cautiously. That was Pali's mantle, a pool of brown on the foyer floor. And it was too quiet now. The hairs on the back of his neck felt prickly. Had Pali dropped the mantle, or was she here, in the building? If she was here, where was Grant? Maybe Erica was right. He should call the police. Bill paused in the middle of the second flight of stairs.

Without warning, light and pain exploded in his head. He knew nothing else.

Grant pulled up next to the factory where half a dozen police cars were parked at odd angles all over the street, their red and amber lights twirling. He got out slowly. Ever since Tom had reached him on the cell phone, Grant felt like he was stuck in slow motion. Driving, thinking, breathing, walking through the front door. A giant hand threatened to tear out his heart at the same time it stopped him from going any closer. *Dear God in heaven.*

"Grant."

The voice belonged to Tom Chainey, Portland's chief of police. Grant noted he wore the same rumpled brown suit as the last time they met. But that had been for dinner two months ago. Now they stood in the foyer of the building where Grant lived and he was supposed to—identify the body.

"Hey, you okay?"

No. He was not *okay*. He had just come from the hospital where his father lay unconscious in ICU. Critical condition.

"Let's get it over with." Tom took him to within a foot of the black rubber sheet and gave a quick nod. Another policeman lifted the sheet away. "We've got pictures already, so we can turn her over if you want."

No, he didn't need that. Grant backed away, both hands shoved into the pockets of his jeans. The sick feeling in his gut hadn't happened in a long time. Not since the first time Ellyn had died. "Her name was Pali. I don't know a last name."

"It looks like she fell from your apartment, after they beat her. We don't know yet if the fall broke her neck." A wave of Tom's hand allowed the coroner's team to start loading Pali's body onto a gurney.

Only by looking at the skylight far above them could Grant control the surge of emotion. Erica and Joey were missing. Pali was dead and his father was—close to dying. If the Sikh had been so brutal with Pali and his father, what had they done to Erica? What had they done to that poor little boy?

"Grant." Tom touched his arm, gaining his attention. "Don't believe what those doctors said about your dad. He'll make it."

"It doesn't look good."

"Yeah, but you Stevens men are stubborn as all get out."

"Does that mean you'll let me help catch the guys who did this?"

"I was hoping you'd say that."

❡ Three ❡

Hot air surged down tin walls to storm Erica's overheated skin. A skylight set high in the roof had been her first reason for hope. But that was hours, perhaps even days ago. She wasn't sure. Pain often robbed her of consciousness. There had been several awakenings, several attempts to gain a foothold in reality before this one.

Now it seemed reality gripped her so firmly she couldn't catch her breath. Beyond the skylight, sunshine was burning to death in a wide sky. Within, drunken shadows swayed upon walls stained blood red and gold, taunting her not to be afraid. The air was thick with dust and a dozen assaulting odors, most strongly fuel.

Erica struggled to her knees amid crates and steel barrels. It was a cavernous space and her little corner seemed a million miles from the doorway. Her hospital scrubs and Grant's sweater were soiled, torn in places. She had lost both shoes. And her wrists were bound with layers of duct tape.

Fortunately, her teeth were strong. She began tearing at the vile tasting tape as one plan after another was formed and discarded. If they hadn't gagged her, that meant she wasn't near enough for people to answer her cries for help. The door—a double, sliding affair—was probably locked from the outside. She would need to get out a different way.

Oh, dear Lord, help me.... The longer it took to chew through the tape, the closer she came to panic. Another half hour passed. Total darkness hooded the skylight. She heard new sounds rising against the walls of her stifling hot prison; a slight wind rattled the tin, that same wind carried strains of music.

Finally, she peeled back the bottom layer of tape and with it a few layers of skin, leaving her wrists raw and bleeding. Tears stung her eyes. Once she was on her feet, it seemed as if the dirt floor became a pool of quicksand, tugging at heavy limbs, threatening to stall her escape. She fell twice before reaching the door. It was locked, which meant she couldn't go through.

But she could go under.

Erica fell to her knees and began clawing at the dirt, driven by images of Pali being beaten and thrown down the stairwell of Grant's apartment.

Slipping through to the outside was like breaking the surface after being underwater too long. Warm, sweet air filled her bursting lungs. She stumbled around the side of the building, back pressed against its corrugated wall, eyes scanning a strange, nighttime world.

The flat earth beneath her feet melded into mounds upon mounds of darker shapes—hills, marking a definite horizon. In one direction, a field of thick grasses whispered as constant background for the occasional scrubbing of bushes. In the other direction—*Oh, Lord....* Erica pushed herself clear of the building, then took a hesitant, disbelieving step.

In the other direction, cradled by the hills, a haze of light charmed its way upward into the darkness, undulating with song and celebration and the sound of a thousand voices. A thousand voices speaking a language she had not heard since her childhood.

India.

Erica took another step, then another. Tears dampened her

cheeks. She had come back so many times in her dreams, perhaps part of her had never left. India was in her blood, and this was not a dream. She was alive. She had survived thus far, and for some reason she had been brought to India. To give up now would mean failing so many—Ellyn and Pali.

And Joey.

Grief ripped through her heart. She could not fail them, not again.

She ran. She walked. She fell often in the slippery sand and picked herself up again. The music was dreamlike, never seeming to change in tempo, not even a long while later when she wove her way down through shadow to hover at the very fringes of the village festival. Everywhere she looked it was a seductive dance of color, women flowing in bright saris, men striding in loosely fitted tunics and pants, but few wore turbans. Like the Sikh.

Erica sagged into the narrow shadows between several solid block huts. The Sikh could not be far away, and if they found her, what then? Would there be endless questions, endless demands, endless ways of punishment twisting round and round, taut as a rubber band, until something snapped and they completed what they had threatened all along—killing her? A silent scream swelled within Erica to remember how Pali had been thrown to her death.

She could only stop the scream by moving away from it, by leaving one shadow for the safety of another. Why hadn't they killed her in Portland? Why was she alive? Laughter swirled up around her. Jewels glimmered and jangled. Bullocks roamed free. Camels endured service. And always the music...so very beautiful, so very familiar.

As a child, she had experienced the Hindu festivals many times. Mercifully, those memories comforted her now. She felt less lost and more certain that she would somehow survive to bring the Sikh to justice. But it would not be easy. She carried no money and had nothing of value to offer the vendors in exchange for the anonymity that would keep her alive.

First, she must find clothing. If she looked like one of them, she could search out someone who spoke English rather than Hindi. Then she would find a phone and transportation away from here. The farther and faster the better. As soon as the Sikh found she was gone, they would raise an alarm.

Erica spent an anxious few minutes slipping through the darkest walkways, watching and waiting for the right moment. So many thronged the canopied booths, haggling for the best bargains, it was a wonder more goods didn't disappear through dim, forgotten corners. A handful of silk here and there. A scrap of white choli. A few missed heartbeats and murmured prayers, then she fled into the shadows again.

Her hands were shaking, which made it as difficult to strip off the old clothes as it was to arrange the silk skirt and form-fitting white blouse. Hopefully the deep sapphire silk would make her blend into the night. She wrapped a similarly shaded mantle over her blond hair, around her neck, and over one shoulder. It was still so long. But she didn't know how to do it properly and every thought now urged her to find a way of escape before the bearded men found her.

She plunged, head lowered, into the world of no turning back.

Beneath her bare feet, the dirt became an uneven street. A cow wandered into her path, or she wandered into its. Erica stumbled away, aware that she was dehydrated. Weariness invaded her body. She could not afford to let it take over.

So many people. In stretching the mantle to cover her lower face, another part of the slippery cloth loosened. When she smelled food, her long-empty stomach revolted. A crowd of people, all moving in the same direction, swept her through the worst moments of nausea.

Suddenly, in her struggle to focus, Erica saw individual faces leaping out of the revelry: a toothless old woman and her baskets, the spice man with his engaging grin, a heavy man who shouted at his reclining camel, a pair of teenage girls looking like fresh flowers. A bearded man.

Desperately, Erica slipped between two booths. *Escape.* She didn't dare run; yet she was soon out of breath and hopelessly lost in the maze of narrow passageways. No one could possibly have followed her, so frantically did she twist and turn through the village. The moment of stopping became less of a choice, more of a necessity.

Everything appeared to blur together.

When the dizziness passed, she found herself beside a stone temple. And she had made a mistake. Bright flames lit the temple, flames that burnished her blond hair and fair skin, now that the mantle had slipped to her shoulders.

The shock chased her gaze from wavering firelight, round dozens and dozens of such temples, to a small lake set in the center. Placid, undisturbed, the lake was at rest with this adoration of light upon its face. Truly, it did not mind.

Erica was terrified. She turned to flee.

And saw him.

He stood opposite her, beyond the leaping flames. Though he wore the traditional loose-fitting shirt and pants, white in color, he seemed different than the others. Not his hair, which was dark and thick and well cut, nor his intense black eyes, nor the clean-shaven duskiness of his skin. Taken separately, none of these would have set him apart. Combined, they created an image that *was* India.

The children standing in front of him were clamoring for his attention, pressing closer and closer. He laughed at them. Soon, he pulled coins from his pocket and the children were laughing, too. A few words on his part sent them all racing to a candy stall on the other side of the open market.

The sight of them began to blur with Erica's dizziness, so she turned to the man again. It was a desperate turning. And he was already watching her, as intently as she had watched the children. Perhaps he knew just by looking at her that she wanted to be like one of them. Except she needed his help, not his coins. *Please, Lord. Let him help me.*

The man moved. Before she could react, the distance between them had vanished. She held her breath as he, in a single, smooth motion, lifted the mantle from her shoulders and wrapped it about her head, covering her hair and part of her face. "Others are staring at you," he said.

Her alarm must have bled through to the hand he placed beneath her elbow, yet he said nothing more. He simply directed her closer to the lake. Erica was aware that he shifted her to his other side in order to block most of the light from touching her face. She was also very aware of feeling small beside him. Though he was not unduly tall, among his countrymen he was taller than most. Lean, controlled. He carried himself with greater discipline.

When he spoke again, she was mesmerized by the sound. "It is easy to confuse the temples if you do not first visit them by day. This confusion, it happens often, especially near *Kartik Poornima,* the Autumn Festival. When the moon is full, thousands more will gather to worship. Many of the women will seek Roop Tirth."

"I'm not...sure what that means. I—" Slowly, she shifted her gaze up to his handsome face, wondering if he cared that her voice was hoarse. She hadn't used it since screaming Pali's name that day at the apartment. Did he care? "I don't know where I am or—"

"Pushkar Lake." By his deliberately calm tone he seemed to convey that she should not lose control. The way he spoke made it sound as if she had come to worship at some temple. He didn't know the Sikh were chasing her. He didn't know about Ellyn and Pali and Joey. The slight pressure of his hand on her elbow silently encouraged Erica to focus outward rather than inward.

"The legend," he continued, "tells how Pushkar was born when the great god Brahma passed overhead and let a lotus flower slip from his grasp." With his free hand, he fluidly demonstrated Brahma's actions. "Where the petals fell to earth, water sprang forth. *Pushkar* means lotus flower. Have you ever seen one? A lotus flower?"

"I don't remember. Could you...help me, please? I need help."

"There." He indicated a set of steps rising from the edge of the lake, upward into a hill overlooking the village. At the top was another temple, larger and more impressive than the ones they were leaving behind. "Lord Brahma has no other temple in all of India. Behind it is a temple dedicated to his first wife, Savitri."

He was strong enough to catch her when she faltered. At once, his arm slid round her waist and they proceeded upward. Though he continued to speak about temples and gods and worship rituals, she realized he did not expect her to respond. It was a ruse for anyone attempting to overhear his conversation. Somehow, he knew theirs must be an unremarkable, perfectly quiet disappearance.

At one point, having gained Lord Brahma's temple, he delayed an elderly man passing by. Words were exchanged between them. For the most part, Erica was hidden by the width of her rescuer's shoulders and did not see the old man's reaction to whatever was requested. He was already gone when she found herself being led past sacred Hindu firelight into darkness. Perhaps even divinely appointed darkness.

Ahead of them was the looming, black outline of Savitri's temple. No worshipers. No firelight. No bearded men. Yet to reach it required climbing another longer set of stairs, and Erica's legs threatened to buckle at the mere thought. She raised her head to tell him so, but he knew.

She was swept off her feet into his arms. "I'm so—sorry."

"Do not speak."

No, she should save her strength for telling him the worst parts. She closed her eyes to stop the fragmented images. Would she ever forget the look in Pali's eyes just before she was pushed down the stairwell? And Joey. A moan escaped her lips.

"No," the man whispered, his breath fanning her cheek. "Please."

Of course. Someone might hear, and he was moving so carefully, so silently. Her head rested high on his shoulder, feeling the heat of him through his white cotton tunic. His heart beat solidly against her ribs. Almost there now. Almost free. In looking at the sky, she thanked God for sending the clouds. She thanked Him for sending this man to rescue her, for sparing Grant and Bill from the Sikh. Or had they been caught up in it too? *Dear God, let them be alive.*

A sudden coolness enveloped her. Erica opened her eyes to find they were inside the temple, moving through murky darkness with an assurance that told her this was not his first time to walk across the polished floor. He stopped only because they reached the back wall. "Are you able to stand now?" he asked, still in a low whisper.

The fact that she didn't answer was answer enough. Being in the cooler temple may have started her shivering, but it was a sudden return of anxiety that sustained it. The mantle was hardly adequate to handle anxiety. *This is India...India! And the Sikh want to kill me. And God wouldn't want me in this temple. And my life is in the hands of this stranger.* He shifted her so that she was on her feet but leaning heavily into the wall, his hands on either side offering support.

Hot tears welled in her eyes, not because of the pain, but because of his kindness when she had just been wondering if he could be trusted. She was brought out of her private thoughts by the touch of his hand to her temple, where the Sikh had left a swollen, bruised reminder. Though it was too dark to see his expression, she could feel anger in him. He mastered it to speak in the richly toned voice that made her feel secure.

"You have been injured and should not be walking about like this."

"I had to—get away." Erica looked down at her arms because he was holding them, and the pressure, though slight, was nonetheless intense. "These men—the Sikh—came to the place where I live and they killed people, a woman and a boy." He became very still, like one of the stone gods. A shiver moved through her entire body. "I don't know why they didn't kill me, too, but I am in danger. Please? Will you help me? I...don't know what to do."

The fingers he laid upon her lips silenced her anguish, and her tears. "I have sent the man to get you something to drink. Then, when you are able, I will take you to my home." One of his hands cradled her aching head, while his thumb raised her chin. She could feel him looking at her, more intently than anyone had done before.

"I don't even know your name."

"Sajah."

But that sounded like something... She thought hard, forcing long-buried memories to the surface until they tangled with the pain in her head. Her father had talked about men, powerful men—the Rajahs and Maharajahs. His name sounded like that. Erica smiled. "Are you a king or—?"

"A prince," he said quietly. "Only a prince."

❦ FOUR ❧

TEN STEPS BY FOUR STEPS. Grant had paced the hospital room often enough lately to know how small it was. Sitting down didn't help either. The chairs were ultramodern, more plastic than upholstery, which equaled more torture than relaxation. He didn't feel like relaxing anyway.

As he paced, his gaze shifted from the door to the clock to his father. None of them moved. Maybe it was all right for time to stand still, but he had a few bad guys to catch. Grant checked his wristwatch, just to make sure the clock on the wall was still alive.

Frozen by the moment of impatience, he heard the clock ticking. The IV machine had its own peculiar sound, as did the feet passing along the hallway beyond that closed door. Doctors walked with clipped steps, hard soles on hard tile. Nurses made less noise, moved with lighter steps. Family, loved ones, moved without purpose, waiting, shuffling sometimes. He separated a faint "ding" from the other sounds. Hopefully Tom was on that elevator.

"Grant."

He pasted on a smile before facing the bed.

"What are you listening to?"

"What makes you think—"

"You're standing there like you just turned on your bionic ear." Bill started to move himself into a more comfortable position, winced, and lay still again. He looked worse now that the bruises were fully blown, purplish green. At least he had color. It was more than the doctors had predicted. The concussion would keep him bedridden a while longer. "I'm thirsty."

"Ice chips?"

"Coffee."

Grant chuckled. "I don't think so, Dad. Why aren't you sleeping?"

"Maybe because you make me nervous, all that bouncing off the walls." Bill opened his mouth to receive an ice chip. Even that small movement taxed his strength. "I hate feeling weak as a baby. When are they going to take out these hoses?"

"IV tubing, Dad. Maybe tomorrow or the next day. If you're nice to the nurses, they might slip you some ice cream."

There was a knock at the door.

Bill groaned. "If it comes with a needle, I'm not buying."

"It's probably Tom."

"Tom Chainey?"

The squeaky question was answered easily enough. Grant pulled open the door, allowing Tom to step inside, right behind a huge bouquet of flowers. The man was grinning from ear to ear. "For the record, these flowers were the little woman's idea, not mine. I smuggled in a deck of cards, a few hot rod magazines, and a candy bar the size of Texas. You ain't looking so good, Bill."

"Neither are you."

Tom laughed until Grant grabbed the vase and made room for the flowers on an empty windowsill. "Thanks. You know, Grant, I expected that I'd have to show my badge to get in here. What gives?"

"He's cooking up something," Bill said with a pointed stare in Grant's direction. "I should have Tom put you under house arrest, make you go home instead of baby-sitting me twenty-four/seven."

"Have another ice chip, Dad. Your throat sounds scratchy." Grant spooned in the chip when his father started to protest. "To answer your question, Tom; yes, I did pull strings to get you here. I want you to promise me you'll watch over Dad while I'm gone."

"Gone?"

Both Bill and Tom said the word. By virtue of health, Tom continued the question. "You found something? When did this happen? I thought you were going to share information with me."

"Whoa." Grant held up a hand. He could handle Tom easily enough, but he didn't want his father getting upset. There were weeks of healing time ahead of Bill Stevens. "First off—I'm going to India."

"But—"

"Give me sixty seconds, Dad. No interruptions. Agreed?"

Bill almost nodded, but that would have hurt so he settled for a grunt instead.

"That reporter from Washington is still missing, but I got a copy of his phone charges. He took several collect calls just before the story broke, all from India. Then there's a fax transmission from him to India."

Tom interrupted. He hadn't agreed to Grant's code of silence. "The article you got with the photographs was a fax copy, right?"

Grant nodded. "It didn't end there. The reporter started making phone calls to India, a lot of them. None of his files on the desktop computer indicated it, but I think he was working on another story. Probably storing notes on a laptop."

"Why did he go to London instead of India?"

"I don't know yet, but I'd say it's somehow connected to the fact a private jet from England flew into Kennedy Airport on Friday and out again late Saturday afternoon."

"That can't mean much in an airport the size of Kennedy."

"I called a friend in England who owes me a favor. He's checking to see if the flight originated in India. He should have solid information by the time I reach London, but I'm betting it leads straight to the Sikh. I've got some people pushing the India visa through. The passport and hooking up a private flight were easy fixes."

"This ain't a walk in the park, Grant."

"I know." He glanced down at his father, noting worry in his eyes that moments ago had been filled with tiredness and pain. "It feels like I need to do this, Dad."

"I know. It feels right, but I don't like it."

"Pali lied to us. I have to figure out why."

"Because she was scared."

No, it was more than that. Grant remembered the last time he had seen Pali alive, when she pleaded exhaustion and insisted that she stay behind at the factory instead of going with him to the airport. True, she had promised to return to the apartment, but she had also told them there was a will in the airport locker.

There was no will. There was only a whole lot of money and a whole lot of mystery. That mystery seemed to have swallowed Erica and Joey out of sight. Grant had already vowed that he wouldn't lose Erica like he had lost Ellyn. Something inside told him she was still alive. He wasn't coming back without her.

❧ FIVE ❧

SHE STUMBLED INTO A LONG HALLWAY lit only by lamps placed far from one another. Darkness and a lamp. Darkness and a lamp. Darkness... After a dozen steps through quicksand, she leaned heavily against the wall, taking deep breaths.

So many doors. They marched before her eyes, blurring into nothingness. Where was he? She had to help him. Erica pushed herself from the cool stone, just before it swallowed her. She had to help Joey now. He was slipping so far away.

Panic grew inside until it was choking her. With each step, she became more aware that she would not reach him in time. Too many doors, too many Sikh. Joey spun away from her grasp, whirling into the dark nothing. Her scream was long and silent. The pool of quicksand boiled beneath her feet.

But there was someone who would not let go. Someone who would not let her sink down to the dark place where there were no thoughts of Joey. It hurt to be pulled back. It hurt very much.... Consciousness returned slowly, and with it came pain, too much pain. When she moved, there were a dozen explosions of light behind her eyes.

"Please to lie still. You have concussion." The voice formed with an image, one feature at a time, and only with great concentration. A teenage girl. Round, pretty face. Black hair drawn to the back of her head in a long braid. Simple clothes. A servant. And this room, so blinding white with morning sunshine, must be part of—Sajah's palace.

"Only a prince," he had said. Last night before the quicksand feeling pulled her into unconsciousness, everything had happened as Sajah said it would. An elderly man had delivered tea. Hot and slightly bitter tea. Outside the Pushkar temple, Sajah had lifted her onto his horse, a black-as-midnight animal. Then he mounted behind her, holding her sideways, keeping her safe.

She remembered how grass became sand then became a liquid, flowing race over the desert. But that's all she remembered. He must have carried her to this room. Across from the bed were open windows graced by intricate carvings; carvings that had been softened by the passing of time. The walls were of pink-white stone and unadorned. The floor white tile. The furniture old and exotic. Her bed was covered in white silk. Her bruised, tired body was covered with a white nightgown.

Erica brought her troubled gaze back to the girl's face.

"You have strange nightmare," she said in her very best English. There was a frown on her youthful face. "Is pain very bad? I give pill doctor leave."

"No." Erica shrank from the thought of being drugged. "Please, I just need to see Sajah."

For a moment, that dark gaze skimmed Erica's face as if the girl were years older than she appeared. "The Rajah Ajari ask I take care you. A bath. Food. Any things you need."

What she needed most was to see him. But it was clear the girl did not intend to summon Prince Ajari until Erica was more presentable, and she did not have the strength to argue.

Throughout the time it took to bathe and eat a little of the food from the tray, Erica held back a sense of distress. She learned the servant, Amreli, was fourteen and lived with her family in a small village not far away, a village owned by Sajah Ajari.

"May I see him now?" Erica asked as she sank onto the bed. Her hair was still damp from washing it. Her feet were bare, but she wore a clean sari, the color of new spring leaves, and the food had helped settle her stomach. "Please, Amreli. I really must see him." Though Amreli had barely taken time to draw breath over the past half an hour, she certainly was silent now. In fact, she rushed about the room, straightening things that did not need to be straightened. "If he is here, would you tell him I have asked to see him?"

There was neither a yes nor a no before Amreli sailed out of the room, leaving Erica alone again. With some effort, she peeled herself off the bed and moved across the tile floor to stand at the wall of windows.

The view unfolded for miles and miles. Hazy mountains rested on the northern horizon. Nearby, there was a meandering river and ripening wheat to hold back the desert sand dunes. Teams of workers were planting rice in another irrigated field. Nearest to the palace she saw low cotton bushes. So much land. As Erica leaned against the windowsill, she felt drained.

The escape, fleeing to Pushkar, being rescued by Sajah, and now being sheltered in his palace—she could see God's hand in all of it, but there were still things she couldn't understand. And there was Joey.

Tears slid down her cheeks. In the nightmare, she had known a desperation to reach Joey, now she felt only the remnants of despair. Every time she relived those moments at the apartment, it was like losing Joey all over again. The Sikh leader had ordered her nephew to be taken away. Then he had tortured her with vivid details of how Joey would be sacrificed, in such a way and in such a place that the people of India would not doubt the Sikh had triumphed.

The weight of a sob pressing in her chest caused Erica to sink to her knees. Through a blur of tears and grief, she wished India would vanish and leave her unscathed back in Portland. She wished Ellyn had let her help before it was too late. She wished Grant were around to tell her everything would be okay. She wished her heart did not feel broken by a lifetime of loss. Her entire family was gone.

Through her tears, she saw movement. Sajah... He appeared almost directly below her, two stories down, emerging onto a stone courtyard. Though today he wore a white shirt and black pants, he still carried himself like an Indian prince. Erica found it difficult to stand again. As she did, just before she called out his name, another man appeared. A bearded man in flowing robes and a heavy turban. Sikh.

Fear rioted through her.

The two men exchanged Hindi words; Sajah's voice remained calm, even bored. At one point, he swung his back to the Sikh and glanced up at the windows of Erica's room. His nod was slight yet commanding. She immediately melted into the shadows, knowing he meant she should stay hidden.

Now what? The man could not have come alone. Other Sikh were probably swarming the palace while Sajah was distracted in conversation. If they found her, Sajah would be forced to pay the price. He was powerful, but not against men willing to kill innocent people for their own twisted purposes. She had to find somewhere to hide.

Adrenaline swam in Erica's veins, torturing her, even more so when she was outside the room because she found herself in the hallway of her nightmare. It was the same towering passage, sunlit now, but still flanked by a dozen closed doors and so completely silent the only whisper of sound came from Erica's quickening footsteps.

Somewhere, a clock struck the half hour. She did not know which half hour, but she followed the sound until she finally reached a staircase. After stumbling down the wide steps, she raced to the next staircase. Chandeliers hung high above the tiled foyer. They would have dripped diamonds of soft light to every corner had they been turned on. They were not. Instead, sunshine cascaded through tall windows.

Erica stood poised at the top of the stairs, staring along its curving length to a massive set of doors. The doors that stood between her and freedom—unless the Sikh caught her first. Step by step, Erica moved downward. Her heart was pounding so furiously, she thought for sure it would explode.

Slowly, Erica. Carefully, quietly. Which direction did she turn? Who would help her in the unknown world outside those doors? Grant was so far away. Maybe he didn't know if she was still alive. Having reached the bottom step, she hovered between flight and purpose. She had to keep her thoughts clear, now more than ever. In a place such as this, there would be a phone. Even dozens of phones. If she found one, she could call Grant. On the other hand, once she stepped through those doors, that action might not be possible.

She had no money, no identification, and no right to be in India. Even if she made it to someone in authority, the Sikh could turn the reality of her situation into lies—as they might now be doing with Sajah. Yes, she must contact Grant.

One more step and she was opening a set of double doors, then swiftly closing them again, sealing herself inside a huge room, a library. All three inner walls were solid bookshelves. Chairs and tables were grouped here and there. A large desk stood in front of the windows.

And on the desk was a telephone.

The handset felt cold, like pressing something foreign to her ear. The thought collided at once with the fact that she didn't know Grant's phone number. Someone would find her soon. She had to hurry. Operator... A voice came on the line at the same time the door opened.

Erica spun around and found herself staring straight into startled, very tired black eyes. The woman was of small stature and beyond middle age, at least in her sixties. Yet her deep gold-colored sari and many jewels lessened the physical maturity.

In their mutual silence, it was possible to hear the operator's voice.

There was a measure of panic in the older woman's expression. Erica's mind whirled with the same sensation. As soon as she saw the woman turn to the still open door, she dropped the handset into its cradle and rushed across the room. "No, please don't." With one hand, she pulled the woman back inside, with the other she slammed the door shut. Then Erica stood there breathing deeply, back pressed against the solid wood, eyes trying to focus. "Don't leave. There are men trying to find me."

"What men? Where?"

"Outside. Talking to Sajah."

The woman's hand closed like talons around Erica's wrist. "Come with me."

"No, please." Erica felt the strength draining from her. "Please, don't tell them where I am."

"Silly girl." The door was eased open. "I am going to hide you."

They went up one flight of steps, then along a maze of increasingly darker hallways, deeper into the palace. An airless, dusty chill began to seep through Erica. She did her best to follow the woman.

Such underlying confidence accompanied this flight from the Sikh that Erica realized the woman must be Sajah's mother. There was little resemblance, but she could see a final vestige of beauty to match Sajah's handsomeness; a trace of regality to remind her of Sajah's power and control. Even the woman's hair seemed to be a soft crown of white. "Are you Mrs. Ajari?"

"Silly English words. *Shrimatee* Ajari," the woman corrected without looking back. "In here. Quickly." She opened a door and pulled Erica forward into a vast space. "You must wait here. Silently. If you hear someone approaching, hide yourself."

"Where?"

A spark seemed to light the Shrimatee's dark eyes. A smile

brought more life to her face, animating a fine network of graceful wrinkles. There was a casual wave of her bejeweled hand. "The choices are endless, just do not choose wrong. That would be endlessly tragic."

"Wait." Erica caught at the hem of her mantle. The woman seemed small, even frail. "Thank you, Mrs. Ajari. For helping me."

"Shrimatee. Shrimatee Loralai." The insistence was followed by another unexpected smile. "What a silly, dear little girl you are. If you escape murder today, it is unwise that you try to phone anyone. The Sikh could trace your calls to Sajah, and it would put him—and you—in more danger."

Yes, she was right. Erica felt guilty she had not thought of it before. "I don't know what to do, Loralai."

"My dear, you can do nothing until you have regained your strength."

Yes, but what else would go wrong in the meantime? Tears flooded her eyes as Loralai whispered good-bye and slipped through the door. The hinges gave a heavy sigh as the door closed. Some kind of latch clicked into place. Then it was quiet.

Then Erica was alone.

The room was windowless, seemingly abandoned. A massive table dominated the cold tile underfoot. Two dozen chairs guarded the dark width and length of the table. Stone walls rose toward a rim of carved balcony, then rose farther to a glass dome, the only source of light.

Erica brought her gaze downward again, to the alcoves hewn into all four walls. Perhaps a hundred or more shrines ringed the room, housing all manner of priceless idols. Where there were no idols, wicked-looking weapons hung in readiness for war.

War with the Sikh? Anxiety overshadowed the pain throbbing in her head. If Sajah was taking chances by hiding her here, she would rather leave. Last night, she had been too ill to think straight.

Today, her situation was not much improved, but at least she knew it wasn't right to involve the Ajaris.

She had to get to the police or the U.S. consulate. Perhaps not right here, wherever here was. Near Pushkar, she remembered that, but did not know where the lake might be found set against the vast expanse of India. She didn't know how to elude the Sikh outside this palace.

She wondered if they were within the palace now. If so, they might hurt Sajah and Loralai because of her. Erica stumbled into the nearest shadow, a corner beneath the stone steps that led to the balcony.

She had no difficulty imagining those chairs filled with Sikh. Fierce men, all talking at once about bloodshed and conquering the enemy. Pounding fists upon the dark table. *Dear Lord, help me.*

In her dizziness, she knocked a sword off the wall. It clanged mercilessly, the echo taunting her again and again, chasing her toward another shadow. Where would she hide if the Sikh came?

So tired. Erica moved along the wall. There was not enough strength in her to make it to the balcony. She should just give up. No, she couldn't do that. They had killed Joey. She went back for the sword, closing her hand around the leather hilt with a prayer that God would use it to avenge Joey's death.

Silly little girl. Loralai's words loosened her grip. The sword fell to the floor a second time. It was silly to think she could fight the Sikh. Resignation dragged her to the table and chained her to one of the chairs. Erica laid her head on folded arms.

Sounds came marching past crushed defenses into her imagination. Her breaths became the breathing of a hundred Hindu idols. An outer breeze along the stone parapet became rumors of war, swirling round and round. *Hide me from the enemy, Lord.* Footsteps along the hall, running closer and closer. A metal latch. Sighing hinges.

When the door opened, she could barely lift her head.

Sajah. His image was blurred by the tears, and thoughts of how Joey had looked like a little man in his white shirt and dark pants, and memories of Pali's suffering. She thought of her dead sister. A sob strangled her next breath, as well as the sound of Sajah's name.

He did not speak but came to her and squatted near the chair. He must have run up the stairs, too. The warmth of him, the male warmth and strength of him made her more aware of the cold, dark room. Like the night before, one hand was lifted to cradle her face.

It was an intimate gesture, making Erica believe he somehow knew her need to trust him. "I—thought they would—find me," she choked out. "They killed Pali and—Joey and—Ellyn." And she couldn't have stopped the Sikh. "There is so much to tell you, Sajah."

"There is time."

"But they will come back."

"No." As he straightened, he scooped her off the chair. "They will not come back. You are safe here."

Safe. The dark room disappeared, replaced by a confusion of lights and stone and gold and Sajah. She had to quit looking at him and close her eyes. Someone followed them as Sajah carried her up the next curving staircase to the upper rooms, her room.

When he laid her on the white bed in the white room, she saw it was Amreli who hovered in the doorway, awaiting the prince's instructions. *The Rajah. And I am only Erica Tanner from Portland, Maine. Dear Lord, this can't be real.*

Sunlight sprinkled Erica's pale green sari, a delicate contrast from the white silk sheets, a fitting compliment to Sajah's noble bearing. She had never known a man who moved with such fluid strength.

"You must take these, Erica," he said, picking up a bottle of medicine from the table near her bed. "Amreli said you refused before."

"I—can't sleep, Sajah. The Sikh."

"The Sikh are gone." He poured a glass of water, then startled her by sitting on the bed. With the sunlight behind him, his face was not so rugged. "I will not let them find you. What I will do, though, is to stay until I see that you take the pills."

Perhaps it was his tone. Perhaps his half-serious, half-amused expression, but Erica suddenly pictured Joey asking Bill for peanut butter and jelly.

"Erica?" She took the tablets from Sajah's hand. He had to help her with the water. He did not have to help her brush the tears from her cheeks, but he did anyway. "Why are you crying?"

"I keep—thinking of Joey. His little white shirt." She touched Sajah's sleeve. "He—sounded like you, a little prince. He wasn't—afraid, not even when the Sikh came. He didn't know they would kill him. I remember his face when they—took him away. He wasn't afraid." Erica's gaze touched Sajah's face, thinking how Joey had looked like a little man...a little prince.

"Amreli, fresh water."

The girl bowed and scurried into the bathroom, pitcher in hand.

Sajah had done it on purpose. The moment of disbelief in Erica's eyes could not be mistaken. Fortunately, she had taken the pills first. They would soon overpower her struggle. "Go to sleep, Erica."

"I never told you my name."

"You did not have to." Sajah watched her shrink from him and he felt a churning inside. Her fear made the trouble in Portland even more real than Bashtar's recounting.

"Are you—were you Ellyn's husband—Sam?"

"No, Sambhal was my brother." His words were absorbed slowly. He could tell she was trying desperately to fit impressions together in her mind. The confusion was still too great. "Why did you leave this room after you saw me in the courtyard?" His question sounded cool, impersonal because he was accustomed to handling people that way, not because he was unaffected by this woman.

She could not, in her weakened state, make her tone match his. Perhaps she was incapable of such passive emotions. "You want to know the truth, Sajah? The truth is, I left because I wanted to protect you from what the Sikh can do. I felt guilty for having dragged you into the middle of my problems."

Muscles began to tighten across his back. If Amreli had been older, more like Pali, he would have simply let the servant deal with Erica Tanner, but Amreli was a mere child. He gave the girl another order, sending her back to the lower level. Sajah was not certain he appreciated being alone with Erica.

It was unpleasant to feel how she was now shaking, to witness the betrayal in her striking blue eyes. "You've been working with the Sikh all along, haven't you?"

He said nothing.

"Ellyn never realized that you were behind the threat." Erica rubbed a hand over her forehead, accidentally touching the bruise. The tears that flooded her eyes were denied release. "Why, Sajah? Why would you do this to your own family?"

Again, he chose silence.

Erica turned her face from him, forcing Sajah to set a hand alongside the softness in order to make her meet his gaze. She was fighting the drug that coursed through her body, the very drug that would numb her pain. She struggled to focus on him. "Was Sam—Sambhal—older than you?"

His nod allowed her to follow the frantic chain of thoughts, for now.

"Then Joey would have inherited all this. That's why you killed him. You caused the airplane to crash, too, didn't you? You planned everything, except Pali brought Joey to Portland. You didn't count on that. Pali was a witness, she knew too much. That's why your men killed her. But me? Why didn't they kill me, Sajah? What am I to you?"

"You are exhausted. We will talk after you sleep."

"No. We'll talk now. Does your mother know you killed her grandson?" Though Sajah abruptly pulled away from her, Erica grasped the material of his sleeve. "Did the Sikh bring me here because they couldn't finish your orders to kill everyone who knew? Grant and Bill know. Which means you're using me as bait to draw them here. What if they don't come? How long will you wait before you kill me, too? When I am well enough to feel every moment of torture like Pali? Or will you wait until I am desperate enough to do it myself?"

"Your bravery is admirable, Miss Tanner."

"Downing a bottle of pills demands little bravery compared to being held as your prisoner."

He released her hold and stood. "You are not my prisoner."

"No? Then I could have remained in the hangar rather than dig my way out with my bare hands?"

Anger flared through his entire being. "Until I received a phone call, I did not know you were kept in the hangar. It was inexcusable. I—apologize for the way you were treated."

"You *apologize?*"

"Since I cannot, with all my power and riches, turn back time— yes, I apologize."

Her silence was more painful than words. It also revealed how quickly the drug was pulling her toward unconsciousness. "Last night, when you helped me, I thought you really cared. I thought— I felt something happen in me that was so close to hope. But I was wrong, Sajah. I was wrong last night. I will not trust you again."

"No, I would not expect it." He paced a few steps away, wanting to leave yet not wanting to leave.

"Sambhal must have hated you."

"To the contrary," Sajah answered with tight control, retracing his steps.

"Then he would have hated you now for the blood on your hands." Erica's expression changed, became more open, allowing him to see her confusion. He had never battled against caring for someone as he battled against instinctively caring for her. "What went wrong, Sajah?" When she shivered, he covered her with a blanket from the foot of the bed. "Why did you change?"

A dozen more accusations burned in her startling blue eyes, but she did not have the strength to speak them. Not even a minute passed before she sank into what he knew would be a troubled sleep.

Before he left, Sajah took the bottle of medicine and slipped it into his pocket. He wasn't willing to trust Erica Tanner either.

Early morning sunlight stung her weary eyes. Aided by regular doses of the powerful painkillers, Erica had slept for the better part of two days, automatically succumbing to Amreli's ministrations when necessary. Her world, her life was cocooned in a thick veil, and while her body healed during that time, the same was not true of her grief. It stayed with her, growing inside the cocoon until it formed its own shell.

Since the night when she had braved an ocean of quicksand only to find herself locked inside the room, Erica accepted the fact Sajah Ajari could do anything he wanted. He had been blessedly absent from her alert moments yet conveniently present in the troubling nightmares, joining the Sikh in their enemy role. The sound that had awakened her on the third day came again—a key turning in the lock.

Just before the door opened, Erica rolled onto her side, unwilling to face Amreli's hopeful smile. She couldn't allow herself to befriend that kind of innocence, not again. Better to let Amreli believe she was still asleep. Except Amreli would never let the door bang open as it did. Silence followed, charging the air with an energy she had experienced before—in Sajah's presence.

"Namastey, Erica."

She rose from the bed with graceful, if not apprehensive movements; the pure white nightgown hardly fitting armor. Today, the prince was dressed in a black suit and white shirt, no tie. If the gods he served had molded him to their liking, he wore the honor well. Every feature was cut to perfection, every movement a study of energy and life. Yet the fire in his dark eyes is what added spirit to him; the spirit that had drawn Erica that first night in Pushkar.

"Namastey, Rajah Ajari."

He resented the formality. She could tell as much by the further darkening of his already black mood. When he held out a piece of paper, she had no choice but to walk closer and take it from him. As soon as she read it, fear inserted itself over any sense of calm, even more so when she looked up at him. "Are these names?"

"A list of the men who hurt you. Nothing—no one—is beyond my reach, Erica." He nodded toward the paper now crumpled in her small fists. "You must learn that."

"What have you done?"

Sajah's jaw clenched more tightly. "It is enough that they know I have identified them." He turned to leave.

But she could not let him go without knowing. "Sajah." When he faced her, she was lashed by the unmistakable frustration in his dark eyes.

"Do not ask me for explanations and do not—*do not*—attack me with your moral accusations. I did not come here to battle you, Erica Tanner."

No. He had come to ease her burden, a puzzling action from a man capable of cold-hearted murder. "What will happen now? I assume you will not turn yourself in to the authorities."

"I am an Ajari. I will do what I must to protect my family."

"What family," she whispered. "You—they *killed* your family."

The fact that Sajah strode out of the room without answering her should have deterred Erica from pursuing the conversation. Instead, a heartache of grief and fear and anger drove her to the armoire for clothes. Prince Ajari had stolen enough from her life; she could not allow him to steal her conviction, too.

Unlike before, Erica found the hallways filled with activity. The servants seemed to be busy cleaning or running errands, though most of them paused to watch her. She didn't meet their eyes. All she wanted was to find Sajah and demand that he let her leave.

If he did let her leave, though highly unlikely, she would go to the nearest authorities and tell her story. If he didn't, she would escape and do the same thing. Either way, Sajah was going to pay for his crimes.

Her search through the palace for Sajah Ajari meant she fairly stumbled into her second meeting with Loralai. When Erica rushed through an open doorway, she found the older woman seated alone in a tastefully decorated room. The room was airy and swathed in the same soft shade of rose as Loralai's sari. Clearly, the prince's mother was surprised by Erica's abrupt entrance. Yet she recovered more quickly than Erica did. "Oh dear, you do like shocking people. Are all Americans so...impulsive?"

"I'm sorry."

"You are looking for Sajah." They were calm words, serving to somewhat slow Erica's racing thoughts. Loralai tilted her head at a motherly angle accompanied by a smile that sympathized with Erica over the most recent upper room dilemma. "Come, dear. Sit down before you collapse all over my expensive rug."

Erica sat down on the ottoman at Loralai's feet with a flounce of sapphire blue silk and a sigh more frustrated than tired.

"I am much relieved, Erica."

Of course the amused words captured Erica's full attention.

"To see you with some color in your face," Loralai explained, folding fragile hands together upon her lap. "The first time I saw you, in Sajah's library, it was quite disturbing—the bruises and your pallor, even your blond hair and blue eyes. Do you believe in ghosts, my dear? No, well I wondered if you had come to haunt me. How silly, don't you think? That's why I took you to the war room. There are many ghosts in the war room to keep you company. Are you enjoying your stay with us now?"

Erica stared at her in bewilderment. "Mrs. Ajari, I—"

"Shrimatee, remember." Loralai raised her eyebrows expressively. "I am your best ally here, Erica. It would help if you learned to recognize your allies from your enemies."

"You mean—"

"Yes. Pali." A tragic sigh accompanied how Loralai shook her head. "She raised Sajah, you know. That is why he came to love her more than he could ever love me."

"Loralai."

The hand Erica reached out was patted and stroked once or twice, then pushed away. "It is true, my dear. And I warned Sajah. I told him Pali was the enemy, but he would not listen. Now—this." Loralai's countenance suddenly changed, became unyielding. "Do you give me your word?"

Erica held her breath.

"Well, speak up."

"I don't know what you mean."

"Oh, stop pretending." Patience was replaced with irritation.

"Betul. You want to see him, don't you?"

"Betul?"

"A pity you do not believe in ghosts, my dear. Especially, little ghosts."

Joey... Erica realized they were talking about Joey. She also realized Loralai Ajari was quite insane. To rise from the stool and calmly back away took great self-control.

Loralai watched every move, her eyes narrowing until they were dark, empty mirrors of a tortured mind. "You would have made a good ghost, my dear. Such white skin. Stay...stay and talk with me about Betul. I will let you see him. He visits me, you know. Erica...oh, Erica?"

She fled the sound of Loralai's laughter. She even closed the door on it, but nothing could have stopped its echo. A slight motion at the other end of the long hallway drew Erica's attention. Sajah must have just entered the palace by way of the courtyard. Beyond the glass doors, she saw a servant holding his black horse in readiness. Closer, almost halfway between where she stood and where Sajah stood, a door opened.

A little ghost flew out.

As quickly as his legs could carry him, Joey ran straight for Sajah, delighting in, even anticipating the way Sajah caught him and swung him high into the air. While Erica clung to the nearest door frame, Joey clung tight to his uncle in a hug with arms and legs and his whole heart.

That's when the shattering began.

"Will she be all right, Sajah?" Betul swiveled until he could see his uncle's face. They had already ridden far across the hot sand. Beneath them, the midnight black horse was masterfully controlled lest he go too fast. Sajah had moonlight white horses, too. When the time was right, Betul would learn how to ride both kinds of horses. For now, he preferred to feel his uncle's strong arms on either side.

He felt safe riding with Sajah. In truth, he felt safer here than in the city where Pali had taken him. He knew this place, how the lazy river and the brown-gray hills protected the growing crops. But he wasn't sure that Aunt Ricky liked it here. "Should we go back to the palace now? Aunt Ricky may be worried about us."

"You should call her by the other name."

Betul shrugged his shoulders against the solidness of Sajah's broad chest. "As we are Ajari?"

"No." Sajah smiled. "As you are Betul."

"Oh! You mean Erica. I like her very much, Sajah. She said funny things...until the Sikh came with Pali. I think Aunt Ricky was afraid of the Sikh."

The horse was slowed to a walk.

Betul glanced at his uncle's face again. He did not seem angry because Pali's name was mentioned. "Where is Pali, Sajah? I asked Amreli, but she did not answer me. Is Pali still in America? Can she not come home? I miss her. Temnah will miss her, too." When one of Sajah's arms wrapped around his tummy, Betul hugged it close.

"Do you remember when we talked about your parents, Betul?"

He nodded but did not like to remember that time. The adventure with Pali had helped him forget. Now Sajah was bringing it all back. "Yes, I remember. They are dead, and I will never see them again. That's why I am with you because you will care for me like they did. That's why Pali and I moved here to the palace."

"Yes, Betul." Sajah's voice rumbled deep in his chest. "When Pali took you to America, I did not know where you were. Pali did not ask me if she could take you there."

"So, you will punish her?"

"No...no, little man." There was a rare sadness in Sajah's words. Betul had only ever heard it once before—the night Sajah came to tell him of his parents. "Pali has not returned with you because there was an accident in America and she is dead."

"Like Mother and Father?" Betul squeezed a frown onto his brow. "Did it happen when I was with Erica? Because one of the Sikh took me away and I thought Erica was going to stay with Pali, but then they came running out, carrying Erica. I was frightened, Sajah."

His uncle said nothing. Betul tilted his head to look at him. "They told me Erica was sick, that's why she slept so long. I held her hand all the way here, so she would not be alone."

"That was very good, Betul."

"I did not see her after the airpla landed. But I knew you would take care of her, like you took care of her today when she fell down in the hallway. Is she still very sick, Sajah? I want to see her. I hope she is not worried about us."

The horse was guided to turn around and begin the long journey back. "Do you understand about Pali?"

"I think so. I didn't want to leave Pali alone."

"It is complicated. You must not worry, Betul. You did the right thing."

Betul felt reassured, mostly. There was still something in his uncle's expression that he hadn't seen before. Perhaps Sajah felt a little sad, too. Galloping would make him feel better. "Let's go faster, Sajah."

They did go faster, until Sajah said the horse was tired and they returned to the stables. Betul sat still on the saddle, waiting for Sajah to lift him down as he always did, with an extra hug along the way. "Now we may see Aunt Ricky?"

"Erica," Sajah reminded. "But you must go wash first and put on clean clothes. And I must speak with your grandmother."

Oh, but that talking could take a long time. "Amreli could show me where Aunt—where Erica's room is. Please? I want to see her very much."

Sajah ruffled his hair. "You said that already, little man. All right. Amreli may take you and I will join you there when I can. But you must be quiet around Erica. Agreed?"

"Agreed." Betul ran off to the palace, already calling Amreli's name.

Hours had passed since Erica had fainted in the lower hallway, yet she was still not prepared to see Joey walk into her room, dressed in an outfit so similar to Sajah's white tunic and pants she wondered why she hadn't known their relationship from those first moments in Pushkar. Joey approached her timidly at first, then broke free from Amreli to run the final few steps.

She sank to her knees. For the past few days, she had believed he was dead. Yet now he stood within the shelter of her embrace. If she cried, it might upset him. If she held him with too much desperation, he would wonder why, and the answers were complicated beyond belief.

Amreli must have felt uncomfortable with their long hug because she cleared her throat and asked if they would like refreshments.

Joey turned toward her, wearing a serious expression and looking more like Sajah than ever. His gesture, commanding Amreli to stand at a distance from them, wrenched something in Erica. The influence Sajah held over Joey was unmistakable, even at his tender age.

Satisfied with Amreli's compliance, he took Erica to the room's damask-covered chaise. "I know you have been sick." The tightness in her chest increased, especially when Joey tilted his head to one side with all of the Rajah's intensity, studying the changes he saw in her. "I prayed for you."

"Thank you. Sit down by me, honey."

He did. "I prayed to many gods because I wasn't sure which one would help you." The way he clasped his tiny hands together and bowed his head dissolved Sajah's shadow so that he was Joey again. Not Sajah's little man, not Loralai's little ghost, only a very confused little boy. "I was—afraid you would go away, like my parents. Like Pali."

"No, Joey." Erica gathered him close. "I won't go away. I promise."

He snuggled into her. "So, it was all right that I prayed?"

"It was especially all right. God heard your prayers, Joey."

"God." He raised his eyes to look at her. "The God who lives in heaven?"

"The only God." Erica brushed the hair from his forehead with a gentle hand. "Do you remember your mother praying?" He nodded. "She prayed to God."

"But what does He look like?"

A smile crossed Erica's mouth, her first smile in a long time. "I don't know. Nobody knows."

"Sajah knows everything. Perhaps I should ask him about God."

The comment caused Erica a moment of panic, until she realized Joey was too young to understand what he was saying. To him, there were no boundaries between the teachings of his parents and the beliefs of his uncle. He acted out of innocent love in trying to grasp as much of both worlds as he could.

This glimpse of his fragile spirit made Erica realize they were at a turning point. If she did not help heal the wounds left by Ellyn and Sambhal's deaths, Joey would be scarred forever.

"Erica?"

She smiled for him, drawing away from the revelation God had just given her.

"Are you sure you don't know what God looks like?"

"Well, let's see." She patted her lap and he settled himself there, one arm around her neck. "When I think about God, I see a bright light and it makes me feel warm inside and safe."

"Even at night?"

She knew what that question meant; Joey was having trouble sleeping. "Yes, honey. Even at night. God is with us all the time, no matter where we are."

"Is He with Sajah, too?"

Innocent hope. Erica glanced toward Amreli and saw that the girl was listening to every word. "We'll have to pray about that, Joey."

"Sajah calls me Betul."

So did Sajah's demented mother. For a moment, defiance rose within Erica. But defiance and determination were not the same thing, and only a steady determination would help Joey now. "Would you like me to call you Betul instead of Joey?"

"Oh yes!" The little boy practically bounced up and down on the cushions in excitement. "Yes, yes. It is the ancient Ajari name. Say it again, Erica. Say it again! You say it funny. Say it again!"

"Betul," Sajah spoke from the doorway, adding enough authority to remind Betul of his promise to be quiet. Now that he had made his presence known, pain burned as a fire in Erica Tanner's eyes. "Amreli, please take Betul downstairs."

The girl bowed.

The boy protested. "But Sajah—" he slid off the chaise—"I only just came. Ten more minutes? Please? I wanted to tell her all about your horse. Have you seen Sajah's horse, Erica?" When he turned back to her, he squeezed her hands tight. "There is no stronger horse in the whole world!"

"I have seen him, but I don't know his name."

"Rama's Shikari. *Shikari* means 'hunter' and—" He looked to Sajah. "What is *Rama* again?"

"Rama is the hero god. The mighty warrior who protects us in battle."

"Oh yes. Rama's Shikari. Hero's hunter. Sajah named him. It is a wonderful name, don't you think so, Erica? Can you ride a horse? I will show you how. It is easy, I think. Sajah taught Temnah how to ride."

"Who is Temnah?"

"Oh, you will like her."

"Enough, Betul." Sajah had moved across the room and now laid a hand on the boy's shoulder. "You will tire Erica with so many words." Besides, she looked close to biting through the delicate skin of her lower lip in an effort to withstand the underlying tension. "Amreli."

"Yes, Rajah." Amreli came at once to take Betul's hand.

He was still reluctant to leave and seemed to drag his feet in following the girl. "Please come with us to Jaipur, Erica. Please. I miss you so much."

Sajah waited for the moment when she turned her gaze on him, for he had already learned she was quite eloquent in speaking without the use of words. He nodded his approval. Besides, it would be best to keep an eye on her until Bashtar resolved the threat of attack.

"Oh, good! Good!" Betul ran back for quick hugs, completely happy. Completely unaware of the price Erica had just paid for the privilege.

It seemed significant that they could hear Betul's excited chatter after he left the room. Then it was silent. Too silent. Sajah paced to the windows and back before giving voice to the first of his rules. "Until now, your door has been locked to keep the more curious servants away. That is no longer necessary. You may go anywhere in the palace that you wish, but you must never leave the grounds."

"Unless you accompany me, of course." She outlasted his severe stare. "Jaipur. I assume that it is outside the grounds, unless your kingdom includes vast cities in keeping with your arrogance?"

He smiled, pure reflex because she had no idea.

She had, however, a very quick temper. "When were you going to tell me about Betul? How long were you going to let me think you are cold and unfeeling before removing all doubt?" The fact that she stood inches shorter than him did not seem to bother her. At any moment, he expected to be punched by one or both of her clenched fists. "I grieved for him, Sajah."

Not a physical punch, but an emotional one.

"I'm beginning to wonder," she continued, "if you aren't as insane as your mother."

"I assure you, my mother is not insane. She is, however, very clever."

"Like mother, like son?"

"I doubt if that is the most important concern you have at the moment." When she took a step back, Sajah took a step forward. "Come now, Miss Tanner. Your letters to Ellyn profess a great affection for Betul."

"I love him, Sajah."

"And I do not?" he challenged. "Your letters to Ellyn also professed a great faith in Jesus Christ. Where did you hide that faith these past few days, I wonder? I certainly saw none of it. You were quite ready to believe I would murder my family for the sake of an inheritance. Did you not once stop to wonder why I was called Rajah? I already hold the inheritance, Miss Tanner. Could you not have taken time to pray for the truth to show itself above your wild imagination?"

Erica obviously felt the sting of his words. Yet in the next moment, he saw something else in her expression—profound relief—as if a huge weight had given way within her. Sajah knew it was a huge weight because it transferred from her to him, pressing against the things that had yet to be said between them.

"The truth, Miss Tanner, is that I did not kill Sambhal and Ellyn. Their airplane crashed in a mountain storm. I did not kill Pali. A group of Sikh extremists reached Portland first. For years now they have been doing what they can to threaten my family. As for choosing to keep Betul from you, it was not as cold and unfeeling as you may think. I was away, attending to matters concerning Sambhal. Since I wanted to be here when you found out Betul was all right, waiting was my only option."

Erica appeared quite shocked now. The way she kneaded the tender spot near her temple indicated a depth of contrition he had, quite honestly, expected all along. He felt the tension dissolving between them, leaving behind pure truth.

"I—don't know what to say, Sajah."

"Neither did I." He motioned that she should be seated on the chaise. When she complied, he sat next to her. "I have some questions, if you feel up to answering them?"

"Of course."

"Betul talked of giving you a secret letter. Was it from Ellyn?"

"Yes, she wrote about sending Joey to me, how I was supposed to have full custody.... You didn't know?"

He leaned forward, forearms on his thighs, hands clasped. "Did you see a will?"

"No, I only saw Ellyn's letter."

"She wrote it? You are sure it was her handwriting?"

The longer Erica remained silent, the deeper his perception of the turmoil she felt. Sajah startled her when he touched her arm. Her blue eyes swam with uncertainty. "I was trying to remember if she signed it. The letter was typed, but I—don't know if Ellyn signed it."

"Were her other letters to you typewritten?"

She gave a slight nod. "All except one part, a Bible verse Ellyn put at the end and her signature. Is it important? Anything in the letter can be proven by the will. Grant went to the airport that day to get money and a will. Even if you can't get the copy Pali brought to Portland, there is an original somewhere. Wouldn't Sambhal have used your family lawyers?"

"I do not know."

"You could check with them. A simple phone call would give you the answer."

"Nothing about this is simple."

"I'm sorry. I was only trying to help."

He stood in an attempt to shed her apology. He didn't want to feel guilty for her injured tone.

"Say something."

"I am thinking."

"Then think out loud." Erica was on her feet, too, earnestly waiting for information he could not give her. "Sajah, please."

A flash of anger burned through the reins of his self-control. "Sambhal was my brother, Erica, my twin brother and the friend of my soul—until Ellyn came between us. Our honesty changed overnight. I resented what she did to him, how she could so easily mold him into someone he was never meant to be."

Erica took a step closer.

His expression stopped her. "The rift lasted until Betul was born. From the first day I held him, it did not matter to me that your sister's blood moved within him because I knew...*I knew* he would always be more Indian than American. I vowed to do everything I could to make sure he knew what it meant to be Ajari. I will not forsake that vow, especially now."

"He carries your family name, Sajah, but Ellyn and Sambhal wanted me to raise him. I have an obligation to their choice."

"And *I* have an obligation to our Indian heritage that says I must raise Betul to take his rightful place here. The Vedas recognize no greater purpose than to have and raise a son who will make offerings to the ancestors. Betul is that son."

"So your Hindu texts are more binding to you than Sambhal's will?"

"The will has not been proven to exist."

"You don't want it to exist! You'd rather just—take over Betul's future."

"An action that is not beyond the reach of well-paid lawyers, Miss Tanner."

"I don't believe you would do that to Betul."

At the moment, he did not care what she believed. Sajah turned to leave. "I have changed my mind. You will not go to Jaipur."

He made it a good distance to the door before Erica Tanner drove the air out of his lungs—without so much as touching him.

"Sajah, wait!"

By the time he swung around, she was not two steps away, her cheeks flushed from the effort, the sapphire sari framing her to perfection, an even more alluring image than the woman he had created in his mind when reading her letters.

"Just one more thing.... Please tell Betul I hope he is not too disappointed that you changed your mind about Jaipur."

❧ Six ☙

Jaipur, Rajasthan's capital city, appeared suddenly at the foot of the blue-gray mountains. From her first sight of its strong, crenellated walls, Erica felt her heart being wooed closer to where her soul had been all along. Heart and soul met where the emptiness had been, so powerfully she knew it had been a futile effort on her part to fill a need only God could span.

The car passed through one of several towering, arched gateways and into the essence of her little girl memories. Even though she was sure her family had never visited this city, what made Jaipur familiar was the way it embraced the very breath of India. At first, wide, tree-lined streets welcomed them, introducing the newest and best in offices and shopping. But soon they were deep within the city where the streets were narrow and the guardian trees were replaced by ancient architecture.

Centuries of practice allowed noon sunlight to gently bathe Jaipur's older buildings. It was a ritual attended by few, observed by many. Few people walked along the street. Many observed the tradition of resting through the day's worst heat, no matter what the season.

Erica saw a bicyclist or two weaving swiftly among cars that were much smaller than Sajah's. Carts she thought were unattended in fact shaded sleeping owners. Animals she knew were unattended ambled along at their own noonday pace, except for the occasional bullock being treated to handfuls of dried grass by less than sleepy children.

Betul suddenly leaned over the back seat. "I told you she would like it, Sajah. Her eyes are shining."

"So they are."

Erica was shy about meeting Sajah's gaze. Ever since dawn when he had sent Amreli with the message that Erica should prepare for the trip to Jaipur, she had felt a little awkward. She had all but black-mailed the man. Common sense told her Sajah had merely chosen the less complicated of two choices. Still, her spirit would not give up echoing the "do unto others" verse. In which case now—as Sajah parked the car—would be a good time to extend the olive branch. "Thank you for letting me come."

There was a nod from Sajah.

Perhaps, for a prince, answering with a nod was sufficient.

After eating at one of the many restaurants, they spent hours in and out of the shops. Erica learned it was Loralai's birthday soon and that Sajah and Betul had made a special trip to buy her a gift. Without knowing exactly what the gift should be, it became a difficult task.

Obviously, the shopkeepers knew Sajah well. Each of them presented their most expensive and beautiful wares for his approval. Jewelry of gold and silver and glass, ornately engraved bowls of copper, shimmering silk saris of every color.

It was no wonder Betul finally grew bored with the process and begged to visit the outdoor stalls. Erica added a silent plea of her own until they were actually outside, moving among so many people.

The press of heat and bodies and noise snatched her back to the memory of Contai. Four years old, in the middle of a street. All alone. Left all alone. So many people. Too many.

"Yes, Betul." The sound of Sajah's deep voice pulled her back.

"But do not run too far ahead. Agreed?"

"Wait." Erica caught Betul back. "I'll hold your hand, okay? You can show me all the best places. Sajah will stay with us, too."

Sajah did not agree. He loosened her hold on the boy. "Go ahead, Betul. Erica and I will only be a few steps behind."

Though she wanted to stop Betul again, the pressure of Sajah's hand around hers cut off any protest. With a few lopsided skips, Betul hurried off, secure in the fact that his uncle would keep an eye on him. Oblivious to the threat of Sikh.

Erica hovered between alarm and anger. Sajah canceled that, too. "You need not panic. I have men watching us today. They have been watching us since the moment we left the palace. They will continue to watch us until I decide otherwise. Betul is perfectly safe."

If she couldn't see the men Sajah spoke about, if she hadn't noticed them all this time, how could they possibly be close enough to keep Betul safe?

"You do not believe me," Sajah said. He was prepared to defend his statement. "Your shining eyes—they reveal more than they conceal."

"I believe you. I just feel—overwhelmed by all of these people and the busyness, the noise." Erica self-consciously twisted her hands into the folds of the pale blue mantle Amreli had wrapped around her shoulders.

Today, her skirt was white, like the choli, and she wore sandals. The outfit seemed formal when compared to Betul's jeans and red polo shirt or Sajah's customary black pants and white shirt. None of the men she saw dressed like Sajah, which meant the men watching over them were dressed to blend in. Did the Sikh use that trick, too? How could Sajah know for certain that the Sikh wouldn't jump out of nowhere and try to hurt Betul?

"Are you coming?"

Yes. It was better than being left alone.

She prayed as Sajah led the way to a stall filled with lovely carvings and silver work. Betul was there already, carefully examining a delicate necklace that he in turn showed to Sajah. While she waited for them, Erica's gaze wandered to a group of silver statues representing various Hindu gods. Seeing them, face-to-face, disturbed her more than she wanted to admit.

Sajah worshiped those gods. He believed in a religion that was based on acts, on working and sacrifice, totally denying the redemptive power of Christ. No wonder he was prepared to fight for custody of Betul. The battle itself was an act of devotion, a test of his sincerity to raise the boy as a Hindu. She felt a very real pain at that thought and turned from Sajah's idols.

There were dozens of baskets at the next stall. Loralai, insane or otherwise, would have no use for a basket. She was not convinced that the old woman was in her right mind. The war room, ghosts, demented laughter—no, Loralai Ajari could hardly be considered sane.

A few yards ahead, Erica saw a stall that sold handmade shawls. Perhaps that would be an appropriate gift. The materials were soft, encouraging the time she spent looking for just the right texture and color. Finally, she found one that was particularly beautiful: a pure, luminous white that looked as if it was spun of pearls. "Sajah, look." She had turned to show him, but he wasn't there; neither was Betul.

People pressed in all around her, but none of them were familiar, none of them was Sajah. Waves of sound broke over her. None of the voices belonged to Sajah.

Amid a rain of Hindi words from the stall's insistent owner, Erica dropped the shawl onto the nearest pile. The man would not let her leave. He blocked her way, gesturing with his hands and the shawl, a dozen shawls, swirling them off the piles until she felt trapped in a kaleidoscope. "No, please. I do not want them."

A bearded man stepped out of the nearest alley. Another was moving closer. Colors flew before her, choking her. She tried to brush them aside. Where was Sajah? *Dear Lord, help me!*

Remembered terror gripped her the instant a hand closed around her arm.

Though Sajah had been prepared to show Erica how angry he was, seeing the expression on her face made him realize she hadn't lost him on purpose. After the initial fear, she actually sagged against him in relief. "You are unharmed?" Sajah cut the stall owner a look of such censure the man began to back away.

"Yes, Sajah. I'm all right. Really." Erica allowed some kind of inner strength to overflow her fear, especially when she faced Betul. "I think I found something for your grandmother. Please, sir, the white shawl."

It was eventually found among the flow dangling about his robust person and handed to Erica, with a wariness respectful of Sajah. Actually, the man's enthusiastic salesmanship became comical. He couldn't seem to talk fast enough or use enough flattery. No doubt the moderate price was based more on these efforts to please than on the shawl's value. Sajah paid the necessary rupees, saw that the package was properly wrapped, and gave Betul the honor of carrying it. In all, he guessed the transaction took fifteen years off the vendor's life.

"You are smiling, Sajah."

He glanced down at Erica and found her smiling too—a dangerous situation. She stopped walking because he did. She stopped smiling because he accidentally brushed her throat when he so carefully arranged the mantle from her shoulders to cover her head. "Given enough time, you will learn a prince can smile quite often. He can tell jokes, too, though not very funny ones." Erica began laughing. He had never heard her laugh before.

The moment was lost when a bicyclist shouted for a clear path, and Sajah had to pull Erica to one side, out of harm's way.

"You're just like Grant, always rescuing me." She faltered over the words because he could not hide his reaction. Even if the comment was innocent, he would not allow her to compare him with Grant Stevens. He had heard time and again from Ellyn how close Grant Stevens was to Erica. The relationship had not bothered him until he met Erica for himself. Now, for her to mention Stevens was like throwing up a wall of division.

She must have read as much from his expression. "Well, we should catch up with Betul, before he gets in trouble."

Like she had just created trouble? Betul's kind of trouble he could handle. Erica Tanner was a different matter entirely. Sajah scanned the crowd, the outdoor stalls, the sky.

"Are you ready?"

He was beginning to doubt if he could ever have been ready to meet her. Finding and reading the letters had not prepared him to meet the spark that fueled her honesty, nor the passion that embraced her gentle words.

"Sajah, are you ready?"

He was ready to tell her just how much he had desired to meet her, but that was a discussion best saved for a more private setting.

It was not long afterward that they left the market. In addition to the shawl, Sajah had chosen a book of poetry and several gold bangles for his mother. He knew the question dancing in Betul's eyes before the boy could ask it, but Erica looked tired now. His hand upon her arm brought her gaze upward.

Several times in the past few hours, he had seen the same unguarded expression. When she looked at him like that, they could easily have been two friends, sharing a day together. But they were not friends. Neither were they strangers. The emotional connection between them had never allowed them to be strangers. He dropped his hand from touching her. "Betul."

"Yes, Sajah?"

"Do you believe you can find the *Hawa Mahal* by yourself?"

"The pink palace! Oh, you will like it, Erica! It is beautiful!"

"You will take her directly there." Sajah's tone encouraged the boy to take the assignment seriously. The way Betul immediately held Erica's hand was a bonus to the promise of adventure. "No stopping along the way. I will deliver the packages to the car and meet you there. Agreed?"

Betul nodded.

Erica nodded too, a silent communication for his benefit. She wanted him to know that she trusted his men would watch over them.

In no time at all, the Hawa Mahal, the Palace of Winds, had captured Erica's heart. It was like a dream castle, so delicately carved out of rose pink sandstone she almost believed it was an illusion. Lush gardens surrounded the palace, but her gaze was drawn upward, past sweeping steps and massive doors to the palace windows, tier upon tier of windows, and each window was surrounded by filigrees of swirling stone that defied the word impossible. Could human hands have made such beauty?

Betul did not let her linger long. He wanted to walk through the *Jai Niwas,* the Palace Gardens. It was an enchanted place. Ornamental fountains dotted emerald green lawns. Exotic flowers filled the air with their sweet perfume. Peacocks strutted about, adding their own brilliant display of color. But Betul's real destination was the ponds, mostly because he enjoyed watching the creatures that lived there. "They are ugly, Erica. Huge monsters." She agreed and kept him from getting too close, though he constantly pulled her forward.

"Wait until one yawns and you see its teeth! We could count them, if we're quick."

"No, thank you. Shouldn't Sajah be back soon?" She hoped so anyway. But he was nowhere in sight. Even if the crocodiles were well fed, she wasn't getting close enough to count their teeth. She was almost relieved when Betul, in his own little wobbly way, tried to sneak up on the peacocks—a fruitless, five-minute endeavor. "Let's go look at the statues now, Betul." A statue was better than live animals any day.

Betul adapted to the idea with the rebound of a four-year-old. "I will show you the biggest statue." They practically ran there. "They are lions! Strong, growling lions. Like this." He growled for her until they both started laughing. "Sajah!" Betul ran past her to launch himself into his uncle's arms. Sajah swung him high into the air, reminding Erica of the first time she had seen them together.

The rush of emotion she had experienced then came tumbling back, forcing her to turn away. It seemed a lifetime before her eyes actually focused on the lion statue. Beneath the ferocious looking beasts were two Hindi words. *Satya—*

"*Satyameva jayate.*" Sajah startled her by speaking almost directly in her ear. She could even feel the heat of him through her silk clothing. "It means 'truth alone triumphs.'"

Truth. Deception and violence had driven her on this collision course with Sajah. It was no wonder that in many ways, she felt ignorant of his truth, the foundation that supported him. Watching Betul innocently run along the path made Erica realize she couldn't afford to remain ignorant about Sajah Ajari.

"Do you remember seeing it as a little girl?"

Erica shook her head. "No, my memories are sporadic. I was only six."

"But you remember sounds and smells. I found your descriptions quite intriguing." Sajah moved farther along the path. When she lagged, he accommodated her by turning and talking and moving all at the same time. Not only a show of agility, but also the way his hands were clasped behind his back accentuated the pull of white shirt across sculpted chest and flat stomach.

Erica looked away, hoping he thought her blush was due to the little girl stories she guessed were coming. "I doubt if my letters were that intriguing to someone who has lived here his entire life. You probably had to fight off sleep while reading them."

"Would you like me to quote from the letters?" He didn't wait for her to agree. "You remember the shuffle of rag-bound feet upon temple stairs, slowly, tiredly moving toward the golden gong with its rippling song. You remember the Hindi voices raised in prayer, undulating with a rhythm that captivated your sadness. And smells—the sweet sting of smoking incense you tried to chase away with a sacrifice of fragrant white flowers until your father came and promised you a piece of candy if you stopped crying.... Did you? Stop crying, I mean."

"I think so. Daddy tickled me if I wouldn't smile for him. Have you truly read all the letters I sent to Ellyn?"

Sajah's nod was both regal and amused, a feat only he could have accomplished. "Here, Miss Tanner. Tell me, do you like this statue?"

She joined him beside the massive gray stone. "Whose dog is it?"

"A hound that belonged to the Rajah Jagat Singh."

A prince was telling her about a prince. How appropriate. "The Rajah must have liked the dog very much to have such a large statue made." Erica looked up just in time to see a definite gleam come into Sajah's dark eyes.

"One may say that, yes." He turned to locate Betul.

"You are smiling again." In fact, he had been teasing her since the statue of the Lion Asoka, but the teasing had a new depth to it now, one that made her feel a little flustered. "I suppose there is a story to explain the statue?"

"There is." Sajah placed his hand on her elbow to guide her around the stone. Today, his touch was like being plugged into a live electrical current. "Jagat Singh was proud of the dog's intelligence and his loyalty."

Erica expected him to go on, but he didn't. "And?"

Sajah raised his eyebrows a little, but politely answered her question. "The Rajah had a harem of women, there, across the garden." Erica felt even more heat rush into her face as he pointed out the building. "It is said that the Rajah spent his evenings sending love letters back and forth to his women via the dog. All of the women were beautiful, of course."

"Of course. Indian women are beautiful and mysterious and beguiling."

"They are, which makes it especially challenging for a prince to choose." Sajah purposely phrased the response to let her imagine he faced the same royal challenge. "The Rajah Singh came upon a clever plan. The nightly exchange of letters was a contest, to see which woman could write the most amusing words. Whoever amused him most would be chosen to entertain him."

"Thank you, Sajah." She couldn't help but smile. "That is a very interesting story."

"But you must hear how they did this entertaining. They—"

"No, stop." Erica's hands flew up to cover her ears. She ruined the whole blushing maiden reflex by giggling.

Sajah changed that. Without warning he stepped closer and turned her laughter into breathlessness.

When he touched her throat this time, it was quite deliberate. She felt his fingertips graze the place where her pulse was beating, then he brought his hands up to cover hers, twining their fingers together. The mantle fell onto her shoulders, letting a breeze caress her hair.

The emotions kindling between them wouldn't allow her to pull away. With his thumb he traced the outline of her lips as if to memorize the way they felt. She watched Sajah's gaze drift over her face, from the curve of her cheeks to her blue eyes, from her slightly parted lips to the fading bruise upon her forehead.

"I am hungry."

Betul's announcement alerted them that he was back. His grin told them he had been back for quite some time, long enough to observe what had just taken place. Now he was looking at them with his head tilted to one side and his eyes dancing with delight.

Sajah recovered before Erica. "How about if you ride on my shoulders, little man? That way you can spy out the best place to eat before we must leave for home."

Home...home. The word vibrated through Erica's quiet contemplation, both during the ride back to the palace and while she helped Sajah get a sleepy Betul ready for bed. The boy's room was spartan, bereft of the toys she expected to find. Betul had a bed, a dresser, a chair, and little else.

But he had Sajah. There was tenderness in the way he covered Betul with a blanket, pausing to smooth the tumbled hair like she would have done. A feeling of grief descended on her, carrying her from the room before Sajah had finished saying good night.

The thought of going to her room and being alone was depressing. Erica changed directions and went to the courtyard. From the windows of her room, it had appeared smaller, crowded with potted trees and flowering plants. In reality, she found it to be an inviting and open space, even under the black veil of nighttime.

Lamplight followed her from the palace, becoming more shy the farther she went. Time had worn the stones beneath her feet. She impulsively removed her sandals and the blue mantle, leaving both of them near one of the trees being rocked to sleep by a gentle breeze.

Her destination was a sliver of silvery pool meandering along the edge of the courtyard, separating it from the formal gardens. Two steps up and she was balancing along the rim of the pool. She wanted to picture Ellyn doing this, but it was unlikely.

Ellyn was—had been serious, focused on doing more than enjoying life. Sambhal must have given Betul that certain zest for adventure. Or perhaps Sajah. She dipped her toes into the rippling water, half expecting them to come out silver tipped. *Silly girl.* Loralai would scold her for being here like this.

Erica looked back at the palace and saw Sajah standing in the doorway, watching her. After a moment, she dipped her toes again. The water was warm, silky, like the movement of the white sari against her legs. "How old is the palace, Sajah?"

"Older than your country. Why?"

"Because it seems like whoever built it wasn't thinking of the children who would grow up here. Everything is so—opulent, so serious. Except this spot." Erica watched Sajah come across the courtyard, until she remembered the intimate moments in Jaipur. Then she did a daring twirl upon the ledge and started making her way to the opposite end. "Once upon a time, I wanted to be a ballerina."

"You are not disciplined enough."

She looked at him so quickly, she nearly lost her balance. "How do you know?"

"Is it true?"

"Yes. Very true." Time to dip her toes again. She smiled at the moon's reflection in the water. "I think my imagination would have gotten in the way of practice. What did you want to be, Sajah?"

"You will laugh."

"I promise not to laugh."

"I wanted to be a lion tamer in the circus."

She laughed until Sajah levered himself onto her ledge and confidently closed the distance. Erica backed away, skirts in hand. Time for a diversion. "What does Betul want to be when he grows up?"

"That depends on the day. Sometimes an equestrian, other times an astronaut, most often he would choose to be a prince."

"Like you."

Sajah nodded. "You are now at the end, Miss Tanner. Where will you go from here?"

"To this side." She ran around the curved end, putting herself on one side of the pool and Sajah on the other. Less than three feet separated them. He had the advantage because the palace lights were behind him. "I think Ellyn always wanted to be a missionary."

"I could tell."

When she moved, Sajah did the same. When she paused to dip her toes in the water, he let her. Erica smiled again. "Did you get along with my sister? Or did your serious natures conflict?"

"Honestly?"

She stood still, the white skirt floating down around her ankles. "Of course, honestly."

"I tolerated your sister."

"For Sambhal's sake?"

"Tolerance is a way of life for followers of Hinduism. Our pluralistic philosophy allows for many paths to salvation, thus many types of religion, Islam and Christianity included, even though they would use conversion to dominate us. The *shloka* states—"

"Wait. Just wait a minute." Erica lifted her skirt and would have jumped over to his side of the pool, but Sajah anticipated her action. He set his hands around her waist, lifting her over. "You're talking about religious tolerance, Sajah. You're digging in your heels, preparing for a long discussion about philosophy and theology. All I asked was if you got along with my sister."

"I did not see her often."

"But when you did, you got into these kind of—conflicts?"

"Her conflict. My tolerance."

His hands were *still* on her waist. Erica pulled back and would have fallen into the pool except that Sajah steadied her. Time to put some distance between her and the prince. She felt flushed as she hurried along the ledge.

"Are you running away, Miss Tanner?"

"No. I'm hungry." The courtyard stones were cool. "Do you have any ice cream? Or doughnuts? Doughnuts are at the top of the list. Could we raid your refrigerator?"

"Erica."

She didn't want to turn around, yet something in his voice compelled her to wait, to listen. Sajah was the one standing in light now. It reflected off the white of his shirt, the blackness of his hair, even the depth of his eyes as he moved toward her.

"When you left Betul's room a few minutes ago, you were running from sadness. I could see it in your eyes. Now you run from speaking of your sister. Are you feeling her loss more tonight?"

Her nod was enough.

"I apologize if my candor has upset you even more, but you should know the truth from the beginning." He paused, as if expecting she would remind him of the days she had spent needlessly mourning Betul's death. There was no reproach in her for his decision. Reason told her he was not the kind of man who would willfully hurt anyone. What he said next challenged her reason. "The truth is, my tolerance has worn thin. It will be best for all of us if Ellyn and Sambhal's work dies with them."

Erica was thankful to see the first signs of sunlight peek into her room. After a quick shower, she dressed in a choli and the sapphire blue sari. The matching mantle was left in its drawer.

As quietly as she could, she made her way downstairs to Betul's room. Somehow, this place seemed to demand quietness, soft steps and whispers. Perhaps it was the passing of centuries. Perhaps it was because of who lived within these walls: a prince, his crazy mother, and a legion of servants.

And Betul.

She still could not think of this as Betul's home. He had spoken of playing in the war room and drawing pictures in the library while Sajah worked. He had told her about falling asleep in Sajah's bed and waking up to tickle his uncle's ear. Such tales could only be born out of extended stays. Had Ellyn and Sambhal made that choice or had Sajah insisted on maintaining a vital role in the boy's life?

Perhaps a combination of both.

She was at Betul's room now, but his bed was empty. After her initial surprise came disappointment. Erica wanted—no, she needed—to spend the day with him. That need pulled her farther into the room, to where his tiny white shirt lay across the bed. Ellyn must have done this many times, smoothing wrinkled sleeves, crushing the shirt close in a one-sided hug.

Maternal love swelled so quickly, it flooded the sense of loss. For her, the spontaneous act of loving Betul would forever keep some part of Ellyn alive. It was like breathing, this desire to protect him, to give and give and give.

To hold on to him as tightly as Sajah was holding on.

Jealousy ripped through Erica like white heat, exposing a conflict that she had not wanted to admit before last night. Sajah Ajari was bound by his religion to tolerate her presence, but he would never let that interfere with his duty to Betul. Either Betul was raised Hindu or Sajah would fail. There was no room for grace in the Hindu life of obedience and sacrifice.

If it came down to it, Sajah would take the case to court. She had no means of fighting him except for what India's Hindu judges would consider an unreasonable fear of letting Betul be a little prince instead of a little boy, her little boy. They would not tolerate sentiment any more than Sajah.

A slight noise drew her attention to a door she hadn't noticed the night before. Erica went there, hoping it was a playroom and that all her worries about Betul having a normal childhood were for naught.

It was true that sunshine spilled in through the room's windows, but that was the only impression Erica formed before she caught sight of Betul at the far end. He was kneeling on a red cushion in front of a shrine.

Loralai was there, too, seated in a special chair, her white-robed lap filled with white flowers. Curling tendrils of smoke stung the delicate blossoms. A strange, rushing sound filled Erica's ears as Betul repeated the words Loralai chanted. Then Loralai handed him some flowers.

His hands—*his* hands placed the sacrifice before the gold shrine. More chanting. More incense. Betul bowing down before the idols. He couldn't do this! Erica took no more than a single step into the room before a hand was clamped over her mouth and a strong arm literally picked her up from behind.

She knew it was Sajah. Her anger mounted when he didn't set her down right away but carried her out to the hallway. All in an instant, Sajah let go of her and reached back to firmly close the door of Betul's room.

Erica swung around ready to lash out. "You beast!"

"Be quiet!"

"I will not be quiet." She winced as he grabbed her arm and pulled her down the hallway. "Let go, Sajah!" He did, but only after he had taken her to his library and closed the doors behind them. A sleepless night and the thoughts that had occupied her mind fed

Erica's anger. "You had no right to keep me from him."

"You have no right." Sajah towered over her. "Until the will should prove otherwise, by reason of his birth in this country I am his guardian."

"Well, I won't stand by and let you teach him to be Hindu!"

"He is already Hindu. Nothing you say or do will change what he is."

"No! He is not Hindu. He's going to know my God, not yours."

"Betul will worship the same gods his father worshiped and our father before him. He is Hindu, Erica."

"He is Ellyn's son, and Ellyn wanted him to be raised knowing the one true God. Sambhal wasn't a Hindu anymore, Sajah, or had you forgotten that? Your brother—"

"My brother was a fool! A fool to be blinded by a woman who was self-centered and manipulative."

"Ellyn wasn't like that. She cared about people. She loved your brother very much. How dare you try to cheapen their love."

"It was not love!" He flung the words at her. "They were like two teenagers who cared for no one but themselves and did exactly what they wanted. They met and were married within a week's time. No responsibilities. No second thoughts for this family. You cannot say that is love!" When he was finished, Sajah whirled around and strode to the windows.

In those brief moments of silence, it seemed to Erica as if the mood changed between them. Their anger had been swift, ugly, even hurtful. Their conviction was lethal. Erica had never fought for anything like she fought to make Sajah understand. "I think what makes you so angry is that Sambhal had the courage to do what you have never been able to do. He wasn't afraid to step out of this—fantasy world you Ajaris live in and discover that you've been wrong all this time."

"You don't know what you are saying."

His too quiet words warned her to be silent, but she didn't heed that warning. "Yes, Sajah. I do know. I know why you want Ellyn and Sambhal's work to die with them. Because you're afraid to admit that everything you've been taught your whole life is a lie. Sambhal wasn't afraid. He listened to Ellyn. Not just because she loved him, but because she showed him Christ provided a way out of the emptiness. Ellyn showed Sambhal how much Jesus loved him."

"Jesus!" Sajah ground out the word. "If your Jesus loved them so much, then why are they both dead?" He may as well have physically slapped her across the face. Every word he spoke, every step closer drove his point straight to her heart. "Why, Erica? Explain to me why your Savior allowed that airplane to crash into the mountain. Explain to me why your Savior allowed Sambhal and Ellyn to lay there for hours, broken, in pain, bleeding until the very life had drained out of their bodies."

Erica bit down on her lip until she tasted blood inside her mouth. Even when she closed her eyes, especially when she closed her eyes, she could see the things he was describing.

"They suffered because no one was there to help them. No one stopped their pain. It was a horrible death, Erica, a horrible end for the faith they put in your Christ. Remember that when you say your prayers at night."

She stared up at him, knowing he said it because he had watched her, heard her praying the night before. "You were still in the courtyard?"

"It is my palace."

Yes. Very much so. She walked past him toward the doors.

"Where are you going?"

"To my room...to pray."

❧ SEVEN ☙

SHE DIDN'T GO TO HER ROOM. At the first landing, she decided to search out the war room. If any space in this vast palace suited her mood at the moment, the war room with its weaponry and imposing atmosphere seemed a perfect match.

Finding it was not as difficult as she expected. She let her impression of those moments spent in Sajah's arms carry her there. Morning had not yet reached the glass dome; although that didn't account in total for the darkness she entered. It was a spiritually dark room, too.

Erica prayed her way around the table, trying not to let herself imagine what must have taken place there through the past two hundred years. Rather, she concentrated on collecting an impression of what God could do through her in this place. At one point, she looked up at the glass dome, expecting to see heavens made of brass.

Her prayers, however earnest, stopped somewhere up there.

Breaking through took several more trips around the table and a journey up to the balcony. It was truly the first time she had felt God's peace since the Sikh had taken her from Portland. To have that peace grow until it filled her was exactly what she needed. Even if God did not reveal how her problems would be resolved, this peace was an answer to the prayers she had just poured out to Him.

"Silly girl."

Erica rushed to the balcony railing and looked down. She had not heard Loralai enter the room, yet Sajah's mother stood at the great war table, still dressed in her white sari. It was entirely possible that she liked dressing as a ghost.

"What are you doing up there, dear? Do you not know that the entire household is searching for you?"

Oh no! Sajah was going to be furious. Somehow, Erica quelled the churning uneasiness by the time she was standing next to Loralai. "I didn't mean to make everyone worry."

"Of course you did. Come."

The talons were not as vicious today, perhaps because the older woman seemed out of sorts rather than in control. They were soon outside the war room and moving down the hallway. "Is something bothering you, Loralai?"

"Sajah left."

"Did he?"

"Do you think I lie?"

"No." Erica hastened to soothe her. "Of course I don't think you're lying. I was just surprised. He didn't mention that he was leaving. Where did he go?"

"Why, Betul is in the music room."

Trying to follow Loralai's conversation was like riding a roller coaster—too many ups and downs. "I meant Sajah. Is he gone for the rest of the day?"

"Bow!"

"What?"

Loralai snapped her to a halt beside a large idol residing in the hall. It was a goddess with many arms and many weapons, riding a tiger and—smiling. "Do you not know who this is, dear? Durga. The power of the supreme being. If you don't bow, you will make her angry."

"I doubt it. She's dead. A dead goddess has no feelings."

The talons tightened. Then, seconds later, Loralai let go and dropped to her knees before the idol of Durga. Her chant was more like soft wailing than actual words. Erica left her there.

By following the sound of Betul's laughter, she discovered the palace music room. Erica traveled another hallway on the second floor until she guessed she was almost directly below her white bedroom. A pair of arched doors opened into a delightfully sunny space.

Her first impression was that it would make a wonderful theater. The dais was raised only two steps off the floor, yet it occupied the wall with windows, a lovely frame for Amreli and Betul. Erica watched them unnoticed for a few moments.

Betul was the enraptured audience, fawning upon the steps, and Amreli was an acting troupe of one, performing all roles in what appeared to be a make-it-up-as-you-go comedy. The girl spoke Hindi, so Erica could not understand what was said. It was enough to see Betul's delight.

When he began clapping, Erica made her entrance. "Well, what have we here? May I join in the fun, too?"

"Erica!" Betul ran to her, full of excitement. "Where have you been? You missed breakfast. We ate in the courtyard. I want to sing, but Amreli cannot play the piano."

"I think I may know how to help you there." In fact, her fingers were itching to play the grand piano set to one side of the platform. Betul soon had her seated at the keyboard. "I don't know any of your Indian songs, but I will teach you some of my favorite songs, okay?"

Both children pressed right up to the shiny black surface, fascinated by the movement of her fingers. Erica smiled at them. They learned the first song in no time and begged for another. By then, a middle-aged servant came to stand in the doorway.

Erica invited her inside.

Every few minutes another servant came. Some sat on the chairs; some pretended to clean the room while they listened. An elderly man, his eyes dimmed by cataracts, chose to stand right next to Betul. The songs changed from upbeat to sentimental to the classical pieces she had memorized in college.

Even when her arms and fingers began to ache, Erica was reluctant to quit. She felt something special taking place that transcended the language barrier. Music did not need an interpreter. Amreli absorbed the notes as if they found an answer in her soul. During one song, the man set his wrinkled hand on Betul's shoulder. Betul liked that.

Erica had never thought of her music as a ministry, but it was that day. And that evening. And the next morning. In between exploring the palace grounds, playing with Betul, and getting to know the servants, Erica gave them her music. If she had listened to Loralai, the music would have stopped because "ghosts loved to hear the piano and would congregate every single time Erica sat down to play. It was dangerous to let the ghosts congregate. There would be trouble."

So be it. Erica merely shrugged her shoulders and reminded Loralai that the ghosts were as dead as the gods and goddesses. What did it matter if she offended them?

Apparently it mattered to Loralai. By the second afternoon, Sajah's mother took up a constant vigil in front of Durga, refusing food or drink, turning the air blue with incense.

She was still kneeling there after dinner when Erica took Betul for a long walk through the palace gardens. She was there when Erica returned to her room and the luxury of a bubble bath. Though determined to put the woman's odd practices out of her mind, Erica found herself praying for Loralai.

That is, until she heard Amreli shouting from the bedroom. "Miss Erica!"

"In here."

"Hurry, Miss Erica. Hurry, hurry!" One of the white towels was snatched off its rack. Amreli probably would have pulled her out of the tub, too, if given half a chance. "Please to hurry! Shrimatee Loralai birthday. You hurry or miss party."

Loralai, for one, would not miss her, though Betul would be disappointed. And if Betul was disappointed that would make the Rajah angry. "Has Sajah come home for his mother's birthday?"

"Of course. Hurry, Miss Erica."

"Where is the party?"

"Shrimatee Loralai sit room."

"Sitting room," Erica automatically corrected. "Give me a few minutes to get dressed, okay?"

"Okay," Amreli mimicked, with a very adult aptitude for Erica's nervous tone. "You wear prettiest sari *and* prettiest smile."

It was twenty minutes before Erica entered the drama unfolding in Loralai's rose-colored sitting room. Other than Sajah, who appeared quite tired after his two days away from the palace, no one noticed her arrival. Sajah wore the dark suit again, the cut of his jacket underscoring the use of expensive fabric. He stared at her so intently, Erica wanted to stare back and understand why.

She chose to look away. All of the servants had gathered to wish their demented mistress a "Happy Birthday." Dressed in a black satin sari, Loralai resided in one of the high-backed chairs, accepting the servants' gifts. Her response to each was the same polite set of words, handled like brittle glass.

Any moment, the glass was going to break. At least that's what it felt like to Erica. She was perplexed how the obviously poor servants could give such beautiful and expensive gifts. More to the point, how could Sajah stand there, letting his mother accept such a sacrifice as if it were owed to her?

Betul suddenly, impatiently inserted himself into the scene. "Here, Grandmama." He dumped the gifts from himself and Sajah onto Loralai's lap.

She scowled at him. Erica held her breath. Then the crazy old woman started laughing, a sound like brittle glass breaking. "Open them, open them," she said. "Just like your father, aren't you? Very well." The servants were dismissed with a cool nod.

As they were leaving, Betul caught sight of Erica and ran to her, quickly forgetting all else. "Erica, where have you been? I waited for you."

Unquestionably, Loralai could have gone on waiting. Erica saw how the woman deliberately brushed Betul's gifts onto the floor. Though he would have taken the hand Erica held out, Betul now rushed back to repile the gifts onto his grandmother's lap.

"Namastey, my dear." Loralai's sugar-sweet greeting was accompanied by an acidic stare.

Perhaps after tonight Sajah would agree his mother was quite insane. Erica didn't look at him again. She did, however, try to checkmate Loralai's little game. The lady wasn't prepared to receive a kiss on her withered cheek. "Good evening, Shrimatee. Some day, you will have to teach me how to sing 'Happy Birthday' in Hindi."

Loralai hesitated, scowled, and waved Erica to a place on one of the stiff rose sofas, a lesser place reserved for troublesome guests. "Betul, you will sit there." The ottoman, for the beloved grandson. Sajah was left to do exactly as he pleased. After what Loralai had said about Pali, Erica got the feeling Sajah was always left to do exactly as he pleased. He was the Rajah.

Wrapping paper flew off the first gift. "A book?" Loralai thrust it out at arm's length, almost hitting Betul in the face. "You know my eyes are bad."

"Sajah will read it to you, Grandmama. Here, let me hold it while you open the others."

"Open them, open them." She laughed, a softhearted grand-mother's laugh that sent Erica's gaze straight to Sajah. It was unavoidable that she wanted to know what he was thinking. No specific emotion seemed to enter his dark eyes, yet she sensed he was on guard tonight, even wary. Not because of his mother. No, Erica knew it was a direct response to the argument that had taken place between them the last time they had seen one another.

"Bangles!" Loralai's exclamation caused Erica to start nervously. "Oh, pretty bangles!"

Betul helped her retrieve them from the tissue paper, dropping the sleek metal rings several times in the process. "Ohh, look at this one! They are pretty, aren't they Grandmama?"

"Too pretty for an old woman. Come, dear." Loralai beckoned for Erica to leave the guest seat and kneel at her feet. "Come, come."

"I cannot take them, Mrs. Ajari."

"Shrimatee, remember?" Loralai's hands felt cold when she caught Erica's arm and forced the gold bangle onto her wrist. "There. And this one." The process was repeated.

"And this one, too, Grandmama." Betul had found a silver bracelet among the servants' gifts. "Give her this one, too. Erica does not have pretty bangles."

"Yes, yes… Find the necklaces, too, Betul."

"Mother." Sajah stepped forward, but his mother was already fitting a chain over Erica's blond curls. "I do not think this is neces-sary."

"The long strand next, Betul. We shall adorn her in bangles until she falls into the piano, they weigh so much!"

Betul giggled. "Oh, Grandmama, you are silly."

No, she was insane. Erica pushed herself from the woman, and though she wanted to snatch Betul to a safe distance, India was not big enough to get away from Loralai Ajari. "Open the last package, Loralai. I helped pick it out, you know."

Paper was torn off. Then there was a long silence. For a moment, Erica feared the shawl was all wrong, a mistake. It surprised her then to see a tragic little smile on the woman's face as she sought out her son. "Sajah."

Say the right thing, Erica urged him silently.

As if she had spoken the thought out loud, he glanced at her before going to stand behind Betul, hands on his nephew's shoulders. "You had one like it years ago. I remember Father and I picked it out together."

"Really?" Betul's eyes were wide. He tipped his head back to see Sajah. "You didn't tell us that in Jaipur."

"Because we had almost lost Erica and it was not the time for storytelling.... Speaking of time, it is now past the time for all little men to be in bed. Erica will take you tonight."

Whatever had possessed Sajah to allow Erica the coveted time alone with Betul, he certainly couldn't have imagined God would use it to bring about a change in her spirit. She knew that her anger had been wrong. Arguing with Sajah in the library, saying those things about his family—that had been wrong, too. Nothing could be accomplished if she let bitterness rise up.

"A soft answer turneth away wrath." A soft answer might turn away Sajah's wrath. It might even alter Loralai's strange mood swings. At any rate, she vowed to rely on God before she opened her mouth rather than calling on Him to right the damage after the fact.

"I do like parties," Betul said sleepily as he snuggled beneath the blankets.

"I know you do." Erica smiled down at him. He looked so tiny lying there. "Your mother liked birthday parties, too. She especially liked when it was her own birthday."

"She was very pretty, wasn't she, Erica?"

"Yes, she was."

"Will I remember her always and forever?"

"I think you will, Betul." Her voice wavered with emotion, but she held steadily to his hands. "I think you'll remember what she looked like and how her voice sounded and the way she held you in her arms. And deep down inside, you'll always, always remember how much she loved you."

"Father too?"

"Yes. Your father loved you, too. We all love you." Her good night included a prayer for God's blessings. Betul seemed to like that, which told Erica it was something Ellyn and Sambhal had done. She left a light burning near the doorway, just as she had the night before. Even if he didn't need it, the action made her feel better.

She had nearly reached the curving staircase when she heard Sajah call her from the doorway of Loralai's sitting room.

"Mother has asked that you join us again."

No. I really don't want to. Erica struggled against the thought, knowing it was terribly unfair, knowing if she really trusted God, she could endure a few more minutes of the woman's company. Not only endure, but also show genuine kindness.

Sajah watched Erica retrace the steps she had just taken. She seemed different tonight. Not ruled by emotion, but by the same inner strength he had witnessed in Jaipur. He wasn't sure he liked the changes that had taken place during his absence. Indian women were much easier to understand.

They walked into the sitting room together. Erica chose to sit on the ottoman, for which his mother showed instant consternation. An uncomfortable feeling began to settle around Sajah's thoughts. He knew his mother's moods. The great Shrimatee was up to more mischief.

"Betul is asleep then?" his mother asked.

"Almost."

The softness of Erica's answer sent Sajah to the windows where he stared out at the darkening world. The entire two days had been spent trying to forget their argument. Now he realized he had wasted his time. The words they had said to one another could not be extracted. By its very nature, the circumstances that threw them together were explosive. The threat increased when his mother spoke again.

"Do you wish to go home, my dear?"

Sajah swung around. "Mother, I've told you Erica cannot leave until we are assured all threats are erased."

"That is nonsense." Loralai dismissed his admonition with a wave of her hand. "Well, Miss Tanner? Do you want to go home?"

Erica was dumbfounded. "I would like to speak with Sajah about it."

"Arrangements have been made for you to leave here tomorrow at noon. You may take that onerous piano with you."

"Mother."

"A car will take you to Jaipur. You may choose to fly out from the airport there or you may travel on to New Delhi. If you travel by car to New Delhi, I will ask the driver to let you see the Taj Mahal in Agra. It is haunted, you know. By the most dreadful ghosts!"

Erica sat forward, clasping her hands until the knuckles were white. "What about Betul?"

"What about him?" Loralai inclined her head slightly.

"I won't leave here without Betul."

"But of course the little ghost will stay. After you sign the papers, Betul will no longer need to see you."

"What papers?" Erica twisted upright until she could see Sajah. "What papers?"

He remained stone-faced while his mother hurried on with her plans. "This is between you and me, Miss Tanner. I have heard from the goddess Durga. In exchange for Betul, you and the piano will be allowed to leave."

Although Erica became pale, somehow, incredibly, she was able to compose herself and give a firm response. "No, Loralai. I will never sign such a paper. Betul isn't a thing. He isn't a little ghost. He's a little boy and I won't sign him away. I can't."

"You fool!" Loralai shouted, half rising from her chair. "You tear him between what you want and what is best for him! Your sister did the same to Sambhal. I will not—allow you to disrupt Betul's life!" She fell backward, hands clutched to her chest. "He is Ajari! He—is not—yours!"

"Loralai." Erica tried to keep her from curling into a tight ball. "Sajah?"

He was already there. The lines around his mother's mouth were set in pain. She fumbled for his hand, silently pleading that he do something. "Your medicine, Mother." He worked a locket out from beneath Loralai's blouse and sprung the hinge. It contained two pills.

Erica took them. "Under your tongue, Loralai. Yes, that's right. And take slower breaths. Think about how happy Betul was tonight."

"I will call the doctor."

"No, Sajah. Let the medicine work. Her pulse is slowing already. She just needs to be kept quiet for a few minutes."

"And if it is another attack?"

Erica looked up at him. Their eyes locked. It was a moment when he needed to trust her, and he wasn't comfortable with that role.

"Sajah?" When Loralai reached out, Erica moved aside so he could kneel next to the chair. "So much—gone wrong—is killing me. Make it—go away. Make her—leave."

The medical crisis seemed to have passed; the emotional one was more intense than ever. Erica tried to take Loralai's pulse again, but the old woman pulled away.

"I will take her to lie down now." Sajah stood, then lifted his mother into his arms. "Wait here, Erica."

She would much rather have gone to her room, but after the incident with Loralai, it wouldn't do to upset Sajah further. Being alone in the rose-colored room drove her first to the windows, then to look at the expensive paintings gracing the walls. Really, she saw none of it. Her mind was on other things, more important things. Everything she had seen in Sajah's actions toward his mother belied what Loralai had said about Pali. Sajah loved his mother. He was devoted to her, respected her. Perhaps he had loved Pali, but he loved his mother more.

Minutes passed. She went to the windows again. It was black outside. She could see nothing except her own reflection in the glass. It didn't please her to think the silk sari fit perfectly with this room. No matter what she wore, she was still the same on the inside. Still the same Erica Tanner.

But that wasn't true, either. Being in this place had slowly peeled away the layers of paper finery she had added to her life. Erica went to the pile of paper wrappings by Loralai's chair and began stacking them together. A white ribbon trailed to the floor. No matter how carefully wrapped, the gift inside is what lasted; the gift inside was worth keeping, not the wrappings. Her gift was a connection to India.

Everyday she was remembering more of her childhood here. It wasn't just the sounds and the smells. She remembered waking up at night to find her father kneeling beside her bed and her mother kneeling beside Ellyn's. With the memory, God brought awareness of how Betul had been entrusted to her care. Sometimes, like now after Loralai's ultimatum, she was overwhelmed by the responsibility attached to loving Betul as her own son.

Sajah stood just inside the door, watching Erica without her knowledge. Very few of the Indian women he had known would look as quiet in the palace as Erica did just now. She seemed unaffected by her surroundings. Each graceful movement of her creamy white arms, each folding of that blue sapphire silk around her feminine curves drove desire through his veins.

When he saw her lift and caress the white ribbon, he forced that desire into the pit of his stomach. It was not right. His voice reflected every ounce of restraint. "There are servants to straighten the room, especially if you play your music for them."

She did not look up at him. Instead, she placed the paper atop a box and began folding the shawl, the bangles chiming with her movements. "How is she?"

"Better."

The shawl was laid over the back of Loralai's chair before Erica apologized. "Sajah, I'm sorry about tonight. I shouldn't have discussed the issue with Loralai, not after she was exhausted from worshiping all afternoon."

He moved to lean against the same chair, arms folded across his chest, body held in a falsely relaxed stance. His mother's words may have unsettled him and raised questions in his mind, but Erica's genuine regret chased those thoughts to the background. "Ellyn not only would have heatedly discussed the issue, she would have added a Scripture verse or two, then my mother would have banished her from ever stepping foot in the palace again and Sambhal would be forced to make amends. Your sister was dynamic. Very sure of herself."

"And I am—"

"You are not like her."

Erica looked down at her clasped hands. "Sometimes I wish I was like her. I wish I could know exactly what to do."

"You knew how to help my mother tonight when she was in pain."

"Because it's what I'm trained to do."

"And you are not *trained* in this thing called faith? You are not sure of what you believe?" Sajah pushed himself from the chair and moved closer. Perhaps too close. "Well? I asked you a question. I want an answer."

"And you always get what you want?"

He should have looked away from her lips, the delicate rose color of them. By the gods, she was a beautiful woman. The scent of jasmine blossoms. The way lamplight touched her blond curls. She was not prepared for the way he drew her into his arms and kissed her, deliberately at first, then with growing passion. He was not prepared for the way she felt next to him, small, perfect, captivating.

Sajah abruptly pushed her away.

Yes, he always got what he wanted, but sometimes he couldn't have what he wanted most. He left her standing in the middle of the room.

❧ Eight ❧

NOW THAT THEY WERE ACTUALLY STANDING inside the door of Sajah's library, Erica wondered if she should cancel Betul's plan. Midmorning sunshine graced the room yet it failed to reach the desk. Sajah, who had been concentrating on some papers, didn't appreciate their interruption. In fact, he sat back with a definite sigh.

It was then that Erica reached for the boy's hand, intent on leaving before they disturbed him any further. Sajah's tone held her there. "What do you want?"

"We were—"

"May we go riding, Sajah?" Betul asked hopefully. "Please?"

There wasn't an immediate answer. Sajah only switched his gaze to Erica's face. "Do you know how to ride?"

"Yes."

"Wait downstairs then." His gaze had already returned to the papers. "I will be done in twenty minutes."

Betul literally pulled Erica out the door. "I told you he would go."

So he had. But that didn't mean it would be a pleasant outing. Erica kept such doubts from showing on her face. "I need to change out of this skirt."

The boy thought a moment. "Would you fit my mother's clothes?"

Yes, but the idea of seeing Ellyn's things made her hold tightly to Betul's hand as he took her to a room very near his own. It contained the bare minimum of furniture and few personal touches. Erica watched Betul haltingly move to a dresser where he stood looking at a picture.

The man resembled Sajah, but she knew it had to be Sambhal. It was painful to witness how Betul traced a finger over the image, the gesture one of pure longing.

"Betul?" He looked up as she drew near to him. Erica knelt, bringing her eyes level with his. "Tell me what you liked best about your father."

"Everything."

Yes, it would be hard to decide at four years old what one thing made a father special. Erica reached for the picture, studying Sambhal, remembering how Sajah had called him a friend of his soul. "I think your father was very handsome. You look like him."

"I do?" Betul took the picture back. "He promised to teach me how to read."

"I can do that."

"He promised to show me how to climb a mountain."

"Oh." Erica shrugged her shoulders. "Maybe Sajah can show you. I don't do mountains."

"Maybe Sajah can show both of us?" There was a smile on Betul's face when he looked at his father again. Perhaps it was all right now to leave him alone with his thoughts.

Erica hurried to find something to wear. The closet held a few dresses, both modern and traditional. Contrary to Sajah's opinion, perhaps Ellyn had not always been in contention with the Shrimatee. Jeans. Erica pulled a pair off the hanger, then found a short-sleeved, white cotton blouse. The closet was spacious enough that she changed there. Although the clothes were a bit large for her, they would do fine for a day.

Betul must have thought so too because he smiled when he saw her.

"Do I pass inspection, sir?" She twirled around for him, stopping suddenly when she faced the door.

Sajah's tall form filled the doorway. The clothes he wore now, black riding pants and a white shirt, should have made him appear relaxed, at ease. Just the opposite was true. One look at his face and Erica knew he disapproved of finding them in Sambhal and Ellyn's room. "Are you ready to go?"

Without saying anything, Betul stretched high to replace the picture.

Rama's Shikari was saddled and waiting. So was another horse, a lively gray mare. Obviously, Sajah had told someone to prepare for their ride. As Betul was lifted high onto the black horse, he flashed Erica a smile that gave her the confidence to mount the gray mare. So far, so good, but the leather reins felt strange in her hands.

Sajah turned his horse toward the flat grassy field. Erica did the same. It was soon apparent that the gray mare had it in mind to keep up with Rama's Shikari. When Sajah began to gallop the black horse, Erica and the mare also increased their speed.

They traveled quite a distance from the palace, running beside the river. Nothing but fields surrounded them, beyond that was the desert. She could see no sign of Pushkar or the hangar where she had been kept prisoner.

Through no fault of her own, Erica began to relax a little. The sun felt pleasantly warm on her shoulders. And they really were having fun. From the corner of her eye, she saw Betul say something to Sajah. They laughed together. It was the first time in days Erica had seen Sajah happy.

He must be missing Sambhal, she thought, *as much as I am missing Ellyn.* They hadn't really talked about the grief part. Guilt pressed down on Erica to remember some of the things she had said to Sajah about his relationship with Sambhal. Besides that, she had basically thrust a load of impossible problems on his shoulders: finding the will, dealing with Pali's death, confronting the Sikh, tempering Loralai's frequent outbursts. *You have been such a selfish fool, Erica Tanner. Such a fool.*

Suddenly, Sajah reined his horse around to head back the way they had come. Erica tried to do the same, but the mare decided to exert her independence and kept going straight. It took all of Erica's strength simply to hold on. Of course, the mare mistook Erica's actions on the reins as a signal to go faster. The ground blurred beneath the horse's hooves. "Sajah!"

Rama's Shikari was whirled around, giving Sajah a full view of how the gray mare traveled at a full gallop. The way she was hanging on, it must have jarred every bone in Erica's body. Sajah swore fiercely and slapped his legs against Shikari. The horse responded instantly. Betul simply held on.

Desert sand flew up behind the mare. The animal had been bred for such conditions. But Rama's Shikari had been bred for speed in such conditions. Sajah's hands upon the reins demanded that the black horse fly over the loose sand. They were closer, but not close enough.

Again, Sajah kicked his heels.

Finally, he cut Rama's Shikari directly into the mare's path. His action was enough to startle the other horse to a standstill. Erica pitched forward in the saddle, clinging to the mare's neck as if her life depended on it, which it certainly did.

"What do you think you are doing?"

"You'd better ask the—horse that."

Betul giggled at her answer, but after glancing up at Sajah's face, quickly hid his smile behind a tiny hand. Sajah moved Rama's

Shikari forward one slow step at a time. "You are in control, Erica, not the horse."

"Right now that's highly questionable." Erica straightened herself somewhat. The way she bit down on her lower lip must have been painful, unless she did it to prevent any more perky, revealing comments. If so, such restraint came too late.

Sajah felt suspicion edge its way to the surface. "You have ridden before?"

"Once...when I was twelve years old for exactly ten minutes before I ended up sitting in a mud puddle."

Sajah turned his gaze to the sand dunes. There was a long silence. As long as it took him to constrain the disquiet her admission caused him. "You will stay next to us," he finally said. "Exactly beside us, all the way back to the stables. Agreed?" He saw her glance at Betul. They must have shared some secret communication because Sajah could feel the boy trying not to laugh. "Erica, agreed?"

"Agreed, Rajah."

"Did you enjoy the ride, Erica?" Betul asked while Sajah was lifting him down. He sounded concerned more so than curious.

"Yes, Betul." She laughed a little. Truthfully, she had never been happier than the moment her feet touched solid ground again. "I did rather enjoy my ride. How about you?"

He ambled up to slip a hand into hers. "It was great fun to chase you and the gray—" He lowered his voice then and added for her ears only—"though Sajah was angry."

It wouldn't do for Betul to sense how often lately she and Sajah seemed to be at odds with one another. Erica squeezed the boy's hand, vowing to protect him from ever finding out.

"Betul." Sajah gained his attention. "Amreli is waiting for you in the gardens. Why don't you go play for a while?"

"Okay, but may we ride again sometime soon?"

"Perhaps."

Apparently the answer was sufficient because Betul gave one more smile, then ran off toward the big palace, legs and arms pumping with energy to reach there as quickly as he could. Such a little man. Erica noticed he always concentrated hard, even at the normal childhood things like running and jumping. His premature birth must have forced him to work that much harder to keep up.

"Why did you lie?"

Erica swung around, unwilling to let Sajah's mood provoke her into another battle. "I didn't lie entirely. I agree that your experience outdistances mine, but I was determined to do something special for Betul. Going for this ride pleased him."

"You could have been injured. The gray is a spirited horse."

"I know." Her eyes met his with a challenge to keep the contention at bay. "Were you worried?"

"Not in the least." His dark eyes returned her challenge—strength for strength, subtlety for subtlety. "But the horse is a valuable animal."

"I'll try to remember that next time." Erica started to turn away. Sajah's hand closed around her arm, halting her forward movement. In the next moment, he was walking to where they had left the horses. No. He wouldn't! He wouldn't make her get back on the gray!

It was worse than that. They stopped in front of Rama's Shikari. "Get on," he commanded. She shook her head. "Get on, Erica." She looked anywhere but at the giant horse. Sajah used his strength to lift her into the saddle. When Shikari sidestepped a little, Erica was forced to hold on to the saddle horn or risk falling off. Sajah swung up behind her, his strong arms coming around her to hold the reins.

"Where are we going?"

"You will see."

As Rama's Shikari set off at a gallop, Erica was at once thankful and uncomfortable to feel the hard muscle of Sajah's chest pressing against her back. It was impossible to move away from him. The wind felt cool on her heated skin. "Sajah?"

"What?"

His voice rumbled a reaction in her stomach. She tried to concentrate. She had to concentrate. "Why did you leave the palace so suddenly?"

"It was not because of you."

The way he so easily guessed her concern made Erica feel strange. "Was it because of the will? You have never said if it was found or if there is anything I might do to help you."

"I have a friend taking care of the matter. It has been difficult because Sambhal traveled to many cities. He could have had the will drawn up in any one of those places, by any number of lawyers."

"You checked with your usual lawyers already?"

"Do you not think I want to find the will as much as you do? Besides—" he shifted her slightly—"finding the will does not solve the problem of your safety. I have been cautioned not to let you leave."

"So, you're stuck with me?"

"I would not put it that way. Betul needs you nearby. Cease that squirming, Erica. You are making the horse nervous."

"Sorry." She found it easier after relaxing against Sajah, easier physically. Emotionally it felt like a tug-of-war was taking place in her brain; one side telling her she was attracted to this enigmatic prince, the other side arguing he was Hindu, devoutly Hindu. She tilted her head back until she could see his face. "There were other letters delivered in Portland. One for myself and one for Grant. Do you think Pali gave us those, too?"

Sajah's brief glance was as disturbing as the way he slowed Rama's Shikari to a walk. "I would have to know what was in the letters." Erica told him exactly, down to the handwriting on the outside of the envelopes. It seemed like a long time before he responded. "I do not understand Pali's actions. If she had the will in hand, why would she need to take Betul out of India? He was more protected here with me."

They were nearing a village. Sajah commanded the horse to stop. Erica looked up at him again. "What if she thought the Sikh were going to try another attack?"

"How much did Ellyn write to you about the Sikh?"

"Nothing. I only knew about them because of her phone call right after the accident in Cawnpore, but I always sensed she was worried about them getting Betul. She told me over the phone that the Sikh wanted to hurt Sam's—Sambhal's family. That's why I believed Betul had been killed, because I've lived with the thought for so long."

"Please, Erica." Sajah's arm came around her waist, holding her still. At least that was his excuse. It felt like something more to her, like he wanted to convey regret for the pain he had caused her without saying it in so many words.

Erica stared toward the desert, feeling small in that space between Sajah and the vast emptiness. Rama's Shikari pranced restlessly beneath them, sensing as she did the tension in Sajah's body. "After they took Betul away from me that day, they said he would be sacrificed, so people would know that the Sikh had triumphed again. Maybe Betul would be safer away from India."

"Do you not feel he is safe with me? I would give my life for him, Erica."

"So would I." She had told the Sikh leader as much that day. He had laughed in her face. Then he had waved a hand and Pali was thrown down the stairs.

Images of that day in Portland were set aside as Sajah guided the horse into the village. When Erica let the concerns fade, a natural interest in her surroundings surfaced. As a child, she had visited numerous villages like this one, yet it seemed brand-new seen through adult eyes.

No matter whom they passed, young or old, there was a respectful bow to which Sajah inclined his head slightly in answer. In the center of the village, he stopped near a stone well, tying the horse to a post before he reached up to help Erica. His hands easily spanned her waist, forcing her to brace herself by placing her hands on his shoulders. "Welcome to my fantasy world, Erica."

Of course, he couldn't own the people, just the land they lived on, and the houses they slept in, and who knows how many of life's necessities. Erica followed Sajah as he began making his way down the dusty street. "If you own all of this land, how do the people earn a living?"

His eyebrows rose expressively. "They pay me rent on the land. Whatever is left from the crops is theirs to keep."

"What if the crops fail?" She had to take two steps to each of his. "Do you still make them pay the rent?" He purposefully chose not to answer, which only frustrated Erica all the more.

The whitewashed huts were built of mud and reinforced with straw. The roofs were slate tiles. There were no glass panes over the windows, only wooden shutters to be closed in the evening and against the cold. "Where do the children go to school?"

"One of the larger huts."

"Do they have books to use? Paper to write on?"

"Yes. The villagers have everything they need, Erica. Books. Tools. Food. Clothing. Temples. Animals for their sacrifices." He glanced at her briefly. "Do you think me a complete Hindu tyrant?"

"No, I'm sorry." Erica released a sigh but could not do the same with the guilt his honesty caused. "I just remember Ellyn describing some of the places she and Sambhal visited. I didn't mean to make it sound—judgmental."

Sajah's princely countenance was set toward his village. "It is the law of the dharma that I take care of these people. Beyond that, I find myself caring about their lives."

She realized that by the way the villagers were responding to his presence. Now that word of his arrival had spread, nearly every doorway was filled with inquisitive people. They bowed as he passed. "The dharma, that is the caste system?"

"Svadharma is the philosophy supporting the caste system. Each person is born to perform a certain job, marry a certain person, eat certain foods, and beget children who do likewise."

Oh. Then svadharma was the underlying constraint she felt, the reason why—even here in this relatively small village of two hundred souls—there appeared to be clear divisions. Some of the people wore nicer clothes. Some wore more expensive jewelry. Some held themselves with more pride. Only the children seemed unaffected by these social divisions.

When Erica moved to pick up a tiny girl, Sajah prevented her from doing so. "Not yet. I wish to show you something first."

He took her to one of the village temples, the largest. There was nothing unique about its tan stone nor the stairs leading into the darkened interior, yet Erica felt something twist up within her as soon as her feet touched the first wide step. Sajah noticed her falter and glanced down. "You are frightened?"

No. Yes. "No, I'm fine. Which god is worshiped here?"

"Rama. Are you ill, Erica?"

No...yes, she did feel strange, but Sajah wanted her to see inside his temple and she would continue. "Rama is the hero god?"

Sajah nodded with a finger to his lips. They must not speak now. The only voices were from a trio of red-swathed temple priests who were chanting as they made the midday sacrifice. *And I will lay the dead carcasses of the children of Israel before their idols.* When Sajah knelt among the handful of other worshipers, she did the same. When he leaned forward, touching his forehead upon the stone floor, she could only stare at the priests laying a food offering before the golden idol of Rama. The god held his bow proudly. He was smiling. A quiver of arrows rested against his back. His free hand was raised at chest level as if he wanted to tell her to be at peace.

Oh, Lord. This is so wrong. This place is so cold. Sweet Jesus, I want to run away, but this is too real. I cannot run from the reality of Sajah's world. She turned her stricken gaze to Sajah. His eyes were closed. He was absorbing the ritual as deeply as she was absorbing the emptiness. *Jesus, he is lost. He is lost.*

She had not spoken aloud, but Sajah suddenly looked at her. In the next instant, he was on his feet, pulling her up beside him. Once outside, the bright sunlight blinded her. "Breathe, Erica. I will get you some water."

Yes, water would be good. Cool water to dissolve the fire burning in her chest. Witnessing Sajah's strides toward the village well brought strength back to her limbs. She was able to smile for him when he brought the clay cup of water. "Thank you."

"We will return to the palace."

"No, please. I'd like to see the rest of the village before we leave." Just no more visiting the temples. She took a step toward some of the children, but Sajah blocked her way. Sunlight glinted off his dark hair and dusky skin.

He was still disturbed by her physical reaction to the temple. "Ellyn and I had several discussions about your childhood."

Erica tilted her head to one side, waiting.

"She said you would sometimes become ill when visiting the temples with your parents."

"Did I?"

"You have suppressed that memory?"

Her gaze retraced the few yards of sand and steps leading into Rama's domain. "The time I chased incense from the flowers, I think I got away from Ellyn to rescue them. But I can't—remember being ill."

Sajah's movement made Erica catch her breath. His head was lowered closer to hers, his voice husky with emotion. "I would not have taken you inside if I had known it would affect you this way."

The concern in his gaze both warmed her clammy skin and served to restore the connection she had felt in Jaipur when he talked about reading her letters. "It was strange for me, Sajah. Ellyn wrote so much about the good she was doing here, but all I could write in return were scattered memories, childish thoughts really. I felt so—inadequate, like I probably disappointed her."

"Or you were jealous of her being here."

Erica pulled back, heart pounding because she suddenly knew the source of her restless existence in Portland. She belonged here.

"Every letter I read contained an unwritten desire to be walking the streets of your memories, to be part of all this." Sajah's gesture included the village, even though his eyes did not leave her face. "You may have disappointed yourself, Erica, but you did not disappoint your sister."

"She told you that?"

"I did not read the letters until after Ellyn died. They made sense out of some things I had heard Ellyn say."

"What things?"

He studied her, then scanned the streets surrounding them. Erica knew without him saying anything that it wasn't appropriate for them to be carrying on such an intense conversation in the middle of the village. He was Rajah Ajari. She was the foreign woman. Simply showing up in her company would raise questions in their minds. Add to that these minutes of standing around, exchanging intimacies, and he would soon need to repair the damage done.

Erica blindly chose a direction and began walking. He must never be free from his duties. No wonder he resented the way Sambhal had been converted to Christianity and married Ellyn. In forsaking Hinduism, Sambhal had also forsaken the duties of his family position.

As Sajah fell into step beside her, she gave voice to the thought. "Have you ever wondered what it would be like to live in a different caste? Your family has always been higher than most people. Have you ever wanted to change that?"

"No. Why should I? The gods chose me to be born an Ajari." He nodded to an old man. "Is that not what your God does also? Choosing you to be who you are?"

"Actually, He chose me despite who I was, who I am." She sank her hands into the pockets of Ellyn's jeans.

"You do not feel worthy of being chosen?"

She shook her head. "Do you feel worthy?"

"No." He selected a narrow side street, leading between several huts.

Erica shivered at the lack of sunshine here. She could hardly wait to break into the light at the end of this path. Then when they did, she could hardly believe the changes.

They had entered a section of the village where there were no huts, only ramshackle shelters of sticks, pieces of cloth, and rope to hold it all together. The stench was gut wrenching. The faces of the people were unforgettable. Memories from many years ago flooded over Erica with such intensity she could barely whisper, *"The Harijan."*

Sajah stopped walking. "What did you say?"

Erica's frown deepened. "I'm not sure." Time flung her backward until she was six years old again. In her mind she could see her father taking her and Ellyn through a place much like this one. She could hear Joe Tanner saying, "The Harijan." Ever so slowly, she looked up into Sajah's eyes. "What does it mean? Who are they, Sajah?"

"The Untouchables...the Pariahs."

She shook her head; that wasn't right. "No, Sajah, the Harijan. What does it mean?" Her hand was gripping his arm. Her eyes filled with tears. Her voice was a broken whisper. "Please, Sajah. Tell me."

"The Harijan," he said in the same hushed tone. "Children of God."

Erica turned to look at them again. Yet it was not them she saw. She remembered being a little girl and Ellyn standing beside her, holding her hand so tightly it hurt. It was nighttime. The darkness was all around them except for the flames. Orange and yellow and white hot flames.

Two fires—orange and yellow and white hot... Ellyn was crying.

There was such an incredible measure of despair in Erica's expression. Sajah hadn't expected it to disturb her this way. Ellyn, too, had been touched by these people, but in a different way. Ellyn had seen them as a cause, another reason to express her humanity by helping them out of the hopeless world they lived in. With Erica it was much different. Somehow, she felt their pain, their loneliness...their despair.

He had meant for this day to teach her about his world. Perhaps it was he who learned more about the life inside of her. She did not object when he took her hand and led her to the well where the horse waited.

All the way back to the palace, Erica remained silent. Sajah could feel tension in her body. Even as he helped her off the horse and they walked back to the palace, she only looked straight ahead.

In the foyer, when she seemed to hesitate, he took her elbow, guiding her into his library. Something was very wrong. He watched her walk straight to the windows and stare outside. What was it that had closed her off from him to this extreme? Sajah moved up behind her. "Erica?"

She started a little as if she hadn't realized he was so close. "Where is she, Sajah? Where are Ellyn and Sambhal?" Sajah made her turn around. Her blue eyes were still shimmering with unshed tears. "Their—graves... Where are they buried?"

"They were not buried." When she closed her eyes against the thought, he tried to explain as gently as he could. "In Hinduism we do not bury someone who has died." She didn't seem to understand. There was a distance in her gaze that troubled him. "Erica?" Very tenderly, he brushed the hair from her cheek. Her tears rolled over his fingertips. "After the recovery efforts, Ellyn and Sambhal's bodies were cremated."

A sob seemed to choke her. Her pain was a tangible, living thing. Erica took a step closer and folded herself into his strength with a need that went deeper than losing Ellyn. Sajah felt her sobs increase until they tore through her slim body, like a dam breaking beneath unbelievable pressure.

Without question, without thinking beyond the moment, Sajah lifted Erica into his arms and carried her to the leather sofa where he sat down with her cradled against him.

Then he just held her.

❧ NINE ☙

THE FIRST TIME SOMEONE KNOCKED on the door, Sajah ignored it. When it happened again not a minute later and a male voice spoke Sajah's name, Erica chose for him by withdrawing from the circle of his arms. Embarrassment had set in anyway.

She did not watch him move across the room. Rather, she leaned into the leather sofa, feet curled beneath her, wondering how mere memories could have broken her. Perhaps it wasn't the memories themselves, but the way God used them to erase a barrier between herself and Sajah.

Whoever had come to see Sajah, he chose to step outside and talk with the man. Erica didn't mind. The low murmur of their voices weaving past the open door couldn't have canceled her thoughts. In the week since Sajah first brought her to his palace, she had existed mostly on her own strength with a prayer here and there for peace.

Today, even if he did not fully understand them, he had seen her childhood scars. She had never written about them to Ellyn. It had been easier to hide the pain and vulnerability, but they had not been hidden from God. He brought her to this emptiness. Only in becoming empty could she, in turn, become full of Him.

New tears came to her eyes to think God had chosen Sajah to witness that healing process. There was so much to tell Sajah now. It was an open door. Gradually, Sajah's voice seeped into her thoughts. When she heard her name mentioned, she could not help but become curious. Neither he nor his visitor was visible to her. And Sajah's tone sounded different, very much at ease.

"Is that so?" Sajah's pleasant laugh unfolded Erica from the sofa. "But agreement will suit her even less than servanthood."

"It suits anyone whose life is in danger. Give it to her."

Before she could get over the "life is in danger" part, Sajah had reentered the room—alone. He went straight to the desk. She wasn't two steps behind him. "Was that the friend who is helping you?"

"Yes, but I did not think you would care to meet him looking like you do." Sajah reached around her for a tissue from the box on his desk, then handed it to her. Not exactly a subtle hint. She probably did look dreadful, which made Sajah's gesture of smoothing a hand over her tumbled curls all the more tender.

Erica took more tissues when he handed them to her, dumping the used one into a wastebasket. "Thank you."

He tilted her chin until she was looking at him. "Your poor eyes are swollen. Perhaps you should rest for a while?"

"I'm not some delicate hothouse flower that wilts at the first opportunity. I'm stronger than I look, Sajah. And why doesn't servanthood suit me? I am not bound by your caste system."

"That is something Ellyn would say." Sajah straightened the collar of her white shirt, near the sensitive skin at the nape of her neck. "You take on her zeal at all the wrong times. I would rather hear from the little girl in you, even if she is so broken by visiting the Harijan that she cries in my arms."

Erica did not know what to say. The tissue came apart in her hands.

"I am late for an appointment. Will you be all right?"

Her nod was also a gesture of guilt for keeping him when he should have been somewhere else. "I'm sorry. You should have just left."

"Now you are being too strong. Here." He withdrew what looked like a small pager from his pocket and handed it to her. "A press of the button will summon help. Carry it with you."

"Do you have the counterpart?"

"Myself and enough other men to cover your wanderings around the palace, even your impromptu piano recitals.... Get some rest, Erica." He took a set of keys from his desk and left.

The palace felt imposing after Sajah's abrupt exit. A passing servant informed her that Betul was napping so Erica asked to be shown to Loralai's bedroom. Though the door was slightly ajar, Erica knocked politely and waited for an answer.

"Come in." Loralai's voice sounded strong enough. Erica found her sitting upright in a huge canopied bed, surrounded by so many shrines and idols there didn't seem to be a spare inch in the huge room. The aroma of flower sacrifices mingled with that of over-ripened fruit. Sweet incense to dead gods.

Erica steeled herself to walk across the floor. The book Loralai had been reading was set aside, a cool stare followed. Experience allowed Erica to know what signs to look for. Loralai's color had returned. The pain had left her face. She appeared well rested. And maybe she wasn't quite insane. That was still debatable. "I'm glad you're feeling better today, Shrimatee."

There was a slight flicker of the woman's hand but no invitation for Erica to sit down. Perhaps the tensions were still too high between them. Erica spoke kindly, not wanting to give in to those negative feelings again. "I have never seen some of these idols."

"Would you have in your safe American cocoon? They mean nothing to you anyway."

Wrong, they represented a growing uneasiness in her life. The more she was exposed to Hinduism, the more she had to pray

Romans 8:38—Nothing could separate her from the love of God in Christ Jesus, neither death nor life. Neither angels nor demons.

"You are a strange ghost," Loralai said, cutting into her thoughts. "You hover there in silence. Why do you not scream at me like the other ghosts?"

"I am not a ghost, Shrimatee. Besides, I would never scream at you. Your pain seems to be gone today."

Loralai looked away. "The pain of a broken heart never leaves."

She meant losing Sambhal. Erica decided to follow the subject, no matter how uncomfortable. "I'm sure you must miss your son a great deal, Loralai, but you still have Sajah."

"No one *has* Sajah." Loralai's voice held anger as well as sadness. "He would never permit it."

"But you are his mother."

"I merely gave birth to him. Pali was his mother." She suddenly looked back with an expression of discontent. "You know nothing of my sons. Sambhal was the older in birth only. He always preferred to follow Sajah's lead. My sons were very different from each other."

"Loralai—" Erica sat down on the edge of the bed, ignoring how her jeans and white blouse seemed inappropriate for such rich surroundings—"just because they were different doesn't mean Sajah loves you any less than Sambhal did."

Dark, tired eyes met her blue ones. "Not once have I heard Sajah say he loves me. Not once in all these years. His heart is so filled with other things there is no room for love."

"He loves Betul."

"Perhaps." The older woman plucked at the afghan covering her legs. "Every day, many times a day, I make a sacrifice to the gods that they will let Sajah love me. It has been thirty-four years."

Pity gripped Erica so tightly, she abandoned caution. "I'm sorry you are unhappy. I will pray about your relationship with Sajah."

"Pray to whom?" Her withered hand gestured toward the crowd

of idols. "You do not even know their names."

"I will pray to the King of kings and Lord of lords. The Redeemer. The Savior. The Healer."

"So many?"

"Jesus is all of those things, Loralai."

"Ah yes. Jesus. The One who died for me." Loralai's smile was cold enough to send a shiver up Erica's spine. Her laugh was equally unnerving. "Sambhal told the entire story, beginning to end. Then I went to sunset worship… There is a lovely ghost hovering near you, dear. I believe she wants to play. If you don't, she will start screaming at you."

"Are you trying to scare me, Loralai? It won't work." Not when she was determined to break through this woman's barriers. "You must get very lonely sometimes. I never see any of your friends come to visit."

"I have no *friends*. I have servants and minions and all manner of persons anxious to indulge my every wish."

"Of course." Erica could not help but smile. "Which is why you do not like me, because I would rather be your friend, if you will let me?" Loralai did not answer. It was doubtful she could have before they heard a commotion in the hallway.

Seconds later, Amreli rushed into the room. "Oh, please! You come. You come!"

Erica went to her at once. "What is it?"

"Amreli—brother. Oh, please to—to help him!"

"What has happened to him?"

"The sickness," Amreli wailed. "He be dying!"

"Amreli!" Erica spoke firmly. "You will stop that right now." The young girl nodded, but with no real strength. Erica pushed her toward the door again. "Go tell one of the stable boys to saddle the gray. Hurry! Loralai—" Erica swung around—"are there any medical supplies?"

The older woman's eyes were narrowed in disapproval.

"I *will* go, Loralai. With or without them." Erica was already on her way out the door. "Where are the supplies?"

"I don't need friends. I have little ghosts and big ghosts and all manner of gods."

Erica did not stay to hear the rest. One of the servants showed her where Sajah kept the medical supplies.

An eternity seemed to pass before she was kneeling on the floor by the makeshift bed of Amreli's two-year-old brother. The girl's fear had not been exaggerated. There was little response as she examined Arun. He whimpered but didn't open his eyes. His fever was very high. He was already dehydrated.

The first concern was to get liquids into him. There was a bottle of sterilized water in the medical kit. Erica found it and raised her eyes to Amreli's mother. "Bina, some sugar. Do you have sugar? Sweet? And a very clean bowl." Some of the English words must have been understood for Bina moved away. While she was gone, Erica lifted the little boy from his bed.

The hut could not have comprised more than two or three rooms. From what she saw, it was sparsely furnished. In the main room, there was a fireplace for cooking, a table and two chairs, nothing more. Erica sat down in one of the chairs, cradling Arun in her lap.

By the time Bina brought a bowl and several small cloth sacks, Amreli came running in, breathing hard from her frantic race across the fields. Other people followed. Just as they had done outside, when they saw her ride up on the gray mare, all of the women stood in a cluster. Only the youngest and most bold of the children dared come any closer. Erica noticed that a few of them didn't look well either, but she must help little Arun first.

Given her haste to find the sugar, the ties on Bina's sacks were not easily opened. Finally, she recognized a brown, sugary substance. "Amreli, put some—" Erica cupped her hand to show the girl how much—"put that much in the water."

It was done quickly.

Then, spoonful by spoonful, Erica poured the water down Arun's throat. He wasn't strong enough to resist. When it was almost gone, she asked Bina to bring more water and fresh cloths. They had to cool him.

Erica gently laid Arun on top of the low table. There was a bottle of rubbing alcohol in the canvas bag. He didn't like to feel the cool alcohol touch his skin. Though he whined pitifully, Erica couldn't stop. "Are there others who are ill, Amreli?" she asked quietly as she worked on the boy.

"Many sick."

Erica's heart contracted. How could many be sick, yet she had not noticed them that morning? Had she been so blind, so preoccupied? She looked over her shoulder at the women. "You must keep the other children away from those who are already ill. Keep them outside as much as possible. Make sure they are clean and the drinking and cooking water should be boiled. Influenza like this can spread rapidly unless you take adequate measures." They stared at her with frightened eyes.

It was too much at once. "Amreli, tell them in Hindi. Try to make them understand." She quickly wrapped Arun in one of the clean towels from her bag and handed him to Bina. "Give him more water. One spoonful at a time. As much as he can take without vomiting."

Bina nodded in a numb way.

Erica made herself turn from the confused mother toward the even more confused daughter. "Amreli, I need to help the others now. I need you to take me and speak Hindi. Will you do that?"

"I do that, yes."

———— ◦◦◦◦ ————

The next hour became a blur of faces and stuffy rooms, overwhelming smells and sunken, terrified eyes. Erica worked automatically, trying not to give in to her feelings of inadequacy. The sickness seemed to engulf at least one in every family she visited.

The very fact she had seen so many idle people earlier should have been a warning sign that they were ill. Had Sajah missed it, too? Had he been too preoccupied answering her questions, accommodating her strange temple illness to see the condition of his people?

Guilt told her the answer.

For some, she knew her help came too late. They wouldn't live through the day. Erica laid gentle hands upon these, praying that they might know Jesus as Redeemer, Savior, and Healer. Amreli faithfully repeated the prayer in Hindi, but there always seemed to be one more waiting, and they would have to leave.

A child came running up to them while they were going to yet another hut. Bina had asked for Erica. Amreli broke into tears. Erica grabbed both medical kits and ran all the way there, preparing herself for the worst.

Yet Bina smiled shyly when Erica rushed inside. Arun was better. His eyes were open and his pulse was strong. Erica took the little boy from her and hugged him close to ease the worst of her worry for the others. If God had spared him, maybe He would touch the others, too.

A noise at the doorway drew their attention. It wasn't Amreli but Sajah.

He seemed to fill the small room without actually stepping inside. "Put the boy down."

"He's better, Sajah." She sat on a chair, wishing her hands wouldn't shake as she removed Arun's simple tunic. "Amreli, there you are. Get some cool water for me, please. We need to bathe your brother."

When the girl tried to get past Sajah to bring the water bucket to the well, he refused to move. "I told you to put the boy down, Erica."

"I just need to show Bina how to bathe him. We need more supplies, Sajah. Could you make some phone calls, get a doctor here?"

The Hindi words he spoke were directed at Amreli. Erica watched the frightened girl lower her eyes before the Rajah, then come to take Arun. "Now," Sajah said. "We will go."

"Sajah, please."

"*Now,* Erica."

Erica pushed past Sajah and through the door without touching him. However, she had no intention of meekly following him back to the palace. "Where is the school?"

"Erica."

"Where is it? Unless you care to have the entire village hear what I have to say to you."

He looked nonplussed, as if no one had ever dared demand things from him in such a tone. That reaction only lasted a moment before the prince clamped his hand around her upper arm and took her to the school. On their way past the well, he gave orders for one of the men to return the gray to the palace stables. He did not talk again until he released Erica in the middle of the school's single, large room. "You were told never to leave the palace without me! No one gave you permission to come here!"

She faced him with a silent, inner reminder about her vow—no angry words. "I had to come. Arun and the others needed help."

He moved to within arm's reach of her. "I am not to be crossed, Erica."

"I understand that. But I did not believe even you, the Rajah, would sacrifice lives at the expense of your pride."

"You sound like Ellyn again."

"No, Sajah. I sound like me. The letters only showed you one side of who I am. I have convictions, too. My little girl faith is stronger, deeper. I have a gift in me that cares for people just as much as Ellyn did."

"Evangelizing them is different than loving them as they are, where they are. Loving them even if they never turn to embrace your message. Ellyn set out to evangelize them." Sajah opened his fist directly in her face. The panic button looked black and accusing. "You dropped this in Mother's room."

"I didn't realize."

"You didn't care."

"I wasn't thinking about myself, Sajah. Will you call in doctors?" She watched him move away from her, back held stiffly, his strides no release for the anger. "If you don't, I will."

"You are an insolent female!"

"And you are an egocentric prince!"

Sajah swung around.

"There are people dying out there." Her voice shook with emotion. "I can't help all of them by myself. Either make the call to bring in doctors and medicine or go back to your war room and start planning on how you can ward off the attack of shame I'll pray down on your royal head!"

The school door had never been rocked back on its hinges with quite as much anger as when Erica left him standing alone in that room. Sajah could see her as she made her way back to Amreli's hut. There was no pride in her steps, only tired determination.

His people watched her. She was not aware of it.

On the other hand, when he left the school and they watched him, he felt the full measure of their regard. He had left the car parked haphazardly at the village entrance. When he got closer, he saw that Bashtar was waiting there, arms crossed over his chest, a smile on his face.

"Are you in trouble again, Rajah Ajari?"

"Be quiet." Sajah threw his set of keys.

Bashtar caught them easily. "Let me guess, I am to go back to the war room and begin planning your salvation."

"Give me the phone." It was tossed at him in the same way he had tossed the keys. Sajah flipped it open. "You are to bring me the medical supplies we have on hand. Take whatever men you need."

"They will be relieved...to escape her wrath, I mean."

Sajah scowled and punched in numbers with more force than necessary. "Go, Bashtar. I have had enough of your humor. Arrange to have barrels of water brought over. I'm closing the well."

His call went through as Bashtar signaled two of the men.

Within five minutes, Erica's requests and his own additions were set in motion: doctors, medicine, blankets, nourishing food. The rest of the men who had followed Erica to the village were put to work covering the well and clearing an area for the funeral pyres. Hindu customs aside, they had to burn the bodies as soon as possible to prevent the sickness from spreading even further.

By the time Sajah delegated the most immediate jobs, Erica was gone from Amreli's hut. He found her with the Harijan. She was kneeling in the dirt beside a little girl, stroking the child's tangled hair. Loving the untouchable.

Amid the dull browns and grays of their world, Erica's white shirt and jeans set her apart. Yet her love wiped out all boundaries. Ever so gently, she set her arms beneath the child's wasted body and gathered her close. The stench did not matter. The filth, the contagion did not matter. For the last few breaths of that little girl's life, Erica loved her.

Sajah had never experienced the kind of spiritual strength he witnessed in Erica as she rose with the child still in her arms. When she turned and saw him, the compassion in her eyes burned away every vestige of nobility, leaving his heart exposed.

He walked up to her and took the little girl.

❧ TEN ❧

THEY LEFT THE VILLAGE SOON after the doctors arrived, but that had been two hours ago. Erica knew her body was operating in automatic mode: a scalding shower, disposing of her old clothes, finding new ones in Ellyn's closet—more jeans and another white shirt—forcing down a few bites of their evening meal, reading to Betul, tucking him in bed.

Outwardly, every action was automatic. Inwardly, her heart was centered on the expression she had seen in Sajah's eyes when he took the little girl from her arms. Yes, he had helped her afterward, sometimes working side by side with her, but part of him had become isolated. And she didn't know why.

This went deeper than calling his bluff over the doctors and medicine. This was something twined within his spirit that would have reached out to hers, if he had allowed it. Rajah Ajari had not allowed it.

Since returning to the palace, he had not spoken with her. They shared the same table, then shared putting Betul to bed all without really looking at each other. Erica now found herself alone in the music room, waiting for sunset to entice her melancholy into settling down, down past the horizon. Then she would be free to play a song more full of hope than restlessness.

Until then, her music was alternately frantic and deliberate, passionate and heavy. She would never have played like this for the servants. *So why now, Erica? Why give in?* She drew her hands into her lap and sat quietly as the thoughts chipped away at her excuses.

Ellyn would be telling her to "look up and look out." It was a favorite saying borrowed from Grant. And it was so true. She couldn't find what she needed by looking inside. God's mercies were new every morning, not stored up for future use. Brand new. He would lift her out of the miry clay, set her feet on the Rock, and put a new song in her heart.

A smile tugged at the corners of her mouth, even as she whispered, "Thank you, Jesus.... This one's for You." The sun was at half-mast now. Her spirit was somewhere above that and soaring higher by the moment. The song she played fairly took flight.

At first, she reasoned the goose-bump feeling to her uplifted spirit, but it became more intense, more distracting. Several notes crashed together. She twisted on the bench until she could see the open doors.

The doors were darker than facing full sunset and she couldn't distinguish if the shape was real. Then it—he moved, dissolving backward into more shadows. She held her breath, knowing it was not Sajah. Another movement, from a side door and another near a heavily curtained window had Erica pushing herself to her feet, fumbling to extract the panic button from the pocket of her jeans.

Her heart seemed to collapse when it fell from her hands and skidded across the floor. *Dear Lord in heaven.* Electronic beeps started sounding from seemingly every direction. The shadows, forms moved quickly. So did Erica.

"Sri Ajari! Here!"

He took the steps from the foyer to the landing two at a time. The servant did not wait. Sajah had to follow the old man down the length of one hallway before he saw him again, entering the music room.

The walls of his office had not been soundproof enough to hide the faint rise and fall of Erica's music. Then his pager had gone off. He wouldn't have needed the old man to tell him where Erica had been, but he certainly needed someone to tell him where she was now.

Sajah did not pass beyond the doorway.

"We did not mean to frighten her, Rajah."

"She plays so beautifully."

"We only wanted to listen, not to frighten."

"Forgive us, Rajah."

The handful of men and women would have continued apologizing if not for the severity of his expression. "This was by the piano." The old man gave him Erica's emergency trigger. "She ran through the main doors."

"Did Bashtar follow her?"

"Bashtar was not here, but the men guarding her—they followed."

"Which way?"

"I do not know, Sri Ajari. May we help find her?"

"No." It was complicated enough. He retraced his steps down the hallway, expecting to find at least one or two of the guards within sight. Instead, the wide halls were empty. Why? If it was all a mistake, they would be in front of him now, apologizing as profusely as the servants.

So it wasn't a mistake.

Sajah fought down a surge of adrenaline. He had to think. Where would she go? By the gods, she was probably scared out of her wits. No, Erica would never be that frightened. She thought on her feet, chose instantly, took chances. He paused beside the idol of Durga. The staircase leading up would take him to Erica's room. She wouldn't go there. It was too far from help. The staircase leading down would take him to Betul's room. She wouldn't go there either. Instinct would make her lead the danger away from Betul. Besides, he would have heard something if she had been chased past his office.

Sajah stared along the darkened passage leading to little used rooms, leading to the war room. That's where she had gone, or that's where she had been taken. Bashtar's latest warnings resounded in his mind as he ran. Stevens could not have gotten past the guards! He couldn't have!

She shrank into the narrow space. It was not big enough for her and the sword. Erica could almost hear Loralai laughing at her. *Silly girl. Silly girl to have chosen wrong.* The footsteps were closing in from both directions, the hallway and the balcony.

"Erica!"

Sajah. But the other man was closer. She tried to peer through the darkness.

"Erica!" Sajah was crossing the room with firm steps. "Answer me."

She couldn't. The other man was too close. Both of her hands gripped the leather hilt. Closer... No, farther. He was moving back up the stairs, not down them. She listened carefully, striving to keep Sajah's footsteps separate from those above her on the stairs.

Panic threatened when she realized Sajah had turned and was leaving. He thought she wasn't here. There was no chance to choose. She simply reacted. "Sajah...Sajah, wait." Scrambling out of her hiding place with the sword still in hand was awkward and noisy. The metal blade clanged upon tile. She scraped her back against the steps. "Sajah."

"Erica."

The tip of the sword speared a chair, twisting free of her hand when she rushed forward. It didn't matter anymore. Two more steps and Sajah was holding her firmly by the shoulders.

"Are you hurt?"

"No. There's someone in here. On the balcony—Sajah, what are you doing? He's on the balcony." Erica tried to pull her hand free and stop his mad rush for the hallway, but the prince was much stronger. "Sajah!"

"Be quiet. I won't tell you again."

They went directly to the stairs, past a gathering of troubled servants and down to Sajah's library.

Erica was pushed into one of the leather seats. She popped to her feet again before Sajah actually made it to the desk where he picked up the handset and punched in a telephone number. Then, and only then, did he face her. She felt lashed by his tight-lipped fury.

"Where are you?" he spoke into the phone. "No, that is not *acceptable*. He made it past the guards."

Erica couldn't look away from the panic button when he let it fall onto the desk. The little black case twirled a moment, then lay down to die. Not what Sajah and his friend had planned.

"I will not wait!... It is logical enough. If you cannot tell me whether this was an attack or Grant Stevens, I will make the decision. We leave within the half hour." He slammed the handset into place.

An action that caused Erica to become very still. "Grant and Bill are here? Sajah, tell me!"

"Bill Stevens has been in the hospital since the day Pali was killed."

The hospital? Erica's heart pounded frantically. She would have turned away to hide her confusion, but Sajah stepped forward to keep her from doing so. His dark eyes seemed to bore into hers, confining her words to a whisper. "Is Bill all right?"

"I do not know."

"Did Grant come alone?"

"Foolishly, yes. Come morning, when the guards can sweep the palace, he will realize his mistake. In the meantime, you and Betul and I are leaving."

"You can't do this. Please, just let me see Grant. Let me explain why I'm here."

"You are here because of me, and I do not owe Grant Stevens an explanation."

"He won't give up, you know."

"Neither will I."

As they rode through the black of night toward Sajah's personal airfield, Betul was the only one excited about the trip. Erica knew Sajah was still angry. Soon, the headlights were fastened on a corrugated steel building. Erica didn't mind when Sajah told her and Betul to wait in the car. She had no affection for the inside of the hangar, but she did watch Sajah until he disappeared through the open doors, beyond reach of the headlights. "Does Sajah know how to fly an airplane, Betul?"

"Oh yes. He flies many kinds of airplanes, even a helicopter." Betul knelt on the seat to get a better look out the window. "I see them. Those men are helping Sajah push the Cessna. Some day, Sajah will show me how to fly the Cessna."

He probably would. Erica found it difficult to swallow past the constriction in her throat. Sajah returned for them, pausing only to fling open the trunk and remove the bags packed for them by flustered servants. "Come. Quickly."

Obviously, Betul had ridden in the airplane before. He climbed up and into the backseat like an old pro while Erica remained outside. She still had not moved when Sajah came around to her side of the plane. "Get in."

"Sajah. I—I really can't."

"I wasn't giving you a choice." His words were less than patient. "Resistance will only make Betul nervous. He doesn't need to be reminded of how his parents died."

No. He didn't. But right now, it was all she could think about. Erica numbly climbed into the left front seat.

The preflight check was completed rapidly but carefully. Sajah's hands flew over the instrument panel. "See that Betul is fastened in, then buckle yourself. Do not forget the headphones. Betul's are in the pocket behind your seat."

She did everything as Sajah said, with a smile she hoped Betul would think was genuine. "Are you all right, little man?"

"Oh yes. This is most fun!"

Fun wasn't exactly the word she would have used. Her own seat belt and headphones felt awkward.

At Sajah's command, twin strings of landing lights lit up the length of runway. The Cessna was a small but powerful airplane. Its engines easily lifted them into the air. Erica managed to get rid of the pressure in her ears. Getting rid of her apprehension was not so easy. She gripped both arms of her seat and stared straight ahead.

"You may as well relax," Sajah said into his microphone. "It is a long flight."

"Where are we going?"

"To Darjeeling."

Something about the way he said it caused Erica to look at him. "Where is Darjeeling?"

"Near the border with Nepal."

They flew east, toward the place where tomorrow would appear, but not until a long, dark night passed. Betul slept in the back of the airplane. Erica would have liked to sleep herself but knew she couldn't. Lights from the instrument panel cast red shadows over Sajah's face. He was still angry. By now she was too tired and discouraged to care.

Sajah turned suddenly and caught her unguarded look. He didn't speak until he had flipped a switch to turn off Betul's headphones. "What is it?"

"Nothing," she lied, wishing the electronics would somehow change her answer to assertive rather than wimpy. Apparently it didn't work.

"You are upset that I have taken you away from your Grant."

"He is not my Grant. He's just a friend."

"Ellyn told me of your *special* relationship with him." The words revealed annoyance. "Any man who travels thousands of miles to find one woman, then bypasses armed guards is not just *a friend.*"

"If it bothers you that much, why didn't you let me go?"

"And leave you to the Sikh?"

"Perhaps they would be more reasonable than you."

Sajah's hands tightened on the controls.

There remained a strained silence between them for several minutes. During that time, Erica felt God prompting her to apologize. But she didn't want to. She didn't want to always be the one who did the bending, the one who backed down in order to bring a foundation of peace into their relationship. *The one who was empty of self, in order to be full of God.* She sighed at the thought.

When her gaze moved to Sajah again, the words tumbled out as if she couldn't say them fast enough. "I'm sorry, Sajah. I shouldn't have said that." His eyes remained fixed straight ahead. "Grant wouldn't try to take me away. Not like you think."

"Wouldn't he?" Sajah checked some instruments. "Your military trained him to be a fighter. Then as a New York policeman, he was decorated many times for heroic acts, for placing his life on the line. He is not the kind of man who leaves business unfinished. He will try."

"Did Ellyn tell you those things or did you have your friend check out Grant's background?"

"Does it matter?"

"No. Not really. Grant was in love with Ellyn, not me."

There was a quick glance. "I realize that. I also no longer wish to discuss Grant Stevens."

Erica stared out the window, at nothing. No lights below them, none above. It was like flying through a vacuum.

She had slipped into her private world again, a fact that registered somewhere near Sajah's growing wariness. Despite what she had said about Grant Stevens, he knew the man was more than a friend. Whatever past they shared wasn't enough of an excuse for Stevens's actions. No, there was something more going on.

Sajah felt the muscles along his jaw clench and unclench. His hands tightened on the controls. Never in his life had he experienced the proverbial green monster of jealousy. The intensity of his feelings gave rise to self-confession. Never in his life had he experienced the range of emotions Erica Tanner created. Physically, intellectually, spiritually—she challenged him at every turn. Tonight, he did not appreciate the challenge.

The controls shuddered beneath his hands. Seconds later, the entire plane rocked sharply to the right. He corrected the Cessna, but not before Erica's head hit the side window. "Tighten your belt. It is too loose."

She didn't move, didn't let go of the arms of her chair, didn't say a word.

"Erica?"

"Yes. I—I think so. I mean, I'm all right." She twisted in her seat to see Betul. Amazingly he was still asleep.

"Tighten your belt for me."

Her fingers seemed to fumble with the clasp. "What was it?"

"Turbulence."

"A storm?"

He would have been a fool not to guess her thoughts. Empathy drifted through the holes in his anger. "No, it is not a storm, just some strong winds. I have moved higher to get above the current."

"Are you sure?" She raised anxious eyes to his. "I'm sorry. Of course you're sure."

"Sambhal and Ellyn's crash was a combination of storm and tiredness and mountains. You are quite safe."

She nodded.

But did she really feel safe? Did she *ever* feel safe and at peace? Sajah adjusted their direction slightly, deciding at the same time that he was unwilling to let her slip back into preoccupied silence. "There is something Ellyn never told me about you, Erica. She revealed no reason for you to react as you did to the Harijan when you first saw them today."

There was a moment when she seemed to measure his sincerity. Like earlier that day in the library, she took a step toward him. This time not a literal step, but an emotional one, a defenseless one. "Ellyn wasn't born here."

"I know. Your parents decided to come to India when Ellyn was three years old."

"They didn't *decide* to come. God called them to missionary work here. They had a burden to help the people wherever, however, God led. I was born two years later in a small village somewhere near Calcutta. There was no hospital, not even a doctor, so Daddy had them put Calcutta on the birth certificate. I really don't know where I was born."

Ellyn had hinted at the story but never with the compelling mixture of wonder and pain Sajah heard from Erica now. What she had experienced today in his village undoubtedly added to those emotions. "Your family traveled from village to village?"

"In an ancient minibus. It was the only home I knew until I was five. I would sit beside my mother and listen to her teaching the children. She was very pretty. I remember her voice. I remember that she and my father loved one another very much." Erica seemed to hold that feeling close for a moment. "When I was five, we settled in one place. Bur-something."

"Burdwan," Sajah spoke quietly.

"Yes, Burdwan." Erica closed her eyes, as if trying to recall every long-ago detail. "We stayed there many months. In a hut. I don't remember much about the people there, but I know they were desperately poor. Daddy would take Ellyn and me for walks to meet his new friends. The Harijan, he said. Children of God."

And seeing the Harijan today had triggered something inside her. A glance at Erica revealed she had been deeply affected by that part of her childhood. No wonder she had gone back to help them. Sajah steeled himself to hear the rest.

"Daddy loved India. Everywhere we went, he told people about God. He was so—strong and he loved helping people. I wish I could have known him better." Erica shrugged her shoulder and turned slightly in her seat toward him, a poignant reminder of how it had felt to have her need him that morning. "My parents loved us, but..." Her words trailed into another shrug. "I don't know. They were always so busy. Ellyn and I spent hours alone. We became best friends when most sisters were still fighting over toys and dolls. We grew up without a lot of things. Especially without the time we needed from our parents. I kept thinking someday, *someday* it would be different."

There was a catch in her words that brought Sajah's eyes to her face.

"That someday never came. I remember many people getting sick. First Daddy went to help them. Then Mom. Ellyn and I were left with an old woman. I'm sure she was kind, but we were frightened. I was too young to understand, but I think Ellyn knew things weren't right. We couldn't go outside and no one came to see us." She laid her cheek upon one shoulder and worried her lower lip in a way that made Sajah want to touch it, to soothe what came next.

"They never returned to the hut, either of them. I—missed our family prayers, missed having Daddy cuddle me in his strong arms. I missed the way my mother brushed my hair." Her voice was hoarse with the little girl disbelief she must have felt. "We weren't a family anymore. They had both died, because of the sickness. Ellyn cried. She held on to my hand and cried and cried. She had always been so carefree and happy before, but that day she was very sad."

"Did you cry, Erica?'

She shook her head. "I couldn't. I never have." Her gaze met his. "Until today when I remembered about them and how the old woman made us watch until the fires were only—ashes. I couldn't cry, Sajah."

He slipped one hand off of the controls and reached for hers, wanting to take the grief from her, wanting to spare her the painful memories. "What happened then? Did you go back to Portland? Your parents were from there?"

"Yes, but it didn't seem like home. I had never lived there. Everything was so foreign to me, so different from India. I think Ellyn grew frustrated with me because I kept begging to come back here."

Her admission surprised him. "Why? Why did you want to come back?"

"This was home, Sajah. India was home."

He squeezed her hand. "Perhaps it still is."

❧ ELEVEN ☙

IT WAS STILL DARK WHEN THEY LANDED at the airport in . As Sajah guided the Cessna to a smooth landing, Erica saw that lines of strain had appeared at the corners of his eyes. Until that moment, she hadn't considered how difficult it must be for him to fly after Sambhal's death. Instinctively, a prayer was whispered in her heart that she would be more sensitive to Sajah's feelings.

Betul awakened long enough to climb out of his seat and into Erica's arms. The little boy whimpered against her neck that he wanted Sajah. But he was already gone, disappearing into a dull, colorless building. As Erica let her gaze wander over the unfamiliar scene, a cool breeze came rushing down from the mountains to make her shiver. She tightened her arms around Betul, not because he was cold, but because she felt a sudden need to hold him closer, to go on holding him no matter what.

The thought frightened her enough that she looked around for Sajah.

He was already returning. Even as he removed their luggage from the airplane, a car arrived to whisk them away. The ride was short. They were soon at a railway station. Apparently Sajah had called ahead to make arrangements because he completely bypassed the ticket office on their way to the long line of waiting cars.

Seven hours later, Erica found herself in mysterious Darjeeling, standing at the edge of another railroad platform, holding Betul's hand. She had agreed with him that it was tall. Indeed, the city rose right up the side of a mountain, three distinct levels. Now all she could see was the fierce, uniformed guard who insisted she show him her permit.

She would have gone on staring at his outstretched hand if Sajah hadn't appeared beside her. Apparently the officer knew him by sight because the suspicious look was replaced with one of respect.

"Miss Tanner is under my care."

"Yes, Sri Ajari. Yes. Good day."

Erica watched the officer walk off and stop the next people along the platform. There were other officers making the same secu-rity check.

"This way, Erica," Sajah said.

They went to a sports utility vehicle that stood ready and wait-ing. Erica copied Betul in settling onto the front seat, but her thoughts were elsewhere. Ever since they had left the palace, things had gone like clockwork—airplanes, cars, trains. It took a lot of connections to accomplish a trip so easily, connections that reached far beyond the palace and the village they had left behind.

Throngs of pedestrians magically parted ranks at first sight of Sajah's vehicle, allowing him to navigate through city streets to country roads. Erica glanced at Sajah over Betul's head. It was not logical that he took them away from the palace, but also to choose the place farthest from Grant's reach seemed deliberately cruel. The sudden flood of disappointment she felt was interrupted by Betul.

"You will like it here, Erica," he chattered. "There is so much to do, so many things I can show you."

"I'm sure it will be very nice." Because the tone in her voice alerted Sajah that something had upset her, he turned his head, long enough to note the tangle of questions in her eyes. She did not hide them from him. He already knew how vulnerable she was. However, she did not know how powerful he was and she needed to know. "What was the permit for?"

"To enter the region."

"Then—" She stopped herself from saying Grant's name. It would only confuse Betul. "Then anyone coming here needs special permission to do so?"

"Yes. It is for military purposes."

Military purposes? And he could just ignore military rules to suit his own objectives? Sajah looked at her. She looked away, suddenly afraid to see him for who he really was. Clearly, he was much more than the Rajah Ajari.

The countryside became heavily wooded as they left behind small villages and lush tea plantations. Mountains began to close in around them. The road became rougher, the going slower.

An hour after they had started out, Sajah turned onto another dirt road, then got out to unlock the gate blocking their way. Erica barely felt anything when Betul pointed to a two-story house far off in the distance at the base of a rich valley. "There it is, Erica! Sajah's house!" He practically bounced onto his knees in order to get a better look. "Sajah owns all of this land, too."

Indeed. Even to her untrained eye, it looked prosperous.

"You will like my friends."

"What friends?"

"The Pabnas. I have other friends who visit sometimes. Temnah likes it here and Bashtar." Betul reached out to open the door for Sajah, then sat back down, eager to resume their journey.

Up close, the house was pretty, still very large and elegant, though not quite as commanding as the palace in Rajasthan. Erica stepped out but kept one hand on the open door while she looked around.

Surrounding the white house was a narrow perimeter of lawn, beyond that were the tea fields: dark green and rugged in their sharp drops and steep plateaus. The only break in so much green was a network of dusty brown access paths, worn by many treks to and from the fields. At the top of a faraway rise, Erica spotted a gathering of huts, no doubt housing for the workers.

The sound of their vehicle brought several curious children running from one of the outbuildings. An energetic boy, about the same age as Betul, was in the lead. "Betul! Betul!"

"Namastey, Hopset! I came to play!" Erica watched the two boys meet in the middle of the driveway. The other children reached them, too. Some of them seemed more interested in Erica than anything else. They whispered behind their hands. One girl smiled. Erica smiled back. Then the whole group took off again, running like gazelles through the tea fields, except Betul. He did not run as smoothly and was soon at the tail end of their little game, struggling to keep up.

The more she was around Betul, the more she realized he was still small for his age and that his coordination should be more advanced than it was. While they were here, she needed to help him get plenty of exercise. Perhaps she could make a game out of it for all the children.

"Are you ready?" Sajah stood beside her, searching her face with his observant dark eyes.

"Yes." Erica let go of the door, aware of the conclusions he was drawing; that she was afraid to step into yet another facet of his life. To prove she wasn't, she grabbed one of the suitcases from his hand and marched up the steps to the verandah, stopping directly in front of the door.

"It isn't locked."

Of course not. She reached forward, but Sajah was already pushing the door inward. He let her enter first, then left the door open behind them. Erica was pleased to see that the plantation house was more comfortable than the rooms at the palace. The furnishings were still expensive and the artwork even more so, but it wasn't like an imperial museum.

She moved to a camel-colored sofa in order to set down the suitcase. Underfoot, the carpets were the same camel color. Actually, camel seemed to dominate the decor. Touches of royal blue and cream had been mixed in here and there. "Did your mother decorate this house?" Erica caught the flicker of a smile on Sajah's face when she asked the question.

"My mother has never been here," Sajah admitted. "She considers the *lifestyle* here too primitive and has always refused even the briefest visit. Besides, she believes this new house, like the old one, is haunted, which is not to be considered as further evidence that she is insane. Agreed?"

Erica inclined her head briefly, then moved around the spacious room, touching the trinkets that interested her. She was very aware that Sajah followed every movement, waiting for her to say something about the permit and bringing them here where it was impossible that Grant could reach them. But she said nothing. She needed time to pray first.

"Your sister decorated this house."

Erica looked over her shoulder at him, then turned completely. "But Betul said it is your house."

"It is. Sambhal and Ellyn preferred to spend their time here, so I let them."

He let them? Erica could not keep a frown from forming. Why did he say it like that? *He let them.* She didn't get a chance to ask.

They both turned when they heard the children's voices again. A plump, middle-aged woman came with them. She was smiling long before she reached the top of the steps and entered the house. "Sajah!"

"Namastey, Ahwa." Sajah allowed very few people to call him by his given name. Ahwa and her family were an exception. The Pabnas had been caretakers of the plantation longer than he could remember. Long enough for their servanthood to become secondary to their friendship.

Ahwa looked past him to Erica. "So, this is the beautiful *Apsara* the children are in awe over."

Sajah's eyebrows rose expressively. "Is that what they told you?"

"Indeed." Ahwa put both hands together over her belly. She was heavy with child and quite pleased by the fact. "What they say suits her."

The comment brought a chuckle from Sajah and, in turn, curiosity from Erica. "You'll have to tell me what Apsara means. I hope it's something good."

He shrugged a little. "That all depends. Apsara is a beautiful damsel for the goddesses. For my people it is a compliment to be considered like her." Soft color spread over her cheeks. She forced her eyes from his. Sajah smiled.

"Oh, see now, Sajah, you have embarrassed her." Ahwa scolded him, but in a teasing way. "My name is Ahwa Pabna, Miss Tanner. Welcome."

"Thank you, Ahwa," Erica spoke quietly. "If you will excuse me, I'd like to meet Betul's friends."

From the open doorway, Sajah watched her move down the steps and onto the grass. Betul ran up to take her hand. There was a warm smile for the other children.

"This one is different from her sister."

Sajah nodded in reply to Ahwa's comment, even though he heard grief constricting the words. He remembered phoning the plantation to tell the Pabnas about the crash. It had been difficult enough for Ahwa then, but now—to see Betul without his parents—

must be far worse. He closed himself to the thoughts. "The autumn harvest went well?"

"Yes, an early and abundant flush. Ved was pleased. The trucks came yesterday to transport the crop."

"And the workers—Ved made sure they received the bonus, the extra weeks of vacation?"

"Has Ved ever disappointed you?"

No. It was only strange to see so little activity at the plantation. Usually there were people working everywhere. Sajah wished he had kept some of the men here, though they were farmers and not bodyguards. "Have you prepared one of the spare rooms?"

"Of course. The blue bedroom is ready, and I have stocked the kitchen."

At the window, he lifted the edge of the drapery in order to see Erica and Betul better. "Thank you, Ahwa. When you go outside, ask Erica and Betul to wait for me in the yard. I will join them after I make a phone call. And tell Ved to come see me." The length of Ahwa's silence, the fact that she did not stir to do his bidding, spoke as clearly as the question that followed.

"What have you done now, Sajah?"

He glanced over his shoulder. "I will let you know if we need anything else. Agreed?"

Ahwa bowed and left the house.

As soon as he heard the door open, Betul jumped up from the bottom step, anxious to quit this waiting. If Erica had not said she was tired, the boy would have had her running a race between the porch and the driveway. Sajah descended the stairs, carrying a basket.

"What is in there? Show me, Sajah! Show me!" Though Betul tried to get a peek inside, Sajah held the basket high over his head. "What is it?"

"You must guess." Sajah held out his free hand to help Erica to her feet. She accepted, though it disturbed her to feel even that simple contact send awareness through her body. His smile could have been for Betul's excited dance or it could have been for her. She wasn't sure.

Betul made several jumps to see inside the basket. "Is it a puppy?"

"Would you like a puppy?"

"Oh yes! A black puppy! But you wouldn't put a puppy in the basket. It must be a picnic," he guessed hopefully. When Sajah nodded, Betul let out a little whoop of joy. "I knew it!"

"But we won't tell Erica where the special spot is, agreed?"

"Agreed," Betul promised. Then, in the next instant, he turned and ran off ahead of them.

Erica and Sajah followed at a slower pace, taking a path that led through the trees. In the places where it was narrow, Sajah politely let her go ahead. Otherwise he stayed beside her. They climbed steadily upward until glimpses of sheer-faced mountains began to appear with increasing regularity.

"Betul," Erica called ahead to the little boy. "Give me a hint about where we are going."

He laughed and ran even farther from them. "You shall see."

Realizing she would get no answers from Betul, Erica turned her eyes to Sajah. "You could give me a hint."

"And spoil the boy's fun?"

No, she supposed that wouldn't do. But she was getting tired. Erica continued to put one foot in front of the other. "Where did you get the picnic lunch?"

"Ahwa."

"She's very nice."

"Hmm." Sajah's agreement reflected that he didn't exactly find it necessary to carry on a conversation.

On the other hand, she couldn't seem to stop her spirit from conversing with God. The distraction of such urgent, wordless prayers drew her into His presence where she needed to be. He alone held peace for what was fast becoming a more complicated situation.

"Hurry! Hurry!" Betul had run back to see what was keeping them. "I can see it! Hurry, Erica!"

"We're—coming." The moment she faltered, Sajah set his hand on her elbow, holding her still so he could study her face. Erica found it impossible to look away.

"It is the altitude," he finally said. "Slow down a little. Betul can wait."

The way Sajah slipped his hand around hers canceled any arguments. Again, there was a stirring in her at his touch. *Lord, what's happening to me? Why am I so torn apart inside by this man? Just when I feel Your peace, Sajah does something and I am back to the doubting again. I do not want to lose Your foundation, Lord.* Though she cried out the silent prayer with all her heart, it failed to ease the tumbling, upside down feeling.

Soon afterward, they reached the top of the hill where Betul waited. Another beautiful valley was laid out before them, all vibrant and green. The sight of it simply took her breath away. Beyond the deep valley were more mountains; mountains that seemed to hold the secrets of time beneath their snowcapped peaks.

"Look, Erica. Over there." Betul drew her attention toward the northwest by pointing to a mountain far off in the hazy distance. "Do you see the giant one?" She nodded, enchanted by its blue-gray majesty. "It is the tallest in the whole world!"

When Erica looked at Sajah, he nodded. "Mount Everest. It is still many miles away, but nonetheless impressive."

Her gaze returned to the far-off mountain. Indeed, it was impressive and overwhelming to think she was actually seeing it in person. Betul went off to collect rocks, leaving Erica and Sajah to stand alone at the edge of the cliff.

The moment Erica let her gaze drop to the valley again, she felt dizzy. *Silly girl.* Loralai would not approve of her dizziness. She closed her eyes, holding on to a deep breath...until she needed to tell Sajah what she was thinking. "There is a psalm I learned as a child. About God being around us like the mountains. 'From this time forth and forevermore.'"

When she opened her eyes again, Sajah was standing close enough to reach out and caress her face with a gentle hand. "Does He know everything, your God?" It wasn't necessary to tell him so. The quietness of her spirit did that. "Does He know what is inside of you, Erica? The little girl who sang songs when her sister couldn't fall asleep at night. The child who could never seem to give away enough of herself. Does your God know those things?"

Yes. God knew.

Sajah lowered his head until his lips touched hers. She could feel beneath her hands how rapidly his heart was pounding in his chest. Hers was surely doing the same. This kiss was very different from the one that had happened the night of Loralai's birthday. So very different.

When at last Sajah drew away, Erica struggled to catch her breath, to feel normal again. The intensity of his gaze made that impossible.

"It is time to eat," he said. "Then we must go back."

Back to the real world. Back to being the Erica and Sajah who were thrown together because each of them loved a little boy named Betul.

Walking along the trail to the plantation house seemed to take forever. It had been a long day for all of them. Once they were inside,

Erica ushered Betul upstairs to settle him for a nap. Betul's room in this house was much different than the one at the palace. There were shelves of toys and books; large windows to let in lots of sunshine and fresh air; a warm cherry red rug on the floor; and pictures of his parents. Even a well-loved teddy bear. Somehow, it made Erica feel better to know he had this room for his very own.

Betul looked up at her as she sat on the bed next to him. "Did you like our adventure, Erica?"

"Yes, I did. Very much. I've never seen Mount Everest before."

"And do you like Sajah?"

She chewed on her lower lip for a moment before answering him. "I don't really know Sajah like you do."

Betul puckered his brow. "But I saw him kiss you."

It was impossible not to smile. "Little boys aren't supposed to be so nosy."

"Oh." He gave her a sheepish look. "Is Sajah nosy, too? Pali said I was just like Sajah."

Erica patted his cheek. "Perhaps he was nosy when he was a little man. Go to sleep now. Maybe I can read you some stories tonight. Would you like that?"

As she expected, he gave an excited nod. "Temnah reads stories when she comes here."

"Who is she? You've mentioned her twice today. Is she one of your friends, too?"

"She was Sajah's friend first, but he shares her with me."

Oh. One of those *kind of friends.* The emotions knifing through Erica were not pleasant. She found it difficult to focus on what Betul said next.

"But Temnah does not come all the time. Pali read to me mostly. Daddy and Mommy left us at the palace, and I got to see some of Sajah's picture books. He had one of a lion and a tiger chasing their tails. It was very silly. Have you read that book?"

"Betul." She laid a finger over his lips. "You will never sleep if you talk so much."

"Sing me a song, please. I will sleep better."

She did sing for him, softer and softer as his eyelids grew heavy and finally stayed closed. It was tempting to curl up on the bed next to him. Instead, she left quietly and dragged herself back downstairs.

Sajah had taken some papers from the briefcase he brought along and sat at the desk in the living room, working on them. He didn't even look up when she passed him on her way to the kitchen. She was thirsty after their walk. Thirsty and cold and confused.

The kitchen was a pleasant room, too, embracing an impression of mellow wood and clay jars and dried herbs. Some of it American, some Indian, and all very much like Ellyn. Erica pressed the loneliness aside to look for tea. Everything seemed to take longer, even heating water in a kettle on the huge gas stove. She found herself back in the living room. Well, not quite in the living room because she hovered in the doorway. "Sajah, I have to know why you did this."

Very slowly, he set down the pen in his hand and stared straight ahead at the wall. "Why I did what?"

"Brought us here. Grant might want to protect me, but it doesn't have to end in a confrontation between the two of you. Our problem is the Sikh extremists. Sit down and talk to Grant. Let him help you figure out what to do."

"He does not want to sit down and talk. The way he broke into the palace proved that."

"What if it wasn't him? Grant wouldn't have scared me like that. He wouldn't have gone sneaking around the war room."

"He would if he was cautious about who heard him speaking to you before he had you in a secure place."

Did the man have an answer for everything? Erica sagged

against the wood frame, arms crossed over herself to hold in a riot of emotions. "What makes you sure it wasn't the Sikh?"

"They are not so—subtle."

"Except if they wanted to show off a little by sneaking past the guards. The Great Rajah's defenses breached by a single Sikh. It would make for spectacular headlines."

When Sajah finally faced her, he hooked one strong arm over the back of the chair. "A single Sikh?"

"Only one man followed me." She tilted her head back. It didn't ease the ache throbbing with every word she said. "I thought there were more men in the music room because there was so much movement, so many shadows and shapes and alarms. But I'm sure there was only one man coming down from the war room balcony. If there had been more Sikh, wouldn't they have joined in the final attack?"

Sajah pushed his chair from the desk and stood, aligning square shoulders over lean hips. "How many alarms?"

"What?"

"In the music room. How many alarms did you hear after you pressed the emergency trigger."

"I didn't press anything. The button fell out of my hands. I wasn't about to go crawling around in the dark, trying to find it again." Especially when her life was in danger.

He repeated, "How many alarms?"

"It seemed like a hundred."

"In reality?"

She didn't know. The kettle on the stove began to whistle. "Five or six."

"From all directions?"

"Except the hall doors, which is why I ran that way. Do you want tea?"

He faced the desk instead of facing her and picked up a handful of papers. "No."

Fine. In the kitchen again, Erica turned off the flame and filled her lonely teapot with hot water. Just when she thought Sajah was softening a little, he threw up the do-not-disturb sign again. It wasn't fair. The thought of standing around while her tea brewed was agonizing. She took up position in the doorway. "Sajah?"

His entire body became rigid. "I am working."

"I'm not going to bring up the Sikh again. I want to use the phone to call home."

He dropped the papers and picked up another batch. "Home where?"

"Portland. Considering that it may take some time to find the will, I need to get in touch with the hospital and tell them I'm taking a leave of absence. They deserve to know I won't be back for a while."

"I do not recall discussing that you would go back at all."

Oh. Time to lean against the door frame again. "What does that mean?"

His explanation was tempered by a businesslike tone. "It means if the will states that you are to be Betul's parent, removing him from India would entirely destroy my relationship with him. If the will states that I am to be his parent, removing yourself from India would mean yet another loss in his life."

"So, neither of us can go back to the way things were before Ellyn and Sambhal died? I can't return to Portland and you can't shut me out of Betul's life."

He glanced at her long enough to measure her listless tone. "I believe it would be more accurate to say that if you *choose* to return to Portland, you will leave alone. I have some business calls to make."

End of discussion.

The tea was overbrewed now. Erica didn't attempt to try a second time. She did, however, take her cup onto the front porch where she sat down in one of the wicker chairs. The longer she stayed there, clinging to the warmth of the cup, the more she wished she had looked in one of the upstairs rooms for her sister's clothes, a jacket or sweater. Anything to dispel the awful chill.

Her eyes strayed over the unfamiliar scene.

Alone. She knew what alone felt like. It went deeper than being lonely. Work and church and people could fill up lonely. They couldn't change alone. Lonely was a choice. Alone was just there, sitting in the bottom of your soul, waiting for God to create contentment.

He had done that for her back in Portland and she had accepted it. This time, accepting contentment waged war with a desire to petition God for more—and that scared her. Nothing was impossible with God, but how much did she dare believe He would choose for her life?

She lifted the mug to her lips. The tea tasted bitter. Even so, she sipped at it, trying to ignore both the churning in her stomach and the churning in her heart. No matter what the will said, she wanted Betul to be hers and to be God's. Beyond that...it was all so tangled up in Sajah she couldn't think straight.

After another sip of tea, she leaned her head against the back of the chair. God forgive her for ever wanting the lukewarm existence in Portland over the unbelievably heated challenge of India. What would she be giving up anyway? She had so few roots in Portland, being transplanted in India would be relatively painless.

Relatively. There was Grant. She could picture his face very clearly. And Bill. Sajah had said Bill was in the hospital, which meant the Sikh had hurt him that day. Perhaps Sajah would allow her to call Portland. Surely even the great Rajah had some amount of compassion for a man who had been injured trying to protect Betul.

She tried to drink more tea, but the churning in her stomach sent out definite warnings now. When every part of her body screamed for sleep, she resisted. She needed to make some kind of plan so Betul didn't have to lose either herself or Sajah, but her thoughts felt all muddled.

It was no longer possible to ignore how her hands were shaking around the cup. She was sick like the people at the village. Very sick. Waves of cold rolled over her heated skin. Fever and nausea. Erica swallowed hard. It didn't work. She stumbled to her feet. The cup fell from her hands, crashing onto the porch. Somehow, she made it to the door. It was already opening from the inside.

She had to push past Sajah in order to reach the kitchen in time. Chills wracked her body as she clung to the sink, vomiting repeatedly. Sajah was there, helping her stand. She was too sick to send him away or to feel embarrassed.

When the worst was over, he handed her a towel, then a glass of water. Water. Raising her eyes to Sajah's face was painful. "I drank water—from the village. I forgot I—drank the water." She was dizzy, like at the cliff, but even worse.

Erica clung to Sajah's arm, then clung to the sink unable to stop vomiting. When it was finally over, he lifted her into his arms and brought her upstairs to a blue bedroom. She moaned as her aching body came in contact with the bed. "Sajah?"

"I'm here." He held one of her hands.

"Betul...t-take him away." She swallowed painfully. "Don't let him near me."

"He will be all right. I'll take care of him."

"No." Erica moved her head restlessly upon the pillow. "No, you—must stay away from me. It could spread through contact, too. Please."

"I will not leave you here alone, Erica." Sajah spoke firmly, but gently. "Now, be quiet and go to sleep."

"Please, Sajah." She struggled to keep her eyes open. "Please. I don't want you to get sick."

❧ TWELVE ❧

THE IMPOSING PALACE HAD BEEN SHOCK ENOUGH, but to actually find the *queen* in residence put Grant way beyond making polite conversation, especially when Loralai Ajari silently commanded that he sit down—on the far side of her rose-colored room. "No, thank you, Mrs. Ajari. I prefer to stand." And he didn't care if he stepped on her royal toes in the process. "Where is she?"

"She?" Innocence was pretended only long enough to bring Grant's frustration to the surface. "She is not here."

Keeping both hands clenched inside the pockets of his brown leather jacket helped him maintain control—but barely. He tried saying a quick prayer. "What do you mean, she's not here?"

"Exactly that, Mr. Stevens. Now if you will please excuse me, I have another appointment."

He doubted it. Grant switched directions on her and went to stand beside the room's tall windows. It was a cool, gray day—perfectly suited to his mood. He had driven straight through from New Delhi, over roads that defied description from someone accustomed to America's freeways.

After piecing together a profile of Sajah Ajari, Grant probably shouldn't be surprised to find Erica gone. Too much hope was a dangerous thing. "It would save us both a lot of time if you tell me where she is." No answer. The old lady was composed. He'd give her that much. Probably had ice running through her blue veins.

Grant faced her, arms crossed over his chest in the typical tough cop stance. "Let's try another subject then. Why didn't your son want to be investigated by the reporter from Washington?"

"I know nothing about a reporter."

"The one who turned up dead in London about the time Sajah had Erica and Joey carted back here?"

She remained impassive.

"Pali contacted the man first, to spill the news about Cawnpore. I'm guessing she wanted to force him to dig into the Sikh angle more than he did. It backfired on her somewhere along the line, like when the guy started getting snoopy about Sajah."

"A delightful story, young man, although it could use a few ghostly characters. Do you believe in ghosts?"

Grant gave Loralai Ajari a dose of her own medicine. He didn't answer. Rather, he studied a shelf of expensive trinkets and wondered what his father would do about now.

"We have ghosts in the palace. They visit me often, but I am not afraid of them."

"Speaking of Pali," Grant inserted, "I have a warrant with your son's name on it." Some of the color drained from the woman's already pasty cheeks. The warrant didn't exist, but—for now—it could be an effective trump card. Grant's eyebrows arched with interest. "Perhaps you would be willing to tell me about Sajah's involvement before I go to the authorities?"

"You have no right to threaten us."

"Wrong, Mrs. Ajari." He swung fully toward her. "I do have the right. An innocent woman is dead. Your son may not have been there, he may not have beaten her bloody then thrown her down those stairs, but he is responsible." Loralai would not look at him now. Clearly, she had never expected to be backed into a corner. "It was very interesting, the things I learned in New Delhi. What interests me most at the moment is the fact that your son has close ties with the

Sikh. How close, I have yet to uncover. But believe me, I will. Now, where are they?" Grant's question startled her. "Calcutta? Darjeeling?" She would not answer. "Do you have any idea how wrong this is? I would at least have expected some guilt for what you've done."

"Love is stronger than guilt, Mr. Stevens."

"Love?" He spoke with great control. "What you feel for Joey is a matter of pride, not love."

"How dare you speak to me like this!" Her eyes were flashing noble offense.

"How dare you and Sajah assume Sambhal wanted his son raised like this."

"You know nothing of Sambhal. He was destroyed by Ellyn Tanner. She made him give up everything! This home, his title, his standing among the Maharajahs. The same will not happen to Betul!"

"I take it you didn't like Ellyn?" When her very expression said it was an understatement, Grant launched himself even further into the old woman's enmity. "There's something I don't quite understand. Why has Sajah been so tolerant of the Sikh extremists who kept threatening Ellyn and Sambhal? A man like Sajah didn't have to spend five years playing this little game of tag. All he had to do was exercise some power and *poof*, they're gone."

"Perhaps you underestimate the Sikh, Mr. Stevens."

"Perhaps you underestimate your son, Shrimatee."

"Get out."

Grant inclined his head at an astute angle. "Of course. I will leave you to entertain your ghosts." Just before he left the room, he stopped and turned to look at her one more time. "By the way, tell Sajah to call off his henchmen. It won't work."

Grant made his way to Pushkar. The town was small by American standards, but that could work to his advantage. Someone was sure to know where Sajah had gone. He parked his rental car near the center of town.

People stared at him, then hurried about their business. The two men in the black car had stopped a few hundred feet away, where they were partially concealed by a string of vegetable stands. Grant had a good mind to walk right up to them.

They had been following him ever since Jaipur. Before that it had been a couple of men just like them with dark skin, long, scruffy-looking beards, and flowing robes. There was nothing the least bit discreet about them. They'd never make it on the streets of New York.

Pushkar's usual tourist spots were bypassed on his way to the marketplace. Within five minutes, he knew there was a system to the busyness. The old men especially liked to haggle over prices. Five more minutes and Grant knew which old man was the most ruthless dealer, and thereby the one most likely to crave *baksheesh*— money in exchange for the information he gave. The fact that he spoke English was another plus.

Grant slipped behind the old man's stall, whispered a prayer of apology to God for what he was about to do, and waited. A break in the conversation meant the man's customers were gone. It also meant Grant should make his move. He literally pulled the old man past a display of hanging rugs and into the nearest shadowed alley. "Don't say a word, understand? All I want is a little information." They went clear to the back where Grant pressed the man against a wooden door. His own heart was pounding, so he could imagine what the Indian felt. "I need to know where Sajah Ajari is."

"The Rajah?"

Too much respect, too much downright hero worship. Not a good sign. Grant pulled out his wallet, allowing the old man to see the money he carried. "Ajari left for somewhere. He took a woman and a little boy with him. Tell me what you know and I'll pay you for the information."

The man shook his head, especially after he happened to glance toward the mouth of the alley. Grant understood. The thugs were hanging around. Not much time. It didn't feel good to tower over the old man, to intimidate him by size alone, but Grant needed answers. He stuffed a few bills into the man's hand. "Where did Ajari go?"

"The plane. Day before this."

"And he was flying to…?"

"Darjeeling."

"How do I get there?" When the man drew back a little, Grant pulled out another bill. The bearded men were firmly in view now, pretending to examine rugs at the old man's stall. "Well?"

"No can go. Is—" He frowned. "Darjeeling is strict."

"Restricted?"

"Yes, restricted. You need papers go there."

"Can I get permission? How? Where?"

Both hands were held up against Grant's barrage of questions. "Take many days. You go bureau at New Delhi ask them. Take many, many days."

"I don't have many days."

"Sorry, man. Sorry." A worried look came over the man's face at Grant's displeasure.

"Can I fly back to New Delhi from here?" It would save him some time.

"No airport in Pushkar."

"Then how did Sajah do it?"

"Rajah own airplane, many airplane. He has buildings and landing place and—he has men who no like I answer question."

A pointed way of telling him that the risk demanded more baksheesh. Grant extracted several bills and held them at a tempting distance. "This is yours, as long as you promise to keep my friends out there busy until I slip away from town. Ten minutes. It won't be hard. Just pretend I hit you on the head or something. Act confused, like you need their help."

The old man's gaze moved from the money in Grant's hand to the money in his own hand. He did not hesitate to shove all of it back at Grant. "You keep. I no want business with any man think Sikh fools." With that, the man attempted to walk past him.

Grant grabbed him by the back of the collar. "What does that mean?"

Somehow the man managed to glance down the alley at the same time he grabbed the money back from Grant's hand. "Sikh one time enemy Hindu, long past. But they smart, they—shake hands powerful Maharajah, gain much. Yes?" Grant nodded to show he understood so far. He also hoped it wasn't going to be a long story. "Some kind of Sikh smart. Some kind of Sikh smart and fighting. American fool to think more smart, more fighting than those Sikh."

And one couldn't just ignore a warning like that.

Grant found an alternate route back to his car, all the while hoping he was two steps ahead of the bad Sikh. He jerked open the door with an impatient tug and climbed inside, automatically checking the rearview mirror to see if they were in sight.

Oddly, one of the men was now in the black car, just sitting there. Grant searched the street and spotted the other one walking out of an office.

As soon as they were both in the car, they took off, driving right past him. So much for all the subterfuge. He should have known Loralai would get Sajah to call off the men.

Grant released a tired sigh. At least now he wouldn't have to keep looking over his shoulder. That took care of one problem. Reaching Erica wasn't going to be as easy.

❧ Thirteen ❧

Erica forced her eyes open. Except for a bit of moonlight filtered through the windows, the room was dark and she was sick, very sick. She remembered pleading with Sajah that he should take Betul and leave. That's why she was alone.

With great effort, she pushed herself off the bed. Then she used the furniture as support in reaching the hallway. There was no light there either. A surge of nausea drove her into the bathroom next to Betul's room.

For several long, desolate minutes, Erica couldn't move off the bathroom floor. Would Sajah come back? If he did, would he get sick? Tears fell relentlessly. One thought chased another until everything was a blur.

Erica pulled herself upright and went along the hallway, stumbling as a new and deeper weakness overtook her body. A huge, yawning hole had opened up with Ellyn's death. No parents, no sister, no family—except Betul. She was alone. *Alone.*

In her fevered state, shadows twirled around the silence, growing, pressing down on her. She clung to the banister. Tears continued to eclipse her vision until she could hardly see. *God, don't leave me alone. Don't send me away from here.*

Erica stumbled into a low table, gasping as pain shot through her leg. The door. Maybe she could find Sajah, tell him she didn't want to be alone. Two more steps and she reached the sofa. Another few steps and she was at the door. So dizzy. She leaned her forehead against the wood for a moment. *Help me, Lord. Help me. I don't want to be alone.*

As soon as she opened the door, cool air stung her heated body. A shadow. No, a person came across the field, running toward her. Erica sank to her knees, whispering Sajah's name.

He reached her as quickly as he could, racing up the steps. "Erica." She didn't even have the strength to lift her head. Someplace inside of him ached to see her so completely helpless. He should have never left to talk with Ved. Sajah placed his hands on her face and made her look at him.

Her eyes refused to focus. "I didn't know—where you were. If you would—come back." The last words were drowned by a sob.

"Shh, it's all right now." As tenderly as he could, Sajah helped her to stand. It took forever to get across the living room, so he lifted her into his arms and carried her the rest of the way upstairs to the blue room. Once there, he laid her down, covered her trembling body with a quilt, and sat beside her.

She couldn't seem to open her eyes. "Betul?"

"He is fine. I took him to Ahwa. He will stay there for a few days until you are well again."

"Don't let...Ahwa come here."

"I know." They could not risk exposing the pregnant woman. Sajah had rejected the idea almost as soon as it formed. He would rather take care of her himself.

Pale moonlight deepened the evidence of sickness on Erica's face, the lines of pain, the dark circles beneath her eyes. When he stood, she sensed it and moaned restlessly. He leaned over her, supporting his weight with one arm while softly touching her face. "Tell me what to do for you, Erica. Tell me how to help you." She pressed her cheek against the comfort of his hand, causing him to draw in a deep breath.

"You want to stay with me?"

"Yes, Erica. I will stay."

"Tired."

Yes, too tired, too feverish, too selfless for her own good.

A soft light came on in the room. As if from far away, Erica heard Sajah asking her to take some pills. He helped her sit upright, then held a glass of water to her lips. Her stomach wanted to rid itself of the medicine, and though she fought the reflex, it required much of what little energy she possessed. Sajah laid her back down.

Suddenly the weight and warmth of the quilts were gone. Erica tried to draw them back, but Sajah pushed her hands away. "You are too warm already." He tried to be gentle when he made her sit up again, but every muscle ached. All she really wanted was to sleep, to drift away into the blessed oblivion of sleep. "Erica." She shivered. "I found a nightgown. You need to change...Erica." This time, his tone was not as gentle. "Change into the nightgown. I'll leave you alone for five minutes. No longer."

Those five minutes seemed like five hours. Somehow, she managed to do what he asked. The effort cost her dearly. By the time she had changed into the cool white poplin, she was too dizzy to stand anymore. Her last thought before lying down on the bed was that she had to turn her head on the pillow so Sajah wouldn't see her tears.

It didn't work. Sajah's fingers on her chin forced her to look at him. He placed a damp cloth on her forehead. The throbbing it caused gave her an excuse to let more tears slide from her eyes. "Does it hurt?" She nodded. Sajah took the cloth away but was quick to replace it with another. Despite her pitiful protests, he kept exchanging the cloths.

After almost an hour of constant pain, Erica began trembling uncontrollably and the ordeal ended. Sajah took the last cloth away, then covered her with a lighter quilt. "Do you feel any better now?"

"No," she whispered through clenched teeth. "No, I don't—feel better."

"So you will hate me for what I have done to you?"

Focusing on his face was difficult. Focusing on his mood was impossible. She sensed he meant more than the cold cloths, more than trying to relieve her fever. Yet all she could do was give the answer her spirit told her to give. Erica reached out to set her hand over his. "No, Sajah. No, I don't hate you."

Without saying anything, Sajah lifted both her and the quilt. Her head rested against his shoulder as he carried her to a chair and sat down with her still in his arms. She could hear the steady beating of his heart beneath her ear. Slowly she placed a hand over the spot where it beat the strongest. "Sajah?"

He drew her closer. "Yes, Erica."

"I'm afraid to be alone. Everyone is gone—my family. I don't want to be alone. I want to be in India. Please, I need to stay."

His hand rested upon her hair, his lips brushed her heated brow. "Of course you may stay."

"You won't send me away?"

"No, Erica. I won't send you away."

It was morning when Erica began to stir. The constant force of sunlight pressing upon the bed had awakened her. She turned toward the warmth and saw French doors opening onto a small balcony. Beyond the balcony was a view fitting for the Rajah—snowcapped, blue-purple mountains, rising edge upon supreme edge as far as the eye could see.

Although she wondered where Sajah might be, she calmed the

need to know by letting her gaze discover the blue room. The furnishings and bedding were sky blue to almost navy with a handful of shades in between and crisp white accents in the airy curtains and woodwork. It was a peaceful room. Is that why Sajah had chosen it for her?

Erica pushed herself upright against the pillows. She didn't have the strength to do any more than that. Though she guessed her temperature was down, her fever still wasn't completely gone. She remembered enduring the cool cloths and being held. She remembered feeling Sajah's heart beating beneath her hand.

Dear Lord, how can I let myself feel this way about him? How can I feel so close to him one moment and so wary of him the next? Because her life was spinning out of control. That's why she felt this way. A chill overtook her chaotic thoughts, so did a sudden need to be in Ellyn's bedroom.

The hallway was empty. She bypassed Betul's room. The door to Ellyn and Sambhal's bedroom was closed. Erica felt renewed grief to push it open and walk inside. Green—Ellyn's favorite color. And Ellyn's favorite perfume still lingered in the air.

Erica went to the dresser where the perfume bottle sat on a mirrored tray. She did not pick it up. Rather, her hands closed around the worn leather cover of her sister's Bible. Not Ellyn's everyday Bible, but the small little-girl Bible that had been a gift from their parents. Erica had one like it back in Portland.

Slowly, she opened the cover to read the handwriting inside...

To my darling Ellyn—
May God always be with you.
Love, Daddy

"Oh, Daddy." Erica touched his signature. An image of him, blond hair and laughing blue eyes, appeared in her mind. She remembered his tireless energy. Her mother had been dark haired like Ellyn with a warm voice and gentle arms. She remembered how God had always been with her parents.

There was a soft chair set directly in a patch of morning sunshine. Erica took the Bible there, folding her legs beneath her as she found the book of Ezekiel. The entire sixth chapter was underlined. She stared at the black marks a moment before reading the words Ellyn had written at the bottom of her letters.

And I will lay the dead carcasses of the children of Israel
before their idols; and I will scatter your bones round
about your altars. In all your dwelling places the cities shall
be laid waste, and the high places shall be desolate; that
your altars may be laid waste and made desolate, and
your idols may be broken and cease, and your images may
be cut down and your works may be abolished.

Perhaps she had been wrong to think these verses were Ellyn's way of warning her against the Sikh extremists. If Ellyn had marked the passage, it seemed unlikely she felt a growing sense of hopelessness. Maybe the words were a spiritual battle cry; a declaration to the enemy that Ellyn would not sink into the pluralistic, multiple paths to salvation philosophy of the Hindu religion.

Erica stood and carried the Bible back to Ellyn's dresser, praying for discernment about the verses. God was the only One who could show her now. The drawers opened silently, releasing more fading wisps of her sister's perfume. From a lower drawer, she pulled out a heavy red sweater and slipped her arms into the oversized sleeves.

"It is too large for you."

She swung her head to the doorway. Today Sajah wore jeans and a black sweater. He was clean shaven, his hair still damp. "Namastey," she whispered quietly.

"What are you doing in here?"

"I don't know." She hugged the edges of the sweater. "I just needed to be with her." Yet all she could think about was the way Sajah had of looking at her that made her run on pure emotion. Last night, even when gripped by fever, she had said things that forced her across a line. Today, she wanted to go back.

With fluid control, Sajah moved from the doorway to where she was standing and laid the back of his hand against her forehead. "Do you need a doctor?"

"No. I'm just tired."

"This is no time to be stubborn."

"I'm not being stubborn." She could not keep the strain from her tone. It rose up in waves that threatened to undermine her already shaky footing with Sajah Ajari. "I'm being practical. You chose the plantation because it's remote, isolated. There are no doctors here. We're a million miles from the real world."

"More to the point, you are centered in my world. I see you are filled with regret this morning." He picked up the Bible. "Because you have been reading this?"

Erica took it from him. "No. Because I wasn't careful about my words or my emotions."

"And that is what you regret, Miss Tanner? The idea that you have trusted me with your emotions even when you do not want to trust me."

"It's not about trust, Sajah." She watched him, but there was no relaxing of the defensive stance, no crumbling of the invisible wall. Erica tried to rub the pain throbbing behind her forehead. It did not go away. "Okay, you're right. It is about trust."

"Enough. You will return to bed and sleep."

The knot in her chest tightened painfully. "I don't want to sleep, Sajah. I want to talk. Here, in their bedroom. I want to talk about my sister, and I want to hear about Sambhal."

His eyes darkened. "No."

"Why not?"

"Because in your weakened state, you will end up crying over every little remembrance."

"I've told you, I'm not a child. Don't treat me like one." Erica took herself and the Bible to an armoire across the room, near the window. The first door flew open at her touch. She calmed herself in opening the second.

"What are you looking for?"

"The letters I wrote to Ellyn."

"I have them."

"Where?"

"If you promise to be good, I will show you."

"I promise to slug you in about two seconds if you keep talking to me like I'm younger than Betul!"

Sajah's unexpected laughter made the room feel warmer. It warmed her, too. Erica's tension ebbed into a feeble puddle at her feet. *Silly girl*. Loralai wouldn't have been wrong to call her a silly girl today. Choosing to smile was not as difficult as she expected after hearing Sajah laugh.

She was also tickled by the neat lineup of clothes in front of her. "Sambhal must have been a neatnik."

"A what?"

"A person who liked to be organized." She gestured toward the armoire. "Ellyn was terrible at keeping her stuff in order. It's about the only fault she had, so I used it against her a lot."

Sajah had moved across the room and stopped behind her, his hands on her shoulders. "Sambhal had many faults, the most frequent of which was confessing to me he had many faults. He was a humble man."

"Never a prince?"

"No, never a prince, but very near to a scholar. He loved learning."

"And you didn't?" Erica turned beneath his hands.

"Sambhal loved it and prospered. I endured it and prospered. We were very different. Come—" his hand slipped down to take hers—"the letters are in my prayer room."

As soon as he said the words *prayer room,* Sajah could feel Erica struggling with her conscience. He should have brought the letters to her, instead of bringing her to the letters. But there was enough stubbornness in him to follow through with his instincts.

They went to the end of the hall where he let go of Erica's hand to open a pair of heavily carved doors. Then he stepped back and let her enter first.

"It's like a moon!"

"Only a half-moon." He watched her gaze fly from a deep blue ceiling down to the dozen soft, moonlight white columns curving around the outer edge. Seamless glass joined the columns together. The expression on Erica's face joined Sajah's spirit to her spirit.

"I feel as if I could just stroll right through those columns and into heaven. It's incredible, Sajah. How did you do it?"

"Master craftsmen," he said as he followed her into the glass-encased room. "I told them what I wanted—*Chota Chand.* A little moon. They brought it to life. It is much different than your little girl memory of dark temples sticky with gold and blood red silk, hot with the devil's breath."

Erica turned around, the Bible clutched to herself much as a new warrior held his shield—too close, too desperately. "How often do you read the letters?"

"I have a photographic memory."

"You do not."

He smiled, one eyebrow cocked at a daring angle.

"You do?" She relaxed her hold on the Bible and came closer to him. "I shall test you. What year did Great Britain begin ruling India?"

"See, there you are getting yourself into trouble, Miss Tanner. If you mean what year did the British East India Company *cease* ruling, that was 1857. If you mean what year did His Majesty the king *take up* ruling, that was 1858 after the Indian Mutiny. Do you want more?"

"I have a harder question, for a man that is. When was Ellyn's birthday?"

"Too easy."

"When is my birthday?"

"Easier. But did you know you were born during *Raksha Bandham?*" Sajah waited for her smile to disappear. It did, but in its place was a look of curiosity that prompted him to continue. He could have done so without touching her. He chose to take her right hand, marveling at the silkiness of it against his fingers. She made it very difficult to concentrate on explanations.

"Of all the Hindu festivals, Raksha Bandham is the one most full of love: sisters for brothers, the shopkeeper for the Harijan, the prince for the princess. We tie a thread called a *rakhi* around the wrist." He traced her wrist with a fingertip. "Traditionally, it was done by maidens before the men they loved went into battle. Even though circumstances separated them, they were bound by that one fragile piece of thread. They say it is significant when a person is born during Raksha Bandham. The love within them, the passion is consuming."

Erica pulled her hand free and moved to the east wall of windows, where the morning sun was the warmest.

"Did I offend you?"

She shook her head.

Then he had stirred her as she continually stirred him. Sajah lowered himself to one of the large, tan cushions on the floor. Yet his gaze never left Erica. She was a quiet image set against sunlit mountains, the white nightgown beneath that old, red sweater. "Was there not a boy in Burdwan who gave you a special birthday gift when you turned six? He was Indian. Ragged hair that you wanted to brush out of his shy eyes. His hands were dirty, scarred by long days spent picking through the garbage heap for food.

"I believe you wrote that he was an orphan. He wore someone's castaway coat for warmth and a pair of cutoff trousers, no shoes. He ran up to you in the market and stared at you for the longest time. You were the first to reach out, the first to smile. That is when he showed you the blue thread."

"He couldn't speak."

"No, but you accepted his gift. When it was lost a few days later, you tried to find the boy again. Your father took you to the Harijan. You searched a long time, never meeting him again. Sometimes you still feel the weight of that thread around your wrist—light as a whisper, heavy as an iron band. Sometimes you still wonder what happened to him. You loved that boy, Erica."

She turned, resting against one of the smooth white pillars. "You do have a photographic memory, Rajah. I wrote that letter years ago."

"But they are all new to me." He opened an ornate wood chest and removed a thick bundle. The letters, her letters, were tied with a blue thread. Sajah watched Erica stumble forward to take them. In her stillness, he set his fingers around her wrist, gently pulling her down to the cushion. "No fainting. Agreed?" She nodded. "It seemed appropriate to bind the letters together with a symbol from one of your memories."

She smiled at him as she undid the blue thread. He wanted to hold her hands still, just to rein back the release of feelings he knew was coming. By the gods, if he needed the power of Rama it was now, to fight this falling in love with a woman who was untouchable. An American. A Christian. Untouchable...no, very touchable.

His touch upon her curling hair brought Erica's gaze to him. "Will you read them to me?"

"No." He settled her into the circle of his arm, then settled himself against the wood chest. "You will read them to me, so that I might hear your voice as I have heard your heart."

Erica was determined to make it downstairs by herself. She dressed in the white choli and blue skirt, alternately shivering and feeling too warm. Most of her reaction was the fever; although some could be due to spending hours in the prayer room when she should have been resting.

Not quite a full day had passed since she last made the journey downstairs. Instead of complete darkness, glowing sunset colors washed through the house. Beneath her bare feet, the floorboards felt cool. The smell of food being cooked reached her from the kitchen. She was thankful the thought of eating no longer repulsed her. Erica took a moment to lean against the post at the bottom of the stairs.

"And where are you off to?" Sajah spoke from the doorway of the kitchen, a towel thrown over one broad shoulder, still wearing the black sweater and jeans. Despite the distance between them, Erica was relieved to see amusement in his eyes. If he was smiling, then he must be in a better mood than the brooding contemplation that had overtaken him while she read through the letters.

She offered a smile, too, pushing herself from the support of the post as Sajah walked up to her. "I am off to climb Mount Everest, of course."

"Perhaps you should save that small feat for tomorrow's adventure?"

"Perhaps." She reached out a hand to him. It felt good to be anchored to something solid, though once he saw her seated, Sajah moved back to the kitchen. "Are you preparing dinner? I didn't realize you can cook."

"I cannot," he called from the other room. "Ahwa provided food."

"Are you sure Betul is all right?"

"He is busy playing with Hopset and the others."

"Will you go get him tonight?"

"No. Not until you are stronger." Sajah came from the kitchen carrying a tray. "Four-year-old boys take a lot of time and energy." Erica drew both legs beneath her to make room for Sajah at the other end of the sofa. "When you are feeling better I will let him come home."

"But I'm—" She stopped because Sajah gave her such a discerning look. "I'm sure tomorrow will be fine."

"For a nurse, you are not inclined to take proper care of yourself. I will see to it myself if I must. Agreed?"

"Agreed, Rajah." He responded to her teasing by handing her a plate of plain rice and pieces of cut-up fruit. "Thank you."

"Do you feel up to eating?"

"Actually, I'm starving." In their companionable silence, Erica studied Sajah from beneath her eyelashes. He had a scar near his right temple. Why hadn't she noticed it before? And there were highlights of brown in his black hair. "Do you like it better here in Darjeeling than at the palace?"

"Why do you ask?"

"I don't know." She wasn't sure really, just a feeling. "You seem more—relaxed here."

"Darjeeling is only a place like any other." Sajah took a drink from his glass of water, then chose to let the subject evaporate into thin air.

She tried another. "Tell me about your mother."

"Do you wish to start an argument?"

No. After a moment, though she had barely eaten a bite, Erica handed him her plate. The ease she had felt upon seeing him as she came downstairs no longer seemed part of the equation. It didn't feel like they were on equal ground anymore. He was the negative to her positive. The same as it had been just before he called a halt to reading the letters. And now he was staring at her, no doubt trying to read her thoughts. What he finally asked could not have been further from the real problem.

"Why did you never marry, Erica?"

Warmth flushed over her. "I nearly did once. But he turned out to be a different person than I thought he was. Why did you never marry?"

"I have never needed to marry." His carefully chosen words made her blush even more. "Does that startle you?"

She rubbed one cheek against her shoulder. "I suppose it shouldn't. You are old enough to make your own choices."

"Yet you disapprove."

She looked anywhere but at him until he physically turned her toward himself, with enough insistence that Erica's heart pounded erratically in her chest. This was the princely side of him, the person who always got his way, who made people listen. She was definitely listening.

His dark gaze locked with hers. "From now on, you are not to back down from what you wish to say. It is happening more and more. Soon, every time you open your mouth you will worry about offending me."

"That's not why I back down."

He tilted his head at that disbelieving angle and waited.

"I made a vow."

"To be passive at all the wrong moments?"

"I made a vow," she continued, "not to speak in anger. When we argued that morning in the palace library, I said things I shouldn't have said. I don't want to do that again."

He relaxed against the cushions. "As I stated, you made a vow to be passive at all the wrong moments. I am not surprised. Do you have any *real* idea why you disapprove of my lifestyle?"

She had plenty of ideas. Erica chewed on her lower lip to rid herself of the feeling she was running in circles. There was a Bible verse that said she should be bold, though remembering a verse and doing what it said were worlds apart. She cast a sidelong glance at Sajah and found him smiling at her. Fine, he had asked for it. "I'm sure you have women falling at your feet, Rajah, but that doesn't make it right. God never intended for people to live outside of marriage as if they were married."

Sajah's narrowed gaze never left her face. "But I do not live beneath your God, Miss Tanner."

The truth stabbed through her, effectively laying bare *God's* reason for her not to be intimidated by Sajah Ajari. "What about your gods then? Don't they care?"

"I suspect you know next to nothing about the Vedas?"

"I suspect I will have to learn, now that I know you." She anticipated the anger that flashed in Sajah's eyes. "I could study Hinduism twenty-four hours a day. I could even become an expert on what you believe and why you believe it, but doing so would only give me a firmer foundation in Christianity."

"And you will feel perfectly safe on your 'firm' foundation."

"No." She kept her words calm. "I will be perfectly saved. There's a difference. Feeling perfectly safe is what Hinduism promises. Knowing you're perfectly saved is what Christ promised for me when He died on the cross."

"And did this *Jesus* also promise you would triumph over the evil Hindu Rajah Ajari?"

Erica shifted uncomfortably at his sarcasm. He was certainly doing his best to challenge her vow. When she remained silent,

Sajah stood, but he did not leave. He knelt before the fireplace, laying wood on the grate.

"Do you mind if I start a fire?"

"I'm sleeping."

"Answer the question. I would not want to cause you nightmares about your parents."

But he did want to cause her hours of lost sleep over his lost soul. Her silence lasted long enough that Sajah turned partially toward her, hands on his thighs, dark eyes a mirror for the tight rein he held on his own feelings. "No," Erica managed. "I don't mind." In fact, she felt chilled and joined him on the floor before the fireplace. Soon, there were red and orange and brilliant white flames licking at the logs.

"What are you thinking?"

"I was praying." She looked up to see how he would react to her honesty.

"I worship too, Erica. You needn't look at me that way."

"Do you have a schedule to follow in your prayer room so you won't forget one of your gods and offend him or her?"

His unexpected smile disarmed the moment of bravado. "No, Erica. I worship the god who will fill my particular need at that time. Usually it is Rama."

She thought back to the temple in his village, when being in that same space with Rama had made her sick. "The hero god... Did you pick Rama as your patron god or did he pick you?" The smile left Sajah's face. "It's difficult for me to understand your Hindu worship. God takes care of any need I have. When Jesus died in my place, it opened the way for me to bring any need, any concern, any dream before God. He doesn't have to—to send me down the line until I happen upon the right answer."

"Hinduism is not like that. It isn't a game my people play."

"I know." She stared at the flames. Despite the fire's warmth she felt uncomfortably cold and wrapped both arms around herself. Perhaps it was self-defense, too. "I know it's not a game. That's what scares me so much." He remained silent. "My parents came here, they *died* here because they knew it wasn't a game. Ellyn and Sambhal died because they knew it wasn't a game."

Sajah's movement caused her to flinch, but he only reached for a woolen blanket. She let her gaze drift over his face as he drew close and wrapped it around her shoulders. Firelight only enhanced his regal bearing. "Are you angry with me again?"

His hands curled around her shoulders. "Should I be?"

"No."

"Not even when you try to prove to me you are right and I am wrong? To prove you are perfectly saved and I am not?"

He would have pulled away, but Erica held onto his arms. "No, Sajah. It isn't like that at all." The tremor in her voice could not be disguised. "I don't want to prove you're wrong. I just want you to know that there is more beyond what you've been taught. I want you to know my God because—" She stopped suddenly, catching her breath, casting her expressive gaze from his.

But he wouldn't let her hide this time. His hand alongside her face forced her to look up again. New tears shimmered upon her long lashes. The answer was there in her eyes, yet he wanted her to say it out loud, to admit the truth. "Why, Erica? Tell me."

"Because I don't want you to stay lost in a way of life that cannot last beyond this." A single tear slipped down her cheek. She closed her eyes before more tears followed. "Because I care, Sajah. I care very much."

He caught the tear with his fingertip. "Look at me, Erica." When she did as he asked, he traced the petal-soft outline of her lips. "Say it. Say you trust me. I have seen it in your eyes since Jaipur. I have felt it drawing us closer together, as it did last night."

"Last night I was sick."

"Last night you were honest with yourself." Gently, he touched the back of his fingers to her cheek. He touched her brow and threaded his fingers through her hair. "Last night it was just you and me. No one else. We were both being honest."

"I don't understand what you mean."

"Don't you?" He leaned forward and covered her lips with his own. It was just like the day before, the same tenderness, the same seeking. Except tonight, Sajah did not lift his head. His tenderness became passion and Erica melted into his arms.

Her action of reaching up to feel the wild pulsing of the veins in his neck is what drew them apart. Even by firelight, Sajah realized there was little color in her face. He should not have kissed her. Not like that.

Angry with himself, he moved to put another log on the grate. Sparks shot up the chimney, dozens of sparks to rival what had just taken place between himself and Erica Tanner. He spoke without looking at her, forcing all emotion from his voice. "Go to your room, Erica." He heard her stand, unsteadily because she stumbled into a table.

"Sajah."

"Now, Erica. Please." He grabbed the iron poker, jabbing at the fire until more sparks rioted upward.

"I wish Pali was alive."

He swung upright so slowly, with so much pain, Erica automatically backed away. The poker was carefully set in its holder as he prepared to receive her accusation against him concerning Pali's death. "And why do you wish Pali was alive?"

"Because I am afraid." The blanket slipped down her back. She stood there shivering. "Pali brought Betul to me because she didn't want him here, but I—I don't know why anymore. I feel like she was right, like she didn't have a choice, but—watching you and Betul, being with you has made me so confused." Her step toward him was desperate. "Am I right that Pali knew how much you love Betul?"

His entire body was taut.

Erica did not move any closer. "What was she afraid of, Sajah? What came between the way she loved you and the way she trusted you? What killed Pali's trust?"

Though Sajah went to stand by the windows, no distance could have been far enough from the turmoil he felt rising up in Erica. Her reflection in the glass showed him how she knelt before the fire again. If he knew her at all, she was praying. Heart-wrenching, desperate prayers.

Tension consumed her body. To know he had caused that tension made him feel both indignant and guilty. It seemed the war within him increased the closer he came to loving her. No one had ever done that to him before. No one. Sajah left the house as quickly as he could, all but commanding Erica to return to her room.

❧ Fourteen ☙

THE FARTHER UP THE TRAIL SHE WENT, the cooler it became, making Erica thankful she had worn jeans and not the silk skirt. A light rain had fallen all morning long. It still clung to the leaves and the grass where late afternoon sunshine had not yet reached. Erica drew the edges of Sajah's leather jacket close, inhaling his scent.

A few minutes ago, she had tried to sneak past him, out of the house. She should have known better. Sajah was aware of everything that happened around him, even when it seemed like he was engrossed in paperwork.

He had come looking for her during the morning and found her packing Ellyn and Sambhal's things into the boxes she had found in a storage closet. Other than telling her not to become overtired, he hadn't disapproved.

That's when she first suspected that something had changed in him. He had been wearing the same jeans and black sweater. A day's growth of beard shadowed his face. Both indications that he had not slept. The only rules he gave her before she left the house were to stick to the trail and to wear his jacket. The Rajah would have noticed she still had a fever. The Rajah would have ordered her to stay away from Betul.

Puzzling out the changes carried Erica to the end of the trail. Today, the view was even more beautiful. Rays of sunshine caused the clinging raindrops to sparkle like diamonds. She stood there a long time, hands sunk into jacket pockets, gaze focused on the mountains. In her heart, she knew why God had compelled her to come here.

She had found dozens of verses underlined in Ellyn's Bible. Every one of them spoke about God being the strength, the high tower, and the deliverer. In her mind, they were proof that Ellyn had not felt hopeless or abandoned after all.

God was confirming that thought now, not only regarding Ellyn. Coming here was for her benefit, too. It was easier to feel that God could be her high tower and deliverer now that she was looking at the mountains.

God was all around her.

Though he needed to work, Sajah found he couldn't. He was too distracted by thoughts of where Erica was along the trail, when she would walk through that door, if she felt warm enough in his jacket, and had she worked too long upstairs.

Sajah finally yielded to the distractions and left the house, heading down the same trail Erica had used. He had gone only a few hundred feet before he began to feel uneasy. A frown creased his brow. His steps quickened.

Erica's footprints could be seen in the freshly dampened dirt, but there were others there too, larger ones.

"Erica?"

His voice echoed back to him, but no other sound came.

Sajah began to run. "Erica!"

It was as if he lived a dozen lifetimes in the minutes before he actually broke through the woods into the clearing. He stopped, exactly there, though his gaze raced the distance to where Erica was standing. Her breath showed white in the cool air. A current of awareness ran through him, tuning in the smallest sound—animals scampering, wind blowing through the highest branches. Every nerve ending was ready, every muscle surged with adrenaline. From the corner of his eye, Sajah saw when Erica took a faltering step toward him. He went to her. "Are you all right?" She nodded. "Did you hear anyone? See anything?"

"No," she barely whispered the word. "Sajah, you're scaring me."

"You should be afraid." He took one of her hands to lead her toward the trail. "Someone followed you here."

She stumbled a little and held more tightly to his hand. "Who?"

"I don't know. You shouldn't be out anyway. You're still warm."

When she tried to draw her hand from his and break the connection, Sajah would not release her. In fact, he made her stay close to his side all the way back to the house.

By the time they reached the house, Sajah's rapid pace had left her breathless. He pulled her up the steps and inside. "Either sit on the sofa or go to your room."

She chose the sofa, dropping onto the cushions because she doubted her legs would support her another second. The room was filled with shadows. Sajah did not turn on the lamps.

"Who followed me, Sajah?"

"I've told you, I don't know."

"Was it your friend? The one who helps you against the Sikh?"

"No. He stayed in Rajasthan."

Erica noticed him move toward the phone, then change directions as if governed by the thought he should not place the call with her in the same room. A feeling of apprehension burst through her, making it harder to catch her breath. "Was it Grant?"

"He cannot get into the region."

"Then how did we get in?"

A certain stillness swept over the room. "I own this land," Sajah said evenly. "I can get in."

"But I couldn't have." Erica knew she spoke the truth by the way he turned to face her. Sinking into the folds of his jacket was the only protection she had once she took the next step. They both knew it. "Who are you, Sajah?"

He ran a hand across the back of his neck.

"Please, I need to know." She was surprised when he pulled an ottoman close to where she was sitting on the sofa. His knees almost touched hers. Because he leaned forward, his entire manner was more intense.

"Five years ago, I was appointed by the president to serve on the Council, our version of your executive branch. I am like an assistant secretary of state."

"How? You're never gone."

"I was often gone from the palace."

Yes, now that she thought about it, his airplane would have cut down on travel time. What an impossible schedule he must be trying to maintain. A government official. She raised her eyes to him and waited. There had to be more.

"I am also considered to be the head of a political movement that is working to unite India. Too many factions, too many religious beliefs have drained our people from any real strength, from having a stronger voice in government. Among other things, we work to prevent any outside *agendas*, shall we say, from weakening the advancements we have made."

Agendas. The pieces refused to be fit together, to form the picture she knew had to be there, staring her in the face. Perhaps because of her confusion, Sajah's voice became more forceful.

"We—I—am fighting to keep your country from pouring missionaries and religious funds into India. You weaken us. You talk of Jesus and turn India from its true strength."

Her gaze collided with his.

"Yes, Erica." The revelation erupted from him. "When Sambhal married Ellyn, he tore into the heart of what united us as brothers. He shattered me, my family, and the very ideals I have been striving for. My only defense has been to work harder, to keep other Indian families from suffering because of the mistake he made."

"It wasn't a mistake."

"Then tell me why you're here!" Sajah threw himself to his feet. "If it wasn't a mistake, why is Betul so confused about being Hindu or being Christian?"

"Maybe because you are his hero." She didn't feel as steady inside as the words sounded, especially when Sajah looked at her with such a fierce expression. Erica slowly rose from the sofa. "Betul looks to you for the truth. He needs you to make the tough choices. As your mother once told me, do not choose wrong."

Erica did not plan on falling asleep. Illness, work, and stress decided otherwise. She awakened to find that evening shadows crowded the blue bedroom. Beyond the balcony doors, she searched a starless horizon for some sign that God had changed her circumstances in the hours she had slept. But nothing looked different and nothing felt different.

She sat up slowly and went to close the French doors, shivering despite the protection of Ellyn's red sweater. It was so quiet here in Sajah's world. The darkness was still. There were lights in the Pabnas' hut, then nothing, only the looming mass of forest and rock and snow. So very quiet.

Unexplainably, her heart started missing beats. The latch slipped in her numb fingers. Pinpricks of fear ran down the entire length of her body. Something, some suspicion told her to get out of the room.

She half stumbled, half ran to the door. Fear constricted her throat. In the hallway, she hurried to the next door; the door Betul had said was Sajah's room. "Sajah." No one answered her desperate whisper. Erica looked over her shoulder. Again the inner voice urged her to move.

She ran the length of hallway, remembering her flight through the palace. Someone had chased her then. Someone wanted her to be afraid. Erica grabbed at the banister but didn't even take a single step down before a hand closed over her wrist, dragging her back. She whipped around.

The scream in her throat died.

It was only Sajah. He must have been in his room after all, must have come behind her.

"What is it?"

"I was asleep and—the wind blew the doors open. I was frightened... Sajah, where are you going?"

"Stay there."

But she couldn't! Not alone. Erica followed. Fear still pounded through her veins, even more so when she reached her room and saw it was still cloaked in darkness. Sajah stood at the foot of the bed, listening, waiting, just like he had done earlier at the clearing. Erica's eyes shifted over the shadows, too. Then a strangled gasp escaped.

Sajah swung around. "Erica, I told you—"

"The doors. I closed them. I know I did."

His gaze flew to the open doors. In seconds his body flew there, too. It was difficult to see anything from the balcony. Every shred of moonlight was secreted behind a bank of clouds. Searching in that kind of darkness was a waste of time. Sajah went back inside, where Erica was still silhouetted in the doorway.

"There is no wind," she said. "Someone was in here."

"But he's gone now. You needn't worry."

"Does that mean you know who was in here, watching me sleep?"

He owed her the truth. "It was Bashtar."

"Bashtar? Betul used that name before. He's your friend, the one helping you protect us?"

"Yes."

Her confusion increased until she was staring at him with obvious pain. "Is Bashtar Sikh?"

Sajah started to nod, but Erica was already leaving, moving as quickly as she could to the staircase. "Let me explain."

"There is nothing to explain," she flung the words over her shoulder. "You keep company with the people who were trying to kill my sister. You let them visit Betul here. Now you have them guarding me. Somewhere in there, I'm sure you can keep your loyalties straight, but I can't even begin to try."

He was only a step behind her now.

Erica didn't stop until she was in the kitchen, until she had turned on every single light and was standing at the sink with a glass of water in her hand. Most of it spilled in her attempt to raise it to her lips. It was inevitable that the glass fell from her hand, shattering against the bottom of the sink.

"Are you ready to listen to me?"

"I'm ready to ask if this is why Pali brought Betul to me, because she couldn't trust the company you keep."

Sajah reached out and captured her by both wrists, making her face him. "Bashtar is not one of the extremists. He has done everything in his power to protect my family from them."

"Then he isn't doing his job!"

"If not for Bashtar, your sister would have died five years ago. The extremists are a group of Sikh who resent everything about me.

Sambhal, Ellyn, Betul—all of them were considered fair game. Bashtar tirelessly stays two steps ahead of them."

"Except with Pali." Erica's eyes were filled with quiet anxiety. "How could Bashtar not know Pali was taking Betul out of the country?"

"Because he was in London, trying to diffuse the mess Pali had created by speaking with a reporter about Cawnpore. That is also the reason he wasn't in Portland when the extremists killed her and injured Bill Stevens. You and Betul would also have been killed if not for the men Bashtar sent." Sajah reached up to touch her face. "You are safe here, Erica."

"I don't feel safe.... The man who followed me this morning—"

"Was also Bashtar. I phoned him while you were sleeping. The extremists have made another threat. Bashtar came as soon as he heard." Sajah watched her sift through the tortured mess of information and emotions. He wasn't surprised when she slipped her hands free and stepped back. It was her way of regaining control.

"I want Betul with us, Sajah. I need him to be with us. Please?"

"I will call Ved. He will be here soon."

By the time they ate supper, cleaned the kitchen, and played together, it was past ten o'clock. Yet Erica was loath to give up Betul's company. "How about a nice warm bath before bed, Betul?"

"With soap?"

"Yes, silly, with soap. How else do you expect to get clean?"

Betul didn't have an answer for that one. Instead, he pretended to be a mountain climber and the staircase was Mount Everest. He concentrated on counting the stairs—in Hindi. Erica concentrated on steadying him when he became overconfident.

Before long, Betul was splashing contentedly in the tub while she sat on a stool and watched. His game had changed from mountain climbing to seafaring. The small plastic boat became a giant ocean liner, the floating sponge an absurdly large whale. He would have gone on playing forever except the water became cool and Erica reminded him that Sajah was waiting.

"You promised to tell me a story."

"Only if you come out now. Check to see if you're done."

"How?"

She plucked one of his hands out of the water. "Just like I thought. See all those wrinkles?" She smiled at his serious nod. "That means you're done. Any longer and I'll have to iron all those wrinkles away."

"You are teasing, Erica."

"Yes, little man. I am teasing." But it felt good after being so afraid, to know God could restore her spirit. Erica made a game out of helping Betul into his pajamas. He escaped her tickles by running into his bedroom, full speed, awkward motions and all.

"There you are." She heard Sajah say as she followed. "I was about to send the Coast Guard after you two."

Betul giggled with abandon. "They could not have captured us, right, Erica?" He jumped on top of the bed, hopping merrily up and down until Sajah captured him and laid him down. "That is not fair, Sajah. You are bigger than the Coast Guard men." He snuggled his favorite teddy bear into the crook of his arm. "And what of my story, Erica?"

She hadn't forgotten. Sajah made room for her on the bed beside the two of them. It felt strange sitting so close to Sajah, feeling her back rub against his strong shoulder. "What would you like to hear about, Betul?"

"Of Mother, please. When you were young like me." Betul snuggled down into the pillow, waiting for the story to start.

Erica had thought he would ask for a fairy tale or a funny story, not for a story about Ellyn. She searched her heart until one memory in particular stood out among all the others. "When I was very young, about your age, your mother and I lived here in India."

"I know about that. When I couldn't sleep—after Daddy and Mommy died—Sajah read to me from your letters."

Oh, dear Lord, this is hard. Erica couldn't quite catch her breath against the stab of sweet pain. Hearing Sajah's voice only made it worse.

"You must be patient, Betul. Maybe this is a new story."

A new story...a new story. She felt Sajah's fingers weave through the curls at the back of her head. Did he remember her father had done that? Erica turned her head to look at him and caught him smiling.

"You haven't run out of stories, have you?"

"No. I haven't run out of stories. I was only trying to think of the best one."

"Oh." He tickled her neck and that made Betul laugh.

Time to start the story. "We were in the giant city."

"There are no giant cities," Betul said. "Are there, Sajah?"

"Little girls like to exaggerate."

Erica ignored their teasing. "We were in the giant city. Daddy took Ellyn and me to the market, but there must have been a festival that day because the women wore pretty colors, yellow and red and green. I thought they looked like a rainbow dancing in the street. And Daddy took us to a parade. It was the first time I had ever seen an elephant!"

"Did you get to ride one?" Betul asked in awe.

"No. We just walked and walked and walked. When my legs got too tired, Daddy carried me on his shoulders. I felt as if I could see the whole world. There were animals all around. And people riding their bicycles, dinging the bells in time to the music. Ellyn danced along beside Daddy and me. But soon, it was getting to be night-time, and we had to go back to the village and see my mother.

Daddy drove the minibus. Ellyn and I were sitting in the back. She talked on and on of the things she was going to tell Mother. When I got tired, Ellyn let me rest my head on her lap."

"She was a good sister." Betul's voice sounded a little sad.

Erica held his hand tightly in her own. "Yes, Betul. She was a good sister. A very good sister, because on our way home to the village, I fell asleep and she was the one who made Daddy stop the bus. They woke me and we went out on top of a big hill. Do you know what was out there?" Betul shook his head. "Stars, hundreds and hundreds of them; so close that I wanted to run and catch them, but Daddy held one of my hands and Ellyn held the other. 'See, Ricky,' she whispered to me, 'God sent all the stars down to earth just for this one night so they could take our most special prayers back up to heaven with them.' We stood there for the longest time and prayed together."

"What did my mother pray for, Erica?"

"I don't remember." Though she tried to hide the sudden hint of tears in her voice, Sajah sensed her emotions. His arm came up to rest on her shoulder. Erica had to resist the urge to turn toward him.

"What did you pray for?"

"Well." She smiled at Betul, a sad sort of smile. "I prayed that the stars would come back and visit me. Every night."

"That was a silly prayer," Betul scolded. "Everyone knows you can't tell stars what to do. All they want to do is play hide-and-seek the way they twinkle so."

"But if you wanted a star to visit you—" Sajah's tone was gentle— "don't you think you could find one that would listen? Or two or three?"

Betul's face crinkled up as he thought about that a moment. "Well, if it did come to visit how would it get back to heaven?"

"Maybe stars can fly, Betul. Maybe God whispers to them and

they obey His voice." Erica smoothed the dark hair from his fore-head. "Does my prayer still seem silly?"

He shook his head. "No, it seems just right. Is that the end of the story?"

"Yes, honey. That's the end." She leaned over to place a soft kiss on his cheek. "Time to go to sleep now. Good night, Betul."

After Sajah said good night too, he followed Erica into the hallway. Even as he closed the door, he sensed a certain amount of caution in the way she looked up at him, almost as if she expected him to be angry over the reference to God. "May we talk, Erica? Outside on the verandah." True, the question was canceled by the statement and by the way he headed to the stairs before she could disagree. But she did follow.

At the outer doorway, he let her go ahead. It was possible to dis-cern her uneasiness as she passed him. When they were both on the porch, she just stood there, waiting. Sajah buried his hands deep into the front pockets of his jeans. His white shirt appeared gray in the dim porch light. Erica's darker clothing all but made her disap-pear into the shadows.

In his continued silence, she moved to the porch rail and looked up at the sky for her stars. It was a little girl gesture. A pow-erful, little girl gesture. Sajah felt the impact of her faith all over again. She had matured into a remarkable blend of dreamer and believer. She would need both after what he asked her now. "When I spoke with Bashtar earlier, he said something that I need to tell you."

"About the Sikh?"

Sajah took a step toward her, then stopped. "Yes, about the Sikh and about us. There are rules—unwritten rules—between the Hindu and Sikh. It is a matter of honor that they have not attacked me."

"Only your family."

"Only my brother's family. They would never attack a Rajah or a Rajah's immediate family. If Sambhal had not renounced his title, the Sikh would have felt free to kill me."

She made her way to the top step and sat down, arms hugging her knees.

"The title was not mine to give away, or I would have done the same thing in order to protect Sambhal."

When she spoke, her voice was unnaturally steady. "Sambhal was protecting you?"

"In a roundabout way, yes. Because he converted to Christianity, he could never have kept the title."

"So, if you adopt Betul, if he becomes your son, if he remains Hindu, it would stop the Sikh from trying to hurt him?"

"Yes."

"Then why are you even trying to find the will?"

"To be fair to you. Until today, we had time to wait."

She was staring into nothing but darkness, seeing more inside her imagination than Sajah wanted her to envision. "Bashtar said you couldn't wait anymore, right? You have to legally adopt Betul, but you need me to sign papers. Even if the will is found, even if Ellyn and Sambhal wanted me to be his mother, I can't let that happen. I have to give up any right to custody."

"Erica."

"Yes or no, Sajah? That's all you have to say—yes or no."

In two strides he was lifting her to her feet, turning her around to face him. "Betul loves you. I will never deny that. Until today, I could not see a way for you to remain part of his life without jeopardizing him at every turn. Being around me would put you in constant danger from the Sikh...unless you become my wife."

"Marry you?"

He held tightly to her arms to prevent her from pulling back.

"Yes. I am asking you to marry me. It is the only way to keep both you and Betul safe."

Her eyes did not hold disbelief, only shock. "It would never work, Sajah."

"It will if we make it work. There are ways—"

"Ways to buy people out of knowing you married a Christian?"

He drew breath against how her honesty stabbed through him. "Your position on the Council. Your role in the political party."

"My private life is my business."

"You don't have a private life, Sajah. You have a very public life. That's the whole crux of their revenge. As Betul gets older, he'll begin to realize just how much you've sacrificed to help your people. I can't be part of the compromise."

"Then you choose to remain part of the problem? Or will you take yourself out of the picture altogether and move back to Portland?" He hated how his words chased the color from her face, leaving her pale and speechless. "I don't want that, Erica. I don't want Betul to lose you or you to lose him. Will you become my wife?"

"I don't know."

"I will expect an answer tomorrow."

✒ FIFTEEN ✒

AFTER BREAKFAST, BETUL AND THE PABNA children escorted Erica on a trip around the plantation. They teased her about looking like a tree among the dark leaves. Perhaps it was true. She had found a lovely nutmeg brown sweater and matching knit pants while packing away Ellyn's things.

At the time, she thought they looked comfortable. The children's observations were probably more accurate. She had only to stand still with her arms outstretched and birds would come to perch on her bark.

If Ahwa hadn't complimented her on the outfit, she would have run back to the main house and changed. Then the children would really have teased her; five voices clamoring that she was wasting time. Better to pull up the droopy sleeves and enjoy being a tree.

While she held Betul's hand, she was very conscious of the fact that Sajah's friend, Bashtar, was out there somewhere, guarding against the Sikh extremists. Perhaps there were other guards, too.

The only man she saw was Ved Pabna. From a distance, Erica guessed he was nearer to fifty than forty. His clothes were common—brown trousers and a cream tunic—not quite a tree. Although he accompanied them on the plantation tour, he didn't speak until it was noon. Then he stepped in to tell his children they must run home to eat before their mother started fussing.

As for Erica, she learned that Sajah was waiting for her in the stables. Betul was quick to invite himself into the picture. "If Sajah is going for a ride, may I go too?"

Ved hesitated. Erica did not. "Why don't you run ahead and ask him, Betul? He should be there." The boy took off, so eager to reach Sajah he fell once along the way. Erica held her breath. Betul simply picked himself up and continued the headlong race.

"He is very much like your sister," Ved stated evenly without taking his gaze from Betul. "Ellyn's faith was always a rush forward, a running determination to do as much as humanly possible. She fell many times, too."

There was that burning inside of her again. "What do you mean?"

"It happened mostly with Sajah. Perhaps with Loralai." Ved shrugged. "Ellyn's desire for them to accept Christ was so—consuming, she would run at them like a child looking for more and more attention. She wanted to make them listen."

"But they didn't."

"God is the only One who can make the deaf to hear and the blind to see."

"Ellyn and Sambhal shared Christ with you?"

His smile, like the rest of him, was quiet. "Ellyn and Sambhal shared Christ with everyone who crossed their path. But, yes, I accepted Him."

"Does Sajah know yet?"

"The time hasn't been right to tell him…. He is a good man, Erica."

"I know." She sought steadiness by looking at the mountains. It seemed strange that they had only met a few hours ago, yet they were talking about personal things. Ved was the first person she had met in India who knew so much about Ellyn and Sambhal and Sajah. His insight brought forth a desire to trust him with what she said next. "Sajah asked me to marry him."

Ved's silence lasted a long time. "What will you do?"

"I'm trying very, very hard not to run."

"Away from him or toward him?"

"Both. I'm trying very hard to find God in all of this."

The stable was not far from the place where Ved left her. It was a long, low building, much like the one at the palace. There were many access doors. She chose one quickly, although hearing Sajah's voice made her stop just inside.

"Tell me what you have been doing all day, little man."

"We took Erica exploring."

"Oh, and what did you and your friends find while you were exploring?"

Erica moved until she could see where they were standing—in the tack room. Neither of them had noticed her arrival.

"Not very much." Betul shrugged his shoulders. "Ved said we could not go past the lawn."

"He was right you know." Sajah lifted something off the wall. "I spoke with your grandmother today."

"She is well?"

"Yes. She is well."

The two of them shared a moment of companionable silence, thinking their own thoughts, content to be together again after the brief separation Erica's illness had caused. Then suddenly, Betul blurted out, "Do you like Erica?"

There was a soft chuckle from Sajah. Erica waited, her hand going to the rough wood wall for support. "Of course I do."

"No." Betul awkwardly climbed onto a bench in order to be the same height as Sajah. "I mean really *like* her, as my father liked my mother. Hopset's sisters were whispering about her being very beautiful."

"She is very beautiful." Sajah set down the bridle in his hand in order to take the boy in his arms. "Would you want me to like her in that way?"

"Oh yes! It would be ever so much fun! You could be my new father and Erica could be my new mother. We could be a family just like the Pabnas."

"Slow down, Betul," Sajah cautioned. "I have not said if I liked your Erica."

"But you do. I can tell."

"Oh? And how do you know so much?"

Betul held his head proudly. "I am a little man, Sajah. And I know."

"Then do you also know if your Erica likes me in that same way?"

Erica held her breath, waiting as Sajah did for Betul to give an answer.

"No. But I will ask her for you." Quick as a wink, Betul slipped out of Sajah's arms to the floor. He stumbled a little, but his actions still made Erica shrink against the wall lest she be discovered.

"Not so fast there." Sajah caught him back. "We shall let Erica decide for herself, no?"

"Don't you want to be my new father and have Erica be my new mother?"

Sajah took Betul's hands in his larger ones. "Yes, Betul. I want that very much, but we must wait until Erica is ready to want the same thing." Betul hung his head in disappointment. "No long faces, now." Sajah put a finger beneath his nephew's chin.

"But waiting is ever so hard."

"I know it is, Betul. Waiting is a test of patience and strength."

"Oh." Betul suddenly stood taller, as if to prove himself worthy of the test.

"That is better. Let's see if Erica is ready."

"I am."

Both Sajah and Betul looked toward her. Only Betul moved forward. "Wait until you see Sajah's horses, Erica! You won't believe how strong they are."

"Really?" Even to her own ears, her voice sounded strained.

It helped some to have Betul slip his hand into hers. "Come, I will show you."

There were four horses in the stable, all of them pure white with huge, dark eyes. Betul rambled on about each in turn until they came to the one Sajah was saddling. Then Betul didn't get quite as close and his hand tightened in Erica's. "This," he said in a lowered tone, "is Parvati."

It wasn't like him to be afraid of the mare. Erica instinctively tried to ease that fear and stretched out her free hand to touch the animal. The moment she did, the horse pulled back sharply and snorted a warning. Sajah calmed it by placing a firm hand on its neck.

"Parvati." Erica repeated the name Betul had used. "Is that one of your gods, Sajah?"

"No. Parvati is a goddess. One of the most powerful. She demands respect but is not very well loved."

In which case, Erica could understand why this horse was named after such a goddess. Sajah indicated with a gesture of his head that she should touch the horse again, for Betul's sake. She did. "You try, Betul. I think Parvati is prettier than the others."

"Prettier. Horses are not pretty." He reached out a tentative hand. "I like the others better."

"A horse can sense your feelings," Sajah said. "You should always be in control."

Betul's hand trembled slightly, then slipped off the horse altogether. He didn't try to pet it again. "Why can't I go with you today, Sajah?"

"Some other day, perhaps. Today you must take a nap."

"Naps are for—"

"For young men who want to go to Diwali."

A smile came over the boy's face.

"Go now. Ahwa is waiting for you."

"Have a good ride!"

"We will." Sajah turned back to saddling Parvati as Betul ran from the stables.

It was quiet then. Erica wandered to the other horses, stroking their noses, wondering why Sajah wouldn't let Betul go on their ride. But she didn't ask. Another question came instead. "Which one will you saddle for me?"

"None. They are spirited animals. You could not handle them." With one final pull, he tightened the cinch, then picked up the reins to lead Parvati outside to the yard. Erica was careful to keep her distance, so much so that Sajah had to look over his shoulder to make sure she was there. "Parvati will not bite."

"I wouldn't be too sure."

Sajah stopped and held out his hand, waiting patiently until Erica walked close enough to take it. In the next instant, he was helping her into the saddle. Before he climbed up behind her, Sajah said a few words into Parvati's ear. Hindi words that Erica couldn't understand. She was barely able to hold her curiosity until he was settled and they had started forward. "What did you tell her?"

Because Sajah took his time in answering, Erica tipped her head back to see his face. The opportunity was not wasted. Sajah bent his head, touching his lips to hers. "I told her to behave herself because you are a very special lady."

All around them the world was bright with sunshine. Parvati ran gracefully over the fields, only slowing when Sajah commanded her to do so. The house was long out of sight when he reined the horse onto a narrow trail strewn with rocks and fallen trees. She handled the obstacles without faltering.

Altogether, it would have been a pleasant ride. Erica ruined it by revealing she had listened in on at least part of his conversation with Betul.

"I heard what you said earlier, Sajah, about liking me. Betul is more vulnerable than ever now. You shouldn't have lied to him."

"I wasn't lying." Sajah not only heard her sigh, but felt a certain strain in her. "Do you not believe me?"

"Should I?"

So, she was in a mood to be quarrelsome. "It would help you to make your decision, would it not?"

"Are you trying to force me into saying yes?"

He spoke close to her ear again, but his tone was not as gentle as before. "Are you intent on twisting everything I say?"

"I was only asking for the truth."

"It *was* the truth!"

Erica started a little. So did Parvati.

Sajah brought the animal under control again. Unfortunately the feelings between himself and Erica could not be as easily harnessed. He pressed Parvati forward more quickly than he should have.

Finally, they broke through the trees into a quiet, sheltered clearing.

"What is this place, Sajah? A temple?"

He glanced down, touched by the wonder in her voice. "No, it is a tribute, a declaration in stone."

"It's...floating."

"An illusion." One that served to dissolve the world they had left behind until it was just this moment. Just the two of them. Even as he stopped the horse and lowered himself to the ground, Sajah could feel the change in Erica. Without saying anything, he lifted her down beside him. The brown sweater with its dangling hem and sleeves made her appear younger, and very lovely. "What you heard me say to Betul was the truth. I want very much to be his father. I want you to be his mother."

"But part of you would always hate me."

"Because of our difference in religion?"

"Would you expect me to give up being Christian?"

"It did not cross my mind. What *has* crossed my mind is the way you have made me want you so much that I let you bend the rules. All of the rules." Sajah knew she would have backed away, but Parvati was behind her. "I have thought of how you beguiled me; first with your tender words, then with your tender ways. Every time that I intend to deny this truth, I am instead filled with a desire stronger than any I have ever known. There is no part of me that can hate you, Erica, because you have already made me love you."

He watched most of the color drain from her face. "All business with the Sikh aside; I would still want you to be Betul's mother. As much as he needs you, I could have changed that. Eventually, I could have made him forget what he feels for you. I could have filled his life with a kingdom of things that would keep him content without you."

When an expression of pain shot through her eyes, Sajah brushed the back of his hand against her cheek. His words held the same intimacy. "Betul could live without you. Even I could live without you. But I have seen the kingdom and it is not big enough, it is not rich enough to keep me content. I want you to be my wife."

Erica searched his face. She knew every line there, every way his eyes could hide what he was feeling. Was it true? As incredible as it was to believe, did he love her? "I'm not sure how I feel about you, Sajah."

"But you are willing to marry me? Without knowing?"

"I need time."

Sajah took a step away from her. "We do not have time. I explained that last night."

"You explained that the Sikh were closing in. If it will throw them off, if it will unbalance them to say you are marrying me, then say it and God forgive me for being this desperate, but I need time to know what is right. Not what's easiest, Sajah. What is right, for all of us—Betul, me, you." Especially you. That was the conviction burning strongest in her now. "Please, Sajah?"

He held out his hand. "Come, I want to show you something."

Outside this shadowy place, the sun was shining. Inside, Erica wondered if winter moonlight had not come to rest upon an earthly bed. She held tightly to Sajah as they moved around the white marble wall. A dozen thick columns formed the curved side of the moon shape. Amazement held her words to a whisper. "It's like the prayer room."

"No, the prayer room is like this."

Wall and columns supported a domed roof, the underside of which appeared to be deep blue mosaic tiles. The celestial figures she had seen in the prayer room were replicas of the ones carved into the capital and base of each column. The open space between columns gave her brief glimpses of charred marble, a chilling stain upon such pure white.

"Before they were married," Sajah said, "the first Sajah Ajari built this tribute for the woman he loved. The story says that he wanted to create something worthy of her beauty. A little bit of heaven, a little moon. Chota Chand."

Sajah continued speaking while Erica slowly moved away from him; her gaze, even her heart absorbing the temple's sadness. "Each stone was of the finest quality, hand cut, flawless. Nothing else would do. Servants worked day and night to complete it before the wedding. Finally the day arrived. It was an elaborate celebration. People came from many miles. They had never seen such a perfect love. They said the gods had made the match."

Erica was now standing before the only set of stairs, the only visible anchor between earth and this place of sadness. A crude rock wall blocked the entrance. Sajah joined her there. "When it was almost evening, the Rajah and his new bride left the celebration and the people behind to come here. Just the two of them. At last, it was time to share his secret—the thing he had most wanted to give her.

"The setting sun was an orange and red fire in the sky, lighting the white marble until it came alive with the colors. Sajah and his bride spent their first night here as man and wife. The next morning they rode home. As the months passed, they knew they were to have a child; a child created from their love on that special night. Both she and the child died during the birth."

Tears shimmered in Erica's eyes now.

"The Rajah brought them here to Chota Chand. It became their beautiful funeral pyre. He would not allow anyone to share in his grief nor would he allow anyone ever again to enter Chota Chand." Very gently Sajah lifted his hand to brush the tears from her face. "The stone wall is deliberately ugly. He placed it there as a reminder that death may interrupt heaven but never transcend it. It is an Ajari tradition that each new bride-to-be is brought here, to the temple, and that she is told the story."

Erica's voice was a whisper. "Why?"

"To strengthen the love she feels in her heart. To make her see that such a love will become the most important thing in her life." Sajah caressed the hollow of her cheek with his fingertips. "And to bestow upon her heart the desire to hold on to that love, so she will never, ever let it go."

Erica reached up to capture his hand. "Sajah, I'm sorry."

He silenced her apology with a long kiss, pulling back when he felt her tremble. "You may have the time you ask for, Erica."

Dinner that evening was shared with the Pabnas. The adults could hardly get a word in edgewise over the excited chatter of the children. Because Sajah was waiting for an important phone call, it was decided that Betul would ride into Darjeeling with Ved and Ahwa. They would all meet again later to share in the festivities.

After Ved bundled everyone off in his car, the house seemed incredibly quiet. Erica changed into an iridescent pink sari she had found among Ellyn's clothes, then wandered aimlessly around her room, waiting for Sajah to come for her. During the past few hours, her anticipation for the evening had somehow changed to nervousness. Though she couldn't quite explain why, neither could she push aside her feelings.

The night was warmer than it had been. There were no clouds in sight as she stepped out onto the balcony. She inhaled a deep breath of fresh air. It was hard to believe Sajah owned this land. She probably didn't know half of the things and places the Ajari family owned. An assistant Council member; head of a political movement; a prince—the magnitude of it was a bit intimidating, especially when she contemplated becoming his wife.

There was a pinging sound behind her. Even as she swung toward it, something whizzed past her, striking the window casing. She felt a terrible pain sear the bare flesh of her forearm. Another ping.

The next bullet shattered the top pane in one of the French doors, spraying her with a dozen shards of glass as she stumbled inside. She all but fell into the nearest corner. Then it was silent, except for the voice screaming inside her head that someone was trying to kill her.

"Erica!"

Sajah! She couldn't call out to him. Her voice, her body seemed severed from reality. He came running through the door, saw her, and quickly plunged the room into darkness. The next thing she knew, he was pulling her out of the corner, blinding her with pain when his hand closed over her arm.

Somehow she found herself in the bathroom. Lights came on. Too bright. Erica closed her eyes. *Dear Lord.* Her arm throbbed with each wild pulsing of her heart. Sajah forced her to sit on the floor. A white towel stained with blood. Erica leaned her head against the wall and watched as Sajah found a washcloth and ran it beneath the faucet.

He was so calm, so controlled. "Someone tried to kill me. Sajah—" she gripped his sleeve—"someone tried to kill me."

He freed himself, quite deliberately. "They only wanted to frighten you."

"Oh, really?" She tried to catch the anger back, but none of this was fair! With her one good arm, she began pushing herself upright. Sajah tried to help, but she twisted away. "Well then, they got what they wanted, didn't they? With a little blood mixed in for good measure."

"Erica."

"I guess I'm lucky they were in such a kind mood."

"Yes, you are."

Shock pooled in the pit of her stomach, made her feel sick. This time, she did not avoid Sajah's touch. She needed it. She needed him to calm the riot of emotions. Erica leaned into him. "I'm sorry," she said quietly.

None of this was his fault. He had done everything he could to protect her. Now wasn't the time to think of things being fair or unfair. Now wasn't the time to put up the walls God was tearing down. Erica forced herself to think clearly, in doing so, she left the comfort of Sajah's arms. "I need some disinfectant, rubbing alcohol or peroxide. And something to bandage my arm."

While he was gone, she prayed for the fear to leave her. Incredibly, it did. So much so that when he returned, she was able to take the small brown bottle from him without shaking. "Thank you."

"What else?"

The wound was bleeding heavily now. It probably needed stitches, but that wasn't possible. "Have you ever heard of a butterfly bandage?" She told him what to pull out of the first-aid kit. Now for the alcohol. It stung like crazy. Erica held out her free hand. "Gauze."

"I will do it."

Yes, maybe he'd better. Erica leaned into the sink, trying to keep her arm still. Once in a while, she gave him instructions. Mostly, she just kept quiet. By the time he was done, her skirt and choli were stained with blood. "I have to change."

"We do not need to go to Darjeeling."

"Betul is waiting."

"Are you always so stubborn, Erica Tanner?"

They smiled for the first time all day. "Always, Sajah Ajari."

The ride into Darjeeling was a quiet one. Erica stared out her window most of the time. Yet, as they reached the top of the last hill, she suddenly sat forward. "Sajah." Her hand went to his arm. "Stop...please."

After he pulled to the side of the road, they both got out and walked to the front of the vehicle. Erica's gaze had not left the city below them. Not once. Every window in every house held a burning lamp, but the lights looked like stars, hundreds of stars.

Sajah set his hands upon her shoulders. "The festival you

watched with your father and Ellyn was Diwali." Erica half turned to look at him. A glimmer of little-girl enchantment had lit up her face. "I wondered if I should even bring you. I didn't want you to be disappointed."

"Oh, Sajah. I always knew they couldn't have been stars. It was just a story." She found herself being turned around to face him.

"Your memories are more than stories, Erica. They are the fiber, the fabric of who you are. Like the gossamer veil."

She smiled self-consciously. "You were right the first time. I do have an overactive imagination. The gossamer veil was mosquito netting mother placed around my little-girl bed…. I'm all grown-up now."

"Being all grown-up doesn't mean you must lay aside the veil." Sajah tucked a curl behind her ear. "In truth Erica, I think I started loving you when I read about your lights of the veil. The man in me knew they were the lamps by which your parents read to you at night. The little boy in me watched through your eyes, through your gossamer veil, as the lamps became your visiting stars, eavesdropping on so many wonderful, fantastic stories…. Don't lose the veil, Erica." He lowered his head to kiss her. "Never lose the veil."

The music rose and fell, making it seem as if the crowd moved in singular rhythm rather than as hundreds of individuals. Keeping track of Erica among so many people would have been impossible except that her sapphire mantle slipped every now and then to let blond curls show. Plus, he was determined not to lose sight of her.

Fifteen minutes earlier, when all his waiting had paid off and Sajah drove into Darjeeling, Grant had felt a surge of relief. Now his gut was telling him that Erica might look all right on the outside, but he shouldn't trust appearances.

Every time Ajari touched her arm, every time the man bent

his head low to answer her questions, Grant became more certain that things were going to be a lot different with Erica. When Sajah moved her along through the crowd, Grant followed.

They weren't just pleasure walking. Sajah kept scanning the street. A couple of times, Grant had to slip behind the stalls, but the prince was distracted enough not to notice. He was distracted enough not to notice Erica was going into full alert mode. Even from fifty feet away, Grant felt it.

She moved stiffly, held her head at a certain angle, and rubbed that worrisome pain in her temple. If he were closer, he'd be able to pinpoint the telltale frown that went with her awareness. His opportunity to get closer was canceled without warning.

Sajah's name was called out from the crowd. Grant slipped behind a stack of baskets, watching, waiting. An older man ran up to them. Words were exchanged. Something was wrong.

The moment Grant stepped out from his hiding place, Ajari and the other man hurried Erica away. Despite Grant's efforts, the three were soon lost in the crowd. He ran through the streets to where he had left the car that he had been able to rent from an enterprising young man.

Enough was enough. He was going to Ajari's house—even if he wasn't welcome.

It was more difficult than he expected to find the plantation. Earlier in the afternoon, when Grant had first arrived at Darjeeling, he asked directions from an old man at the hotel. Actually finding the plantation in the dark was another story. He was forced to stop half a dozen times and make sure he was going the right way.

Finally it came into view. Grant parked outside the locked gate and got out of his car. Several of the house's windows glowed with lamplight, but nobody was moving around. He grabbed his jacket from the front seat. Ready or not, Sajah Ajari was going to start answering some questions.

Grant thought it was strange not to have anyone stop him, especially when he moved onto the porch. His heart pounded so hard beneath the chambray shirt he wore, he thought for sure it would sound as loud as his trio of knocks. Rapid footsteps approached from the opposite side of the door. Then suddenly, he was standing face to face with Sajah Ajari.

Sajah showed no sign of being surprised to see him—an indication of adequate intelligence. All he did was move aside to let Grant enter. Okay, above average intelligence. Grant's eyes briefly scanned the room before he turned to face Sajah again. "Where is she?"

"Upstairs. In Betul's room."

Before the answer was finished, Grant was on the steps, heading up.

"You have ten minutes with her, Stevens. No more."

"Wrong," Grant called back without stopping. "You've had her for the past two weeks. I'll decide my own time."

His strides carried him to where light seeped into the shadowy hallway. Once there, he paused in the door. Erica was on her knees, curled up in a tight ball next to the child's bed, her head buried in both arms. Very slowly, Grant moved into the room. She literally flinched when she heard his footsteps.

"Go away." Her words were muffled. "Leave me alone."

"That's a fine thing to say to someone who's gone through agony to find you." She became very still. "Erica?" Grant reached out a gentle hand, turning her toward him. Her eyes expressed shock. Her face was pale. The red sweater she wore over the choli and blue skirt hung on her slim frame. She was shivering. She had lost weight. He tried a smile, but that only brought tears to her eyes. "I don't recall that you cried when I rescued you from the riptide."

Erica bit down on her lip, unable to keep from shaking, unable to make his name more than a whisper. "Oh, Grant."

He lifted her onto the bed, then sat next to her, keeping one hand linked with hers. "What is it, kid? What's wrong?"

"They took Betul."

Concern creased Grant's brow. "Who took Betul? The Sikh?"

"Sajah was going to get the papers. He was going to keep Betul safe, but it's too late. They should have come after me. They should have left Betul alone and come after me."

"Hey, slow down," Grant spoke calmly. "You're going way too fast for me here. What kind of papers was Sajah going to get?"

"He was going to adopt Betul and keep him safe from the Sikh, but I messed things up. I got in the way. Sajah would have gotten the papers already except I got in the way."

"I'm sure it didn't happen like that."

Erica pushed herself off the bed and went to the shelves where there were framed photographs of Betul. "He must be so—afraid. Look at him, he's only a little boy."

Grant joined her, standing close enough that he could feel her torment. God had led him to India and opened a few doors. But God had never told him it would be like this. He reached for a picture of Betul and Ellyn near the front of the shelf.

Yet Erica suddenly knocked his hand aside, knocked frames aside to reach one sitting in the back. When she withdrew it, all trace of color withdrew from her face.

"Erica?" He tried to take the picture from her, but she held on to it so tightly the frame cut into her hands. She was staring at the face of the man holding a younger Betul in his arms. And Grant didn't like it at all that she was so perfectly still. "Erica...breathe, kid."

She avoided his hands. Shock drove her from the room, but also purpose. "Sajah!"

Sajah was already on his way up the stairs. They met in the middle of the hall. The way Erica held out the picture—both hands, arms rigid—impaled him. He grabbed the frame. "It is Betul and Bashtar."

"Bashtar?"

"Yes. Bashtar!" Sajah did not welcome Grant's cautioning hand upon his arm and shrugged it aside. "Betul and Bashtar are friends. You knew he was Sikh, Erica. I told you he was Sikh. Bashtar has always been part of Betul's life. Betul trusts him."

Erica's perceptive gaze skidded to Grant.

That's when Sajah dropped the picture and gripped her arms, held her right in front of him. "If you are afraid of something, you tell me. *Me*, Erica."

"Afraid? No, Sajah." She shrugged loose from his hold. "Not afraid. Stunned, angry, deceived. Bashtar was one of the men who killed Pali."

"He was in London."

"I saw him, Sajah! He was the one who sent Betul away from the apartment. That's why Betul wasn't afraid. 'Because Bashtar has always been part of Betul's life. Because Betul trusts him.'"

Sajah's hands slipped down her arms.

"I saw him," she repeated. "Bashtar isn't protecting you from the extremists. He's leading them."

God had never told Grant this was coming. Not that he expected God to let him in on all the details, but this time it would have helped. On the other hand, he probably wouldn't have believed a twist like this unless it struck him between the eyes in thunderbolt form. Grant broke Sajah's long silence. "Excuse me, but if we could go get coffee, sit down and talk, that would be better than—"

"You will need an extension on your permit," Sajah said evenly.

His expression was even, too. Not only was the man intelligent and proud, but he had a good handle on the self-control issue. "I will make the necessary phone calls."

"Thanks."

"No, thank you." Erica set herself between the two of them. "You can't stay, Grant. The minute you step into the picture, you become a target, too."

"Yeah, a big target with moves they haven't seen before. Not to worry, kid."

"You can't do this!"

"Sure I can. I'm trained for it." Grant deliberately shifted his concentration to Sajah, trying to forget that Erica looked like she needed a big-brother hug. "Before we get into details, I'd like to know if you trust Bashtar?"

"Yes, I trust him."

"No!" Erica held herself so stiffly it seemed as if her body would break in two. "No, Sajah! You can't trust him!"

"With Betul," Sajah said firmly, "I will trust him."

They never did get coffee. In fact, they didn't make it a step closer to the stairs before the phone rang. Sajah moved first, rushing to Sambhal's room where he picked up the handset. "Namastey."

"Ah, Sajah. It is good you answered."

"Bashtar." Anger swept through Sajah. He heard when Erica and Grant came and switched his words from English to Hindi. "Where is he? What have you done with Betul?"

"Nothing," Bashtar replied coolly, using the same language. "Nothing yet. I am disappointed that you know, Sajah. What a pity I cannot even tell you the elaborate story I devised about the Sikh extremists taking Betul. A great pity."

"How long did you think you could go on lying to me?"

"As long as I wanted."

"But you didn't count on her, did you?"

"So," Bashtar's voice changed. "Erica is with you, and you still try to protect her from the truth. No, friend. I did not count on her. I planned to kill her along with Pali, but there was something sweet about her. It was difficult making sure she did not see my face while you were at the palace, but I did enjoy watching you fall in love with her."

"You are a fool!" Sajah's anger was quelled when Erica came closer. He continued to speak so she couldn't understand. "No matter where you're headed, you are to bring him back. Immediately. Do you understand?"

"Taking Betul is only a means to an end. You know what I want."

"Never."

There was a long silence. "You are the fool, Sajah. The woman is worth nothing. I will not give up until I have made the sacrifice I was asked to make."

"Asked by whom?"

"Ah, so you are still discovering the depths of my commitment."

"This is insane! Tell me where you have taken Betul."

"*I* have taken him nowhere."

"You are still here?"

"I am still here, but where is Betul? That is your dilemma, friend. Unless you, with all of your power, can stop time from ticking away, Betul slips through your fingers and Erica Tanner is still as good as dead. Do you really want Betul's blood mixed with hers?" The connection was severed.

Sajah swore fiercely and slammed the handset into its cradle, staring at it.

"Did he—hurt Betul?"

There was such uncertainty in Erica's voice that Sajah reacted by pulling her into his arms, cradling her head against his shoulder until she relaxed. Although he whispered that Betul was all right, he couldn't tell her how volatile the whole situation was. He had never heard that crazed quality in Bashtar's voice.

It would have been impossible to forget that Grant watched them. Sajah looked at the other man, noting how Stevens seemed unchanged, even now that he had seen the truth about his feelings for Erica. No display of jealousy, no anger, nothing other than that rock-steady gaze. Sajah was ready for the steps Grant took toward them.

"Bashtar expects you to comply?"

"Yes."

"It ties together, but neither action is logical unless he's got a separate main objective."

Erica drew back enough to look over her shoulder at Grant. "Would you just grow up, Stevens! I don't need you talking some stupid secret code. Bashtar wants to kill me."

"Erica."

"It's true. And he's not the only one. Tell him, Sajah. Tell him who ordered Bashtar to do this."

Sajah's hands slipped over hers where she was clutching the front of his tunic, but she tore away and reached for the phone, blindly pressing buttons, any button. He snatched the handset from her. "Go downstairs."

She stood still.

"Do it, Erica."

After one last devastated look, she did what he asked. Grant followed her.

Each number he pressed added to the black anger swelling inside his heart. Even when the call was completed, Sajah was forced to wait for a servant to awaken his mother. He had grave misgivings about calling her, yet part of him needed to know for sure—one way or the other.

Finally, Loralai's voice came across the line. "Sajah! What in the world made you call me this time of night?"

"It is Betul, Mother." Sajah heard her sharp intake of breath. "Bashtar has taken him."

"What do you mean? That's impossible!"

"Betul has not been harmed. Bashtar has said he will not hurt Betul as long as he gets Erica."

"Do it!"

So quickly, so painfully, Sajah had his answer. He sank onto the bed, running a hand over his face. His own mother. "You were the one to give Bashtar orders to kill her?"

"Yes! And you will let Bashtar finish the job."

"Did you also ask him to kill Pali?"

"She overheard me talking to Bashtar. She knew the things I had done."

"That's why she took Betul to Portland. She was frightened of what you would do to him."

"I would never harm Betul!"

"Not physically, Mother. Mentally, emotionally." Sajah fought the anger into submission. "Is there a will, Mother?"

"I refuse to tell you. You do not appreciate the cleverness of everything I have done."

"Cleverness? No, Mother. Erica is right. This is insanity!"

"I did what I had to do. I know what's best for us."

"You do not know!" Revulsion seared through him, loosing a dozen lesser wrongdoings free from the tomb in which he had tried to bury them. "You may think Bashtar is playing along with your game, Mother, but he is the clever one. He's using you to justify harming me. That's all he's ever wanted."

"No, Sajah. Bashtar does what I tell him to do."

"Exactly. Then he weaves it into his plot to destroy me. You were his pawn, Mother. Not the other way around." He hung up on her.

Sane or insane? Vindictive or reckless? Cunning or terrified? Will or no will? The questions pursued Sajah all the way to the top of the staircase. Then vanished.

It was the sight of Grant Stevens praying with Erica that scattered all other thoughts. He was praying with her, sharing her faith, loving her in a way that shook Sajah to the core of his being.

The sound of his footsteps drew the two apart, but neither of them rose from the sofa. Erica's expression was pensive, strained with pain. Grant's was unreadable. Sajah continued down the stairs, then went directly to the kitchen.

One A.M. No wonder he was tired. He barely had the bottle of aspirin in his hand before Erica was behind him. "What happened?"

Sajah turned on the tap and filled a glass with cool water.

"Did she ask Bashtar to kill me?"

"Yes." He emptied two of the white pills into the palm of his hand, finding it impossible to prevent the way events locked together in his mind. His mother's plans were only the springboard to Bashtar's deception. A terrorist attack for every personal attack against his family, a national distraction for every personal distraction. Bashtar was right; he could have gone on lying a long time before the pieces of the puzzle began fitting together. Bashtar had been the one to frighten Erica at the palace. In fact, he had set up the entire emergency system as a giant ruse to make it seem like he was doing his job.

Sajah slammed the pill bottle onto the counter. "Here, take these."

Erica shook her head. "Grant already made me take some."

The idea that Stevens could know her unspoken needs so easily made Sajah angry all over again. "Then go to bed."

"Sajah."

"Do what I say and do it now."

"I'm not some servant you can order around!"

"And I am not someone you can disobey!"

"Excuse me," Grant spoke from the doorway, drawing their undivided attention. "I think neither one of you needs to be yelling right now." He pushed free from the frame and moved farther into the room, both hands sunk deep into the pockets of his jeans. "It won't help get Joey back."

Sajah turned to dump the aspirin and water into the sink. As had happened upstairs, the moment Sajah looked into Grant's unwavering gaze, he felt torn by an emotion he had seldom encountered before—regret. Grant Stevens was disciplined, filled with integrity, and driven by a faith stronger than any Sajah had ever seen.

In his silence, Erica started asking the painful questions. "Where is Betul? Did Bashtar tell you?"

"No. He will hide Betul until he gets what he wants."

Grant spoke again. "Hide as in make you figure it out or as in cover his tracks?"

Sajah rummaged through the cupboards now, searching for coffee. "You think he wants me distracted?"

"That's pretty much a given, but I was thinking more along the lines of using his shrewdness to outsmart you, if possible."

"It is entirely possible. He's done it for the past five years." No sooner did he turn around with the can of coffee, then Erica was taking it from his hands. "I'll make the coffee."

"You don't know how."

"I *do* know how." He took the tin from her. "I may be a prince, but you assume too much into the title and not enough into the man." He turned away, but he didn't suddenly become deaf.

"I assume? You were the one just ordering me to leave your presence. Excuse me for finding it difficult to see a heart beneath the royal attitude!"

"My attitude is just as strained at the moment as yours. I am very human, Erica."

"From out of the abundance of the heart the mouth speaks."

"You are being like Ellyn again."

"Good! Ellyn obviously had more of an effect on you than I have. Get your hands off me, Grant!" She shrugged his hands away once but not the second time. Sajah watched the man grab Erica from behind, his arm immobilizing both of hers. Then Grant literally swept her off her feet, a move that left her suspended above the floor, not above the anger. "Put me down this instant!"

"Say pretty please."

"You're hurting me."

"Liar."

No, she was serious. Sajah saw the pain in her eyes and realized the bullet wound was directly under Grant's iron grip. "Let her go, Stevens."

Grant set her down. Erica couldn't get away fast enough. Every single one of her steps was purposeful. "Hey, kid. I was just trying to lighten things up a little."

"Erica." Sajah waited for her to turn around. She didn't. "Where are you going?"

"Outside."

"You can't."

"But I will," she threw over her shoulder. "Maybe Bashtar's bullet will find its mark this time!"

Sajah swore fiercely and started after her. He didn't get more than two steps before Grant got in his way.

"What does she mean by that?"

"Earlier tonight Erica was injured when one of Bashtar's men tried to shoot her."

"One of Bashtar's men? Not Bashtar?"

"Bashtar would not have missed."

"Stay here and listen for the phone." Grant was already hurrying from the room. Seconds later, Sajah heard the front door slam.

It was darker now. Warm and breezy. There! Grant missed a few steps on the way down. "Slow down, kid."

She kept walking as if demons chased her. "If you can't keep up, go back."

"No deal." He finally caught up with her. "Where are we going?"

"To the road and back—a hundred times."

One of Grant's eyebrows rose in amusement. "Sounds like you're confused about which Stevens you're talking to. That's my dad's thing, not mine."

Mention of his father brought Erica to an abrupt standstill. "How is he?"

Now that's what he had been waiting to hear, some of her old tenderness, her old compassion. Grant shuffled one tennis shoe through the dirt. "The last time I called, he was giving the hospital a run for its money. To hear him talk, you'd think there was a revival going on. He must have converted half the patients on his floor by now." Erica wouldn't hold his gaze, a habit from her teenage years. "Don't worry about him. It was touch and go for a while, but he always lands on his feet."

"But it's still my fault that he was hurt."

"Says who? You're one of the victims too, Erica. Or have you set that aside in order to play the martyr role?"

She started walking again in the direction of the gate, faster than before. That is, until Grant reached out and set a hand on her elbow.

Then she had to keep his pace—a slow, aggravating stroll. All the while, Grant remained alert to every movement, every sound. "Speaking of martyrdom, stay close, okay? Sajah told me what happened earlier tonight."

She looked up at the sky, down at the ground, anywhere but at him.

"I guess that got lost somewhere with all the other stuff you had to tell me, huh? The Portland scene, Loralai, the village. There wouldn't be anything else you didn't have time to say, would there?"

"Sajah asked me to marry him, Grant."

His heart screamed no, but he couldn't let her hear it so he answered, "That's interesting." It got more interesting. Erica had a list of reasons for Sajah's proposal, all of which were moot points now that the truth was out about Bashtar. "Let's just take this one step at a time, kid. The thing about you being Sajah's wife is way on the back burner." Which should give God plenty of time to stir some common sense into her boiling emotions. "Tell me what you're thinking about Bashtar."

"He's evil."

"Come on, you can do better than that."

"He's unpredictable, underhanded, vile, ugly, loathsome."

"Ugly, too? I admit he's not in the same category as Prince Charming Ajari but ugly?"

"Are you jealous of Sajah?"

"Naw, big brothers don't get jealous. If you weren't my kid sister, now then I might be jealous. Hey, are you crying?" He looked down at her, wanting to see past the shadows that hid her expressions from him. Maybe he was wrong about the martyr thing. The way she bowed her head spoke its own troubled answer. "Things will work out, Erica. Just hang in there, okay?"

She shrugged her shoulders.

"Right now, you're tired and scared."

"Is this the 'things will look better in the morning' speech?"

Obviously a bad idea. Grant's hand closed over her arm, keeping her there. "We'll cover this in prayer, okay?" She released his hold, gingerly. The action was enough to make Grant capture her hand and pull back the sleeve of the sweater. Against such darkness, the white bandage somehow looked worse, and remembering how he had manhandled her back in the kitchen was worse yet. "Sorry if I hurt you before. Is it very bad?" She murmured some answer, but it got lost in the tears that thickened her voice. Time for the big brother hug. "I've missed you, kid."

"I'm sorry. This is such a mess."

Okay, it was a mess. With Betul's life on the line, he had to be brutally honest. Grant turned Erica back to the house, but it didn't seem like she was in a hurry to get there.

A bank of clouds moved in front of the mountaintop, hiding what little moonlight there had been. He automatically moved closer to Erica. If Bashtar wanted her dead, this would be a perfect opportunity. Dark, no barriers. All it would take is a nightscope and a high-powered rifle.

"Why did you come here?"

Grant smiled because Erica's tone was both hesitant and defensive. A familiar combination. "Think of me as your guardian angel."

"I don't need one."

"Huh." He knew her better than that. They were at the verandah again. Erica went first, then she suddenly stopped and turned around. Now that she was two steps higher, they were on the same level. Porch light touched his face, while hers was still hidden in shadow. He reached out to take her hand. "You want to know why I really came? I came because after I read Ezekiel 6:7, God didn't give me a choice. Something big is happening here, kid. Something real big."

❧ Sixteen ❧

Dawn was still traveling toward the horizon. From where Grant stood at the kitchen window, he guessed the mountains had another hour or so of sleep before it was time for them to roll out the red-gold-purple carpet in honor of morning. Altogether, it had been—would be—a very long wait.

He listened intently but heard no movement from the other room. Necessity, more than anything, pulled him forward until he stood in the doorway. "Sajah?" The other man looked up briefly, then looked toward the sofa.

Erica was finally asleep. They could talk now. Sajah rose, flexing against the stiffness in his body after so many hours of sitting at the desk. There had been phone calls to dozens of places around the country, trying to stay ahead of Bashtar's men before they could hide Betul.

Grant had come to respect the way Sajah operated under pressure. Because of Erica's presence throughout the night, some significant things had been left unsaid between them. Now it was time to change that.

Once Sajah was in the kitchen, Grant handed him a cup of very strong coffee. They sat opposite each other at the table. He came straight to the point. An envelope was extracted from the inside pocket of his jacket and slid across the width of the table. "You'll want to see this."

Sajah took it, staring at the handwriting. "Pali?"

"I don't know. Since it had your name on the front, I didn't open it."

"Where did you get it?"

"It was left in the room where Pali hid out while I went after the money at the airport." Grant watched Sajah tear open the seal. "Pali told Dad there was a will with the money, but apparently not because there was only money in the bag. It took me a while to find this."

Sajah was unfolding a thickness of papers, reading, scowling.

"Is it the will?"

"No."

"Is there a will? Sajah—"

"Pali destroyed the will."

"What?" Grant sat straighter in his chair, catching the top paper when Sajah sailed it in his direction. "This is written in Hindi."

"You do not trust me to tell you what it says?"

"No, I'm just surprised. What are the other papers?"

Sajah also sailed those toward him, one at a time. "A copy of the article written by the reporter. An account of the conversation she overheard between Bashtar and my mother. And this." He held the final paper in both hands with enough tension that Grant feared the page would tear in two. "This is a letter from my brother."

Written in Hindi. "Do you want to tell me what it says?" Grant saw a definite darkening in the other man's eyes. "Okay, do you want to tell me why Pali destroyed the will?"

"Neither of the issues is important unless we get Betul back."

True. And Sajah didn't quite trust him yet. Grant set out to change that; first by dropping the questions, second by picking up some of the burden over Betul. "No holds barred, Sajah. Does Bashtar really expect you to deliver Erica into his hands?"

"Yes."

Grant leaned forward, arms on the table, waiting.

The explanation came, full force. "These hours since taking Betul, since the phone call, Bashtar expected me to spend in prayer. He expected me to reach the same conclusion my mother reached—that attempting to deny the Shrimatee this satisfaction would be considered a great demerit on my part."

"Demerit?"

"Demerits hinder the quality of *samsara*...rebirth."

"So, if you don't let Bashtar have Erica, you'll be reborn as what? A worm? A rock?" Grant didn't feel like backing down from the fierce scowl on Prince Ajari's brow. "Before you have me thrown out of India for sacrilege, at least consider that all these little pieces of information let me know how desperate Bashtar thinks you are. The more desperate and distracted, the less likely you are to come up with a viable solution. So, back to the thing about demerits, Bashtar knows you don't have a system of grace in Hinduism, no chance of redemption if you mess up."

"There is *moksha*." Sajah's words were tight, razor sharp. "Moksha is release from the process of rebirth through the renunciation of all worldly desires."

"He's figuring, either way, you lose Erica. The proverbial dilemma of being caught between a rock and a hard place."

The way Sajah stood and went after more coffee proved he wasn't about to let himself get caught in anything, least of all a discussion on religious viewpoints.

Grant twirled his half-empty cup, watching the black liquid gyrate from side to side. "Do you think Bashtar was counting on me being around for this?"

"No."

"Wrong answer." He glanced over his shoulder and saw another scowl. "Somebody had to open a door somewhere for me to get in.

Bashtar could do that, drop your name a few times and presto—
Grant Stevens is suddenly cleared for takeoff."

"Another distraction."

"Which is leading me to wonder why so many deliberate distractions."

Sajah came back to the table and began gathering the papers,
stuffing them into the envelope, every gesture rigid with concentration. "Deliberately focusing me on all of India makes it harder for me
to see one little part of India. Perhaps this little part of India."

"That's what I'm thinking." The cup was pushed away. Grant sat
back in his chair, his manner as intense as Sajah's. "I'm also thinking
Bashtar wasn't here shooting at Erica because he had to be the one to
take Betul. Last night you said Betul and Bashtar are friends. You also
said Betul was excited about being at the festival. Bashtar must have
enticed him away with something more exciting. Some kind of bait."

"Horses. Bashtar knows Betul loves horses."

"If he took Betul away from the festival on horseback, they
couldn't have gone far from Darjeeling."

"If he simply promised Betul a midnight ride, perhaps a ride
with myself and Bashtar, there would be no reason to ride horseback
from Darjeeling to here." Sajah's hand closed in a fist around the
envelope. "Did you bring a gun?"

Grant stood now too, lowering his voice like Sajah had done so
as not to awaken Erica. "Yes. You know where they are?"

"Bashtar used a strange phrase during our phone conversation.
Instead of saying he wouldn't stop until he had finished the job my
mother told him to do, he said he wouldn't stop until he had made
the sacrifice. He has taken Betul to Chota Chand."

They probably would have tried to ride off without telling her, but
Erica had awakened in time to hear the tail end of their little kitchen

conference about Bashtar. The instant they stepped into the living room, she knew she had a fight on her hands, but she refused to budge from blocking their path to the door. "I'm going with you."

"No." Sajah moved to get around her. She countered. "You are wasting my time, Erica. If I must force you to stay, I will do so."

"That goes for me too, kid."

She didn't bother looking at Grant. He undoubtedly wore a man-of-steel expression similar to Sajah's. Superman in duplicate. Not what she needed. "If Bashtar sees you ride up without me—"

"Bashtar will not see us ride up."

"Oh, a blind-sided, two-man, hero-type attack? Let me see, that puts Betul somewhere in the middle of things, right next to the crazy man." She wanted her voice to sound sarcastic. It came out closer to spastic, especially when Sajah went to the desk phone. He was dialing and shoving papers into his briefcase all at the same time, proof positive of his determination. Well, she was determined, too. "I won't stay behind!"

"Erica." Grant stepped in front of her. "You aren't helping by throwing this tantrum."

"This isn't a tantrum!"

"Okay, wrong word. It's panic."

"It's love. I want Betul back, Grant. I just want him back." She looked beyond him to Sajah, until Grant caught her chin in his fingers and forced her to pay attention.

"If you want him back, you will calmly and quietly let us walk out that door. Sajah doesn't need a scene from you right now. Neither do I. The situation can be resolved without violence if Sajah has a chance to sit down and talk to Bashtar. A season of prayer on your part wouldn't hurt either."

Grant had no idea how much it would hurt if they left her behind. Besides, a season of prayer couldn't make someone like Bashtar disappear.

"Ved?"

He turned from the porch railing to face her. By Sajah's orders, he would watch every move she made. The role did not fit him. Dressed in his simple caretaker's clothing, he appeared as unsettled as she felt.

"How long will it take them to get there?"

"Thirty minutes or more because of the darkness. Even when daylight comes, they must travel with caution. If you will please change now, I wish to get back to Ahwa and the children."

"Of course. Five minutes."

"Erica? Bring your sister's Bible, please."

"Why?"

"Because there is something I must show you."

It didn't take her the full five minutes to pull on jeans and a clean white T-shirt. She bypassed Ellyn's red sweater in favor of Sajah's leather jacket, taken from the back of his desk chair. She should have apologized before he left. She should have let him know that she trusted him.

The sound of footsteps pacing along the porch reminded her to hurry. As soon as she opened the door the man turned toward her, a dull shadow in the predawn murkiness. She knew for certain by the way he held himself that it was not Ved. Bashtar's step forward threw her heartbeat out of rhythm.

"Good morning, Miss Tanner."

"What are you doing here?"

"Think a moment. I'm sure the answer will come into your pretty head. By the way, Ved is with Ahwa and the children."

"And Betul?"

"Yes, Betul is also there."

"I don't believe you."

"I thought that might be the case." He gestured toward the

Pabnas' distant hut. The door opened. Betul appeared in the door-way, looking small beside one of Bashtar's men. "Wave to him, Miss Tanner. Pretend you are happy to see him."

She waved.

"Good. You are learning." Another gesture on Bashtar's part sent Betul and the man back indoors. "He has been told that I will give you a riding lesson as a surprise for Sajah. You see, I am not such an evil man after all. I would not want anything to alarm the boy." When she made no comment, he smiled at her. "I believe you have lost your sense of humor, Miss Tanner. No doubt it is the same with Sajah. I am anxious to see his face when he rides up to Chota Chand and finds you there. He did not plan on me doubling back like this."

"He didn't plan on you doing a lot of things."

"A fatal mistake."

She couldn't help but take a step back when Bashtar took another step closer. She ran out of room before he did. He contin-ued until she was pinned against the door, Ellyn's Bible the only shield between them.

"Ahh." He took it from her. "God's Word is quick, powerful, sharper than any two-edged sword. Do I remember the verse cor-rectly?"

"Yes."

"There were many others, but I was particularly amused by that one. Why do you stare at me so? Is it the turban I wear? Perhaps you wish to know if beneath the turban I am shorter than Sajah?"

She remained silent.

"The answer is yes, Miss Tanner. Perhaps it is my beard." He stroked the scraggly, dark length of it. "Or my Sikh clothes. The short pants are traditional. The tunic and long vest are traditional. Of course, I do not dress like Sajah and this is the reason you stare at me."

"I was looking at your eyes," she admitted. "Your eyes show me what is in your soul—hatred."

"Hatred? An insignificant word compared to what I am feeling." He dropped the Bible onto the porch floor, disregarding how Erica cringed. "Come." The touch of his hand around her upper arm reminded her of Loralai's claws.

He took her around the side of the main house to where his horse was waiting. Because she hesitated, he forced her to mount the black animal. "Your cooperation would be appreciated, Miss Tanner."

"I'm sure it would."

Bashtar's raspy voice, the touch of his arms around her, his male sweat—all these impressions combined to chill her through to the bone. He knew that. "You are not as brave as you pretend to be. A pity. The bravest among us make the perfect sacrifices."

Taking the most direct path to the Chand would have been too risky. Instead, Sajah took an unmarked route through rougher terrain, and Grant made his way through the forest, parallel to the trail Sajah said led to a view of Mount Everest.

For Grant those forty minutes passed like ten years. He had seen the expression on Ved Pabna's face when Sajah told him what was going on. Anxiety of that magnitude wasn't something easy to hide. In fact, Ved was probably pacing back and forth on the porch about now, wishing he could do more than stand guard over Erica.

The white horse moved restlessly, too. Grant stopped at the edge of the clearing where there was enough daybreak to peer at the crude map Sajah had drawn for him. Another mile or so north. He stuffed the paper into the pocket of his jeans. He should have changed; blue didn't exactly blend in with the surroundings. He should have made Sajah change, too. White was worse.

Maybe it didn't matter. He had yet to see any sign that Bashtar had posted a perimeter of watchmen. If there were men watching him now, they had been given orders not to shoot. Grant urged the mare forward into the open space. No consequences to his boldness. He frowned and moved on. One step at a time.

The trees were so thick, it was impossible to see. Grant felt impatient, then realized the foliage was hiding him from Bashtar. He moved a few feet, crouching behind another tree. There, that was better. He scanned Chota Chand again.

Sajah had described it to the last detail, inside and out, just in case. Something twisted in Grant's stomach to see the rock wall tumbled in a broken heap upon the ground. He straightened behind the tree trunk, drawing in a deep breath. Sajah had fifteen minutes yet. Fifteen minutes of waiting.

Grant turned himself a little, hoping to catch some sight of Betul. Nothing had changed since his arrival. Two horses—one for Bashtar, one for the guy standing in readiness on the front steps—there were packs by the steps. Empty, padded packs. He frowned. Then searched the temple stones again with greater care.

There. And there.

His heart began to pound faster as he noted every hiding place around the lower rim. Bashtar was not very subtle. He was also no fool. Grant brought his gaze farther along the rim, seeking and finding the illusive supporting stones. Every single one was connected to Bashtar's network of detonators.

"Come out, Mr. Stevens."

He flattened himself against the tree, feeling the bark dig into his back.

"Perhaps Miss Tanner will help you decide."

No. Grant ground his teeth together until they ached. No! He swung around the tree so fast, it surprised the man standing next to

Bashtar into firing, but Grant was already going into a roll. The bullet splintered into the tree behind him. When he came up, he was on his feet, gun held firmly in both hands, eyes filled with anger.

Bashtar did not react, except maybe to tighten his hold around Erica's neck. "Let me make this easier for you to understand, Mr. Stevens. Now that you have spurred Sajah into action, I find you no longer have a purpose here. I wish you to leave before Sajah's arrival. Miss Tanner has promised to be very cooperative."

Cooperative? Grant began moving forward. Cooperative didn't include being slapped around. Her jaw was already swollen. Her wrists had been tied together. She was trying desperately to tell him things with her eyes. He continued moving toward the Chand.

Bashtar took a step backward, dragging Erica with him. "My man has been waiting to take you back to the plantation. Heed a word of advice—stay there. You will be released at the appropriate time, after it is too late to stop me. Should you try to leave the plantation, Betul and the others will be forced to watch your execution."

After a moment, Grant slowly lowered the gun. "Tell me something, Bashtar. What will you gain by carrying out this plan of yours?"

"It is not what I will gain, Mr. Stevens. It is what Sajah will lose." Bashtar said more, but it was in his own language—orders to the man who went to get one of the horses.

Things seemed to happen quickly then. The man took Grant's gun, gave him a push toward the path, adjusted his hold on the reins, and followed. On foot. Big mistake. It was easy to overpower a man who made careless mistakes. All he had to do was bide his time until they were out of Bashtar's range...

When Bashtar threw her against the marble pyre, there was pain. Erica struggled to push herself away from the charred stone slab.

"You do not cry out, Miss Tanner."

Her eyes raised to meet Bashtar's. She did not lift herself off the floor. "Why should I? Don't you already have satisfaction in knowing you inflict pain?"

"Of course, but never enough satisfaction, Miss Tanner. Never enough pain." Bashtar reached for the can near her feet and began emptying fuel along the half circle of cloth he had set out. "You do not ask why I destroy Chota Chand. Are you not curious?"

"No." She wasn't curious. She found it difficult to stand when he eyed her so fiercely.

Bashtar let the can clatter to the floor; the sound echoing on the same discordant tone as his words. "Loralai ordered that I take care of you. Not only you, but your ghost. All of the ghosts. She delighted in the idea of scattering her tormentors to the heavens, sending them beyond the moon so to speak. I delight in the violence of it all."

He was obviously frustrated that she said nothing.

A knife was ripped from the sheath at his waist. "This is where it all started, you know—the place where Ajari men first received their warrior strength, their fierce devotion, their passion for life, their desire for beautiful women." He took up position behind her and pressed the point into the tender flesh of her neck. "Sajah will come soon, Miss Tanner. Let us hasten his arrival. Let us watch how the flames turn as blue as your eyes." With the flick of his wrist, Bashtar sent a burning lighter toward the fuel.

Heat instantly filled the chamber. Erica tried to hold her breath. She held her breath so long it was impossible to distinguish the pounding of her own pulse from the pounding of horse's hooves, racing closer. Beyond the wild tangle of waist-high flames, she saw Sajah on Parvati.

Seconds later, he stood at the top of the stairs. "Let her go!"

Bashtar's laugh was hollow, dead.

Sajah thrust his way inside, stopping only when he saw the knife pressed to her throat. "You will let her go now!"

"Or what, Sajah?" Bashtar used his free hand to jerk Erica to her feet. Then he pulled a remote device from his pocket. "Once I press this button, you have twenty seconds before the temple blows. Save yourself, Sajah. Or choose to come for her, and you both die." He pressed the button.

Bashtar turned. So did Erica. Actually, she threw herself at him. Her ropes became entangled with his arm. His momentum tumbled them through an opening in the columns and over the edge. Seconds ticking. Bashtar righted himself.

Seconds.

He dragged Erica to her knees, to her feet. The knife flashed toward her. Seconds. Sajah's voice came from behind them, yet Erica caught a movement nearby. Grant! She couldn't draw breath before his fist smashed into Bashtar's face. Seconds. The knife sliced downward into Grant's shoulder. Bashtar whirled, his foot driving Grant head first into the blocks. Erica did not have time to scream. Bashtar's powerful arm scooped her off her feet. He ran. All the seconds ended.

The explosion drove them to the ground. Every bone and muscle in her body felt the impact. It seemed to go on forever—the noise, the debris, fire flying through the air. She thought of Grant and Sajah. She thought of dying herself.

But Bashtar was dragging her upright again, making her run.

Bashtar took her to the edge of the cliff. The same place where Betul had so excitedly shown her Mount Everest, where Sajah had kissed her...where she had told God she would trust Him. Erica looked up into Bashtar's eyes as she drew air into her aching lungs.

"It is time to say good-bye to this world, Miss Tanner."

"That doesn't scare me."

He set one hand on her face, forcing her eyes to stay locked with his. "It should."

She tore herself from his hold, slipping on the dew-covered grass. If her hands had not been tied, she would have slapped his face. She had nothing to lose now. He was going to kill her.

As if he read her mind, Bashtar held his knife before her face. The dried blood on its sharp edge, Grant's blood, sickened her to the point of wishing it was over with already. "Do you want me to kill you before I throw you over or shall you die at the bottom?" His words made her heart stop. "Come, Miss Tanner? Surely you must have a preference."

"Bashtar!"

They turned and saw Sajah standing at the edge of the clearing. Erica instinctively moved toward him, but Bashtar caught her with one strong arm around her neck.

Sajah was breathing hard from chasing after them. His eyes swiftly scanned her face, then he looked at Bashtar. "Let her go."

"You arrived a moment too soon, my friend. Your troubles would be over by now if you had not interrupted me." Bashtar took a step backward, holding the knife threateningly close to Erica's bare throat.

Sajah took several measured steps closer. "Whatever my mother told you to do to Erica is no longer your concern. She is to be my wife. You would be as good as killing me if you harmed her now." As he spoke, Sajah carefully moved to within arm's reach of them.

"Are you offering yourself in her place?"

Sajah's eyes narrowed considerably. "We have known one another since we were boys."

"Yes, and you have always won over me—the money, the land, the women, the connections and respect.... It is my turn now. The gods have decided who shall be greater."

"And that is why you have increased the terrorist attacks? That is why you have abused our friendship by using my planes, my money, my name to accomplish your subversive goals?"

"Yes." Bashtar's grin was wicked. "It took you a long time to figure things out. We are stronger than you thought, yes? *I* am stronger than you thought."

"No, you are weaker. A stronger man, a stronger friend would have stood face-to-face with me. No lies." There was deadly conviction in Sajah's words. "Let her go, Bashtar. You have what you want. I will take her place."

"No!" Despite Erica's desperate plea, the knife was lowered. "Sajah!"

Afterward, Sajah would wonder how something that happened so quickly could be so firmly etched in his mind. At the same moment that Bashtar braced himself to shove Erica away, his feet slipped and he began falling over the cliff. Instinctively, the arm Bashtar held around Erica tightened, but Sajah was just as quick in reacting to stop their fall.

His hand tightened around Erica's arm pulling her toward him. While they fell to the ground, Bashtar desperately clutched for anything to stop his own fall. Sajah grabbed for his hand, catching it just before it was too late.

Thus began the struggle to stop Bashtar from falling and himself from being pulled over the edge. Behind him, Erica wrapped her tied hands around one of his ankles. She could do nothing else. The muscles in his body tightened. With his free hand, Sajah groped for a more secure hold on the ground. "Pull—up, Bashtar!"

"You will die with me."

"No! Pull up!" Their two hands began to slip away from one

another. He wouldn't let go. He wouldn't! Sajah stretched farther. Bashtar's fingernails raked his wrist, his palm.

"The gods—curse you!"

"No!" Sajah felt blood sliding between their fingers. He couldn't hold on. A moan came from deep inside of him as Bashtar slipped away.

Time passed, seconds seeming like hours. Sajah could not tear his gaze from the hidden bottom of the valley, not even when he heard Erica struggle to her feet.

"Sajah?"

He stood, too, but did not look at her.

"Sajah, help me!"

Bashtar was dead.

"Help me!"

The plea carried enough panic to bring his eyes to her face. She was trying to free her hands. Sajah remained immobile.

"Sajah, please!" A sob choked her words. The first tears slipped down her cheeks. "Please!"

He picked up Bashtar's knife, staring at the dried blood, but Erica wasn't cut.... With one swift upward slice, the ropes fell from her hands. She ran then, toward Chota Chand.

It looked like the end of the world. Fire still burned in the center. Huge stones were piled upon one another. Erica's heart pounded erratically when she reached the place where she knew Grant should be. *Dear Lord, let him be alive! Let him be alive!* She fell to her knees.

The stones cut into her bare hands, but she kept digging. *Lord, let him be alive! Dear Lord!* Prayers poured from her as fast as she moved the smaller stones. Finally, she found a shoe. *Oh, Grant!* Her tears were brushed away, but more came. The stones were so heavy.

Dear Lord, help me! Blood from her palms dripped onto the white stone. Let him be alive! She pulled again, but the stone didn't move. *Help me, Lord!*

Erica cried out when two strong hands came around her arms, drawing her back.

"Let it be, Erica."

She twisted in Sajah's arms. "Help me. Help me move the stones."

"No."

"Sajah!"

"He is dead, Erica."

She shrank from the words, from the look in Sajah's eyes. "No...no, he can't be! You have to try! You have to!"

He released her so abruptly, she almost fell. "Grant Stevens is dead."

No! She wouldn't give up. Erica swung back, pulling at the bloodstained stone, yet a movement from the trees arrested her actions. It was Parvati emerging from the smoke. She was alone, all the other horses had left, but Parvati returned. Erica knew why. "Sajah, use her to move the stones. Please. Grant isn't dead."

"Go to the other side of the clearing."

"God sent you help!"

"Go!" In his next breath, he whistled for the horse to come.

By the time Ved arrived from the plantation, Sajah had used Parvati to move two of the larger stones. Erica watched the men hook Ved's horse to the same rope. Her mind and body were numb. Bashtar was dead. Bashtar's men had scattered—for now.

She wrapped both arms around herself but couldn't stop the shaking. She reminded herself that Betul was safe. That didn't stop the shaking either. Both white horses strained against the rope now, pulling, pulling with all their strength. Sajah urged the animals forward, pulling with all his strength on the reins. Stone ground against stone. Parvati's scream echoed the one in her head. Still, Sajah would not let the horses rest.

When she saw Ved run forward to the jumble of stones, Erica thought she would never breathe again. Sajah moved too, pushing past Ved. Finally, she saw Sajah stand. He looked her way, then he was walking toward her. She still couldn't move. He reached her. She looked past him to see Ved kneel next to the place where they had found Grant's body.

❧ SEVENTEEN ❧

"SRI AJARI?"

Sajah looked up, feeling impatience for yet another interruption when he had so much work to finish. His secretary did not move past the door she had opened. "What is it?"

"Security called. There is a Mr. Stevens asking to see you."

"Let him through." Though his tone sounded normal enough, Sajah felt a rush of emotions—most of them uncomfortable. He went to stand by the wide window behind his desk. Blue sky stretched itself over New Delhi. People, hundreds of them, thronged the streets below with hopes of completing their errands before the shops closed.

In the week since his return, it had been easy to distance himself from the rest of his life—uncle, son, prince. Now, those thoughts pulled all else aside, stretching his conscience from northeast to southwest. He fought to center himself again. If Grant Stevens was in New Delhi, that meant he had proven the Calcutta doctors wrong. It meant he had made a miraculous recovery to go with his miraculous escape from death.

Sajah could clearly imagine the ruined Chota Chand. Its image had burned in his heart for days now, beside the words Sambhal had written in the letter. He kept waiting for both to be consumed and give him some peace. Yet the fire did not consume. It only burned.

"Well."

He glanced over his shoulder first...then turned.

The action spoke volumes to Grant. It said Sajah Ajari wasn't ready for this visit. He crossed the room anyway, limping a little, comparing his jeans and white polo shirt to Sajah's expensive black suit and tie, noting details about the well-appointed office. "Quite the guards you have here, Sajah."

One eyebrow rose.

Obviously no red carpet today. Grant lowered himself into the leather upholstered chair in front of the desk. There. That was better. His leg still hurt sometimes. "I hear you're resigning." Not that it was public knowledge yet.

"Who told you?"

"Doesn't matter." Grant massaged a sore spot below the bandage on his shoulder. "I wanted to say thanks for everything you've done—the helicopter, hospital, jet. Then there's all that stuff you did for my dad back in Portland." He paused, deliberately, but it wasn't easy to rattle a man like Sajah Ajari. "My plane leaves in forty minutes." No response. No visible response anyway. The Rajah did, however, face the window again. "I talked to Dad last night. He told me what you did, about your mother, I mean."

They both knew Loralai's confession, the one Sajah had forced her to make, was merely an act of survival. If Sajah had chosen the way of silence, he could never have lived with the guilt. Age and ill health prevented Loralai from standing trial for her part in the deceptive activities Bashtar had pursued. Unlike Bashtar's men, who were lying low at the moment, Loralai Ajari would never serve prison time. Something told Grant her prison was self-made. The punishment—a lifetime lived beneath the Rajah's condemnation.

Quite abruptly, Sajah moved from the window and resumed his

seat. He even held Grant's steady gaze. Those few moments took on a new tension, and it had nothing to do with Loralai's part in Pali's murder.

Grant watched with curiosity as Sajah opened a drawer. When an envelope was held out for him to take, he did so. "What is it?"

Sajah leaned back again. "It's a reason for you to return to India."

Another long look passed between them before Grant actually read the letter. A frown formed. By the time he finished reading, he was well into a prayer for self-control.

"Will you come back?"

It was tempting. Too tempting. Grant started to replace the single sheet.

"I was going to mail this." Sajah held out another letter. "It's for your father."

"I suppose you created a job for him, too?"

Sajah rested both elbows on the arms of his chair and linked his hands together. "Erica thinks a great deal of you and your father."

"Which is why you're making sure we aren't her excuse to leave India." Grant threw his letter onto the desk, then threw himself to his feet. "Do you know what I think, Sajah? I think you don't know her at all, and that scares the life out of you! That's why you haven't told her about the letter Pali gave you or about the will being destroyed. Do you know how many times I've wanted to rip that little secret out of your gullet?" He should leave now. Right now, before he said something he would regret.

Sajah stood too but didn't move around the desk. "Stevens."

Grant stopped at the door.

"Where is Erica?"

That was the irony of it. Grant set his arms across his chest even though the gesture irritated his wound. "She was going to storm the U.S. Embassy and tell a wild story about how she'd been in the country for almost a month without a passport or visa." Though he watched Sajah's face carefully, the man was a master at hiding all emotion. "I talked her out of that. Actually, I bribed her with a wad of money. She's getting some clothes that fit her instead of wearing her dead sister's stuff. After that, she promised me she'd get her hair done, but I doubt if that will happen. She'll probably end up giving the money away to some little kids on the street."

Still the same controlled expression. Grant tried harder. "I can tell you're real worried, Sajah, but before I left her I made sure to point out the half dozen good guys you have tailing her every move. She accepted them because she knows the bad guys are still out there. She also accepted that you won't let Betul come home until the so-called 'adoption papers' are final. That one is breaking her heart."

Sajah said nothing.

Grant felt the muscles tensing across his shoulders. "I don't like it when her heart gets broken, Sajah. And I don't like it when she makes life-changing decisions and you sit around on your stupid pride! She asked me to close up her apartment in Portland. The hospital got a call. So did her insurance company. Her mail will be forwarded here. You see where this is going, don't you? Despite your silence, despite the fact you can't come to terms with whatever was in that letter, God is still working behind the scenes. Erica is staying because her heart keeps telling her it's the right thing to do, and that, Sajah, is called trust."

No reaction.

Grant shifted and released a sigh. "Trust is also the only reason I'm getting on that airplane." Now, he got a response. Sajah dropped his eyes to some papers on the desk. "If I didn't trust God and what I've seen in Erica all week, I'd be camped on your doorstep. As for you, if you can't trust Erica, trust what I just said because you're walking a fine line with me, and don't think I won't know what's going on back here. I've got my sources, too." He left without saying good-bye.

Shopping was a bore, or maybe her restlessness came from within, feeling as if every person who walked past her wanted to know why she carried so many packages. Because she had been kidnapped to India...because she liked spending Grant's money...because she thought shopping would make her forget that Grant was leaving. None of the excuses that swam through her thoughts could tell what was really going on in her heart.

She squeezed her way between a young man and an elderly couple. Anytime she wanted to, she could flag down Sajah's men and have them whisk her off to Assistant Secretary Ajari's office. Erica didn't want it to happen that way. She had a mind of her own, resources of her own. Most of all, she had a backbone and it was time to use it!

There had to be ice cream in a city this size, didn't there? She paused at a corner. Two men half a block ahead, one on either side of the street, two men picking up the rear. Yup, they were all in place. Had Sajah lived like this since being appointed to the Council? Or longer? Had his family's position always required this kind of security?

A crowd of people crossed the street with her. There was a grocer ahead. He didn't have ice cream, but the vegetables and fruit looked mouth watering. And chocolate! She hadn't tasted chocolate since being abducted from America.

Erica spent almost an hour in the grocer's company. When she left, it was with a very full, very heavy cloth bag. The sidewalk was not as crowded now. The shadows were longer as night descended on the city. One man in front. She turned her gaze. One man in back. That was all.

Perhaps the others had gone home to their families. Erica stood in front of the grocer's contemplating if it would be best to find her own way to Sajah or just succumb to the luxury of lifting her finger and having it happen. The men decided for her. They converged with lightning speed on the spot where she was standing.

"Miss Tanner. You will come with us now." One of them took her arm, the other took her packages. A third man waited in the car she hadn't noticed.

It was done so quickly, she didn't have time to wonder about it until they were zigzagging through traffic at a reckless pace. "Where are we going?"

The man behind the wheel looked at her via the rearview mirror. Neither of the other two seemed to have heard her question. Minutes later, they drew up to a tall building. Again, one of Sajah's men opened the door and the other took her arm. She had a fleeting impression of marble and dark wood, of silent halls, and a swift elevator. Then she was shut inside a darkened room with her bags.

Her first coherent thought was that they hadn't put her in a room but in an apartment. Her second thought was stronger— Sajah's men had to learn some manners!

Two minutes was all the time she needed to know for sure that it was Sajah's apartment. Though why he chose to live in such an impersonal space, she couldn't comprehend. Everything from artwork to furniture to the towels in his bathroom matched a theme—neutral. Sajah Ajari was *anything* but neutral.

Erica ate some of her chocolate bar. She spent the next hour alternately reveling in the other half, sitting by the low windows in the living room, and taking a shower. After the shower she dressed in some of her new clothes—a silky pantsuit the prettiest shade of blue lavender. The pants were loose, flowing. The top had long sleeves and was sculpted to her shape. She fastened a simple pair of silver earrings to her lobes. The touch of silver embroidery at the blouse's collar had inspired her to buy the earrings instead of cutting her hair.

Besides, she liked how the curls could be tucked behind her ears, how they framed her face, making it look a little softer, a little more carefree. *Silly girl.* She took the remembered admonition with her to the living room windows. Lights were still popping on here and there. Perhaps Sajah would come soon. She hoped so.

Making a meal for the two of them took up the next hour. Then she found herself at the windows again, with no real excuse against curling up next to the cool glass and waiting. Strange how her day alone had only made her more lonely.

Back in Portland, she had become used to spending time by herself. She had even enjoyed it. But this wasn't her apartment...and she hadn't known Sajah then. She hadn't experienced his gentleness or honor. She hadn't seen his dedication or felt the passion he could raise within her.

Admitting the facts was easier than examining them.

What was she thinking to let herself fall in love with Sajah Ajari? He was a prince. He was Hindu. God couldn't have designed this. Perhaps her feelings were more about ardor than love? It was entirely possible. One minute she wanted Sajah to kiss her, the next minute she wanted him to be reasonable. He exasperated her and excited her.

Silly girl.

Yes, she was being silly. Sajah hadn't so much as tried to speak with her for the past week. Maybe he was preparing to ship her back to Portland. A sigh escaped to fog the window. She drew a smiley face. Then erased it with one lonely swipe.

Betul would be asleep by now, snuggled up with Hopset in the Pabnas' hut. She missed him so much, missed seeing his smile, having his warm hand in hers. In her heart, she knew it was right for Sajah to keep her separated from Betul. It was logical that the Sikh would pick her as their first target, leaving Betul as the ultimate bargaining chip. Until the adoption was final, until Bashtar's men were found, the danger hadn't really lessened.

A shrill ring shattered the stillness. She froze. The phone rang again. Should she? It rang once more, then was quiet. Erica settled against the window, trying to count the lights in the next building. Most of them had gone out now.

Not even five minutes later, the front door suddenly opened. Erica's anticipation twisted into dread. The man silhouetted against the hallway light was not Sajah.

Somehow, she was able to press herself upright, but she didn't move any more than that. Her heart started to pound erratically. Her legs felt heavy. The man wore traditional Indian clothes. His beard was long. His turban white. His face was hidden in shadow...Bashtar. But it couldn't be! He was staring; she could feel his eyes on her. She could feel his power. *Not again. Dear Lord, not again.*

Light flooded the entrance hall, blinding her for a moment. Unfortunately, it did not reach where she was standing. Erica slid along the windows, backing herself with a solid wall and the nearest weapon at hand—a brass vase. "Leave me alone!"

He came closer. She threw the vase with all her strength. It was easily deflected by his upraised arm. *Silly girl.* There was no defense against Bashtar. A scream caught in her throat, making it impossible to breathe. He had come back to kill her, to end the madness he had begun at Darjeeling once and for all.

He smiled. Erica fumbled for the edge of the wall, just to ground herself against the swirl of dizziness. "You're—alive?"

"Yes. I have been for some time now." He was close enough to reach a hand to her throat. She twisted away, stumbling toward the only way of escape. He caught her with one hand, turned on a light switch with the other. "Miss Tanner, my name is Mahim. I am Bashtar's brother."

"Brother?" *Brother*... Yes, she could see the subtle differences now. This man was younger. Sajah's age. He was not as heavy. His eyes did not burn with hatred. "Bashtar's brother?"

"I am also a doctor who knows nurses sometimes make the worst patients. Will you agree to sitting down, if not lying down until the dizziness passes?"

"Dizziness?"

Again, he smiled, but his smile was charming. Mahim captured her hand and urged her forward to the stiff cream sofa. "Please stay there. Sajah will have my head if I let you faint."

The moment she closed her eyes, Mahim set two fingers on the pulse beating at her throat. She could feel for herself that it was still too fast, pounding out a frantic rhythm. Mahim's next action was to go to the kitchen and bring her a glass of cool water.

He didn't make it back before the front door opened a second time. Erica popped off the sofa too fast and stumbled toward Sajah. He had time to drop his briefcase and jacket before she fell into his arms.

"For goodness' sake, lay her down again, Sajah. Sit on her if you have to."

He didn't sit on her, but he did sit on the edge of the sofa. His expression was so fierce, she couldn't help but smile up at him. "I'm sorry," she whispered, for his ears only. He didn't like that either, because his frown became a scowl. A glass of water materialized above her head.

She and Sajah both looked toward Mahim.

"It's for drinking, Sajah," Mahim said, "not for pouring all over those beautiful blond curls. As for you, Miss Tanner, tell me you didn't eat so much sugar all at once." He opened his other hand to reveal the crumbled wrappers.

Heat rushed into her cheeks. "Not all at once. Well, nearly I suppose. But I hadn't eaten anything else all day and I was hungry."

"No wonder you are dizzy." Mahim tipped the glass enough to

make a drop fall on her nose. She sputtered false indignation. He laughed and left.

Although she reached up to wipe away the water, Sajah did it for her. An action that carried her straight back to feeling breathless.

"Did Mahim frighten you?"

She nodded, inching her way upright. "I thought he was Bashtar."

"Bashtar's body was found, Erica."

Oh. Then she was being a very silly girl. "You look tired."

"You look different." His gaze traveled the length of her pantsuit and back to her face. She didn't quite know what to do when he touched the silver earrings. "Did you have fun shopping?"

"No."

"Because you kept thinking about Grant leaving India?" Sajah handed her the glass of water. "Or because my men were watching you so closely?"

Erica stared at the accumulation of moisture on the glass. "Both...why did you leave Calcutta so suddenly?"

"I had duties here."

"It wasn't because you think Grant loves me?"

"I do not think he loves you, Erica. I *know* he loves you." Sajah rose with unwavering control—controlled anger. She knew from experience that it wasn't a good idea to face Sajah Ajari's anger unless you had both feet on the ground. Erica dispatched the water and her caution. Neither action escaped his attention.

"Grant is like an older brother, Sajah. I've explained that."

"But he is not your brother. There is nothing to keep his *affection* for you from becoming much more."

"Yes, there is." She paced to the other side of the room, a neutral corner in decor only. "I've known Grant my entire adult life. Wouldn't you think I'd realize by now if God had decided Grant and I were to be husband and wife?"

"Circumstances change, Erica."

"That's right. You didn't plan on falling in love with me."

"And you—" he took several steps closer—"did not plan on falling in love with me."

Mahim moved into the room, whistling a popular tune, earning Erica's gratitude. Sajah, it would seem, experienced pure frustration—a reaction Mahim handled with great skill. "Remember me, Sajah? The third wheel. Just so you understand, I tried phoning from the lobby before I came up, but no one answered. Had I known Erica was here waiting for you, I wouldn't have barged in. Since none of this is my fault and I missed dinner, I've decided to invite myself to share your table. Come and eat. Both of you."

"You fixed food?" Sajah asked incredulously.

"Your little *Sitara* fixed food."

Erica wasn't sure she appreciated being called Sajah's little anything. Chances were Sitara was another Hindu goddess, probably the one who acted foolishly at every turn. When Sajah joined Mahim in the dining room, she chose not to follow. "Excuse me," she said tightly. "I am no longer hungry. May I use the guest room?"

Both men stared at her: Mahim with professional concern, Sajah with piercing skepticism. It was Sajah who spoke. "Are you ill?"

"As a matter of fact, yes. My feet hurt because I'm constantly walking on eggshells!"

The delight in Mahim's laughter was silenced by a single look from Prince Ajari. Mahim held up his hands and went to get the food. Sajah crossed both arms over his chest. "I see you have changed since being around Stevens."

"I have not." Frustration rolled right into defeat. "I'm tired, Sajah. Which room may I use?"

"Mine. The guest room has two beds. Mahim will be staying."

"Good night then." She half expected him to stop her from rushing off. He didn't. At the door to his bedroom, she made the mistake of looking back. Those dark eyes were filled with an expression that caused regret to curl upward through her body. Words of apology burned upon her lips, but she could not speak them. Not tonight.

"Do you require something?"

She shook her head, without breaking eye contact. Where had it gone wrong? Minutes ago, she had thrown herself into his arms, needing his comfort and strength. Now they stood on either side of an emotional chasm, each waiting for the other to say something, anything that would erase the distance.

The only thing that changed was Sajah's stance. He held himself in that completely powerful, unapproachable way now. "Sleep well, Erica."

She doubted if she would sleep at all.

The only one at the apartment when she awakened the next morning was a servant, an elderly woman who spoke no English. Erica did not see Sajah until after five o'clock. She had just changed into some of her new clothes, a simple, scoop-necked shell of creamy white with a jewel-toned batik skirt that swirled around her ankles when she turned circles.

Sajah caught her turning circles in front of his mirror.

Color flooded her cheeks. She forced herself to face the man, not his image. He wore a suit again, gray this time. The tie at his collar had been unknotted. Tiredness lingered about his dark eyes. "Hello."

He nodded but didn't move.

Erica moved to the tall bureau where she replaced the brush she had used on her hair. "Is Mahim with you?"

"He left early this morning."

"For Punjab?"

Another nod, and a narrowing of his eyes as if he were wondering how much she knew about Punjab. Perhaps he wondered how many questions she would ask now. It wasn't necessary to ask questions.

"Mahim seems content. He must enjoy his work as a doctor."

Although Sajah crossed the room and stopped close enough to touch her, he didn't reach out. Rather, he repeated his actions from the night before, inclining his head until he looked every bit the Rajah. "Are you working this conversation toward asking about my contentment?"

"No." Erica shifted. "I was just thinking how Mahim seems to tease you with a friend's freedom. Yet there were times when you...held back, when you—"

"I held back because he is a friend, not because I am a prince. From the moment I saw him, I dreaded having to tell Mahim exactly how and why Bashtar died. Did you consider that possibility, Erica?" He seemed to take the answer from her guilty expression. "How much longer will you continue to look at the title rather than the man? My life is filled with people who calculate how my power and position can be used for their purposes or for their demise, whichever state of mind they are in at the moment. I *do not* need to love a woman who feels the same way."

No, he didn't. Erica sat down on the bed, tucking her feet beneath the long hem of her skirt, hugging her knees to her chest. "Tell me more about being a prince."

Impatience laced itself into Sajah's intense gaze. "Is this your vow of temperance showing through? You are unwilling to offend me, so you ask questions instead of releasing the emotion I see burning in your blue eyes?"

"What emotion? It seems I spend my days thinking up ways to torture the prince. I hardly have time to feel any real emotion for the man."

"Now you are being facetious."

"No, Rajah Ajari. I am perfectly serious. I have seen many sides to you as a man, but that's not the whole picture."

He was still staring at her. Erica wet her lips with the tip of her tongue. He was a most disconcerting man. *God help me say the right thing.* "Your life is so complicated, Sajah. I don't understand how you make it work. Sometimes it feels like you run on pure energy, reacting according to some inner set of rules that keep you in balance. Is that your Hindu faith?"

"What do you think?"

"I believe it is." She rocked forward, chin on her knees. "But there is part of me that reasons you would be more content if you were actually fulfilling your dharma." She wasn't surprised when Sajah suddenly turned, took a few steps to the closet, and jerked open the door. "Were you content before I entered your life? On every level—professionally, personally, spiritually? Did it seem like you were reaching the goals you set for yourself?"

"A path, Erica. Hindus set the mind upon choosing a path. Each person has a unique way toward salvation, one best suited for him or her. I have chosen my path to salvation. It is not about being content. It's about making a decision and taking responsibility to fulfill that decision."

When he turned around. One hand held a bundle of shirts. Another held a suitcase. Sajah threw both onto the bed next to her and went back for more. Erica automatically began folding the clothes, then placing them inside the suitcase. Her voice was soft, even troubled when she spoke again. "Don't you wonder sometimes what it would feel like to be content, happy?"

"As you are content?" Sajah's question was muffled. "I have seen spiritual depth in you, Erica, but very little true contentment. How is it that you feel these pangs of regret over my faith without bothering to right what is wrong within yourself?"

"Remove the beam."

Sajah came to dump more clothes and another suitcase onto the bed. This time, he didn't turn away. "What did you say?"

Erica thoughtfully smoothed a wrinkle from the shirt she held in her hands. "It's a verse from the Bible, about me trying to remove the speck from your eye, when I'm blinded by the beam in my own. I'm sorry, Sajah. I was wrong."

His dark eyes searched hers for a long moment before he spoke. "Ellyn never admitted to being sorry." Erica became very still. Sajah took the shirt from her hands and tossed it on top of the others. "No, Erica, I was not content before you entered my life. I was devoted to the responsibility of my path. So devoted, I am finding it difficult understanding how you could suddenly be set upon the same path."

She worried her lower lip, enough to compel him to touch her there.

When his hand fell away, it seemed as though part of his spirit left, too. "We are going back to the palace. Be ready within the half hour."

The stone pool, the night breeze, the sounds of the desert. The palace windows mere sleepy eyes in an aging face. Smooth stones beneath her feet. The flow of sapphire, garnet, gold, and emerald around her legs. Moments before, Erica had entered the courtyard. Now she was just standing there, so still and calm, Sajah wondered if she had forgotten he sent Amreli with a request for her immediate presence.

He stripped the tie away from his neck and tossed it carelessly toward one of the chairs attending the iron and glass table. When it slid to the courtyard floor, Erica moved gracefully to pick it up. The action, as everything else about her lately, served to heighten his awareness. "Did you hope I would let you play in the pool again?"

She was smiling when she rose and faced him. "Yes, actually. Or I thought you might have found some doughnuts. Did you?" The woman glided toward him, unaware that her manner could just as easily be enchanting as amusing. "I ran all the way down here without my shoes, hoping you would have a chocolate-covered doughnut waiting for me."

To prove her eagerness, she lifted the hem of her skirt and wiggled her toes at him. To prove his control, he captured her chin in hand and placed a hard kiss on her delightful mouth. Without the control, he would have taken her in his arms. "You, Miss Tanner, are a tease."

Her blue eyes had widened.

"Why do you look at me as if you are surprised by the kiss?" He raised his hand and gave the signal that brought a blushing Amreli forward from her designated waiting place just inside the palace doors. "Beside the pool please, Amreli. Then you may leave, and ask the others not to bother me, for any reason."

"Yes, Rajah."

After placing the heavy tray on the pool ledge, Amreli backed away from the prince. At some unmarked point, she turned and scampered into the palace. Erica scampered in the other direction, blushing just as self-consciously. Any moment now, she would scold him for letting the girl see their kiss. Sajah rolled back the sleeves of his white shirt in preparation for the latest battle of words.

She did not scold him, verbally at least. She only perched on the pool ledge and ran her fingers through the water in slow figure eights.

"Are you not curious about what is on this tray?"

"No."

"Are you praying again?"

"Yes."

He peeled back the cloth and chose one of the dishes, a spoon, and a napkin, just in case she decided to throw the gift in his face.

"I went to very much trouble to bring you this, Erica. Will you at least eat it before it melts?"

"Ice cream?"

"If you smile like that just because I bring you ice cream, you may have it every day." Sajah let her take the bowl but kept the spoon for himself. "Open up."

"Sajah—mmm, that's cold. It's butter brickle!"

He fed her another spoonful. "I told you I have a photographic memory."

"The orphanage in Calcutta. Daddy told me the stone looked like butter-brickle ice cream, and I envied the children who lived inside because I had never tasted ice cream." She held the bowl for him to scoop another bite, although she playfully turned the spoon back on him. "Do you like it?"

"Chocolate tastes better, but this has a certain appeal." Especially when she was wearing some on her top lip. He allowed himself to wipe it away with a tender gesture. "Erica?"

"Hmm?"

"Have you decided? Will you marry me?"

The way she jerked in reaction forced him to rescue the bowl from her hands. It wasn't as easy to rescue his emotions. The expression on her upturned face hovered between shyness and dismay.

"I know I said I would give you time, but this…waiting, this wondering what you are thinking and feeling drives me crazy!" Sajah slid off the ledge onto the courtyard, then reached for Erica, standing her beside him. Three determined strides brought him to the tray again. "Do you see?" He wiped the cloth aside, exposing the doughnuts. "Chocolate, sprinkles, plain, even the holes. I had them specially made for you. Do you know how long it took the cooks to perfect frying American doughnuts in a country full of people who eat fruit and vegetables?"

"Sajah—"

"Come." His hand around her wrist made sure she followed him inside. In fact, she had to follow him to the second floor music room. He turned on one set of lights. It was enough. "This piano has been tuned by the finest man available. I have given the servants permission to spend as much time listening to you as they want, provided their work is still accomplished. Sheet music has been ordered. I wasn't certain what you played, so there will be boxes and boxes of music."

Erica didn't seem inclined to go near the piano.

He had more to show her.

Directly across from the music room, he opened a set of doors, threw another light switch, and pulled her into a newly refurbished room. Most of the floor had been carpeted in bright colors to compliment the array of child-sized furniture and toys. There was a tiled circle near the windows for playing ball games, an easel for art projects, and a giant teddy bear to cuddle with while reading a book. "Do you think Betul will like it here, Erica?"

"Of course he will."

"But you do not approve?"

She faced him, her eyes clouded by concern. "It isn't that, Sajah. I just—don't understand."

"Perhaps this will help you understand." He held out his hand. She came toward him, slipping her fingers in between his.

This time, they went up to the top floor. Sajah could feel her trembling even before he opened a set of doors opposite her bedroom suite. It was dark inside the open, lofty space. "Go to the middle, Erica...go on." Her steps were hesitant.

Only when she stopped did Sajah turn on the lights.

It was exactly like waking up in her little girl bed. Yet this gossamer veil was so grand, so far above her she felt tiny standing in the center. Yards and yards of fine, glimmering veil had been draped from a ring set in the ceiling. Partway down, it was caught back and up again by golden ropes attached to the walls. Then the full, sheer wings were allowed to float freely to the floor.

The gossamer circle was ten feet wide with nothing inside except a bed fit for a princess, dressed in royal blue, trimmed with gold and cream. Outside the veil were stars, dozens and dozens of soft lights set at random along the deep blue walls. Everywhere she turned, there were lights. Even surrounding Sajah.

Erica held her breath when he moved toward her, under the gossamer veil.

"I cannot give you real stars, but I can give you this little bit of heaven." He withdrew something from his pocket. "Turn please."

She did. The weight of the chain and pendant he fastened around her neck felt like no more than angel kisses. The touch of his hands upon her bare skin whisked her back to earth, where she wanted to be as long as he was there.

His arms came around her from behind, holding her gently against himself. When he spoke, his breath stirred her hair. "I asked them for the diamonds first. Then I saw this blue sapphire, and it reminded me of the stars in your eyes when you speak of your childhood. Do you mind?"

"It's beautiful, Sajah, but—"

"Do not tell me I shouldn't have. Agreed?"

Her agreement conveyed wonder for the priceless gift, more so for the room than the sapphire. She tilted her head back to gaze upon the little bit of heaven he had created for her.

Sajah brushed his lips against her temple. "You were a princess even then, Erica. Be my princess now. Say you will marry me."

She turned in his arms. The white fabric of his shirt was warm beneath her hands. "So much has happened, Sajah. I know I'm supposed to be here, in India. I know that with all my heart, but I don't know how to answer you about becoming your wife."

"I can give you what you dreamed about, Erica. The little girl who mothered her doll with such compassion she wanted ten children. We can have as many children as you want, brothers and sisters for Betul. And they can grow up as fascinated by India as you were. For once, you will have no limit on helping people, even the Harijan, especially the Harijan. You can nurse them, teach them, and play your music for them if you want. You have so much inside you to give."

He caressed the back of her head, as her father used to do. "Look at the future through this veil. There are a million stars for you to invite into your world, my world, and I would love every one of them because they come to me through your heart. Let me love you, Erica."

Her hand trembled in lifting it to where his heart was beating. "There's one thing about my little girl stories you never talk about, Sajah. The letter you never let me read that day in Darjeeling."

"When Ellyn was angry with you and left you standing alone in the Contai market." Sajah captured her hands inside his own. "It tears something in me to imagine what you felt that day. I cannot talk about it."

"But I need to, Sajah." She went to sit on the bed, curling her legs beneath her. Sajah remained standing at the edge of the veil, his face shadowed. "It's my first memory of India, probably because it was so traumatic. When you are a child of four, everything—everyone seems so much bigger and louder and busier."

For a moment, she watched Sajah move around the perimeter of the veil, and then she closed her eyes, concentrating on the little-girl scenes in Contai. "Spicy smells and flowers and dust. It was hot. Mama made me wear one of Ellyn's plain blue American dresses. It was too big. I wanted a silk sari, pink and yellow. Daddy was in a hurry. I don't remember why. I remember Ellyn constantly jerking me forward, and I was tired. She always wanted to move. I wanted to stay and just be there for a while."

Sajah's footsteps told her when he entered the veil. She knew he stood at the end of the bed because she felt him there, sensed his emotions becoming entangled with hers. "I just stopped, in the middle of the market. Ellyn whispered at me that Daddy would lose us, that he wouldn't notice and we would be left all alone. I can still hear her voice, whispering, more and more desperately to make me understand. Then the whispering stopped, and she let go of my hand and walked away.... Do you remember what I did, Sajah?"

"You were afraid. You wrote about the tightness growing in your chest until you wanted to curl into a ball. You were humming a song to yourself so you wouldn't hear all the voices, but it didn't work. People started crowding around you, pointing at you, some of them laughing at the little blond girl in her baggy dress, tears running down her face."

Erica nodded. "I had to pray, Sajah. I had to kneel down right there in the middle of them and pray. Then everything got so quiet. Inside of me, everything was so quiet." Her fingers closed around the smooth sapphire. "They came and found me."

"The Hindu priests."

She could picture their red robes, their serious expressions. "I just looked up and they were there. Why would they do that, Sajah? Why would they clear the market and chase everyone away?"

He did not answer for a long time. When he did, his words were quiet. "I went to Contai after reading your letter. I found the temple nearest to the market. There was only one priest there who remembered that day. He was very old, nearly blind, but he described you as a little girl." Sajah moved around the bed and guided her upright until she was standing. "He described you perfectly, in English. Even if the people do not always speak English, the priests do. They cleared everyone from the market because of the words you were praying."

He lifted a hand to catch the single tear that slipped down her cheek. "You were talking to Jesus like He was right there with you. You told Him over and over again that you were sorry for sinning and you wanted Him to forgive you, to save you. To the priests your prayer sounded like something you must have memorized from your parents, but it changed the longer you prayed."

"Changed?"

"You were asking Jesus to bless your daddy and your mommy and Ellyn, to bless all the people and the cows and the men in red. You were asking Him to send someone to help you. The priests were afraid of your little-girl prayers, Erica. They were afraid of that much quiet faith. You weren't running. You weren't crying out. You were just there, a powerful, tiny presence in the midst of their people."

"So they sent people away before Jesus used one of them to answer my prayers?"

Sajah stroked the hair from her forehead. "I have never heard a story like it, Erica. You were still praying for the men in red when your father came to find you."

"Daddy was angry with me, like Ellyn."

"No, he was not angry with you. The priest said Joe Tanner told them they had just witnessed the awesome, gentle power of Jesus."

"He said that? I don't remember that part. I thought Daddy was angry."

"He was upset with the priests."

Erica felt a stirring within herself. "Why?"

"Because they told him to leave Contai and never come back. According to the priest, you never returned."

She wasn't sure. "Ellyn mailed a letter from there once. That's what made me remember. Ellyn never spoke about it, though."

"She told me." Sajah's hands fell away. He even took a step back. "It was shortly after Ellyn married Sambhal. Actually, as I understand it, she told her side of the story quite often. It was one of the tools she used to coerce people into believing that Christianity is stronger than Hinduism."

Erica backed up, too, until her legs hit the bed and she sank onto the covers, a tight feeling growing inside her chest.

"Ellyn's version portrayed you as the innocent child who slipped away from what was best for her. You were helpless, lost in the midst of gathering darkness just like the Hindu people who gathered around to console you. There was no difference between you and them. The Hindu priests could see that. No difference. You were lost and hungry and lonely. Then, Joe and Ellyn Tanner started praying and Jesus heard *their* prayers. Jesus rescued you from the trappings of Hindu and brought you home to your Father's arms.... There were references to a parable from your Bible."

"The prodigal son."

Sajah crossed both arms over his chest. "Things quickly become twisted, Erica. We see what we want to see. I did not, nor will I ever approve of the method your sister and my brother used to propagate conversions. The longer it went on, the more coercive it became. Somehow, the very ideals they were preaching became lost to them. That is why I ask you to let it die."

"I'm sorry, Sajah. I had no idea."

"So retelling your memory of that day in Contai was simply your roundabout way of saying you feel lost in my world."

"Sometimes." When Sajah would have walked away, Erica caught at his arm. The action made her stumble off the bed. He steadied her. "Please, don't be angry."

"I am not angry." But he did loosen her hold on his arm. "What is it that you need, Erica? What more must I say? How can I prove to you—"

Her fingers against his lips silenced him. "I want to be your wife, Sajah."

He captured her hands in his. "Then I will make it so."

"You can't." Tears thickened her voice. "God must make it so."

"And how long will that take?" He used a finger to tilt her face up. "You asked me once if I got everything I wanted. Do you remember?"

She nodded. It was the night of Loralai's party, the first time he had kissed her.

"Pray, if you must. Wait if you must. But do not make me force the answer to that question."

❧ Eighteen ❧

SAJAH FOUGHT AGAINST THE NAMELESS, faceless fear, but it was stronger. It pulled him over the edge of the cliff. Then he was tumbling through midair. Falling...falling. He jerked upright on the bed. The sound that had interrupted his nightmare came again. Someone was at the door.

His gaze automatically went to the clock beside the bed. Eight A.M. No wonder sunshine poured into the room. He threw on a pair of jeans and a plain, white tunic. There was another knock. He strode across the room.

Another knock.

Impatience determined how he flung open the door.

"N-Namastey."

Amreli. Sajah released a sigh. "What do you want?"

"Sri Ajari say I come wh-when Miss Tanner leave palace."

His hand tightened on the doorknob. "Where is she? When did she leave?"

The girl backed away from his barrage of questions. "I ask. She no stop."

Typical.

"Amreli sorry, Sri Ajari."

"It's all right. Thank you. You may go now."

Amreli bowed quickly, then scurried down the hall.

Sajah wasted no time in going after Erica. In fact, Rama's Shikari raced wildly toward the river. Hoofprints in the damp soil led them all the way, right to a thick grove of trees, as thick as the confusion preventing Erica from accepting his proposal. Once at the grove, low-hanging branches forced Sajah from the saddle.

The gray mare was tied to a tree, grazing on the sparse grass underfoot. Rama's Shikari stayed exactly in the place where Sajah dropped the reins. Unfortunately, he was not sure Erica would stay in one place long enough to see reason.

It would have been impossible to approach without making a sound. Sajah was too irritated for that. His strides snapped every twig in his path. Then he entered a clearing and found he was the one snapped—to an abrupt halt.

The woman coming toward him was not Erica.

Today, Temnah's long black hair was coiled into a braid that rested atop her head, adding inches to her diminutive height. Her olive-colored skin glowed with good health, accentuating the play of morning sunlight upon the gold silk of her sari. She looked exactly like the princess she was.

At some unseen distance, shyness overcame her and she stopped. Her head was bent to smell the fragile bouquet of white flowers she held. "Namastey, Sajah. The servants said you were sleeping."

"I was." But he was wide awake now.

"You are not happy to see me," she whispered against the white petals.

Sajah smiled down at her. "I am very happy to see you, Temnah. But it is a surprise. How did you get here?"

"On the mare."

"Oh, all the way from Punjab?"

Temnah's laugh was light, childlike, reminding Sajah that she was still very young. "I came yesterday."

"Because of Bashtar."

The smile was gone in an instant. Several tears slipped from her wide, expressive eyes, down her cheek.

They were Sajah's undoing. He caught them with his fingertips, then gave up the simple gesture in favor of folding her into his arms. "Temnah. You always try to be so brave."

"It hurts," she spoke against his shoulder.

"I know." He was hurting too. In more ways than he could tell her. Sajah's private thought made him wonder where Erica was. He turned his head but could not see past the trees. Had she gone to the village?

"Sajah?"

His eyes shifted again to Temnah.

"Could I stay, please, for a little while? Mother and Father are in mourning. They won't care if I'm around or not."

The lonely little princess. True, she had been cherished her entire life, but she had also been born into a world where, in the end, only male heirs mattered. It was a world that would soon come crashing down. Her family had little money left. For once, he was grateful she did not know. Sajah placed a tender kiss on her forehead. "Of course, you may stay, Temnah...come."

"Where?"

He was weaving his way toward the horses. "To the village. I need to find someone."

Temnah hurried to catch up. "Who?"

"You ask too many questions."

Sajah saw Erica at once, sitting on the ground, cradling a child in each arm—children of the Harijan. She was laughing with them. More children surrounded her—children of a higher caste. The little fool! His heart pounded a fierce rhythm, one beat for each rapid step he took toward her from the well.

One of the children glanced up and saw him. Warnings were whispered. They scattered, except for the youngsters Erica held. Her jeans were dusty. She wore a gray T-shirt. There was a smudge of dirt on one cheek. Obviously, she had enjoyed her visit to the village.

Sajah was very much aware of when Erica looked past him to see Temnah standing beside the well. He chose that same moment to remind her of the restrictions. "You are never to leave the palace without me."

Erica shifted the children until she could stand. A gentle push sent them on their way. Only then did she fully meet Sajah's gaze. "I was lonesome without Betul. I thought coming here would help."

That she spoke so calmly canceled some of his anger, but he refused to give it up entirely. "It won't happen again, agreed? They have not yet found all the extremists. Besides, you have no idea what you're doing, mixing the children together in such a way."

Her eyes went back to the crude huts of the Harijan. "I can't help it, Sajah."

The quiet admission was as effective as a kick in his gut. He rubbed a hand over the back of his neck. Why? Why did she always do this to him? And she did not even beg to remain at the village. Instead, she started walking toward the well.

It was a moment before Erica heard Sajah fall into step beside her. The woman who held so tightly to the horses' reins was very pretty. No. Erica changed her mind as they got closer. The woman was beautiful. Instinctively she knew this was Sajah's special friend, the one Betul had mentioned so often. When she stopped in front of the younger woman, Erica recognized a certain hesitation from her. "Namastey."

There was a shy dipping of her head, a whispered namastey.

No jealousy, no resentment. Erica offered a smile. "You must be

Temnah. I'm Erica." Before she could say anything else, Sajah's hand came to her elbow and he steered her toward Rama's Shikari where he lifted her into the saddle. By the time Erica looked back, Temnah had already mounted the gray. They shared another smile. Then Sajah started off at a reckless pace that left no chance for further communication.

At the palace, Erica was told to go upstairs and change. She accepted the demand without argument. Sajah was in no mood to have her explain why it wasn't necessary for him to treat her like a prisoner. She took a long time to shower and change into the pretty blue-lavender pantsuit.

As she did, her thoughts kept returning to Temnah. If the woman was even twenty years old, Erica would be surprised. Something about her seemed to invite protection and nurturing. Was it the same for Sajah? Perhaps she had been wrong all this time and his relationship with Temnah was like her friendship with Grant.

Erica fastened the star sapphire around her neck. By daylight it was even more dramatic, the white six-sided star gleaming out of deepest blue. The silver chain was delicate. Perhaps she shouldn't wear it except for special occasions. Removing it again was a little disappointing. She overcame that by going to visit the lights of the veil.

In daylight it was less dramatic, a sweet room, a curl up and daydream room. She stood in the doorway, remembering how Sajah had left her the night before, with a warning that she should not push him into taking what he wanted. She had prayed and cried and finally slept upon the bed, but she had found no answer to the troubling questions.

The awesome, gentle power of Jesus hadn't come to quiet her spirit.

Now she was feeling a sudden need to talk to Grant, a heart-to-heart talk. She went to a spare room several doors down the hall.

She had peeked into almost all the rooms by now. This one, though simply furnished, was one of the few to have a phone. The operator took forever to connect her call. Then she endured another eternity waiting out each ring. She was just about ready to hang up when a male voice answered.

"Yup?"

A dozen feelings swept through her at once, leaving her homesick. Erica sank onto the creaky bed. "Hello, Bill."

"Half-pint? That you?"

"Am I surprising you?"

"I'll say. Hands off."

"What?"

"Grant. He's trying to steal the phone from me. You'll spend a few minutes talking to an old man, won't you, Half-pint?"

"I've been praying for you all the time. How are you?"

His chuckle settled some of her fears. "Moving slower, but otherwise no lasting side effects. It takes more than a few Sikh to do me in. Grant—"

"Hey, kid."

Erica smiled. "Hey. You're going to owe him a steak for this one. You ought to get a speakerphone or something."

"Not by the sound of your voice. Where are you?"

"At the palace. Betul is still in Darjeeling."

"No wonder you sound lonely. I miss you like crazy. What have you been doing?"

She traced a hand over the bed's woven coverlet, thinking it was the color of white marble. "At the risk of repeating my conversation with your father, how are you? Did you make a full recovery from Chota Chand? No more aches and pains? Other than the stuff you were born with, of course."

"You're in a teasing mood, huh? You get like that when things aren't looking so good.... Erica? You still there?"

"Yeah. Do you think there's a chance God sent me here just for Sajah?"

"No."

A frown cut across her brow, then Grant went on.

"Think about it, kid. Think about who Sajah is, what he's been doing all these years. It's like the old saying, 'can't see the forest for the trees.' Look at it through God's eyes once and you'll see how much He wants to use you there. Sajah is just part of it."

"That's what scares me the most, Grant, catching a vision of what God can do."

"That shouldn't be scary."

"It is when I think about Ellyn's desire to follow God, no matter what. Sajah told me things last night that—scared me. Things about Ellyn and Sambhal."

"About their ministry."

"You know?"

"I heard plenty when I was over there. They were high profile. It seemed like all I had to do was mention their names and everybody had something to say."

"Like what?"

There was a long pause. Grant's voice was ruled by control when he spoke again. "One old woman in New Delhi told me they saw their converts as Christians rather than Indians who knew Christ. I talked to one of their converts, a boy about sixteen, maybe seventeen. He described a powerful service. He knows he was saved, but he also felt abandoned because Ellyn and Sambhal forgot to follow through with the discipleship, the teaching part of it. It sounds to me like they switched more to evangelism rather than missionary work, which is fine. But it almost seems like they got caught up in the numbers. What they did toward the end caused social havoc in some of the families and villages."

"And Sajah was left to step in with the calm voice," Erica

guessed. "That wasn't right, Grant. It doesn't sound right."

"I know. It didn't sound right to me either until I started connecting the dots. When they left a place, missionaries or trained tribals were supposed to step in and take up the work. It didn't happen that way. Sajah stepped in."

"He stopped what they were doing?"

"Sometimes. More often, people from the political movement used his name and stepped in."

"Didn't the missionaries complain to Ellyn and Sambhal?"

"When they could reach them. They traveled straight for weeks at a time. From what I heard, they were pretty much unreachable. Betul was left with Sajah a lot. If Betul wasn't at the palace, he was at the plantation." Grant sighed. "It wasn't an ideal situation. I guess I keep hanging on to the thought that, deep down inside, Ellyn and Sambhal were ministering the way God asked of them."

"Intensely enough that Ellyn claimed Ezekiel 6?"

"Now that one, Half-pint; I'm thinking that one was for Sajah."

Erica sat bolt upright. "What do you mean?"

"Didn't you say Ved wanted to show you something in Ellyn's Bible?"

"Before the incident at Chota Chand, but he never did."

"Well, I think I know what he wanted to tell you, but this call is costing a fortune. How about if I tell you in person, say in a week or so? Dad and I have the tickets already. Tell Sajah we're coming. See ya then, kid."

"Grant!"

Too late. He had already hung up.

Erica literally flew down the steps. She even stumbled a little at the top of the last flight and had to catch herself before she fell. Of course Sajah witnessed her carelessness because he was standing in the foyer with Temnah. Erica ran down to them. "Why didn't you say something!"

"About what?"

"About Grant and Bill coming." The change in Sajah was immediate. She smiled in hopes of erasing his displeasure. "Grant said to tell you they're coming."

"You spoke with him?"

"I just called. Are they coming to stay, not just to visit? When did all this happen?"

"Before I resigned."

"Resigned? From the Council?"

"Yes."

"But you didn't tell me!"

Sajah's brief glance at Temnah made Erica very aware of the differences between herself and the young woman. Compared to her rush down the stairs and her anxious questions, Temnah presented the very picture of patience. The downcast eyes and folded hands were proof that Temnah had been schooled in how to conduct herself around the Rajah.

Erica felt herself blushing. No wonder Sajah had called her an insolent female. Undoubtedly, the way she asked Temnah to excuse herself and Sajah would not improve matters.

At first, she did not think he would follow her to the library. Then she found herself wishing he wouldn't. No doubt, he was going to be angry for the way she had spoken so directly in front of Temnah.

Seconds after she heard his approaching footsteps, Sajah closed the doors, sealing them both inside with a finality Erica well remembered. She continued to face the windows, waiting for her heartbeat to become normal again—a waste of time.

His silence had the ability to cancel any trace of normalcy.

"Does Temnah know why I'm here?"

"Temnah barely knows how her brother died."

Erica whirled around, all off balance—inside and out. An unreasonable surge of guilt swept through her, making it impossible to speak.

Sajah guessed her thoughts. "Yes, she is Bashtar's sister, Mahim's sister. Her father and mine were friends before it was acceptable for a Sikh and a Hindu to trust each other. I have not told Temnah how Bashtar tried to destroy that bond. There will be a right time and a right place for her to learn the truth. Until then, I wish to protect her from as much pain as possible."

Erica knew he had chosen what was best for Temnah, yet other thoughts crowded her mind, urging her to turn back to the window. The scene spread out before her was a mere blur. Sometimes she wondered if anything would be clear to her again. "Will you demand that I stay away from Temnah?"

"What makes you think such a thing?"

"Because you don't trust me."

"Erica—"

"It's true. That's why you didn't tell me about Grant coming because you thought I would call and persuade him to come instead of letting it be his decision. You didn't trust me enough to tell me." She was startled to feel Sajah's fingers touching the nape of her neck, threading through the curls there. It was harder to speak then, but she had to say this. "You haven't really trusted me since Darjeeling and I don't know why. What did I do there that keeps forcing your feelings into a tight box? It's as if I am that bundle of letters. You tie me up so tightly and push me into a neat corner of your life, expecting to find me waiting when you feel...sentimental. Otherwise I'm left in the dark."

He turned her around, emotion darkening his eyes. "I see your imagination has been given free reign."

"Is it my imagination that you resigned from the Council because of me?"

A smile touched his mouth but not his eyes. "Because of you. Because of my mother. Because of Bashtar. Because the circumstances behind Pali's and the reporter's deaths will be known soon. There were many reasons, Erica."

"But no real excuses for not telling me? Except that you don't want to trust me. You will give me your kingdom, you'll even love me, but you will not trust me." She started to leave.

Sajah set a hand on her arm, dragging her back. The tension she had felt building in him last night surfaced now, full force. "You have no idea how much I have trusted you, Erica. Neither do you have any idea what loving you has cost me."

"Yes, Sajah. I do." By bringing herself closer, she was aware of his power, his control...his confusion. "It cost you a friendship with Bashtar and a career on the Council. It cost the final shred of respect you had for your mother. It cost you peace of mind and being comfortable with Hinduism." Even though his hand tightened upon her arm, she went on. "It cost more than you wanted to give, didn't it? It cost you Temnah."

Friendship did not come between Erica and Temnah right away. Perhaps, if Sajah had not been called away to New Delhi, it would not have come at all Whenever Sajah was near the girl, Erica saw a shy attentiveness to his comforts, his words, his everything It was like stepping back in time to the days when royal families held court and were attended by dutiful ladies in waiting.

More than once that first day, Erica was stung by the thought that she had changed the relationship between Sajah and Temnah. Guilt set in with a vengeance. She spent time praying it away, yet it returned as soon as she saw Temnah wandering the second floor hallway the next morning.

Since Sajah had been called away on business, Temnah was torn between going home or staying It took a split second for Erica to realize the answer depended on her. She took Temnah's hand and led her into the music room. That's when their friendship began to grow.

Erica showed Temnah how to play a simple song, but only after she promised to teach Erica how to ride the gray mare. The discoveries were endless. She introduced Temnah to splashing in the courtyard pool. Temnah introduced her to making beautiful flower arrangements. They spent one morning in the new playroom, talking mostly about Betul and how they had both come to love the little boy.

They spent that same afternoon at the village where Temnah could not get enough of watching the children in school. She told Erica of the times she had traveled with Bashtar or Sajah, how she was always drawn to the children. If there were not enough classrooms or teachers for the children, she would not rest until arrangements were made.

Secretly, Temnah admitted she would love to be a teacher, but it had been decided that she would marry Sajah. She had been raised knowing that was her role in life. Erica did not sleep that night. She wandered around and around the lights of the veil, thinking of all the things she should have told Temnah, but they were not her confidences to tell.

The burden resting over Erica's heart did not lift.

Temnah asked several times the next day if she was ill. It wasn't a physical illness as much as it was emotional and spiritual. She simply asked for time alone to pray. The hours stretched toward what would have been a very long, lonely evening, except that Temnah persuaded her out onto the courtyard for an impromptu picnic.

Evening sunlight warmed a cool breeze. The sun would set quietly.

"It is not like Darjeeling," Temnah sighed.

"Betul said you liked it there."

"Yes, very much. Sometimes, Sambhal would go riding with me."

"Ellyn didn't go?"

"She never learned. I tried to persuade her, but she was always too busy." After a moment, Temnah brought her gaze to rest on Erica's face. "You are so opposite your sister. I could not have one conversation with Ellyn except that she asked to pray for me."

Erica swallowed some of her tea, then sat back in her chair rather than forward in eagerness to hear more.

Temnah sensed the change. "You are a believer in Christ. What is this difference? I understand the...theology of one Savior, one forgiveness of sins, but I do not understand how believers of the same God can be so unlike each other. Does Christ give you different ways to show your faith?"

"Yes, sometimes, but it is a heart difference, too." Erica struggled to put the words together. "It's like when you accept Jesus as your Savior, He puts a fire in your heart. Some people have a consuming fire. They are driven to press forward as God leads them."

"Ellyn had this type of consuming fire?"

Erica nodded. "I believe so. Other Christians receive a sustaining fire, the steady burning kind, the kind that would be placed in a window to light someone's way home at night."

"And this sustaining fire is you?"

Again, she nodded. "They both have their places, Temnah. God knows how to open hearts to receive the salvation of Christ. Ellyn didn't mean to offend you or anyone with the way she lived her faith. She was being obedient to keep the fire burning. It's just that the fire burned so bright, so hot, that it was easy to get scorched."

"But you have a different way. You glow and people come to you, curious, drawn closer by the warmth, not fearing that they will get burned...except Sajah."

Erica caught back her breath.

"I have never seen him so consumed, Erica Somehow, the fire in you has ignited a larger fire in him. I do not think he knows what to do about it." Temnah gestured to the blue star sapphire Erica had worn throughout the day "Ellyn, he could deal with. You he must woo as a prince woos a princess."

"Temnah—"

"Please, Erica, let me finish." The plea was made more poignant by the way Temnah rose from the chair and came to kneel beside her. She took both of Erica's hands, held on tight. "I am not such a child that I can't understand how a man looks at the woman he loves. I wanted to...despise you for changing Sajah's heart, but I see now you have done nothing more than to be yourself. No." She shook her head. "I should say you have done nothing more than be the person Christ called you to be. That is what has affected the change in Sajah Christ in you."

Erica was startled by the brilliant smile Temnah gave her.

"I cannot despise you, Erica. Seeing myself through your eyes, I realize I could not have truly been happy married to Sajah. You complete a searching in me that began when I met your sister. Ellyn's fire was fascinating, but I could not look on it for long without feeling hopelessly empty Your fire—" Temnah squeezed her hands— "your fire fills me with a desire to let the emptiness burn away. Can Christ do that for me?"

"Yes, Temnah. Jesus can do that for you."

Neither of them noticed when Loralai came to stand in the doorway. The older woman's hand turned white upon the cane she now used constantly. Dread clouded Loralai's eyes She felt tired. She felt isolated. She felt as if Sajah were millions of miles away rather than in New Delhi.

Such thoughts drove her back inside. Her son could not love

Erica. It would destroy his life. It would destroy Temnah, too, worse than this talk of Jesus Christ. Loralai went to her sitting room. The huge space rang hollow with her worries. There had to be some way to make Erica Tanner leave.

Pacing back and forth over the thick carpet did nothing to ease the questions. There must be some way. Loralai sank into a chair. Perhaps Sajah did not love her any more, but she was still his mother. She had to protect him. After many long minutes, she pressed the button, calling for a servant.

When the man arrived, she asked him to bring a telephone. Then she ordered him to leave the room. Loralai didn't want anyone to hear what she was about to do.

❧ NINETEEN ☙

DID THE GIRL RUN EVERYWHERE SHE WENT? Grant smiled at her, then hurried to catch up. Her name was Temnah. She was twenty-one. She lived a long way from here, and that's all he knew about her. That and the fact she bounced between shyness and liveliness like a rubber ball. Oh, and she packed a mean tackle.

A few minutes earlier, just as he and his father reached the entrance to Sajah's palace, the door had unexpectedly flown open, releasing this firecracker. He had barely saved her, let alone himself, from being plastered all over the steps. And she had laughed about the whole thing.

"There she is!"

Grant shaded his eyes against the afternoon sunshine. "Where?"

"There, silly." Temnah pointed to a still distant spot of gray near where the fields were met by desert sand dunes. "Come."

The gray mare was closing the distance at a reckless pace. When Erica was still a hundred feet away, she gave up on the horse and slid from the saddle. Grant passed Temnah. He and Erica met in the middle of the field. It was easy for him to span her waist with both hands and twirl her into the air, around and around. Her laugh sounded better than anything he could think of just then.

"Oh, Grant. Put me down!"

"Gladly. You must have gained weight, kid."

Erica hit him as he lowered her to the ground, but he had only spoken the truth. She looked more rested. The jeans she wore fit better. Her white shirt had been knotted about her waist. "Well," he said. "Go on, admit it. You missed me like crazy."

"She did not miss you, Grant Stevens." They both looked toward Temnah, who was already mounting the gray mare. Her playful smile was enchanting. "She had me to keep her company, and I do not tell her she is a kid!"

"That's because you're decades younger than she is."

"Which makes you older than dirt," Erica kindly pointed out, for which Grant pretended to catch her in a headlock.

Temnah laughed at them. "Good-bye! It is a long walk back, but you will not mind, I think." She kicked her bare heels against the mare's sides and galloped away, black hair streaming out.

"Who is she?"

Erica slipped her hand into his before saying anything. "Bashtar's little sister." The hesitation in Grant's steps was more for the suddenly serious tone in Erica's voice than for what she said. He glanced down at her face and saw a myriad of emotions. "She is also Mahim's little sister. He is a good friend of Sajah's, a doctor. They went to college together, in England. From what Sajah said, their families go way back." Erica sank her free hand into the pocket of her jeans but kept her eyes focused straight ahead.

"What else?"

She stopped. They faced each other.

The tears in her eyes surprised Grant. He touched a tender hand to her chin, keeping her head up so he could search out what was wrong.

"Temnah was Sajah's intended."

"And?"

"Oh, Grant." Erica bit down on her lip.

"Do you love him?"

"I don't know." She pulled away. "It—it's such a mess.

Everything is...upside down and turned around and—and I don't know what to do."

"What's a mess? You and Sajah?"

"Yes. But it's Temnah, too." She released a shaky sigh. "Grant, I led Temnah to the Lord."

"You what?" She practically jumped out of her skin he said it so loud. The eyes she raised to his were wide with apprehension. Grant's smile broadened. "Sajah's going to hit the roof."

"I know...I'm so scared."

"Then it's a good thing Dad and I came early." Grant reached for her hand and started walking toward the palace again. Things would work out. Somehow.

"There's something else you should know."

He squeezed her hand because she sounded so uncertain.

"Amreli accepted the Lord, too."

Sajah forced his body to cooperate. Every muscle screamed for rest. He hadn't slept in two days and now the long flight home. He leaned against the car for a moment after closing the door. His briefcase seemed to weigh a ton. So did his head as he lifted it to look at the palace.

When he was little, like Betul, he had imagined the stone walls holding out nighttime. Every light in every window was a guard against the darkness. He would race from room to room just to make certain the guards were on duty. Then he would go back to his bedroom and sleep, content to know that he was safe, that nothing could disturb his happiness.

Real life wasn't like those childhood ideals. If anything, he felt as if he couldn't rest because the outside darkness would break in. It would steal every last thing he held on to. Sajah moved up the steps, vowing not to let down his guard.

Inside the palace, he heard voices coming from his mother's sitting room, yet his eyes strayed up the stairs, as far as he could see without actually walking up them. Where was Erica? He listened again. Male voices. American voices. The muscles across his shoulders knotted in a dozen places. His steps toward the hallway were just as stiff.

"Sri Ajari."

He swung around so quickly Amreli almost fainted.

"A message for you."

"Later." Sajah resumed his pursuit.

Amreli followed. "Is urgent message."

"It can wait."

"But—"

When Sajah stopped, the girl crashed into him. The apologies that tumbled from her mouth were cut short by the way he held out his hand to receive the paper she held. Amreli gave it to him, took the briefcase he handed to her, then scurried away.

He did not notice her exit, not once he began reading the message. His hand tightened around the paper until his knuckles turned white. *The stupid, little fool!* His eyes flew down the hallway, then back to the stairs. Fate decided for him. She was there.

Erica had stopped halfway down the final flight. The pale green silk sari settled about her legs, the mantle slipped from her shoulders. Neither of them moved for a long moment. It was as if Sajah's anger suspended time, burning a path from his eyes to hers, from his heart to her soul.

When he did move, Erica remained quite still. He ascended the stairs slowly, until he was one step below her. But he was still taller; he still looked down at her. "What have you done now?" Confusion colored her eyes a darker blue, rivaling the star sapphire hanging around her neck. Sajah brought the paper right in front of her face, his fist inches from the soft skin. "Jachan has called me before the Maharajahs. He has called *me* before the Maharajahs!"

Erica gripped the banister.

"What in the name of the gods have you done now?"

"Sajah, please!"

His hand opened. Before the paper could fall to the step between them, his strong fingers had closed about her throat, tilting her head far back. "Tell me! Now!"

"I don't know. W-who is Jachan?"

"Temnah's father."

Fear flooded her eyes.

Sajah read the guilt in her expression. A curse erupted to fill the foyer, to drown out the sound of Grant's approach until he was standing directly below them. "Let her go, Sajah."

It was a warning Sajah did not heed. Grant took the steps two at a time. The first push was a test, the second was not.

Erica watched in horror as Sajah and Grant tumbled down to the tile floor. They were on their feet in seconds, fists hammering solid blows. By the time Bill pulled them apart, blood ran from a cut on Sajah's cheek. He wiped it away with the back of a bruised hand; his eyes still locked with Grant's. "Never do that again, Stevens."

"Or what?" Grant challenged.

Bill set a hand on his son's chest. "That's enough. Both of you. It's over."

It wasn't over. Not by a long shot. When Grant looked up at her, so did Sajah. Erica sank onto the step, torn by the fact they had fought because of her. Not even leaning against the railing helped steady her anxiety. Bill was the one who came to her. He sat down on the same step and wrapped an arm across her shoulders. "You okay, Half-pint?"

Somehow she managed to mumble yes. Sajah hadn't hurt her.

She was only scared. He would never hurt her. Her eyes sought his, but he was staring at the place where Temnah stood, almost as if he tried to see the change in her. But how could he know? How could Jachan know already?

Bill shattered the moment when he stood and reached for the crumpled paper. "What does this mean, Sajah?"

"It means—" he ground out the words—"I have to defend myself against Erica's actions. It means everything I have worked for in uniting my people will seem like a lie because she has poisoned the mind of Jachan's daughter. It means I have another choice to make—deny my heritage or deny her."

No one said anything, least of all Erica.

Sajah moved up the steps, every motion deliberate, precise. He took both of her hands in one of his and pulled her to her feet. Then he made her turn around and head back up.

"Sajah." Grant's tone failed to stop him. "If you touch her again, I'll—"

"You spoke of trust, Stevens," Sajah said over his shoulder. "Learn the lesson."

Erica's first thought was that Sajah would take her to her room. Instead, they went up a third flight of stairs she had never used before. The narrow passage made her feel strange, especially because it was so dark. At the top, he reached around her to push open a door. Cool air rushed at them. Erica was hesitant about stepping out. Then her eyes adjusted to the moonlight and she could see that they were on top of the palace.

Sajah set a hand on her elbow to guide her toward the edge. A crenellated, waist-high wall offered much needed support. The stone felt smooth beneath her hands, worn by centuries of existence—Sajah's heritage. Erica lifted her eyes to his face.

There was something very tender about the way she reached up and wiped the blood from his cheek with her fingers, but he did not look down. "Why?" The word rasped from Sajah's throat.

"Because I care about Temnah. I wanted her to know the truth about salvation."

"She is easily persuaded. You had no right to tell her things she cannot understand."

"But she does understand, Sajah. She recognized Jesus is the only way to salvation."

"You will say nothing to me of your faith." Sajah felt Erica shrink from him, drawing into herself. That wasn't what he wanted. He wanted… By the gods, he didn't know what he wanted anymore! He shoved a hand through his hair. "Did you even once stop to think what this would do to me? Does what I feel matter at all?"

"Yes, Sajah." She wrapped both arms around herself. "It does matter."

"Then how could you have done this? Don't you know what influence Jachan holds?"

"How could I? You have never spoken about him."

A cool breeze came, carrying with it a smoky scent. When Erica shivered again and turned her eyes to the distant fires in the village, Sajah quickly removed his suit coat to wrap it about her shoulders, holding the lapels together in front of her. The way she raised her face made him want to kiss her, but he didn't. Instead, he reminded himself what her foolish actions had caused.

As if she read his thoughts, Erica quietly asked, "What will happen?"

"I don't know."

"I never meant to hurt you."

He believed her. Though his mind fought against the truth, his heart believed what she said. A sense of calm overrode any anger that remained. "Perhaps if I speak with Jachan, it will calm the threats." Sajah shrugged. Temnah's father was as unpredictable as Bashtar had been. Yet Jachan was powerful enough to unite Sikh leaders and Maharajahs under one roof. They were already gathering.

"I'm sorry, Sajah."

He laid a finger against her lips, an act that caused a great stirring in him. He chose to give up the intimate contact, and the subject of Jachan. "I spoke with Betul this morning." Moonlight picked up the presence of tears in her eyes. "He sends his love. And no, he is not lonesome for us yet. Even Ahwa said he has done well." Sajah let Erica turn to the wall.

After a moment, he leaned against it too, arms extended, hands clasped. The palace grounds, the fields, the river, and desert—all were stretched out below them in an endless vision of beauty. He could tell by her reaction that talking about Betul would not be best right now. Neither was his next thought, but Sajah could not keep himself from asking. "Does Temnah know **about** us?"

"She guessed."

"She is an intuitive girl. Sambhal and I turned thirteen the day she was born. I think it made her special somehow, knowing the gods had chosen our day for her birth. Since then, I have watched over her. We would visit often. She spent many summers here.... My father was the first one to suggest a marriage. But it never seemed right."

"Until now?"

Sajah turned to look at Erica. "I do not love Temnah in the same way that I love you."

"But you would have married her."

"Yes."

Erica's next words were whispered, fractured by emotion. "I've—ruined everything for you, haven't I?"

He said nothing. In looking east, he could see the moon resting just at the top of the opposite wall. It glowed pale gold, surrounded by a handful of even paler stars. Beside him, Erica rubbed one cheek against the collar of his coat.

"In the Bible, it says a Christian shouldn't be unequally yoked with an unbeliever." She must have known that he was studying the expression on her face because she was cautious now. "I haven't shown Temnah that verse yet. I haven't—explained it to her."

"There is no need. Not when you are the woman I will marry."

"It's no different for me, Sajah."

He stiffened, held his breath until he thought it would burst in his lungs.

"I've been praying for you, that you would accept Christ as Temnah has done."

"Never."

She took a few steps away. "Then we can never be married."

The curse that poured from him was strong enough to make Erica face him. She shrank away when his hands snaked out to grab her arms. "You have lied to me! All this time, you have lied to me! Saying you needed time when you needed this *salvation* to happen!"

"No, Sajah. I didn't lie. God has simply opened my eyes, shown me that I cannot compromise His truth. Not even for Betul's sake."

"And what of your feelings, Erica?"

Her eyes closed a moment, until he chose to slip his arms around her. She placed both hands on his chest. "Sajah...don't."

"Don't confuse you by showing you what is real? Don't remind you of the truth you have buried in your heart?" Sajah lowered his head, bringing his mouth over hers. His kiss was not gentle. It demanded and sought and demanded again.

Finally, Erica managed to break away. She stumbled back a step. The breeze may have cooled her heated skin, but he knew it could not diminish the feelings he ignited. "Where is your God now, Erica? My world may be crumbling, it may seem like your God is in control, but

He can never touch the passion between us. Even if He takes everything else from me, I will still be Hindu and I will still have you."

She turned and ran to the doorway, disappearing inside.

Slowly, Sajah bent to lift her fallen mantle. Though his hand
closed into a fist around the silk, it was not crushed by his power.
Was the same true of Erica? Or would he, in the end, crush her spirit
because he held her so tightly?

He didn't know.

His eyes shot up to the heavens. For the first time in his life, he
didn't know the answer.

It was midmorning by the time Sajah finally left his office in search
of breakfast. That and he had to make sure the Stevens men knew
what they would be doing. As he walked toward the terrace, memories of his nightmare returned. It was always the same sense of fear,
the same falling over the cliff, falling and falling—then waking just
before it was too late.

But last night, something had been different. Erica was falling
with him. He clenched both hands into fists at his sides to rid himself of the gnawing ache in his gut. It was a gesture he had used often
lately; so much so he was able to keep any sign of the struggle from
showing on his face when he stepped outdoors onto the courtyard
and everyone at the table looked at him.

Bill offered a pleasant hello Grant lowered his eyes immediately.
And Temnah...Temnah gave him a shy smile. They were the only
ones seated around the iron table. A fourth chair was empty. Sajah
sat down, flicked the napkin open, and reached for the coffee carafe.
Temnah's hand was already there. She poured for him. "You slept
well, Sajah?"

"Yes. Thank you. Bill, I've made arrangements for you to start
on the village project today. You'll find the papers you need in the

office I have prepared for you on the second floor. Handle the school contracts first. I want construction started as soon as possible."

"Sure. But Grant said something about a work program."

So he knew. Sajah looked to where Grant was sitting. The man must have very good sources. His eyes returned to Bill. "Can you handle both the school and the work program at once? Do you feel strong enough?"

"No promises, but I'll give it a try."

Honest to the core. Sajah lifted his cup but didn't drink any coffee yet. Not until he finished laying out exactly what he wanted Grant to do. "I've cleared your pilot's license with the authorities. You'll need to bring yourself up to speed with my planes, preferably the twin engine first. The jet and helicopter can come later."

Grant nodded.

"You will also have to prove yourself. The Council agreed to a trial period of six months."

"It won't take that long."

Sajah sat back in his chair. "You understand the job carries some risk?"

Again, there was a calm nod.

Because Temnah listened to everything being said, Sajah chose his words carefully. "There was an incident earlier this week."

"Where?"

"Calcutta."

Grant's gaze cut quickly to Temnah, then he focused on Sajah again. "When do I leave?"

"As soon as you can."

"But Sajah," Temnah interrupted quietly, her eyes pleading. "We have already made plans for everyone to go riding. Please? Now that we know you're still here, you could join us."

"Not today, Temnah." He started to take a sip of coffee, then paused. "Why wouldn't I be here?"

Temnah set her chin upon her upraised hands. "Because your car is gone. I thought you left early—" The sudden frown across Sajah's brow stopped her.

It was Bill who offered the most logical explanation. "One of the servants probably put the car away."

"Not unless I order it." Sajah met Grant's eyes. It was just like before. Their thoughts ran in the same direction, drawing the same conclusion. They were on their feet in seconds. Their steps matched as they headed back inside. "Have you seen her this morning?"

"No."

Sajah vaulted up the stairs. Grant wasn't far behind.

They found Erica's third floor room empty. While Grant flung open the doors of the wardrobe to see if she had taken anything, Sajah stared at her perfectly made bed, the bed she hadn't slept in. The Bible was still there though. He snatched it off the nightstand, already pulling a piece of paper from its pages.

Grant came to stand beside him.

Sajah,
You were right. Sometimes I don't stop to think. But please know I am not acting on impulse now. I have prayed and searched my heart. Wait for the letter. It will explain more.
Erica

Grant headed out the door again. "The nearest public airport. Where is it?"

"Jaipur." Sajah's steps were just as purposeful.

❧ TWENTY ❧

No one came to close the door after him. Each step rang hollow on the stone floor. Shadows consumed his progress to the rear of the massive Punjabi palace. His father would be in the office. The doors were partially open so they flew inward the instant Mahim slammed his hands into the solid wood.

He stopped just inside, feet planted wide apart, arms crossed over his chest in a pose fitting for the dark room. A dozen Maharajahs and Sikh leaders looked at him, but his father did not. Scanning the familiar faces provided an answer for why they had laid aside their differences. A gathering like this had not been called for generations. Not since one of their own had betrayed India. "Where is she?" Mahim asked.

Finally, Jachan raised his head. "It is no concern of yours."

"Wrong, Father." Mahim advanced a few steps. "In Sajah's absence, she is my concern. I swore to him that she would never again suffer because of Bashtar."

Jachan stood slowly. Age may have withered his frame to less than that of his son, but he still held himself with all the pride of a Sikh leader. His face was lined now, his dark eyes clouded, yet he commanded respect. Even more so, he commanded obedience. He came around the desk, bearing with him the support of all present, except his son. "Then who will pay for Bashtar's death?"

If his father knew all there was to know about Bashtar, there would be no talk of seeking revenge. But Mahim had also promised Sajah he would never speak about Bashtar. So his father was left to find fault elsewhere.

The old man held himself like a warrior ready for battle. "It is not only your brother, Mahim. Who will be punished for your sister bowing to a strange God?"

Mahim could not keep the pain from his eyes.

"You see how much it hurts, son. I feel the same—the same anger, the same betrayal."

"Where is she?"

Murmurs of dissent ran around the room. Mahim had never really been one of them. He was averse to wielding the kind of power it took to dwell in their exalted ranks. Bashtar had been different. Bashtar would not have hesitated.

A sharp sigh was released from Jachan, but he gave no answer for Mahim's question.

"Know this, Father," Mahim spoke in a low tone, then lifted his head to look at all of them. "Sajah will come for her. When he does...may the gods help you if you have harmed her in any way."

"She has not been harmed!"

Mahim felt relief flood through his body. But it was quickly gone.

His father advanced. "I am an old man, Mahim. An old man who has few days left. When I die, you will become Mahim Singh. You will lead the *Khalsa*." Jachan's tone was low, menacing in its power. "Which is stronger, Mahim? Your friendship with Sajah or your loyalty to this family, to the Sikh people?"

"Father—"

"Make the choice, my son. Stand with us against this woman. If you don't, she will ruin all of us as she has ruined Bashtar and Sajah." Once the words were spoken, Jachan went to his chair behind the desk. "She is in the garden."

After one last troubled look, Mahim left the room.

Erica was sitting on a marble bench, hands clasped demurely in her lap. The pale pink sari she wore was obviously stained by her travels, yet she looked beautiful. Against the backdrop of trees and towering mountains, she stood out like a rose. Mahim approached so silently, she did not realize he was there until he spoke her name. Then she was on her feet and smiling at him. "Mahim! I didn't expect to see you here. How are you?"

"I...am very upset."

Erica's smile vanished. "With me?"

His nod confirmed her suspicion. He watched her turn and face the mountains.

"I'm only trying to help Sajah."

"Then you are going about it the wrong way. Coming here will make things worse, not better." Mahim moved in front of her so that she had to look at him. "You have driven their bitterness deeper, Erica." And she did not fear the reprisals. Mahim saw it in her expression. His first meeting with her, in Sajah's apartment, had been a time to learn her weakness. Now he saw her strength. She would have made an excellent member of the Khalsa, the religious and military order of his people. However, he would not share that thought with his father.

"The woman in the window."

Mahim looked to the top floor of the palace.

"Your mother?"

"Yes." His eyes returned to Erica's face.

"She has been there since I came outside. Could I see her, Mahim? Talk with her?"

It was impossible. "She is in mourning for Bashtar. From the moment Sajah called, no one has spoken with her."

"I think I know how she feels. It's lonely." Erica offered a delicate shrug. "The Maharajahs will not speak with me either."

"What did you expect?" Flaring resentment tarnished his words, causing Erica to lower her head. "If you expected your Savior to open doors for you here, then you have wasted your hope. The doors are closed, Erica."

She moved to a nearby tree, leaning into the solid trunk, even though the rough bark must have dug into the soft flesh of her arm. "I feel sadness in this place, Mahim. It is more than the broken walls, the crumbling grandeur. God wouldn't bring me here to add to the pain." When she lifted her head, the mountains were reflected in her blue eyes. "Before Bashtar died, he told Sajah it was time for the gods to choose which of them was worthy. Maybe that's why I'm here—because it's time for choices."

Her words so exactly mirrored his father's, Mahim felt an expectation rise within him. He could not look away from her gaze. "Those men, the Maharajahs and Sikh leaders, can choose to punish me for Bashtar and Temnah, but it won't change what's happened. They can choose revenge, but the satisfaction would only fade with time. Your father's relief will fade. What he's doing now, the choices he is making, will bring him to the end of his life an empty man."

She glanced at the upper windows, then back to him. "You have choices too, Mahim. You hold the future of this family in your hands. Just as Sajah holds the future of his family. But it goes beyond that."

A sense of boldness raised her chin slightly. New strength sparked in her eyes. "The minute you see Temnah again, you'll realize the change in her. She's found the peace you and Sajah have been looking for. Not the contentment of your work as a doctor, not the fact that you are raising your children according to the Sikh religion. I mean the peace in your soul. That's what Temnah has found. Jesus made that difference in her life. Jesus is the One who proved Himself real to Sajah the day Bashtar died. He's the One laying those choices at your feet, Mahim. You can walk away from them, turn your back on ever really helping your family, or you can open the door and let Jesus show you the truth of salvation."

Tehri, the village that lay at the foot of Jachan's mountain palace, was a buzz of activity. Yet every person within sight seemed to stop what they were doing to watch Sajah stride toward the place where Grant waited beside saddled horses. They knew he would race off like the others had done; Maharajahs and Sikh leaders, Erica, and Mahim. Each name that had been added fueled his determination. The list and the threats ended now.

Sajah mounted the bay gelding in a single frustrated motion. Grant did the same. The first raindrops began to fall, reminding their audience to seek shelter before the storm broke. The only shelter Sajah desired to see was Jachan's palace; a long, hard ride higher into the mountains.

Within half an hour, lightning snaked down from the sky. Rain fell in thick, heavy sheets. The horses became more difficult to handle. The darkness increased. It was like riding straight into confusion. Though Sajah had been on the trail many times, he could barely make out which direction to turn. He only knew to keep heading up along the steep ledge. Then at a clearing, they would head east again.

His arms began to ache from trying to control the frightened gelding. It no longer had sure footing on the rain-slick rocks. Sajah glanced over his shoulder to see how Grant was doing.

"Just keep going," Grant called ahead.

Yes, they had to keep going. There was no choice. Sajah swung to the front again, but it was too late. The horse missed its next step.

He felt himself falling over the edge. Fear clutched him as tightly as he clutched the reins. The leather cut into his hands as it slipped away. Then he was falling.

"Why do you stand at the window?"

Erica was startled by the sound of Jachan's voice. She hadn't known he was in the room with her. By the time she turned, he was lowering himself into a chair near the fireplace. His white hair and lined face showed up brilliantly now that he was closer to the flames. "I was just watching the storm."

Jachan growled his disapproval, then watched her pace to another window. "You are nervous as a cat. I do not like cats." Because his words didn't faze her, he tried again, with greater purpose. "If Mahim continues to delay, I will let the Maharajahs carry out your punishment.... Did you hear me?"

"It's so quiet," Erica said.

He cursed her. "It is quiet because this is a fortress. To keep out intrusions."

Such as herself. But there had been cracks to slip through. Erica saw a streak of white light in the sky. Another chased it into the trees. Voices came from the hallway, then the Maharajahs and Sikh leaders entered the sitting room. They chose various vantage points in the vast space. Some sat on chairs near the fire. Some gathered in a group by the bookshelves. All of them watched her.

In the hours since Mahim left the palace, she had felt increasingly ill at ease. But why? He had promised to send a message to Sajah. He had promised to return in the morning. They were promises she knew would be kept. Yet there was a restlessness building in her. She was only one among so many, and they seemed much stronger. Their silence forced her to spew out the first thought that came to mind. "Were you born here, Jachan?" Too late, she realized she should not have called him by his given name, not in front of the others.

Jachan glared at her. "Yes, I was born here and I will die here. Where will you die, Erica Tanner?"

It was difficult to hide the fact she was shaken by his words. "Where I die doesn't matter. How or why doesn't matter either."

"Because of your *faith*." He released the word as if it were an ugly thing.

"Yes, because of my faith."

The Maharajahs didn't like her answer and murmured against her. Erica exhaled a deep breath. Jachan's reflection in the window showed her that he was now looking at the fire, probably wondering how long it would take to burn her at the stake. "I hear Mahim has a son named Jehmal. You must love him very much, Jachan." Oh. She bit down on her lip, mentally berating herself for making the same mistake twice. "I only meant that you seem to love your family very much."

"You have *destroyed* my family."

No, years of struggling for power and position had destroyed his family. She was only someone to blame for his current state of mind. More lightning flashed over the outside world. This time it showed her a sight terrifying enough to freeze the blood in her veins.

Oh, no...no! Erica moved to another window, then to another. *Dear God, no!* She ran from the room before any of them could stop her. The outer door was heavy. She inched it inward until there was enough space for her to slip through. Cold rain immediately stung her body, but she didn't care. Her eyes were fastened on the horse emerging from the darkness.

"Go back," Grant shouted above the thunder.

She kept running toward them. The horse shied from her when she tried to catch the reins.

"Erica, don't." Grant struggled to hold the horse steady.

Strong hands pushed her aside. When she resisted, one of the Maharajahs gripped her by both arms, hauling her away from the horse.

The others helped Grant.

Sajah was carried into the sitting room. Many hands reached out to help ease him onto a table that was dragged close to the fire. "Careful with his shoulder," Grant cautioned. "It's dislocated."

Erica pushed herself through the Maharajahs until she was standing beside Grant. "What else?"

He knew that was the nurse in her taking over. Hopefully it would last long enough. "I don't know. It was too dark."

Erica pressed closer, already feeling for a pulse. "I'll need more light."

Two of the men left. Grant looked long and hard at the others. Only one held his gaze. That would be Jachan.

"Grant."

He focused on Erica again.

"How long has he been out?"

"Since before I pulled him up the cliff."

"Dear Lord." Her hands trembled in opening the medical kit one of the men brought. Grant judged it to be fairly new. No doubt, compliments of Mahim. She pulled out a pair of scissors and started to cut Sajah's shirt away from his body. Half a dozen hands shot out to stop her.

She was shaking so hard Grant could feel it. He released the hand holding her wrist. After that, the look in his eyes made the others back away from the table. The injuries added up quickly—a deep gash on Sajah's forearm that needed stitches, a dislocated shoulder, another cut, some ugly scratches, a bruise on his forehead, and he was pale, deathly pale.

Erica probed the bruise on Sajah's forehead gently, but not gently enough because he started to moan. Seconds later, his eyes flew open. Grant was there to hold the man down. "Lie still. You're at Jachan's palace. Erica is working on you." At least she was trying. Grant wondered how long she could hold out. "Where else do you hurt?"

"Shoulder."

"No problem. Erica can fix that. Where else?"

Where didn't he hurt? Each time he turned his head he saw another Maharajah staring at him. Then there was the solid wall of Sikh leaders. Sajah winced and not because Erica was feeling over his bruised ribs. He grabbed her hand, startling her. "You are...a fool, Erica Tanner! A stupid, innocent little fool!"

"Excuse me." Grant effectively pulled them apart. "I don't think you're supposed to talk to the nurse that way. With that attitude, she might not take care of you. Might leave you for dead."

Like Grant could have left him on the cliff. Sajah closed his eyes. What had possessed the man to come down after him? He sensed Erica's movement. When he looked, she was sitting on the table, taking his injured arm in both hands. Her foot was placed in his armpit.

"I need a couple of you to hold him down," she said. Grant volunteered, but nobody else did. Erica spared them no mercy. "Do it— right now." Every man in the room recognized the undercurrent of stress in her voice. Those who were most affected by it stepped to the table and held Sajah where she instructed.

"It's going to hurt, Sajah."

It couldn't hurt worse than it did already. He braced himself. Erica pulled as hard as she could, but the shoulder didn't pop into place. Her face was no doubt as pale as his. "Do it...again," Sajah said. "You have to."

It worked the second time. She slid off the table and started throwing out orders. Hot water and more bandages. Blankets. "Okay, Sajah." Erica held his chin in a firm grip. "Follow my finger."

He did. Perfectly. "You know as much as Mahim."

"Not nearly." The extra lamps came. Erica made the Maharajahs stand by, holding them. Then she looked around.

"What do you need?" Grant asked.

"More room."

"Plenty of that." Grant set his hands under Sajah's shoulders. "Time to move, buddy. You're hogging the lady's space." Incredibly, several of the men laughed at Grant's teasing tone. Grant showed his surprise by lifting one eyebrow in Erica's direction. She shrugged a little. At least she meant to. The gesture was interrupted when one of the Maharajahs set his hands about her waist and lifted her onto the table. Then the man actually smiled at her.

Erica was so flabbergasted she smiled back.

Sajah cleared his throat. "I'm bleeding to death here."

"You are not. Set your arm across my lap."

He could just imagine what kind of looks raced around the room at those innocent words, though Erica didn't leave him long to imagine before she spoke again. "Grant, you need to get out of those wet clothes. Maybe Jachan can find something for you to wear."

Sajah's eyes widened. If not for the fact he hurt all over, he might have even laughed. Imagine, Erica Tanner giving orders to one of the most powerful men in all of India. He could just barely see the old man around her slim body. Jachan shared the amazement. Only for a heartbeat, though. Then he stormed out of the room. Grant followed.

A certain quietness settled in the old man's wake, but it held enough tension to make Erica shake slightly as she set the first stitches. "Hold still."

"I am." Sajah studied her profile in the lamplight. "What does a broken leg feel like?"

Erica jerked her head up. "Oh, Sajah. You didn't—"

"No. But you did once. When you were, let me remember, five."

A Maharajah spoke rapidly. Sajah answered in the same dialect, agreeing that Nurse Tanner was an intriguing mixture of gentle and tough. Another Maharajah spoke. Yes, Sajah answered, she did seem irritated by their Hindi conversation. He responded to quite a few more questions in the time it took Erica to stitch his arm.

Finally, she washed it and applied a bandage. Every once in a while, she would scold him for dozing off. Actually, it wasn't hard to remain conscious with her hands constantly moving over his body. He closed his eyes, remembering the day when he had seen her with Arun...

"Sajah?" Her fingers touched the bruise on his forehead.

She did not expect how he reached up to capture her hand. The action pulled her closer. "Do you wish," he said hoarsely, "to make all the Maharajahs jealous so they will throw themselves off a cliff in hopes of having you nurse them as you have done for me?"

Those Maharajahs who were close enough to hear laughed heartily at his words. Color flooded Erica's pale cheeks. Before she could answer, the door banged open and crashed against the wall, causing Erica to straighten. Jachan's expression was ominous. Something changed in the old man, and in Erica too, as they stood there.

Sajah struggled to raise himself. Even as he swung both legs over the edge of the table, leaning heavily on his good arm, hatred poured from Jachan to flood the room. "Will she poison all of you?" He took measured steps inside. "Will you listen to her lies when you know she has killed Bashtar? Will you stand by and watch Sajah succumb to her evil beauty?"

"Jachan."

"No, Sajah! You will keep silent!"

The tone of Jachan's voice made the others wary. They knew where the true power lay It had always been that way, for centuries. Ajari blood was the first of their blood spilled in any battle. Ajari gold was the first of their gold given for freedom. Ajari sweat was poured out in labor for India. Ajari words wooed kings and prime ministers and people of many nations. Ajari men held the real power. Sajah held the real power, not Jachan.

Sajah lowered his feet to the floor and drew himself into a straight line. "Be seated. Everyone."

They complied. Except for Jachan. The old man moved toward the place where Sajah stood. Firelight flickered over his face, show-ing every line, every shadow. When he looked past Sajah, it was to meet Erica's eyes again. "She is Christian, Sajah. In your great-grand-father's time, we would have put her to death."

"Just as we would have put Bashtar to death—for trying to kill me."

The Maharajahs became perfectly still.

Jachan slowly shifted his gaze to Sajah. Beside Sajah's strength, he looked withered, spent. Yet his eyes burned with emotion.

"My mother did not tell you that part of the story, did she, Jachan?"

"The poison of Tanner's God has reached your mind as well as your heart."

"No," Sajah spoke firmly; his voice did not waver. "Your life, my life, has been changed by a different poison. Hatred. Revenge. That is the real poison, Jachan. That is what killed Bashtar. Now it is up to us to stop its spread."

Jachan set both hands behind his back as he began to walk around the room. The eyes of the Maharajahs followed him. "Do you believe what he says, men?"

"Sajah has never lied."

"For her—he would lie!"

"That's not true." Erica's hushed voice drew their eyes, and Sajah's. A silent communication passed from him to her. No matter what was said, she was not to speak again. She turned toward the fire, watching it burn while Sajah answered Jachan's accusations.

"What is the lie, Jachan? And what is the truth? In order to invoke your sympathies, my mother told you things, true things, she had no right to tell. In order to protect your family, I withheld the truth about Bashtar. At what point does one truth cancel out the other? When it becomes painful?"

"No." Jachan stopped. "When it means you place your rights above ours."

"I have never done that."

"Until now."

Sajah ran a hand over his face but could not erase the evidence of his growing impatience. "What you say is wrong. You have taken it upon yourself to interfere in my life. By calling this gathering, you force me to take a stand, you force me to openly challenge your wishes when I have already decided what I must do."

"What you must do?" Jachan sneered the words, his eyes narrowing. "You think you must marry her? You think Sajah Ajari cannot keep his brother's child any other way than to *marry* her? By the gods, Sajah! If I do not force you to think logically, to realize how she has twisted your mind, what hope do any of us have against being overtaken by the same lies? It rests on your shoulders or it lies at your feet. Accept the responsibility, Sajah—or give up being the man we thought you were."

When all remained quiet, Erica slowly faced the room again. Grant was there now, standing just inside the open doorway. The Maharajahs and Sikh leaders, every one of them, were staring at

Sajah. Jachan's face was a mask of stone. She couldn't see Sajah's face, but she could imagine his expression was chiseled in stone, too. It was because of her he had to defend himself like this. Guilt crushed her until the very breath seemed emptied from her body.

Sajah took a step toward the middle of the room. Then another. Then he stopped. His dark, damp hair glistened wherever touched by firelight. His bare chest, his stiffened back, the way he held his head; all showed how royal Ajari blood was deeply ingrained within him. Finally, he looked at Jachan. "As my father did and his father before him, as all Ajari men, I will do what I know is right.... I will marry Erica Tanner."

Sajah felt that he was not alone, but it was a great effort to open his eyes. He tried again. The room was shadowed except for slivers of sunlight cutting through the wood shutters that had been closed over the windows. It was morning then, early morning. He turned his head on the pillow. "Mahim."

"Hello, Sajah."

But where was Erica? She and Grant had stayed with him late into the night. Grant must have taken her to another room, made her sleep for a while. Once more, Sajah brought his eyes to Mahim's face. "Have you seen Grant Stevens?"

There was a nod as Mahim began pulling instruments from a bag on the table. "He filled me in on your little mishap. You are even with him now, no? You saved his life. He saved yours."

"It is not—" Sajah winced as he shifted positions—"the same."

"Really? Both times did not take faith?"

Sajah's head came off the pillow, followed by his shoulders until he was sitting. The soreness of his body was not the only reason he scowled. "Grant Stevens's faith may have sent him down that cliff last night, but it was Erica's faith that made me dig him out of the temple stones."

Mahim unwound the bandage on Sajah's arm, nodding approval for the neat row of stitches Erica had set into the flesh. "Despite the emotion of the moment, she has done well in seeing to your needs. Perhaps I should see how she is doing now that the shock has worn off."

"It is her job, Mahim."

"True...yet it must have taken bravery, even faith. Erica says faith is catchy."

A low humph was Sajah's only answer.

"She says it can travel from one heart to the next without anyone knowing, like an invisible seed which implants itself and sends down deep roots." Mahim ran his hands over Sajah's ribs, checking them as Erica had done. "I'm afraid, my friend, that I cannot give you a shot to prevent you from catching this thing called faith."

"I will not *catch* anything from Erica."

"Then why are you sick with love for her?"

Sajah pushed Mahim's hands away and got out of the bed, searching the room for something to wear. It did not help his mood any that Mahim calmly held out a set of clothes, black pants and a white tunic. He grabbed them. "Where is your father?"

"I do not know. Put this sling on too, and keep it on."

"Where is Grant?"

"I don't know, Sajah."

"Well, what do you know?"

Mahim shoved his stethoscope into the bag. "I know you should stay in that bed another two days, but I also know you won't listen to anything I have to say."

"Your bedside manner could use a little work, Doctor."

"So could your attitude, Rajah Ajari."

Their friction began to ignite. It had been decided long ago that they would never let Sajah's position come between them, that who Sajah was would never influence their friendship. Now Mahim was breaking the rules, and Sajah could easily guess why. He finished dressing and adjusting the sling, then moved to the windows, throwing the shutters open to let sunshine flood the space between him and Mahim. "You are blaming me for Temnah."

Mahim finished packing his things, then moved to the window, too. He did not look at Sajah but at the rugged world stretched out below them. "No one has to be blamed for Temnah. My sister made the choice of her own free will."

"And your father? After last night, he will disinherit you if you remain my friend." He only spoke the truth. Jachan had pronounced the sentence himself, calling for an end to centuries of Ajari leadership. Any Maharajah or Sikh leader who did not cut off all ties with Sajah would find himself isolated with the same kind of severity Sajah had to endure.

"Erica said it would come to this. A choice." Mahim set both hands on the wide stone sill. "My choice was made yesterday, Sajah. Nothing, not even such dire words, can change my mind." He lifted his eyes to Sajah's face. "We are as close as brothers. I will stand by you."

"But—"

"My father is wrong. Someday, the others will come to realize how wrong."

A knock on the door sealed the trust between them. Mahim was the one who bade the person enter. Neither of them expected to see Grant walk into the room. They met him halfway.

"It's late. I thought we should wake Erica and get going."

Sajah agreed.

Mahim didn't. "You shouldn't travel yet. Sajah needs the rest."

"I am not an invalid."

"You will be if you push yourself in recovering from this."

A casual shrug ended the discussion. Sajah started for the door, the other men followed, joining him in the hallway. "Grant, where is Erica?"

"In Temnah's room. We talked with your mother, Mahim. She said it would be all right."

Mahim came to an abrupt halt. So did Sajah. Their eyes met...then they both looked at Grant. "My mother said?"

Caution ruled how Grant nodded. In the next moment, Mahim ran for the staircase leading up to the third floor. Sajah almost beat him there.

The door was already open, slowing how Mahim approached the room, allowing Sajah to catch up with him at the doorway. If not for Mahim blocking his way, Sajah would have barged inside. As it was, he forcibly pushed the other man's arm aside gaining entrance. Quick, silent steps carried him across the room, straight to the bed.

She looked so peaceful sleeping there, bathed in sunlight, wearing one of Temnah's nightgowns—a pale blue one to match the color of her eyes. Sajah tore his gaze from her face to the idol that now lay beside her. Its eight arms twisted at grotesque angles, as if reaching out for her.

Diva...

Anger and fear made him grab the idol. It flew through the air and crashed against the far wall, shattering into a dozen pieces.

Erica jerked spastically, then sat upright on the bed, her eyes running rapidly from Sajah to Mahim to Grant, then back again. It all happened so fast. Sajah dragged her from the bed with his one good arm. She stood there shaking as he picked another idol of Diva off the mattress and threw that against the wall, too. But he was not satisfied. There was a smaller idol on Temnah's bedside table. He set his hand around it.

"Sajah, don't!" Mahim was beside them in a few anxious strides. "Put it down."

"Do *not* tell me what to do!" Sajah flung the idol, barely missing Erica's head. She stumbled backward as its destruction echoed through the huge room. Sajah spotted another Diva on the floor at the foot of the bed. It was made of brass, though, and only made a hollow, empty sound when he sent it into the wall.

Erica's muffled gasp was much more shattering. Mahim was quick to pull a blanket from the bed and draw close enough to wrap it around her shoulders. His actions did not stop her shaking, nor did it stop Sajah from heading for the door.

Grant barred his way. "Where are you going?"

"To see Mahim's mother." Every word was accompanied by unrequited anger.

"What good will that do?"

"It will convince her she cannot call upon Diva's power to destroy Erica! Now get out of my way!"

Mahim spoke carefully. "You are too late." His words had Sajah turning back. An expression of regret filled Mahim's eyes. "You are too late," he repeated quietly. "Just...take her and leave."

"Mahim."

"Now, Sajah. Before they see what you have done."

Sajah's gaze shifted to the broken idols scattered across the floor. How could he have thought for one moment to destroy the great destroyer? Something drew him toward the brass Diva, made him pick it up, and stare at its face.

When Grant spoke, his voice seemed to fill the room. "'That your altars may be laid waste and made desolate, and your idols may be broken and cease, and your images may be cut down, and your works may be abolished.'" Sajah stared at him. "'And the slain shall fall in the midst of you, and ye shall know that I am the LORD.' Ezekiel. Chapter 6. It fits, doesn't it? Perfectly. God led Ellyn to pray those words for you, Sajah. Five years worth of prayers."

The brass tongues of fire around Diva's ring cut into his hand, but Sajah did not loosen his hold.

"First the temple laid to waste. Then Bashtar slain by his own hatred." Grant continued in a calm, even tone. "Think about it, Sajah. Everything you've worked for abolished by the Maharajahs. Broken idols. Seems to me like God knows exactly what He's doing and you're running out of time."

❧ TWENTY-ONE ❧

THE VEIL WHISPERED AS SHE PASSED THROUGH, but the stars, the lights of the veil did not move. Thinking about her little girl story drew her forward, past the bed and more whispering veil. In pressing aside the velvety curtains, she could open the windows. They swung outward at her touch. The breeze floated inward along with a nighttime view of the palace's front lawn.

The moment they had returned to the palace, Sajah had sent Temnah home. It was Grant's idea to use the plane and fly her to Punjab. Sajah didn't object, as long as Grant went straight to Calcutta from there. Erica hugged both arms over herself to remember the feeling she had when Bill finally told her what kind of work Grant would do for Sajah. Investigating Sikh extremist attacks for the government wasn't exactly a nine-to-five, safe-behind-a-desk job. Of course, Grant was qualified. More than qualified. But why would Sajah deliberately place him in danger like that?

She leaned into the windowsill, hoping to hear Rama's Shikari come riding up. It was late. Sajah couldn't stay out there forever. They would have to talk soon. He had to... No. Sajah didn't have to do anything until he was ready.

Her eyes lifted to the sky as she remembered the look on his face earlier that morning in Temnah's room, when he had held the idol in his hands. It was like God had torn the veil in two all over again, allowing Sajah to clearly see the significance of Christ's sacrifice. Now, if Sajah would only let go of his chosen path to walk toward true salvation.

Truth alone triumphs. The words were Sajah's foundation, but his world was built on Hindu truths. He had surrendered to the wrong truth. The possibility that he might retreat further into Hinduism, into the very thing that was most familiar to him, made her heart ache unbearably. Then it started pounding hard, in rhythm with the hoof beats that pounded the ground. Rama's Shikari entered the pool of light coming from the lower floors. She could barely distinguish Sajah from the black horse because he was dressed completely in black. "Sajah!"

He reined the animal in so quickly Rama's Shikari reared up on its back legs. Sajah fought with his one good arm to bring the animal under control, then looked to the top of the palace. "What do you want?"

"I was waiting for you. Where are you going?"

There was some delay about his answer, as if he was trying not to be upset. "To the village."

"May I come?"

Again, he didn't answer right away. "Hurry then."

"But I'll have to change into jeans."

"Just come down here."

He sounded in no mood to wait if she insisted on changing her clothes, so Erica ran from the room and down the stairs, almost colliding with Bill on the second landing.

"Steady on, girl."

"Sorry." She offered a quick smile, then started down the next flight.

"Where are you off to?"

"The village," Erica said over her shoulder, "with Sajah. Don't wait up."

———∞∞∞———

Many fires burned around the open area surrounding the well. Sajah left the horse near the edge of the huts, and they walked the rest of the way Light, enchanting music drifted toward them, much like the night she had escaped into Pushkar. That night seemed like a lifetime ago. So much had happened since then—Jaipur, Darjeeling, and now Tehri. Erica suddenly looked up into Sajah's face. Her inattentiveness to where they were going caused her to stumble a little.

Sajah took her hand. It was necessary anyway or they could have become separated in the crowd of villagers. Once people noticed them, a path began to clear. Just as they reached the inner circle, a hush fell, leaving a single male voice to rise up into the night sky. Erica was glad Sajah drew her in front of him so she could see the marriage ceremony without having to peer over his shoulder.

The bridegroom was seated on a simple wood bench, near the largest fire and the well. Beside him, dressed in the traditional all-red wedding costume, was—Amreli. Erica whirled around. "Sajah."

"Shh, you must be quiet." He turned her around again.

Amreli had seen them. Her tear-filled gaze met Erica's, silently pleading that Erica stop what was about to happen. The Hindu priest's prayer droned on until Erica thought her heart would burst. Sajah's hand slipped from her shoulder to her arm. It tightened, painfully so, letting her know he had guessed the truth. Amreli was crying openly now. The priest motioned for Amreli and the young man to rise. It would be over soon. Erica clenched both hands into fists.

Red silk flashed with firelight when the priest took the end of Amreli's long mantle and the end of the bridegroom's scarf. He would tie the two pieces of cloth together, uniting them forever.

An expectant hush fell over the crowd. They did not expect Erica to move straight to the middle of their gathering, but she did. There was no boldness about her actions. In fact, she was shaking inside. The emotion that drove her to her knees there in the middle of the village was similar to what she had felt as a little girl in Contai.

She needed Jesus.

Sajah lifted his eyes to the heavens. He wanted to curse the God who would put Erica through this again. He wanted to, but the words would not form completely in his mind, nor his heart.

He split through a sea of murmuring, angry voices to reach Erica before the priest laid his hands on her. The argument that ensued was heated and doomed from the beginning. Sajah was Prince Ajari. His power was great enough to stop the marriage.

By the time he gave the final order, the priest was promising a show of disapproval from the gods. So be it. The gods could add this demerit to those he had accumulated in Tehri.

Sajah turned to where Erica was still kneeling in prayer—a powerful, tiny presence in the midst of his village. A powerful presence in his life. She was calm when he reached down and lifted her to her feet.

She was still calm when they reached the palace again and he took her to the library. Sajah let go of her arm and went to the desk. He had kept the envelope there. "Sit down, Erica."

"I don't want to."

"I'm not giving you a choice." Once she was seated opposite him at the desk, he slid the thick envelope toward her.

"The adoption papers?"

"No, I will not adopt Betul."

"But you said you were having papers drawn up by your lawyers."

"I was, until Grant brought me that."

Erica pulled the pages free from the envelope, her voice raw with emotion. "What do they say?"

"You must listen, carefully." Because he couldn't say it twice. Once would tear him apart. Sajah began in smooth monotone, matching the words to his movement around the library. "Pali left that package of papers at Grant's apartment. You'll see there is a copy of the Washington article. I knew about that. There were also two letters, both written in Hindi. The letter from Pali begins by stating her devotion to me. She loved me as a son."

"I know."

When Erica rose from her chair, Sajah faced her. "Pali's letter also confessed there was a will. Signed by both Ellyn and Sambhal. They wanted you to have full custody of Betul."

"No." Her whisper opened a wound in him that had been festering since the morning Grant gave him the letters. "I don't—want full custody."

"They *willed* it, Erica. Sambhal's letter spelled out that the decision was based on religious views. It had nothing to do with trust, nothing to do with brotherhood. They want Betul to be raised Christian. Pali destroyed the will in hopes that you and I could reach joint custody, if not something more."

"Marriage?"

"Yes. Pali realized the extent of Bashtar's deception. She knew that the only true way to protect Betul was if I adopted him and the only way to protect you was if you became my wife. Pali knew all of this before any of us. Her letter confirmed everything we had talked about already."

"Except that now you know about...Betul."

Sajah nodded. "I must honor my brother's wishes."

"What about your honor? What about your religion?"

"My honor is worthless if I can ignore my brother's plea for understanding."

"And your religion?"

"I don't know.... You have what you want, Erica. Ellyn and

Sambhal have what they wanted. If there is a measure of contentment for me in your satisfaction, then that will have to be enough."

It was almost noon the next day before Erica made her way downstairs. She felt no better for having slept so late. If anything, she felt
worse. Her head ached enough that she went in search of aspirin.

She usually went right past the second floor. Today, there was
noise coming from a room across the hall from the war room. Erica
made her way there, then stood in the doorway, smiling a little as
Bill finished singing the closing lines to a hymn—totally off-key, of
course. He looked up when she clapped for him.

"Hey, Half-pint. Thought you'd sleep the day away."

"I was tired."

"You still look tired. He won't like that."

"Who?"

"Me."

She jumped when Grant spoke so close behind her. Ignoring
him seemed like suitable revenge. Her questions were directed at
Bill. "What is he doing here? He was supposed to go to Calcutta."

"Been there, done that." Grant gave her a little push into the
office. "I touched down about an hour ago. The scene was pretty
much bulldozed into nothing by the time I got there. Dad, why
don't you make yourself scarce for a while."

"You're kicking me out of my own space?"

"Something like that."

Bill took his empty coffee cup with him. "R-e-s-p-e-c-t. There
will be a spelling test later, Stevens."

"Yeah, and by the way, your first name isn't k-i-n-g. The palace
is rubbing off on you in all the wrong ways."

Bill waved the teasing aside before disappearing. The silence he
left behind carried Erica farther into the room. "How is it going for

your dad, the plans and everything?" Her question was asked more to fill in the silence than because she really wanted to know.

"Not bad. They're putting up a clinic, as well as the school."

Erica glanced at Grant for a moment, then went to the bookshelves where she pretended to study the titles.

"It was Sajah's idea.... No comment, huh? Well what would you say if I told you Sajah's doing it for you?"

"I know that." The leather volume she lifted was heavy in her hands. "Sajah told me not long ago that he'd give me an entire kindgom. I don't want it. I don't want anything from Sajah Ajari."

Grant drew close to where she was making her stand. "Those are fighting words if I've ever heard them." There was a slight shrug, until he set a hand on her arm and she looked up at him. She didn't object when he led her to a delicate sofa, pure decoration in the otherwise functional room. "Okay." He sat beside her. "I'm ready to listen, if you're ready to talk."

"I've talked myself blue in the face."

"Royal blue?"

Erica focused on her clasped hands. Today, she had dressed in jeans and a white shirt. Ellyn's red sweater kept her warm—at least on the outside. Inside, she felt very cold, almost numb. "Yes, royal blue. He should have told me about Pali's letter as soon as you gave it to him."

"I agree."

"He thinks I'm satisfied now because I get Betul and he doesn't. It was never a *contest* between us."

"No, it was—it still is a conflict between Sajah and his heritage." When Grant leaned back, Erica did the same. Their shoulders touched in a companionable way. "Sounds to me like you're missing all the little miracles just because you want the big miracle to hurry up and happen."

The expression of unquestionable love in his eyes made it all right for her to snuggle into the crook of his arm. Somehow, when she most needed a big brother, Grant was part of her life again. He was there for her. A few tears slipped from her eyes. "Look for the little miracles, Half-pint. Then the big one won't seem so far away."

"Do you think it will happen?"

"I'm praying for it to happen. But only God knows for sure." Grant played with her curls. "It's a test of your faith, too. How much of your life can you place completely in His care? Everything?"

"I want to, but I don't know."

They were quiet for a long time.

Only when Grant shifted a little did Erica remember he had probably been awake since Tehri. She pushed herself upright, offering an apologetic smile as she tried to wipe the damp spot from his shirt. "Sorry I cried all over you."

"No problem." Grant helped her to her feet but kept hold of her hands. "Go get yourself something to eat. I'll meet you here in, say, an hour?"

"Why?"

"Because I'm supposed to fly you to Darjeeling. Sajah went to England."

"England?"

"Is there an echo? He wanted you to spend the time with Betul."

"And the extremists are suddenly on vacation, too?"

"After Tehri, the extremists don't have a motive for attacking Sajah."

"Oh, really?"

"Yes, really." Grant's tone was serious. "Open your eyes, kid. Sajah walked away from the Council. He turned his back on the political party. He destroyed his standing among the Maharajahs. He buried his ambition to bury the missionary programs. The only thing he can't leave behind is his title. The Sikh aren't interested in attacking a title. Sajah's going to fade into the background and become a gentleman prince. No headlines there."

"I didn't make him give up those things."

"Not directly, but you're part of it. In case you're wondering, he said he'd be back in a couple of weeks, maybe longer."

Fine. She started to walk away, but Grant caught her hand. Their eyes met, demanding honesty, no matter how hard it was for Erica to find the words. "He never even said good-bye."

"Maybe because he couldn't."

"Maybe because it's too easy for him to run away rather than stay here and face what's happening."

"If you think it was easy for him to leave, you should have seen his face before he walked out that door. He needs time to think, girl. You have to be patient."

TWENTY-TWO

"WHAT'S THAT FOR?" BETUL ASKED, scooting closer to where she sat on the living room floor. He rested his back against the couch, just like her. And drew his knees up to his chest, just like her.

Erica smiled down at him, feeling a surge of love. "It's another Christmas gift." He eyed the bright red wrapping paper and the white bow she had just tied. During the weeks she had been at the plantation, they had wrapped many such gifts.

"Is it for me?"

"No." She set an arm around his shoulders. "Not this one. If it was for you, I would have been more secretive and kept it in my room, wouldn't I?" There was a halfhearted shrug. "How are you feeling after your nap?"

"Better. Except I don't like taking naps all the time."

"You were tired." She eased the frown from his forehead with a gentle hand, then added a kiss for good measure. It was peaceful in the house.

"What present did you get for Sajah?"

The lack of enthusiasm in his tone set Erica's heart racing a little. For the past week, she had watched him become less active, more pensive. "Nothing yet. Maybe we could go to Darjeeling later and find him a special gift. Do you miss Sajah very much?"

Betul nodded, snuggling closer. "When will he come back? I don't like when he's gone so long."

Neither did she. The two weeks had passed a while back. Sajah's last phone call indicated he might return in time for Christmas or he might stay away. Her eyes went to the phone on Sajah's desk, an action she repeated dozens of times each day. But she never called.

"Erica?"

"Hmm."

"Will you sing me a song about Jesus?"

A lump formed in her throat preventing her from doing what he asked.

"Please? Mommy used to sing all the time. Daddy liked to—to hear her sing."

"Okay, but only if you help."

Betul rubbed a hand over his eyes. "I don't remember the words." Again, he rubbed at his eyes. "Please Erica. Will you sing now?"

"In a minute." She knelt beside him, carefully studying his face. Yes, he had been born prematurely, but those things about his coordination that had disturbed her before now gnawed at her conscience, working themselves into a disturbing pattern—the uneven gait, the hesitations in his speech, the loss of appetite. "Stand up for me, okay?" He did as she asked, slowly, awkwardly. He also did the other things she asked because she made it seem like playing a game.

Afterward, she took him to the kitchen and made hot chocolate. When she said she had to call someone, Betul was content to sit at the table, watching the steam swirl up from his cup.

She couldn't seem to find the right numbers. Finally, the call went through and she heard someone answer, a servant at the palace. Erica asked for Bill, quietly so Betul couldn't overhear. He had talked with Bill a number of times and would want to do so again. She paced to the limit of the cord, then back again two times before she heard Bill's voice.

"Hi, Half-pint. I wasn't expecting you to call so soon."

"Bill, just listen, okay. I need you to find Grant for me. Right away."

"He's in New Delhi."

"Get him on the phone then."

"Wait a minute. Slow down and stop whispering like that."

She glanced into the kitchen. Betul was still sitting at the table, but she didn't speak any louder. "I need Grant to fly here. All the way here, in the helicopter. Then get Mahim to meet us in New Delhi. Have him arrange for a CT scan, an MRI, and a complete neurological workup. Have him find a pediatric—"

"Erica."

Her hand tightened over the phone until the knuckles went white.

"Please, girl. You're scaring the daylights out of me."

"Bill, I need Grant to come, okay?"

There was a long pause. "What about Sajah?"

"Get him to come home. Now." Her eyes filled with tears, but she couldn't cry. "Tell him Betul is sick."

"Erica."

"Bill." She took a deep breath. "Just tell him he has to come home."

The next twenty-four hours were a nightmare. By the time Grant arrived, Betul could barely walk. Riding in the military helicopter with the soldiers Grant brought should have been an adventure, but the little boy was sick the entire time.

Once they reached Bagdogra, Grant switched them to the twin-engine plane. There was more room for Betul and Erica could sit beside him, holding his hand. She was there when the seizures started.

Several radio messages allowed Mahim to meet them at the airport in New Delhi with an ambulance. Erica sat in her allotted space, hands clasped, plagued by exhaustion and fear. Betul looked so tiny laying on the gurney. If he would only open his eyes.

"Erica."

She jerked at the sound of Mahim's voice.

"Start an IV," Mahim said. "He needs fluids."

"I can't."

"You can and you will."

But her hands were shaking. Mahim handed her a pair of latex gloves. It took a few tries before she got them on correctly. Another attendant gave her the proper kit. Her body and mind worked automatically then. Every motion was precise. Somewhere in the back of her numbness, as the siren continued to scream, she realized Mahim had done this on purpose. He made her work because he knew the truth, too.

Erica stared at the MRI films.

"It needs to be done," Mahim repeated, more urgently this time.

"I want to wait for Sajah. Please, just a few more hours?"

The desperation in her words made Grant squat down in front of her chair, his eyes level with hers. "You have to make the decision, Erica. You. There's no time to wait." When she tried to look away, his hand shot out to hold her face. The intensity surrounding them was powerful. "God is in this too, Erica. Just like all the other times."

But they wanted her to agree to something that could cost Betul his life. Her hands moved to grip the arms of the chair, otherwise she became very still. "All right. Do the surgery."

Mahim grabbed the films and rushed out. Now that she had given permission, there were many arrangements to make. The door swished closed, sealing Grant and Erica in the room. It was some comfort that Grant pulled a chair close to hers and leaned forward on the seat, so he could hold her hands. "It's the right choice, Erica."

It was the only choice. "Will you—stay with me until Sajah comes?"

"Of course."

Erica bit down on her lip, hard enough to taste blood inside her mouth. His kindness was melting what little strength she had managed to hold on to. Tiny pieces of her heart started to break away. "You've always been there for me, haven't you? Sajah thinks you love me."

"I do. You're my kid sister."

"And I always wanted a—big brother." Though she pulled one hand free to wipe a tear from her cheek, Grant tenderly did it for her. "I can't believe this is happening. How many people can God take away from me before it's enough? I—I can't lose anyone else. I can't lose that little boy. I love him like he was my own."

"God knows that, honey. Don't give up on what He can do. I've seen lots of miracles in my time, some of them involving you." His smile could not coax an answering smile from her. Not now.

"Oh, Grant," she whispered. "I need Sajah to be here."

"Then we'll go call Dad again. Maybe he's reached Sajah by now." Grant helped her stand. "Sajah has the jet, you know. He'll get here in record time." But they were both wondering if it would be soon enough.

"Miss Tanner?"

She jerked away from checking Betul's pulse to look toward the door and the nurse who stood there.

"You have a phone call."

She looked to where Grant was sitting, but he didn't give her an excuse to stay like she wanted. Instead, he promised to sit with Betul until she returned. The hallway seemed empty, maybe because it was too early for evening visitation. She followed the nurse to a desk, then lifted the handset, hoping to hear Sajah's voice. "Hello?"

"I want to know what is happening with my grandson."

Loralai. Erica controlled her disappointment by speaking very calmly, as she would have done with any other distraught grandmother. "He's very sick, Loralai."

"How sick? What's wrong with him?"

"It's complicated."

"I'm not an imbecile! Tell me the truth!"

She leaned against the metal desk, needing the support it offered. Two days without sleep, getting Betul here, agreeing to the surgery, waiting.

"Well?"

"He needs an operation. They'll be coming for him soon." In fact, she should get back. Her gaze traveled to the door of Betul's room. Yet suddenly she felt more than Loralai's impatience, she also felt the other woman's fear and uncertainty. "I wish you were here, Loralai. Bill could bring you, if you want."

"It is impossible."

"But you could be here in a few hours if you came by airplane. I could arrange everything."

"Stop talking nonsense and tell me what's really wrong with Betul."

The words seemed to stick in her throat, to choke her. "He has a brain tumor. They'll remove what they can." But Betul could die. Erica dipped her head low, torn between hoping and knowing, between what her heart kept praying and her mind kept screaming.

"Are you still there?"

"Yes. I'm sorry, Loralai. I need to go now."

There was a heavy sigh, then the connection went dead. When Erica turned around from replacing the handset, two nurses were just entering Betul's room. She practically ran the length of the hall-way.

Grant met her at the door, firmly holding her back. "He's already asleep, kid. Just let them do what they have to do."

Yes. Erica made herself relax, outwardly at least. She and Grant stepped aside so Betul's gurney could be wheeled into the hallway. There was a moment for her to touch the little boy's hand, then he was gone. The elevator doors swept shut with such finality.

"Erica?"

She couldn't seem to look at anything but those closed doors.

"Let's go upstairs," Grant urged. "We'll stay in the waiting room until Mahim comes."

"No, I want to pray. I want to stay here and pray." Even as she said the words, Erica backed farther into the room. There was a stiff little chair near the empty bed. She lowered herself into it.

"I'm going to call Dad, okay?"

Erica nodded the slightest bit. After Grant left, she reached for the cuddly, brown teddy bear laying next to Betul's pillow. It had been with him all this time, all the way from Darjeeling. She wouldn't let go of it, not until Mahim came. Not until she knew for sure.

By leaning forward, she could lay her head on the cool sheets. The tiredness had become an ache now...or maybe that was her heart. It didn't really matter which. If she could only hold Betul one more time, tell him one more story, sing him another song about Jesus. The ache deepened. Other thoughts started to crowd out the prayers, thoughts about what was happening in that operating room.

Erica closed her eyes to get rid of them. But they returned ten-fold. Panic set in, driving her from the chair. Tears blinded her, sobs ripped through her. Dear Lord, what had she done? Why had she let them take Betul? Somehow, she was in the hallway, stumbling toward the elevator. The doors wouldn't open! They wouldn't open!

"Erica!"

She heard Grant, but he was so far away and she wanted Betul back. She wanted him back!

"Erica." Grant drew her away from the elevator. When she resisted, he gathered her into his arms. "Shh. It's okay.... It's okay now." She clung to his strength, hid her face against him in a help-less way that made him hold her closer, made it all right for him to place a kiss upon her damp brow. "Shh," he whispered. "It's okay. Everything is okay."

A shadow fell across the floor, then stopped, close enough that Grant raised his head to see who it was.

"Let her go."

"Sajah."

"I said, let her go." He made his point very clear by pulling Erica toward him. In the next instant, he swung her up into his arms. He knew how every nurse, every doctor, watched them. Grant was watching. Temnah watched. For that reason, he walked away, down the long, white corridor, his footsteps echoing across the tiled floor.

Since early that morning, when he had awakened with an urgent feeling that he should fly back to India, Sajah had felt numb. Stopping in Punjab to speak with Mahim but finding Temnah instead...hearing her tell of Betul. The whole time he had felt numb. Now he felt angry. It wasn't fair that Betul should be sick.

When he lowered his eyes a little, he could see Erica clutching Betul's teddy bear. She was still sobbing, still shaking. He headed for the waiting room. The one couple there immediately got up and left. Sajah sat down on a chair, still cradling Erica in his arms. Her bro-kenness was something he hadn't expected. She was always so strong, so sure. And now this.

Sajah's breath changed, became more uneven. It was true then.

Betul could die. He swallowed hard, but the lump of fear wouldn't go away. Not when so much love welled up in him, filling every part of his being. He had never loved anyone like he loved Erica and Betul. And now he might lose them. Sajah laid his head back against the wall. Hot tears stung his eyes. By the God in heaven, he would rather die than live without either one of them.

A choking sob became lodged just over his heart. The tears slid down his cheeks. Would Erica's God listen to him? Would He have mercy? *Lord,* his soul whispered the name for the first time, *if You have any love at all, spare Betul. Do not slay him because of my unbelief.* The words tumbled over and over in his mind, fighting to be free. *Do not let me be the reason for his death. Do not steal him away now.* Sajah looked down at Erica again and his arms drew her as close as he could. *Lord,* he prayed again, *show me Your power, Your mercy by letting Betul live.*

❧ TWENTY-THREE ☙

A PHONE WAS RINGING. Erica tried to move, but something tightened around her to keep her still. She opened her eyes just as Sajah said, "Hello." He was really here. Erica lifted a hand to his face, drawing Sajah's eyes to her.

"Yes," he said into the receiver. "We'll be right there."

The bright lights in the hallway blinded her for a moment. She clung to Sajah's hand as he led her to the elevators. They were whisked upward so quickly that her stomach and head did funny things. "What—time is it? How long did I sleep?"

"An hour maybe." Sajah squeezed through the doors before they were fully open. Erica followed, but he was already running ahead, straight to the nurse's desk. Before she reached there, he was moving again, into a room. A room on the intensive care floor, not the surgical floor.

Erica overcame the initial shock to drag herself as far as the desk. Then Mahim was blocking her way. Their eyes met. "Come with me," he said gruffly.

But she wanted to be with Sajah and Betul.

A hand was clamped around her elbow. They went to another room not many steps away. Mahim was already pulling MRI films from envelopes and papers from folders. "Sit down."

She couldn't. Erica winced when he jammed the films into place against the white lights. Then her eyes were fixed on the black and gray pictures.

"The neurosurgeon wanted another set before he would start."

When Erica reached out for his notes, Mahim let her have them. One shaking hand went to cover her mouth, the other gripped the papers.

"Will you tell Sajah or shall I?"

Erica lifted dazed eyes to Mahim's face.

"It looks like I should tell him."

"No." She shook her head and looked at the films again, wishing they didn't say so much. "I'll tell him."

"Erica." Mahim set a hand on her shoulder. "I'm sorry."

She entered the other room so quietly, Sajah did not hear her at first. When he realized she was there, he straightened from the bed. She was pale. His gaze moved from her face to Betul's.

"They won't do surgery."

Something inside of him collapsed, yet his entire body became stiff, unyielding.

"There's another tumor, Sajah. Deeper in his brain. Mahim said it would be impossible for Betul to survive surgery."

Sajah swung around and headed for the door. "Stay here."

"Sajah—"

Outside the room, he paused long enough to find Mahim in the hallway. He was standing with Grant and Temnah beside the desk. All three of them looked up, but Sajah's eyes were focused on Mahim. Angry strides carried him forward. Intense fear forced the words from his mouth. "Make them do surgery."

"No, Sajah."

"Make—them—do—surgery!" When Mahim glanced away, Sajah's hand snaked out to grab the front of his coat. "Did you hear me? Make them operate! Make them!"

Grant was strong enough to pull Sajah away, to pin him against the wall. They stared hard at each other. Not one word passed between them. Words weren't necessary anymore. After several long moments, Grant released the pressure of his arm across Sajah's chest and stepped back. "Temnah, stay with Erica a while. Sajah and I are going for a walk."

They started off at the same rapid pace, side by side, steps matched perfectly.

The streets of New Delhi were not crowded, probably because rain pounded the pavement with a severity to match Sajah's steps. Seconds after stepping out the hospital doors, his black suit was soaked through. He didn't care. The anger still chased him, made him keep going.

God had not answered his prayer. Betul would die. Erica would leave India. His life would be in ruins—just like the temple in Darjeeling, broken beyond repair. The weeks spent in England searching for some sort of stability were erased now. Everything he had decided meant nothing. Nothing!

Grant pulled him back from the path of a speeding car. Sajah jerked himself free again, waited for the car to pass, then crossed the street. On the other side, he glanced sideways. Grant was thoroughly soaked, too. His cream shirt and khaki pants were plastered to his body. Anyone driving by would think them insane, yet Grant had read his emotions well enough to know this blind release of energy was the only way to head off the fear.

Sajah slowed his steps. "Where is your God now, Grant?"

The question did not seem to take Grant by surprise. "Right where He's always been. God never changes, Sajah. We're the ones who change." They crossed another street. "He's in control of everything, even when it doesn't seem like it."

"I know He is in control."

Grant's hand came out again, dragging Sajah to an abrupt halt. Honesty raged between them, just as it had done since the first day they met.

"What you say about God allowing all these things to happen— I do not deny it is true." Sajah wiped the rain out of his eyes with an impatient gesture. "I do not deny that He can take everything away from me if He wants. He has proven His power, His ability to crush me. But I *prayed*, Grant." The passion of Sajah's admission gripped them both. "I prayed for your God to have mercy and let Betul live. Tell me why He remains silent."

"I don't know."

"Then He is not a God of mercy! His Son is not the way to salvation. Not if they choose to punish Betul because of me!" Sajah began walking again, faster than ever, forcing Grant to catch up with him.

"God isn't like that, Sajah. He would never punish Betul. He would never punish you, either. And this has nothing to do with salvation. Betul isn't part of that decision. He can't be or it's like God bribing you to turn from Hinduism. God doesn't use bribes. He uses the truth."

"Forgive me if I have a hard time believing your words!" Sajah allowed Grant Stevens to stop him, though it was unfitting that they stood in front of an ancient Hindu temple.

"The verse from Ezekiel," Grant said, "the verse about everything falling apart. It ends with knowing that God is God. Knowing in your heart, Sajah. Right now you feel His power, but He wants more for you. He wants you to know the truth."

"The truth that He is higher than my gods—" Sajah swung a hand toward the temple—"that He can do anything He wants and I must accept it."

"No, Sajah. The truth that He's giving you a choice. All your life, you've been submissive to a dozen gods, more than that probably. You've worshiped them for what they can do for you. You've paid homage to their idols. You've pledged service and loyalty and strength and money. Whatever it took, whenever and wherever your chosen path to salvation led you, just to please the gods.... But now you've changed. You're starting to realize there's only one true God. It's a whole new way of thinking, Sajah. God will never demand ritualistic sacrifices. He wants you, your brokenness, and your trust, not the things you can give Him."

"My brokenness." Sajah stared at the buildings behind Grant. "My emptiness. If Betul dies, there will be nothing for me.... Erica will leave India."

"She loves you, Sajah."

Their eyes met again. No sense of peace came to Sajah, no relief.

"I can't tell you why this is happening," Grant said. "All I can tell you is that God is a God of mercy. He is a God of grace and forgiveness. Jesus made it possible for you to experience all of those things, but not until you accept the truth of salvation. What you're feeling right now, what you've been feeling for a long time, is your own conscience at war with His truth. Make the choice. Cross the line. Accept what God wants to give you."

"All I want from God," Sajah said quietly, "is to know that Betul will live. If you can't offer me that, Grant Stevens, then there is no more to say." He would have moved on, but Grant set a hand on his arm. So much assurance filled Grant's eyes it cut Sajah to the core of his being.

"Do you know what Erica wants, Sajah? She wants you to believe Christ died on the cross to save you from making this kind of mistake."

"I do not need to be saved! I need this—this Christ to save Betul!"

— ∞ —

The days blended together with a terrible sameness. Sajah tried again and again to persuade Erica to go to his apartment with Temnah, but she never went. She only stayed in the ICU waiting room, wanting to be there more than listening to her body and mind beg for rest.

Though another terrorist attack sent Grant rushing back to Calcutta, Loralai and Bill came. Mahim was there often. So were the Maharajahs and Sikh leaders. They arrived one by one, offering support in ways that dissolved Jachan's strict orders into futile, empty words. Sajah had stood by them many times. Now it was their turn.

Late at night, when only Sajah and Erica remained in the waiting room, the hours seemed to drag by. They took turns going in to see Betul. Every time Erica came back, Sajah wondered if a little more of her strength had seeped away. Then she would smile for him and sit down to read from Ellyn's Bible. Her strength, her faith did not seep away.

There were physical changes. Dark shadows bruised the skin beneath her eyes. She was pale. She ate next to nothing. Yet she never failed to find some source of peace in the words written across those pages. Whenever he sat there, watching her, Sajah remembered Grant telling him what Erica wanted—that he would find his way to the cross and accept Christ. But how was it possible for him to reach toward salvation when Betul was in the very next room, fighting for his life?

On the fourth afternoon, a call came from the Council that Sajah was needed to take care of matters relating to the Sikh attack Grant was investigating. When he stopped Temnah in the hallway and explained, she promised to stay with Erica. Certain uneasiness remained with him throughout the next hours. He found it difficult to concentrate, to focus on doing what he should.

Darkness fell while he was closeted away with the details. Near ten o'clock, he could no longer ignore the sense of urgency he felt. Driving to the hospital was a blur, so was riding in the elevator. From the moment he reached the ICU ward, he knew. Alarms sounded throughout the hallway. People rushed in and out of Betul's room. Sajah started forward, walking, then as the emotions became clearer, running.

No one noticed him step into the room. His eyes focused on Betul's face. It was ashen. His lips were turning blue. *No! Dear God in heaven, no!*

Mahim shouted orders, then moved Erica's hands aside to take over CPR. "Get her out of here."

"No!" Erica tilted Betul's head back, gave him a breath at the right time. "He needs to be tubed."

"He's coded three times."

"Give it to me, then! I'll do it!"

"Someone get her out of here!"

Erica resisted the hands that urged her to the door. Another breath. "Come on, Betul. Breathe! Breathe!" Mahim pushed her away to insert the tube. "Give him—"

"Be quiet! I want a smaller tube. Now! And get Erica out of this room!"

Another monitor went off. All eyes in the room stared at the flat green line on the screen.

Erica moved first. Compressing Betul's chest with a desperate rhythm. Tears fell from her eyes. She couldn't let him die. She couldn't—let—him—die. The strength suddenly went out of her arms. *Dear Jesus, dear Jesus.*

She laid a hand on Betul's forehead, whispering to him that he couldn't leave, that she didn't want him to leave. Along with the words, a prayer went out from her heart. She could hear one of the nurses crying. She knew when Mahim backed away from the bed, stricken with his own grief. Somehow, she knew the man who came to stand beside her was Sajah.

Erica stroked the dark hair from Betul's face. Jesus was there, too. In the room with them. His peace and warmth came flooding over her just like it had when she was lost in Contai. She closed her eyes and continued to pray. The hand covering hers on Betul's chest was Sajah's. But God's hand was over both of theirs.

Erica was the only one who didn't look up when the shrill, monotone beep on the monitor was interrupted by several smaller beeps. It happened again. And again. Life was returning to Betul's body.

Soft lights colored the room. Betul looked around for a moment before bringing his eyes back to Sajah. It seemed funny that he slept with his head on the bed that way. Slowly, Betul set a hand on his uncle's arm. "Wake up, Sajah."

Sajah did awaken. In fact, he sat bolt upright in the chair. Betul's smile eased the frown from his uncle's brow. When he patted the edge of the mattress, Sajah sat there and pulled him into a big hug. "I have missed you so much, Sajah."

"I've missed you too, little man."

The huskiness of Sajah's voice had Betul drawing back to look into his face. "Where is Erica?"

Sajah nodded toward a bed on the other side of the room. "She's very tired. Let's whisper, okay?"

Because he liked the idea of playing such a game, Betul smiled his answer and snuggled into another hug. "Is it Christmas yet?"

"No, Betul. You slept through Christmas."

"May we celebrate today then?"

"Are you feeling well enough for such a party?"

Betul gave a nod against Sajah's shoulder. He liked hearing how

Sajah's voice rumbled in his chest, how his heart beat so strong and steady. "I had a dream."

"What about?"

He tried to remember all of it. "About seeing Jesus." One of Sajah's hands came up to touch his cheek. "Jesus held me in His arms and talked to me. I liked Him.... I think I saw Mommy and Daddy, too. They waved to me. Then Jesus said it was time to leave. I—held His hand. Jesus still has scars on His hands, where the nails held Him on the cross. It made me want to cry to touch them, but He said I couldn't cry in heaven." Betul reached up to touch the tears sliding down his uncle's cheek. "You'd like Him, Sajah. You'd like Jesus.... I'm sleepy now. Where's my teddy bear?"

"Right here." Sajah found the stuffed bear at the end of the bed. It felt good to cradle the bear tight as Sajah tucked him under the covers. "Rest well, little man."

"Sajah?"

"Hmm?"

"I love you."

"I love you too, Betul."

Sajah let himself out of the car onto the tarmac. It was not quite dawn. Landing lights had guided the airplane home from a gray-blue sky. Grant himself executed the smooth touchdown.

The dying whine of jet engines was familiar. Sajah moved toward the sound. He was standing twenty feet away when the fuselage stairs yawned open and Grant exited, missing fully half the steps. The American jeans and chambray shirt were totally opposite Sajah's black suit and white shirt. Yet they came together with the same purpose.

"Betul?"

"He is awake now." Sajah felt relief impact Grant, much as it had impacted him an hour earlier. "I need your help."

"Sure, anything."

Sajah stared beyond the width of Grant Stevens's shoulders. "I need to know if Jesus will give me another chance." The way Grant shifted closer began to undermine the business Sajah wanted to finish. He hurried on. "Intellectually, I know it will seem like I made a deal with God. If He healed Betul, I would accept the message of salvation. But that's not what this feels like, Grant."

"What does it feel like?"

"Betul saw Jesus. I know when he speaks of scars on the hands he held, he means Jesus. Jesus had Betul in His arms. Jesus spoke to him, loved him. Jesus healed him, Grant, *completely* healed him." Sajah rounded his shoulders against the flood tide of emotion. "If Jesus can do all that, then He didn't have to send Betul back to someone like me. Jesus didn't have to give him back."

"But He did because He loves you, too."

Incredibly, unbelievably—yes. "I wasn't worthy of the second chance with Betul, let alone to feel like Jesus is giving me a second chance. I can't turn back to Hinduism after this. None of the Hindu sacrifices I have made can bring me closer to a God who would give me this second chance. I've done everything wrong, yet He wants me to experience love and forgiveness."

"There's only one way there, Sajah. Through Jesus."

"I know. Betul said I will like Jesus when I meet Him."

"You will." Grant's hand settled on his shoulder. "Let's go find somewhere to pray."

❧ TWENTY-FOUR ❧

"GRRR-ANT!"

"Hey, tiger!"

Betul ran across the room, throwing himself into Grant's arms at top speed so that they both tumbled backward onto the carpet. They tickled each other with abandon, Betul squealing as loudly as Grant was laughing.

"Can I join in?"

Grant rolled onto his back but didn't let go. They both looked up at Erica. She wore the sapphire blue sari today because of the celebration that was planned. She also wore a very pretty smile. Betul bounced upright until he was sitting on Grant's stomach. "Girls shouldn't wrestle, should they?"

"Nope."

"Who says," Erica challenged, hands on her hips, eyes sparking mischief. "You're just scared I'll beat both of you."

Betul adopted a doubtful look that he promptly shared with Grant.

That's when Erica laughed. "Well at least get up so I can give Grant a hug."

Hugging again. There had been a lot of that around the palace lately. Betul watched how Grant folded Erica into his arms. He hoped she wouldn't cry like she usually did. The hug lasted a long time. Grant whispered things in Erica's ear. She did start to cry. Even though she tried to hide her tears, Betul could tell.

Afterward, she slipped out of the room, leaving Grant and him alone. Betul moved close enough to set his hand into Grant's. "I don't like it when she cries."

"She's just happy, Betul."

Happy? He hadn't thought of that. "Where is she going now?"

"To see Sajah. He asked me to give her a message."

"A secret message?" An adventure!

Grant smiled down at him. "Sort of... What do you say we go find Temnah?"

"She's with Grandmama and Bill on the terrace."

"Want to race?"

"I'll beat you!" Betul took off running, knowing Grant wouldn't be far behind.

As she neared the stables, Erica could see that Rama's Shikari was already saddled. Sajah leaned against the fence, eyes fixed on the distant expanse of desert sand dunes. In the two days since their return from New Delhi, he had seemed restless. It was no different now, not even with the promise of Betul's celebration.

"Hello, Sajah."

He turned toward her.

"Grant said you wanted to see me."

Rather than saying anything, Sajah set his hands about her waist and lifted her onto the saddle. Then he swung up behind her. She didn't ask where they would go. His quietness let her know such things weren't important.

The horse raced overland, throwing up sand with each powerful gait. A cool breeze lifted the hair from her face, but the clear blue sky allowed morning sunshine to keep her warm. Erica had grown used to feeling Sajah's muscled chest behind her. Of all the times they had ridden this way, today's journey seemed more significant. Perhaps because he took her past the fields and the river into the desert.

At some unseen spot, high atop a sandy dune, he drew on the reins, stopping Rama's Shikari. Erica waited for him to dismount. Their eyes met for a moment, then he helped her down, too. She placed her hands on his arms for support. The white tunic he wore was open at the collar, revealing every pulse that beat in the veins of his neck. Erica almost reached up to touch that place, but she couldn't because Sajah set his hands on her shoulders and gently turned her to face the palace.

"You have never seen it from here, have you, Erica?"

She shook her head. It was no longer a cool, towering pile of stones. It was beautiful, touchable.

"Sometimes it takes moving away, setting yourself at a distance, before you can see things as they really are."

Erica looked up at him.

"That's what happened with me." He brought his eyes to her face again. "God set me at a distance from everything that I held important in my life so I could see it the way He sees it. I found out I don't need those things—the power, the political ambitions, the money, the control."

She dipped her head to hide the tears in her eyes, but Sajah wouldn't let her. His hand beside her face guided her eyes upward again.

"When Betul first woke up in the hospital, he told me about seeing Jesus." Sajah paused to make his voice steadier. Erica's tears rolled over his fingers. "Looking into his innocent eyes, seeing his faith—it broke down every last wall, Erica. I understand now. Grant showed me how to understand."

Erica set her hand over his.

"We've spent hours going through the Bible. He showed me

Ezekiel chapter 6, the verses he thinks Ellyn prayed for me. God has had His hand on me a long time and I felt something, but I didn't take time to really look at who was there. Now I know He is Lord.... I've made things right with my mother. We talked a long time last night. I think, some day, she'll open her heart to God and lay all the ghosts to rest. Will you pray with me for her salvation?"

"Of course, Sajah."

"I love you so much," he whispered. "More now that I know what strength you have had in loving me."

When she moved into his arms, it felt as if nothing would ever come between them again. It felt as if all the waiting and the trials had been worth this moment, this precious moment of hearing him say he had found what she had wanted for him all this time.

Sajah placed a kiss upon her temple. "Marry me, Erica. Today. Right now."

She pulled back enough to smile up at him. "But I have to make sure the lights of the veil are ready. They'll really want to hear this story."

"I'm sure they will. How many times will you tell it, I wonder?"

"Over and over and over again," she whispered. "Forever."

Dear Reader,

As Grant would say, "Breathe, kid!" That's better. If you're at all like me, right about now you need to page back through this little adventure and figure out where your heart started beating so fast.

Do you want to know where I looked? All over the place. From Erica's vigil at Betul's hospital bed to the cliffhangers in Darjeeling. From the little-girl letters and Hindu temples to my first sight of Sajah beside Pushkar Lake. All the way back to Grant's Portland apartment. Then I found it.

Satyameva jayate. Truth alone triumphs (see page 7).

You see, as with any journey—real or imaginary—it's what you choose to take home with you that matters most. I hope you won't soon forget Erica and Sajah, but I *pray* you never forget the nuggets of Truth contained within their story. Whatever the circumstances you're facing, Jesus has won the victory. If it's been a while since you've read the end of that Book, I encourage you to do so. It's guaranteed to really get your heart—and your faith—pumping.

Before I sign off, I just want you to know that it was no accident I included the story about Erica and the stars. I embrace Erica's little-girl spirit of inviting the stars to come visit her so they could share in wonderful, fantastic stories. Think of it as me inviting you to share *Lights of the Veil.* I'm glad you came. Now—get out there and shine bright for Jesus!

In His service and love,

I love to hear from my readers. Write me at:

Patty Metzer

Patty Metzer•Multnomah Publishers•P.O. Box 1720
Sisters, Oregon 97759
Or e-mail: pmetzer@uslink.net

LOVE AND FAITH RENEWED

Returning a mysterious wedding gift leads a disillusioned socialite on a healing journey to a father she'd never known and unexpected love in a savage jungle paradise.

ISBN 1-57673-445-5

IN AN AGE OF DARKNESS COMES A FLAME THAT WILL CHANGE IRELAND AND HER PEOPLE FOREVER...

Fierce warrior queen Maire struggles to understand her attraction to a bold yet humble faith-filled mercenary she takes hostage. Can love spark between enemies?

ISBN 1-57673-625-3

GOD'S LOVE SOMETIMES APPEARS IN STRANGE PLACES

Laurel Binet works for wildlife conservation while Darren Grant tries to save lives in desperate Africa. Can people of seemingly opposing passions find harmony through faith?

ISBN 1-57673-626-1